What October Brings

A Lovecraftian
Celebration of Halloween

What October Brings:
  A Lovecraftian Celebration of Halloween

ISBN: 978-4-902075-90-8

Celaeno Press
CELAENOPRESS.COM

What October Brings

A Lovecraftian Celebration of Halloween

Edited and with an introduction by

Douglas Draa

Celaeno Press
2018

Contents

Introduction

What *does* October Bring? That's a very good question. I know Beggars Night, at the very end of October, would bring us treats. This was one of Halloween's many aspects that make the 31st of October so special. Halloween isn't just about receiving treats. Halloween is also a chance and a possibility. A chance to thumb our collective noses at death and the great unknown, and a possibility, even if for only one evening a year, the curtain separating this world and the next might be drawn back just far enough for us to catch a glimpse of what is waiting for us on the other side. Or using Mr. Lovecraft's phraseology; we might get to meet The Lurker at the Threshold!

I mentioned treats earlier. And that's how I see this collection. I loved all those candies. B-B Bats and bite-sized Baby Ruth bars were great, but those little foil-wrapped Reese Cups were my favorites. And you, the reader are exceedingly fortunate to be holding a literary version of one of those foil-wrapped Reese Cups. On the outside though, instead of foil, you have a beautiful Daniele Serra cover to catch your eye and give you some hint of what awaits you between the covers. Of course you won't find a diabetic coma-inducing mixture of Chocolate and Peanut Butter between those covers, but I can promise you though, that you will still find two great tastes that taste great together; H. P. Lovecraft and Halloween!

Every story in this anthology has been written a current Mistress or Master of the macabre and Lovecraftian. No voice is alike nor are any voices similar. This means that each story is to be savored as an individually wrapped and uniquely flavored Halloween treat. Each one sharing only a seasoning of Mr. Lovecraft's essential Saltes.

So now that the nights are getting longer and the season of the witch draws nigh, turn down the lights and prepare yourself to enter a world of dreams, fantasies and horrors.

Enjoy!

Doug Draa
Nuremberg
August 2018

Hallowe'en in a Suburb

Howard Phillips Lovecraft

The steeples are white in the wild moonlight,
    And the trees have a silver glare;
Past the chimneys high see the vampires fly,
    And the harpies of upper air,
      That flutter and laugh and stare.

For the village dead to the moon outspread
    Never shone in the sunset's gleam,
But grew out of the deep that the dead years keep
    Where the rivers of madness stream
      Down the gulfs to a pit of dream.

A chill wind weaves thro' the rows of sheaves
    In the meadows that shimmer pale,
And comes to twine where the headstones shine
    And the ghouls of the churchyard wail
      For harvests that fly and fail.

Not a breath of the strange grey gods of change
    That tore from the past its own
Can quicken this hour, when a spectral pow'r
    Spreads sleep o'er the cosmic throne
      And looses the vast unknown.

So here again stretch the vale and plain
 That moons long-forgotten saw,
And the dead leap gay in the pallid ray,
 Sprung out of the tomb's black maw
 To shake all the world with awe.

And all that the morn shall greet forlorn,
 The ugliness and the pest
Of rows where thick rise the stones and brick,
 Shall some day be with the rest,
 And brood with the shades unblest.

Then wild in the dark let the lemurs bark,
 And the leprous spires ascend;
For new and old alike in the fold
 Of horror and death are penn'd,
 For the hounds of Time to rend.

Uncle's In the Treetops

Darrell Schweitzer

Yes, I can tell you about it.

It was in the Leaf Falling Time, when Uncle Alazar was in the treetops. He could come close to the Earth then, out of the midnight sky. You could hear him among the upper branches in the forest, sometimes skittering like a squirrel, sometimes hovering there, his wings buzzing and fluttering like those of some enormous insect. Whose uncle was he, precisely? There were stories about that, often contradictory. I'd been hearing them all my life. He was one of us, one of the Burton family, though whose brother and how many generations back, was not at all clear. He dwelt among Those of the Air. He spoke to the dark gods. He had gone to them, out into the night, and had never come back, not really, only able to return halfway like that, and was utterly transformed, beyond humanity altogether. Sometimes we Burtons heard him whispering to us. He reached into our dreams. My father had heard him, in his time, and my father's father, and *his* father; though not my mother, because she was only a Burton by marriage and there was something about the true blood that went back for years and years … but I digress.

Now, mind you, the village of Chorazin may be isolated, and it may be different in its customs, but it's still in Pennsylvania, not on Mars, so we do have some things in common with the rest of the world. We

have Halloween here, and Leaf Falling Time (old Indian name) is pretty much the same as Halloween, so we
indeed have kids in costumes shuffling noisily through
the leaves from house to house, collecting candy. They
travel in groups only, and make all that noise to scare
away Zenas, who was one of us once, so the story goes,
but he too went into the darkness on such a night and
became part of it – whether he was still alive or not was
a matter of some debate – and he supposedly had long,
sharp fingers like twigs, and you really didn't want to
meet him.

It was on such a night, after the candy and costumes
were put away. I'd gone as Darth Vader that year, my
brother Joram as a vampire. We sat on our porch in the
dark with our parents, my brother and I – he was ten,
three years younger than me – and two very distin-
guished visitors, Elder Abraham, who is our leader, and
his assistant Brother Azrael. They questioned Joram and
me closely, and spoke to us both in a very old-fashioned
way that I knew was part of the ritual.

My father sat wordlessly, while my mother let out a
little sob.

This was a serious business. People who went out
into the dark sometimes did not come back.

"Joram," said the elder. "Tell me in truth, hast thou
heard thine uncle's voice clearly and comprehended his
words? Wilt thou act as his messenger?"

"Yes, I will," my brother said.

The Elder turned to me. "And thou?"

"Yeah. Me too."

He reached out, and took both of us by the hand, and
joined our hands together, and he said, "Then you have
to go. Go now. "

I knew the rest, and we didn't have to rehearse it. The
signs had manifested themselves. The stars had turned
in their courses, as if tumblers had fallen into place in
a lock, and gateways in the sky were open, and Uncle

Alazar could come racing back out of the dark depths to speak to us on this night.

It was a very special time. To our people, though not to other Pennsylvanians, I am sure, a holy time.

My father spoke only briefly, to me, "Thomas, take care of your brother."

"I will, Dad."

So, hand-in-hand, my brother and I went. You could conjure up an almost bucolic scene, despite the spooky undertones, two boys holding hands for comfort, or so they wouldn't lose one another, two brothers making their way (noisily at first, kicking up leaves, then less noisily) into the wooded hills beyond the town, to fulfil some ancient rite, like a confirmation or a walkabout, some passage into manhood perhaps.

So we followed the unpaved road for a little bit, then cut across the fields, into the woods, beneath the brilliant stars, and what, I ask you, is wrong with this picture?

There are things I've left out.

The first is that I hated my brother intensely. I didn't show it, but I'd nursed my hatred in secret almost since when he was born. I didn't even know why at first. He was smarter than me, cleverer. My parents liked him best. When we were very young, he broke my toys because he could. He did better in school. (Ours was perhaps the last one-room school in the country, so I saw when he won all the prizes. That meant I'd lost them.) But more than that, *he* was the one Uncle Alazar had showed a special interest in. It was Joram's dreams that Uncle had entered into, so that Joram would sit up in his bed sometimes and scream out words in strange languages, and then wake up in a sweat and (absurd as it seems) sometimes come to me for comfort. And I pretended to comfort him, but I was false, always false, and I held my hatred in my heart.

This was all very distinct from sounds you heard overhead at night, that might have been squirrels or just the wind rattling branches, or a voice you heard from far off, like somebody shouting from a distant hilltop and you couldn't make out what they said, only the wailing, trailing cry. That was all my father had ever heard, or my grandfather, or my great-grandfather, because the gods, or Those of the Air, or even centuries-lost-departed-uncles did not communicate with us all that often, and it was very special when they did. Which of course made my brother very special.

And I was not. That was the next thing.

I had lied to Elder Abraham. I had heard nothing, myself. Once again I was false, and to lie to the Elder like that is a blasphemy, but I did it, and I had no regrets.

I had also promised my father that I would take care of my brother. That promise I would keep. Oh, yes. I would take care of him.

We walked through the woods in the dark, for miles perhaps. My brother was in some kind of trance, I think. He was humming softly to himself. His eyes were wide, but I don't think he was seeing in the usual way. I had to reach out and push branches out of the way so he wouldn't get smacked in the face. Not that I'd mind him being smacked in the face, but that didn't fit with what I intended, not yet. He seemed to know where he was going.

Uncle was in the treetops. I heard him too now, chittering, scrambling from branch to branch, his wings and those of his companions flapping, buzzing, heavy upon the air.

Joram began to make chittering noises, not bird sounds, more like the sound of some enormous insect, and he was answered from above.

I looked up. There was only darkness, and I could see the stars through the branches, and once, only once, did I see what looked like a black plastic bag detach itself from an upper branch and flutter off into the night; or that might have been a shadow.

I let Joram guide me, even though he couldn't see. I had to reach out and clear the way for him, but he was the one who led me on, even as we descended into a hollow, then climbed a ridge on the other side. The trees seemed larger than I had ever seen them, towering, the trunks as thick as houses; but that may have been a trick of the dark, or the night, or the dream which was pouring into my brother as he chittered and stared blindly ahead, and maybe I wasn't entirely lying after all, and maybe I really did feel a little bit of it.

We came to a particularly enormous tree, a beech it felt like from the smooth bark, with a lot of low branches all the way down the trunk to the ground. My brother began to climb. I climbed after him. By daylight, in the course of normal kid activities, I actually was a pretty good tree climber, but this wasn't like that at all. We went up and up, and sometimes the angles of the branches and the trunk itself seemed to twist strangely. Several times my brother slipped and almost fell, but I caught hold of him, and he clung to me, whimpering slightly, as if he were half awake and scared in his dream.

Did he know what I intended? He had every right to be scared. Hah!

Still we climbed, and now there were things in the branches with us, only way out on the swaying ends, and the branches rose and fell and rose and fell as half-seen shapes alighted on them. The air was filled with buzzing and flapping sounds. Joram made sounds I hadn't know a human throat could ever make, and he was answered by multitudes.

Then the branches cleared away, and we were beneath the open, star-filled, moonless sky, and Those of the Air circled around us now. Joram and I sat where the trunk forked, my arm around him, while with my other hand I held onto a branch. I could see them clearly, black creatures, a little like enormous bats, a little like wasps, but not really like either, and one of them came toward us, chittering, its face aglow like a paper lantern, its features human or almost human; and I recognized out legendary relative, the fabled Uncle Alazar whose special affinity to our family brought him back to this planet on such occasions as tonight, when the signs were as they needed to be and the dark, holy rites were to be fulfilled.

Now that Uncle was here, and I had used my gibbering brother to guide me to him, I had no further use for Joram, whom I had always hated; so I flung him from me, out among the swaying branches, and down he fell: screaming, thump, thump, thump, crash, thump, and silence.

I was almost surprised that none of the winged ones tried to retrieve him, but they didn't.

Uncle Alazar hovered before me, his eyes dark, his face inscrutable.

"I am afraid my brother isn't available," I said. "You will have to take me instead."

And they did take me. Hard, sharp fingers or claws seized hold of me from every side. Some grabbed me by the hair and lifted me up.

I was hanging in the air, with wings whirring and flapping and buzzing all around me, and yes, I was terribly afraid, but also I was filled with a fierce, grasping, greedy joy, because I had *done it* and now Uncle Alazar would have to reveal the secrets of the darkness and of the black worlds to *me*, and I would become very great among our people, a prophet, very special indeed, a great one, perhaps able to live for centuries like Elder Abraham or Brother Azrael.

Uncle's face floated in front of mine, filled with pale light. He spoke. He made that chittering sound. It was just noise to me. He paused. He spoke again, as if expecting a reply. I tried to reply, imitating his squeaks and chirps or whatever, and then, suddenly, he drew away, and made a very human "Hah!" sound, and they *dropped* me.

Down *I* went, through the branches: screaming, crash, thump, thump, thump, crash, thud. There was so much pain. I couldn't move. I don't know if what followed was a dream, because the next thing I knew Zenas had found me, he of the stiletto-sharp stick-like fingers, remember? He was naked, and very thin, his body elongated, almost like a snake, with way too many ribs, and his face was partly a man's face, with a wild mass of hair, but his eyes were multi-faceted and there was something very strange about his mouth. His jaws moved sideways like those of a praying mantis or a hornet, and he leaned down, out of my field of view, and came up again with a mouthful of bloody flesh. Zenas was *eating* me. I felt the bones of my legs crunching. I screamed and screamed and he went down and came up again with his mouth full, and gulped it down the way an animal would, and went back for more. I knew this couldn't be happening. It was impossible. I should have been dead by now. I should have bled to death, my guts gushing out like water from a balloon that's been slashed open. I went on screaming and the pain just wouldn't end. It went on and on. I pounded my fists on the ground to try to make it stop, but it did not stop.

At one point he stared into my eyes, and I was terribly afraid that he would take them. But he just remained there, making clicking sounds as if he were speaking a language I did not know. He was there long afterwards in my dreams, with his bloody saliva dripping down onto my face, burning.

And when I awoke, in my own room, in my own bed, I was swathed in bandages. My face was covered by something thick and heavy, but I could see out, and I could see that both of my arms were in casts and my legs were gone.

They tell me I screamed non-stop for another six months. I had to be put in an attic. There are, in Chorazin, lots of embarrassments hidden away in attics.

More than once, after I stopped screaming, Elder Abraham and Brother Azrael would come to see me, always late at night. They stood silently over my bed, regarding me, saying nothing. I could read nothing in their expressions. Once the Elder had a glowing stone with him, which he touched to my forehead. I didn't dare ask what that was about. I didn't dare say anything.

When my reason returned, more or less, and I had healed as much as I could, I was brought down from the attic, and began my new life as a cripple. My father had built a low, wooden cart for me. I could sit in it and reach over the sides to push myself along. No one mentioned Joram.

Almost a year had passed. That year, at Leaf-Falling Time, or Halloween as you'd call it, I sat with my parents on the porch as costumed children came up, fearfully, to receive a handful of candy, then scamper off. I just sat there in the dark, a lump of disfigured flesh. I don't think they knew I was awake, or could hear them when they whispered, "What is it?" and "That can't be him."

It was that year, too, on the evening after Halloween, which would be All Soul's Night (Halloween being the Eve of All Hallows – get it?) and that's what we called it too, that Elder Abraham led us all out into the woods, into the Bone Forest, where generations of bone offerings, our dead, animals, others, dangled from the trees and rattled in the wind. By torchlight he delivered a memorable sermon. I heard it all. The way was too rough for me to get there in a cart, so my father carried me in a satchel on his back, and I crawled up out of the satchel and clung to him, my arms around his neck, and looked over his shoulder and saw the Elder in his ceremonial robe and holding his staff with the glowing stone on the end of it.

He spoke about change, transformation and transfiguration, about how, in time, the Old Gods would return and clear off the Earth of all human things, and only those of us who were changed in some way would have any place in the new world. And he emphasized something that I thought was aimed just at me, that this change comes as inevitably as leaves falling in the autumn, or a tide on the seashore, rushing in. There is *no morality* to it, for such things mean nothing to the darkness and to those who dwell there. What happens merely happens because it has happened, because the stars have turned and the gateways between the worlds have configured themselves *just so.*

If I'd been better read, better educated, I might have called it fate. That year I became better read and educated. I got out more, wheeling my way here and there around the village, sometimes scaring the younger children and making other people turn away. For months I had been desperately afraid of mirrors. I could feel that my face was thick and stiff and my cheeks didn't move properly. I was afraid of how disfigured I might be. But in time was I angry. I had become a monster. I should damn well look like a monster. Finally I dared, and snatched up one of my mother's mirrors and saw that I was indeed hideous, as if my face had been half dissolved and partially reshaped, until I looked a little bit like an insect, a little bit like Zenas, though I did not have multi-faceted eyes and my jaws and teeth worked normally.

Fate, education, yes. There I went, scurrying and scooting around town, the object of horror and fascination. I went to the general store, where Brother Azrael kept his collection of ancient books and scrolls locked away in a back room. Those weren't for just anybody to read, but he unlocked the door to that room, and let me read them. He patiently tutored me in the languages required. He spoke to me of things we had known since the most ancient days, since before even Elder Abraham was alive, and Elder Abraham was over a thousand. ("He remembers when Charlemagne was king," the Brother told me, and later, from a more conventional set of encyclopedias, I learned who Charlemagne was.) That was the essence of our faith, what other people would call a religion, or the beliefs of a cult, that we had no faith, that we knew with certain knowledge that Elder Abraham was indeed that old, and that there are things in the sky and the earth that you can talk to, and that the elder powers will one day rule again where mankind rules now. These things are merely true, we know, from what we have seen and what we have done.

Yes, I even read part of the *Necronomicon.* It should not be surprising that someone as eminent as Elder Abraham or Brother Azrael should have a copy. I read it in Latin, which wasn't hard. For all my brother Joram had excelled me in school, I proved to have gift for languages, once I applied myself.

What comforted me most was that nowhere in all of this was there any discussion of *right and wrong* or of *morality.* It was just as the Elder had said. Things happen because they happen. In the larger scheme of things, by the standards of the Abyss and of the Black Worlds beyond the sky, such human concerns are irrelevant. Therefore I felt no guilt over what I had done. I had suffered much, but I was not sorry. It was like the leaves falling, or like a tide rushing in at the seashore.

I was also still a kid. I was, by my count, more than fifteen, and I should have been getting a bit old for Halloween, but I told my parents that I wanted to go out one last time, and either they felt sorry for me, or maybe they were even afraid, so they didn't stop me as I worked for hours on my "costume." If I was going to have to move around on wheels, I decided, I would go as a tank. I built a shell out of plywood and cardboard, complete with a swiveling turret, and I fit it over my cart, so I could indeed go out disguised as a goddamn Panzer tank from World War II, complete with an iron cross and swastikas painted on it. As a finishing touch, it was a flame-throwing tank. I rigged up a cigarette lighter and an aerosol can in the turret.

This did not work out well. When I trundled up to the first house and shouted "Seig Heil! Fuck you! Trick or treat!" the aerosol can exploded and the tank went up in a fireball and I set somebody's porch on fire, and then everybody was trying to beat the flames out with rugs and such before I burned down the whole village. I was screaming once more, and I was hurt, but my screams gave way to screeching and chittering the likes of which no human throat should be able to utter, and I was *answered*, right there in town, from some point above the rooftops, and I began to understand what was said.

Like I said, I had a gift for languages.

Once again I was in the attic for a while, gibbering. The Elder came and touched me with his glowing stone one more time.

I should mention that I had only one friend during this period. My parents were my parents, and Brother Azrael was my teacher, but the closest thing I had to a friend was the muddy kid, Jerry, or more formally Jeroboam. He was odd like me, not that he was misshapen or missing any limbs, but that his special talent was that he could swim through the earth as if through water, so that any time day or night when he felt the call, but especially on certain festivals, he would sink down into the ground without smothering and converse with our dead ancestors, or with others that lay there. Sometimes he would raise up the dead, or bone-creatures, like skeletal beasts, for us to ride on as we went to places of worship and sacrifice. The result of this was that he was always dirty; even when he tried to wash himself, he never got it all; and he could feel the dead beneath the ground whenever he could touch it with his skin, so he went barefoot much of the year, except when it was very cold. It was hell on his clothes too, so he would turn up at school that way sometimes, barefoot and smeared with mud and nearly naked, but that was just Jerry.

He was the one who told me what had happened in the village during the year I was in the attic. Something about a teacher who'd come from outside, and tried to change things, and who died. I thought it was funny. Jerry thought it was sad. Well, he as younger than me. I think that despite everything, he didn't get it. *There is no morality. Nothing is right or wrong.*

Nevertheless, he was my friend, even if he did betray me at the end, if that's what he did.

⚜

It was at the Leaf-Falling Time, yet again. Such things happen at particular times, because the cycles turn and the gates open.

I was in the attic. I wasn't confined there anymore, but I had grown to like it. It was only because my senses had begun to change, to become more acute, that I heard a very soft footstep on the stairs. Jerry, when he's barefoot like that can be almost totally silent, but I knew it was him, and it was. He had been swimming in the earth. Despite the cold of the season he only wore a pair of filthy denim cut-offs. He was covered with mud, but his face was streaked with tears.

He stood at the top of the attic stairs, looked at me, and said softly, "I know what you did."

And before I could make any argument about leaves and tides and there being no morality, something clumped and scraped and grabbed Jerry by the hair from behind and threw him, yelping and banging, down the stairs.

Joram. I suppose while Jerry was swimming around among the graves, he'd met my late brother, and Joram demanded to be taken to visit dear older brother Tommy, and now that this was accomplished he'd tossed Jerry aside like an empty candy wrapper. I only had to contend with Joram. You don't grow older when you're dead, so he was still ten years old, but he'd changed. He wore only shreds of the sheet he'd been buried in, and he moved strangely because his bones were still broken, and his face was terribly pale, his eyes very strange, his fingers long and thin like sharpened sticks.

He screamed at me, not in words, but chittering, and I understood how much he hated me, how much he resented that I had stolen his role in the future among the stars.

There's no morality. No right and wrong. We do what we do.

He lunged for me, shrieking. His mouth was distorted, almost like an insect's. I could see that his teeth were sharp points. His fingernails were like knives.

But I skittered aside. Since I had very strong arms, and there was only half of me left, my body was light, and I'd learned to move like the half-man, Johnny Eck, in that movie *Freaks*. (Brother Azrael had a secret TV and VCR hidden in the back room of his store. He'd showed it to me.) There were hoops of rope strung all over the attic rafters, and I grabbed hold of them, and swung out of reach, then moved like a monkey in treetops while Joram hissed and shrieked and crashed into furniture and shelves and storage boxes. I made it past him and down the stairs. I skittered right over Jerry, who was still lying there, stunned. Joram came after me.

That was when I heard real screaming, human screaming, from downstairs in the parlor. Two voices, a grown man and a woman, in utmost agony. My parents. But by the time I got to them it was too late. Zenas was there, all awash in blood, looming over them, gobbling. He had killed and partially eaten both of them. There was blood all over the walls and ceiling.

Joram was there. He shouted something to Zenas, who looked up, then began to follow me.

I scrambled out the front door and across the lawn, with Joram and Zenas both in close pursuit.

And came face to face with Elder Abraham and Brother Azrael in their ceremonial robes, both of them holding burning staves. Behind them the people of the village were gathered, costumed, not for Halloween festivities, though it was Halloween, but for something a lot more serious. They all wore masks, some like skulls, some like beasts, some like nothing that had ever walked the earth.

Zenas caught hold of me and lifted me up, and began to strip away the flesh from my back and shoulders, but Elder Abraham struck him with his staff, and he exploded into a cloud of blood and bones and flesh. Then Brother Azrael struck Joram, and he was gone too.

The Elder explained that some who go into the darkness and are changed and come back are failures, or of limited use.

But it would not be so for me.

Though I was hurt and bleeding, someone bore me up, and I was carried at the head of a procession, alongside the Elder and the Brother, with all the people behind us, singing. We filed through the Bone Forest. We went past the standing stones beyond it, into the woods again, on for miles, our way lit by the burning staves. The light reflected off eyes in the forest. I don't think it was wolves, but we were followed. I was even aware that Jerry was with us for a while, his arms crossed across his bare chest against the cold, limping from where he'd banged his knees on the stairs, trying to keep up.

When we came to the great tree, and the Elder bade me climb, Jerry didn't try to follow me. He was of the earth. He was never a very good climber anyway. Besides, he wasn't supposed to. This climb was for me alone. It was my fate or my destiny, if you want to call it that.

Elder Abraham spoke to me, in my mind, in the chittering, clicking language of Those of the Air, not using human words at all any longer. He didn't need to.

All these changes, he said, *all these sufferings and sacrifices, are stages in your transformation, for only those who are transformed, one way or another, have any place in the world that is to come. You have climbed, step by step, up a ladder, never faltering in your course, and that is good. You are the one who will climb on our behalf into the realm of the gods, and learn their secrets, and come back to us when it is the season, as their messenger. For this you must leave your humanity behind. All of it. Shed hate and fear and hope and love like old clothes.*

So I climbed, easily seizing one branch after another, swinging like a monkey.

The air began to fill with presences, with buzzing, flapping wings. Uncle Alazar was there. He bade me come to him, and I let go of the last branch, and allowed myself to fall.

But this time he and his companions bore me up, out of the tree. For an instant I could see the dark hills, and the fields, and the few lights of Chorazin in the distance, but then I was surrounded by the stars of space, and I lost all sense of time in that cold, dark voyage. The black planets loomed before me, Yuggoth, and more distant Shaggai, and others without names, beyond the Rim. We swooped low through an endless valley lined with frozen gods, those that slept and waited and dreamed while the cycles turned. Their immense shapes were like nothing that ever walked the earth, or ever will until the end. They spoke to me, inside my head, in muted thunder, and I learned their ways.

Again space opened up, and we were falling, swirling around and around into a great whirlpool of the void, for a thousand years, I think, or a million, or for all of time, while in the far distance and faintly I heard the throbbing, pulsating drumming that is the voice of ultimate chaos, which is called Azathoth.

There was no morality in all this, no good or evil, right or wrong. These things *were.* They *are* and *shall be.*

Other such notions I had left behind, discarded with my humanity.

That's the story. Uncle's in the treetops. So am I. He and his fellows worship me now, because I went so much farther than even they ever did. I am like a god to them.

Joram is not here. Zenas is not here. Neither are Elder Abraham or Brother Azrael, though they can sense my presence, and we converse.

I returned to Earth, to Chorazin in the Pennsylvania hills, because the time and the seasons and the motions of the stars decreed. I fell backwards through millions of years. But I did not arrive precisely back at the point from which I'd departed.

I manifested myself to my old friend Jerry, who was a grown man now, though he looked pretty much the same, long-limbed and smooth-skinned and always covered with mud. I don't know if he was exactly glad to see me, but I don't think he was afraid.

The Elder and the Brother had not changed at all. They do not.

I can't actually touch the earth. I can't come down. You will have to come to me if you want to know more. Climb.

Down into Silence

Storm Constantine

Sometimes, places are more beautiful in decay, no matter how elegant and grand they might have been in their prime. Gone the straight lines of walls and roofs, gone the smooth roadways, the tidy gardens. The mellow light of October gilds the ancient stone, the defiant spires still standing. The sun falls down the cloud-flecked sky, robed in the colours of harvest. The palette of Fall roars against the dark hills, the trees still clothed in finery, hanging on, perhaps, for the ball, the festival: All Hallows' Eve. Gazing upon such a scene, you cannot help but feel melancholy, grieving for a world you never knew, but which you know is lost forever and cannot truly be restored or replicated, even as a theme park. That lost world was somehow greater than what has come to replace it.

There are few hidden places now, few uncovered secrets—*anywhere*. We know the secrets of Innsmouth, or what the alleged witnesses told us were true so long ago. Nearly a hundred years has passed. The way the town draws her skirts around the truth is clever; those who *did* witness, *if* they did, lost a degree of sanity, could never be thought of as entirely reliable again. Maybe *none* of it was true. The surviving records sound like witch trials to me, more imagination than fact.

And yet, standing here on the bridge over the tumbling River Manuxet, gazing out to sea, I wonder. The fact is, I *want* it to be true, all of it.

I went to Innsmouth to capture the spirit of the town in pictures—this is my hobby, not my job. I visit places of ill or unusual reputation and post the results of my captures on a blog. Halloween seemed an appropriate time of year to visit this allegedly blighted spot. So—I'm on holiday, shooting the memory of monsters, but not with a gun.

I've already begun to compose the text that will accompany my pictures. I think the old stories are *based* on fact but have been exaggerated over the years. The only person who revealed the "truth" was Zadok Allen in the 1920s, and he was hardly a reliable source, being an aged and raddled alcoholic. Robert Olmstead, who collected and revealed Allen's ramblings, proved to be equally unreliable. Claiming to be a "descendent" of the famed Marsh family, he ended his life in an asylum. Records state that a tumour on the brain altered his behaviour and made him prey to delusions. Most historians interested in the town believe Allen and Olmstead concocted the most outrageous of the stories between them. Allen, immersed in inebriated fantasies fuelled by paranoia and plain lunacy, found in Olmstead an eager and gullible listener, who egged him on, drawing ever more dubious tales from the old drunk.

When I first arrived in town, like everyone I suppose, I began hunting for the "Innsmouth Look" in the faces of the inhabitants—traces of a batrachian ancestry, beasts from the sea and their hybrid offspring. But it soon became clear that the majority of the modern population came from somewhere else. There is plenty of work here now. Innsmouth is up there with Salem and Arkham as a tourist destination. There's a huge welcome sign on the main road in, sporting a cheerful fish man waving at new arrivals with webbed hands, claiming "Welcome to the Darkest Corner of New England". I forced myself not to buy a luridly-green, batrachian plushie *thing* from the gift shop I passed, even though I could imagine the toy sitting on my work station and how well it would go with my other fetishes. But regardless of the kitsch appeal, I felt it was more of an abomination than anything that might have happened here in the past. Yet despite the gift shop and the welcome sign, the place is still recognisable as the town that fell to ruin early in the twentieth century. The famous old landmarks remain, even if a couple more cafés have been added to the main square. *The Gilman House Hotel*, the largest hostelry in town, has been renovated to a state of shabby chic—it's now fit to house guests. Those who run Innsmouth must be aware that the greater part of the town's allure—and therefore their livelihoods—derives from what it *was* and that must not be obliterated.

Of course, I *had* to stay at *The Gilman House*. Even though other guest houses in the area had interesting names, *Obed's Rest, Sumatry* and *Eliza Orne's Cottage*, I doubted the people who worked in them were natives to the area.

I registered in the lobby, which was hung with plaited ropes of dwarf corn cobs dyed different shades of red, orange and gold. Before the desk was a pile of plump pumpkins carved into grimacing faces.

When I entered my room, it smelled of spiced soup and candy, undoubtedly courtesy of a seasonally-themed air freshener.

Now, I gaze out of the window. Innsmouth is quite beautiful in the light of the fading day. I wish, though, I was closer to the sea. I'll eat dinner in the hotel, and afterwards will take my initial steps into the town, without baggage; the true start of my exploration. I prefer to absorb the atmosphere of a place, attune to it with my senses, before capturing its soul through my camera. Sniper shots on my phone, however, are allowed.

The Gilman House lies on the Town Square and

my first pictures are taken from my window. There's a fountain in the middle of the square now, with wooden benches around it. Children are playing there. Immense stone fishes with mad eyes vomit water into the wide, sea-shell bowl.

The old families of Innsmouth were supposed to have died out or been killed, but over the years off-shoots of these lines have appeared from other, often distant places. Perhaps they are charlatans, but they have reclaimed their ancestral homes with the blessing of the town council. They too are now part of the tourist industry, even if their eyes don't bulge, and they have discernible chins, the necks beneath disappointingly lacking gills.

According to Olmstead, when he visited this town, he eventually had to escape it, pursued by monstrous inhabitants. I suppose he *could* have been driven out of town, but surely only because the community was closed, undoubtedly inbred, and resented outsiders poking about. It's likely many of them had been deformed because of their heritage. Maybe the legendary sea captain Obed Marsh *did* bring strange ideas back with him from his voyages to Polynesia. But had the inhabitants of Innsmouth bred with fish people? Much as the idea is appealing for someone who loves mystery and strangeness, I don't think so. I accept it's possible they worshipped gods of the sea and believed the agents of those gods were fishlike beings that could come onto the land. The Esoteric Order of Dagon, whose temple still stands, was undoubtedly an offshoot of Freemasonry that embraced the new religion Marsh brought to the town. The people believed in it and their town—particularly their fishing—flourished; the power of suggestion is a powerful thing. Believe something hard enough and you can make it true.

There's no doubt that something shady went on that inspired the government to raid the town in 1927. The official report claims this was bootlegging and no doubt it was. The bootleggers fought back, and many were killed. Perhaps they hid some of their booty beneath the sea, which accounts for the explosions that allegedly took place near Devil's Reef.

There *is* truth there, I'm sure, but also fantasy and wishful thinking.

Still, I must open myself to all possibilities and search. I'll expose myself to the ambience of Innsmouth, sniff out its soul.

The elegant dining room of the *Gilman House Hotel* is Edwardian in theme. The staff are quiet yet pleasant. The dinner they bring me is seafood, exquisitely cooked. I wonder what the ghost of Robert Olmstead would think if he was sitting here with me, observing this lovingly reimagined building. It's easy to picture him there, opposite me. He appears somewhat surly in a shabby dark suit.

"You see, Robert," I tell him silently, "all your efforts did no good. The town did not sink into the sea. The notoriety you enhanced has made it *this*. The food is very good."

Remembered as being an ascetic, if not a miserly man, he no doubt disapproves of the luxurious fare.

I often create invented beings to accompany me on my travels. I see them as tendrils from the deepest pools of my mind that are able to communicate with me. I decide to take this *idea* of Robert with me on my walks. I'll allow him to talk to me, see what comes out of my imagination.

We take the main road across the river, Federal Street, which has the largest bridge. Below us, towards the harbour, the waters throw themselves over the lip of the falls, eager for the sea. The air is full of mist and the perfume of the land—water, wet rock, the tang of salt.

On the bridge across the Manuxet, which feels flimsy above the rowdy waters, I pause to take in the scene. I take a few shots on my phone, place-markers for the future.

Robert is uncomfortable, perhaps afraid.

"It was a long time ago," I tell him. "Nothing can harm you now, not even memory."

It's recorded that, when he died, Robert Olmstead firmly believed he was living in a palace beneath the ocean, so perhaps my *tulpa* of him fears the recent changes in Innsmouth more than its history.

On the other side of the Manuxet, we turn east into River Street and follow this until we reach Water Street and the harbour. Everything looks ancient and faded, but not derelict—a deliberate effect. The tide is in, and the fishing boats rub against one another in the docks. I wonder whether they are still used for fishing or merely for ferrying tourists, perhaps not even that. Along the sea front, there are cafés and fish restaurants, yet more gift shops, and a small maritime museum. There are piles of pumpkins here too, most of them for sale, heaped outside the small shops. Their smell soaks the air, mingling with the aroma of the sea. Seagulls hang in the air, uttering cries that conjure inexorably the boundless summers of childhood. Families stroll up and down the harbour. A child skips by me, wearing a witch's hat and holding a green balloon with a picture of a fishy face on it.

In the water, a few heads of corn are bobbing—an accidental spill from a shop crate or a local custom? I photograph the scene on my phone.

The harbour is constructed around a cup-shaped cape, with the open side to my right. A spit of land can just be discerned across the water. Beyond that, the ocean will be wild, untamed, unlike this waterfront calm. Perhaps the far side will be more like the original Innsmouth. As I stare at it, the place exudes a greater sense of desolation.

As the night draws in and the temperature drops, a

grey veil of mist rises from the prowling sea, but I think I can just about make out the dark smudges of the reef emerging from the far waters to the northeast of the cape, the smash of waves against them.

Robert is being stubborn. When I invite him to talk all he can repeat in my head is "I cannot be made to shoot myself."

Perhaps I should discard him as a companion for a while.

Leaving him to mutter at the water, I head back across the bridge towards the old wharfs, which are picturesquely decayed. A mass of brightly-painted small boats cluster around them, rising and falling restlessly on the high tide, like gulls waiting to be fed. But then I see they are chained together and held to the land with locks and keys. According to a painted sign on the boardwalk, again with cartoon representations of cheery fish people, these vessels can be hired by tourists. In addition, organised trips in larger boats will ferry people out to Devil Reef, where you may peer into the waves and hope to see something scary peering back. I might go there tomorrow.

I find the wharfs beautiful. They have not been overly "prettified" and their sagging boards feel restful rather than an unsettling reminder of inevitable decay.

I wander along the boardwalk, soaking up the atmosphere, taking a few shots on the phone now and again. There are few other people here, as most tourists no doubt prefer the attractions of the harbour and the centre of town.

Eventually the boardwalk sinks into gritty sand, tufted with coarse dune grass. There is a strong salty smell. The twilight comes down and I see there is a figure at the water's edge. It wears a long bulky coat and appears to be poking around in the rock pools. This person is awkward somehow, their movements those of a self-conscious teenager not yet at home in their skin.

The figure pauses as I approach, and I sense within them an urge to flee.

"Hi," I say—not too enthusiastically, hardly more than a sigh, really.

I see it's a woman before me; as yet I can't determine her age, but she doesn't *feel* old to me. She grunts and sidles away. All I see is the gleam of an eye through the lank dark hair that hangs over her face. She's different. She's wary. What's she doing out here?

"Do you live here?" I ask her.

She straightens up and stares at me. She has huge round eyes in a long face, but her jaw is firm and well-sculpted, her lips somewhat thin. She is young, perhaps in her early twenties. She doesn't have the "look", as it's described, yet to me she's... *other.* Her long coat hangs open revealing a fisherman's jumper and trousers tucked into waterproof boots. She carries over her arm a basket filled with shells and stones. "What do you want?" she says in a heavy accent that has a foreign lilt to it.

"I'm a photographer, and I'd like to take your picture."

She coughs out a short laugh then. She knows my sort, doesn't have to say so. She's not conventionally photogenic, so my reasons for capturing her must be voyeuristic in a sense other than sexual. *Freak.*

But she's not hideous. If anything, she's striking: her long hair drifting like strands of seaweed on the breeze, her gaze steady and dark. I can see her in a picture and it would be a good one. It wouldn't be a picture of a freak.

"My name is Maisie Horne." I fish out a card from my jacket pocket. It's turned to felt at the edges from living in my coat too long, but I hold it out to her.

She looks at it without moving.

"When I photograph a place, I seek its inner life, its soul, if you like. I look for interesting people who have stories in their faces..."

I trail off. It sounds ridiculous.

The woman takes the card from me, holds it close to her eyes to study it. "Do you pay?" she asks.

"Yes," I answer at once, even though my funds aren't that healthy at the moment."I pay twenty-five dollars for a few shots."

She sniffs. "Fifty. Take it or leave it."

I can tell she won't negotiate, but the price is still cheap, of course. I nod. "OK. I can stretch to that if you give me a full hour. Tomorrow?"

She puts my card in her pocket. "Has to be morning. Early. Around seven. Have things to do."

"That's fine." I pause. "Would you let me have your name?"

"Kezia."

I'm itching to point my phone at her, but sense this is not part of our agreement; it would seem too eager.

"I'm staying at *The Gilman*. Would you meet me there?"

"I'll be outside at seven," she says and turns her back to me.

I stand there for some moments, because although our scene has ended, we're both still standing in it. It's awkward. I'll go and look for Robert. "Goodbye," I say, but she doesn't respond.

I find Robert sitting on a memorial bench at the harbour. He's staring moodily out to sea. I've seen photos from his medical records, but the man before me now is shape-shifting, perhaps becoming more like what I find interesting rather than what he really was. He's dark, ascetic-looking, but attractive in a gaunt, Gothic way. No one would believe his anguished stories. He's tragic.

"Let's go back to the Hotel," I say to him. "You must sit downstairs in the bar alone, but you have plenty of money and can drink there."

When I'm creating imaginary people, I try to give them some autonomy, the permission to exist when I'm not there. Whether this is effective or not, I of course have no idea.

I meet Robert at breakfast. He's sitting at one of the tables and appears to have been waiting for some time. He's irritated. I sit down and say good morning. A waitress comes to take my order—no buffet meals here. Today is the Eve of the Hallows, the day when the veil between the worlds of the living and the dead is reputedly thin. Perhaps this is true. Robert is vivid across the table from me.

"I'm going to take photographs of a young woman this morning," I tell him. In my mind, I'm talking aloud, but naturally it's not advisable to talk to invisible people in public. Our conversations must remain private, silent. "I want you to come with me and tell me what you think about her."

Robert doesn't speak but stares at me, blinks once.

"I want to believe she's a descendant of an original inhabitant," I say. "Perhaps you'll have more idea about this than me."

He shrugs, then says, "Why do you keep me here?"

"Because you're a witness. You can help me. I'm here for two days, then you can go."

He looks at me with contempt, so I visualise the waitress bringing him a breakfast and he has to eat it. His miserliness won't allow him to let the food go to waste.

After our meal, when we go outside, Kezia is standing hunched on the hotel porch, her hands thrust into the pockets of her coat, which hangs open and looks somewhat damp and mildewy, as does the long black woollen dress she wears beneath it. Her feet are encased in workman's boots. "Can I have my money?" she asks.

"When I've taken the pictures," I reply, then add, "I need to go to the bank. I have no cash."

"Where you want to go?"

"Well, let's just walk, shall we? You must know the streets that are least touched by... change."

I notice she glances to the side of me, where Robert is standing. For a moment I think she can see him, then realise she must be looking into the hotel lobby, which is no doubt a place she's never been.

She jerks her head to indicate I should follow her.

After calling at the bank, where she waits outside for me, we head down to the waterfront, but not to the harbour. We traverse one of the six bridges across the river into a residential area. There are fewer tourists here, even though a fair percentage of the buildings are now guest houses. The decorations on the doors are tradition-al—woven dried grasses, elaborate wreaths of foliage and dried fruit, with the inevitable cackling pumpkins squatting on the porches.

"This town is lucky, in a way," I say to Kezia. We have walked most of the way in silence, with her only occasionally pointing out areas of interest to me.

"How do you figure that?" she asks.

"Well, because of its history, for a long time it was… shunned. This means it wasn't gutted and mauled by town planners. What remains has been renovated with at least some dignity or left alone completely. Have you lived here all your life?"

"It's my home."

"Let's take some shots here."

I position her before the tall, gambrelled buildings of Washington Street, but she doesn't look comfortable. This isn't her area; at one time it was affluent, before it was abandoned, and now it's affluent again. I realise I'm imagining she's lived here since the 1920s, which is clearly not the case. She's no ghost, and if she were really that old, she would've transformed into a denizen of the sea, as the elderly Innsmouth inhabitants were said to do. "Isn't that right, Robert?" I ask silently.

"That's what happened," he says. He's oddly un-moved by Kezia. I was hoping for fear, surprise… something.

"If you were to be photographed in the place you felt you most belonged, where would it be?" I ask her.

"Out by the sea," she says.

"The wharfs?"

"The place I love is the far side of the cape. It's wild. No one goes there."

"Sounds perfect," I say.

"It's a long walk."

"That's OK."

On the way, I take pictures of the houses and occasional shots of Kezia when she's not aware. She feels increasingly to me like a teenager who wants to appear rebellious or different. She's not told me her surname and I realise I'm not going to ask for it; I'll imagine it's Marsh, Waite or Eliot, or another belonging to one of the old families, not a name from somewhere else, somewhere new.

We walk down Martin Street towards the sea and eventually come to Water Street, which follows the harbour all the way round the inner rim of the cape. Gradually the buildings become fewer and shops and cafes are no longer to be seen. As we reach the farthest side, the quays are more widely-spaced, and the boats moored there are mostly dilapidated. Sheds huddle in exhausted groups. A cold wind blows over the land, which is flat and sandy, but for the rise of dunes on the seaward side, and covered in a dry kind of grass that is almost colourless. The only trees are bent and spiny like hunched crones, maledictory branches pointing like fingers. Water Street persists, but is now a sodden boardwalk, occasionally covered by sand. Bleached wooden picket fencing staggers beside it, almost upright in places, but mostly fallen, with grass growing over it.

"Stand still," Kezia says to me. "Listen."

The wind is singing, or perhaps hidden within it is a voice calling from the deeps. Melancholia steals over me. I'm overwhelmed by a feeling of reverence.

"This is the best spot to hear the song of the wind and sea," Kezia tells me.

I realise she's opening up slowly, if not exactly warming to me. "I can see why you love it here," I say. I notice Robert has wandered off towards the open ocean to the east. He's of course drawn mournfully to what he believes lies beneath the waves.

Kezia and I walk in the same direction. The smell of salt and fish is overpoweringly strong. We climb a rise of dunes and, once at the apex, gaze down a stone-littered sandy slope towards the sea. To our left a tall, sagging lifeguard's chair still stands, if leaning dangerously towards the ground. It's hard to imagine that once people spent summer days here, children running in and out of the waves, women lying down on the sand wearing sunglasses. Now, the beach lies desolate and abandoned, as if we've walked into the far future of the world and no one is left alive, anywhere. But what kind of people once came here?

As the wind grabs handfuls of Kezia's hair, I photograph her against the backdrop of the open ocean. Devil's Reef is clearer now, the suggestion of land upon the horizon. If we drew closer to it, we'd be able to see it is jagged and deadly.

The Deep Ones come from below, it's said, to cavort upon the sharp rocks, to take the sacrifices offered to them. Here is the sea priestess, ready to preside over the festival of death. She's disguised in dingy clothes, but her eyes are on fire and her smile fierce. She gives herself to the air, at one point throwing out her arms, her head flung back, a laugh pealing from her. Robert stands behind her, some distance off, a thin black shape amid the dune grass.

In Kezia's moments of joy, it's hard to credit she's a native of this place. Surliness is a documented accessory to the Innsmouth Look. She's in love with the town and its landscape certainly, fascinated by it, perhaps obsessed, but is she that different to me? Has she moved here to live or, when she told me Innsmouth was her home, was that only her dream?

"Have you ever seen the ocean glow?" I ask her.

She glances at me suspiciously, then answers guardedly, dropping back to sullenness. "Sometimes it does."

There's a silence, then I say, "This place is precious. We should be glad people are taking care of it, even if they don't fully realise what it is they're looking after."

"Shouldn't be this way," Kezia snaps angrily, loudly. Her sudden mood change is unsettling. "One man killed old Innsmouth… just one man. Couldn't leave it alone."

I glance somewhat nervously at Robert and say gently, "If it hadn't been him, then it would have been someone else, Kezia. Innsmouth couldn't have stayed hidden for ever. The modern world doesn't allow that. If Innsmouth had—or has—an enemy it is time, the changes in society, not merely the word of one man."

"He was bitter," Kezia says, in a voice craving for vengeance. "He wanted to be here, he was one of them, but he ruined it. They chased him out and then, like a mean little boy, he told tales."

Her impassioned words make her sound more ordinary—rooted in the mundane world—and yet at the same time more credible as the opposite. I realised her summary is accurate. In no single account did anyone ever wonder if the people of Innsmouth had been frightened, could perceive the potential of their own fate in this meddling, damaged man.

"She's right, isn't she?" I say to Robert, not even sure if I've bothered to keep the words silent.

He stares at me mulishly. "I want to go home."

The crossing is easy, of course, at this time of year.

Kezia has also fixed me with a stare. "Can you take him?" I ask her. "He was never quite himself, you know."

Her eyes are fathomless, and she is so still, like a picture. Then she turns to where Robert is standing. I raise the camera before my face but close my eyes as I take the shot.

I remain like that for some time, and when I lower the camera, I'm alone. I leave fifty dollars on the grass and hold down the notes with a stone.

The War on Halloween

Cody Goodfellow

When they were ready to open the doors, the Devil took a velvet knee and led them in prayer.

"Lord," he prayed, "we beseech thee, help us to touch the hearts of both sinners and saved who come to us on this unhallowed night, when the forces of darkness are at their most potent. Let our humble show be the hand on the shoulder that turns lost souls to the light of your divine countenance... And grant us the strength to forgive whoever wantonly vandalized our frontage with spraypaint and, uh... excrement today... I know they know not what they do, but they also know not whom they're messing with... Amen. To Hell with the Devil!"

"To hell with the devil," replied the assemblage of the damned, just before All Souls Southern Baptist Church of Shafter's Devil's Dungeon attraction opened its doors on Halloween night.

The attraction was Pastor Gary Horton's brainchild, and he'd run it for six years out of the abandoned Wal Mart on Main Street with the devoted if not capable support of Leah Dupar, Wenda Orlick and Burt Coughlin. While the other pastors begged for pennies from their aging, underemployed flock, Gary summoned the whole county's godless masses and shoved the wages of sin in their faces every weekend of October, the unholiest month on the calendar, at ten bucks a head. He was the reason the church's youth group was so successful, and God-fearing families with theatrically-minded teens from up and down the state moved *to* the dying agricultural town to work the annual event.

Though they tried to take it from him every year, Horton had clung to the Devil's Dungeon as his family left him and his middle school teaching job was ripped away for ministering to students in danger of turning to the gay lifestyle, and as servants of Satan throughout the county targeted him for advocating a ban on trick-or-treating and secular "Satanic entertainments."

Pastor Gary was a Christian warrior, and Halloween night his annual battlefield for the souls of the youth of his town. But he had never stepped into an acting role himself, choosing to watch from on high and sometimes ambush teens making out in the dead-end corridors of the house.

Dane Duncan was their regular Satan. Waiting at the end of the maze, he judged the pie-eyed rubes as they stumbled out of the last of the five major rooms and were shoved down a spiral slide to the exit.

When Dane missed his call time and didn't pick up his phone, Pastor Horton suspected it had something to do with Trisha, the young ingénue anchoring the abortion room this year. Eating all the snacks in the break room and crying a lot was expected. The role called for nonstop hysterics, but Gary had a director's sixth sense for when it wasn't just acting.

Gary was looking for a substitute when the spirit suddenly came upon him, and he sat down in the chair himself and told Wenda to get busy.

Acting was a dangerous art, but that was exactly why they used it to reach the sinners. They had to scrap the gay rave torture chamber, because the pressure of living such a role for two weeks plus rehearsals put ideas in one's head that never washed out.

They were getting ready to open when Gary did the

final walk-through. Every inch of the Cutting Room, a gallery of teen suicide and self-destruction, dripped pop and rap lyrics, scrawled in stage blood. The Rumpus Room reeked of fake vomit and stale beer, but the old drunk driver's Honda Civic was replaced at great expense this year with a Burning Man scene, where wild-eyed hipster savages in day-glo warpaint put the torch to a screaming Christian family.

The Chat Room was a labyrinth of mirrors and old monitors streaming sexy ads, youtube vids and sexting messages, the screens dazzling you while depraved sex offenders and werewolf child molesters leapt out to ambush and drag you back to their blacklight suicide booths.

The Sacred Grove was set for its endless pagan ritual, where gay satyrs and lesbian centaurs frolicked to New Age Muzak and hooded acolytes chanted blasphemous factoids about evolution.

He skipped the Black Chapel, where he would judge the damned, turned for the exit when he heard voices, felt approaching footsteps through the plywood floor.

His pulse doubled, teeth gritted until he tasted flakes of enamel. Did he hear that rasp and thud, like shuffling, dragging feet? If those darned vandals came back—Did he smell that stink of ammonia, of mothballs and dead animal musk?

No!

Someone ran into him. He screamed and shoved the assailant into a painted flat. The other fell ass-first through the canvas, clutching his throat, giggling like a lunatic.

"Trick or treat, Pastor Gary," he croaked. "Smell my feet."

"Quit clowning, Todd." Gary offered his hand. "Are you high on something?"

Todd giggled maniacally. His glasses hung askew on his face, which was the ashy gray of soap scum, slimy with snot and tears. His hair was shot through white streaks, his eyes like puddles of mud. If it was makeup, Wenda had really outdone herself.

Jaws working, one hand clutched at his neck just under his ear and a gush of glistening red shadow came out his mouth. Then it was gone, just a trick of the light.

Half the time, the kid smelled like pot. Maybe he'd given Gary a "contact buzz." Todd Chicoine was the haunt's semi-official photographer. Never a member of the church, Todd lurked in the corridors and snapped flash photographs of patrons screaming, which generated a nice extra revenue stream.

"Todd, get your act together, we're about to open." He reached for the kid's hand again, but Todd scooted backwards until he hit a solid wall. His movements had the spent, underwater quality of a marathon runner collapsing on the finish line. His camera snapped off a couple pictures, the flash stunning Gary.

"I can't believe it… I'm not… I'm not really out, it wouldn't just let me out…" He touched his neck, then looked at his hand. "*You* did it… *Was* it you? It wasn't *you*… was it?"

"Where have you been, Todd?" He began to wonder if he hadn't solved the mystery of today's vandalism, in the bargain.

Todd stared at him like he'd never seen him before. "Why, right *here*, Pastor Gary. In the *Black Chapel. I tried to leave, but it won't let me.* Where have *you* been?"

"Looking for you, Todd. And praying for you."

A giggle like a seizure shook Todd. "Oh please, Pastor Gary, pray for me!" He pounded the floor with his fist. A blood vessel seemed to burst behind one eye like a shadow leaking out, as he coughed, "Looking for me… I… oh, God… I've been looking for you, too. And I found you, at the end…" He laughed harder, and then he was crying, clearly a candidate for the Burning Man room tonight.

Gary tried to lift Todd to his feet, but the kid screamed, "Get off me, God damn you!" Gary dropped him. For just a second, when they were pressed together, Todd felt wet, sticky, like he was covered in fake blood. Or the other kind…

"Stop talking like that, Todd." He couldn't stop wiping his hands off on his cape. "You don't know the first god—the first thing about God or the Bible."

Todd giggled. "I know all about that part where God and Satan are like, wrecking this guy's life just to see if he'll curse the Lord. Like a rich man making a bet with his chauffeur, about if a loyal dog will bite you, before you kick it to death?"

"That's enough."

"I have it straight from the horse's mouth, it's the only part of the Bible that's true."

"Shut up, Todd."

"I'm just the message in this bottle, man. What did you build this place to show people? It wants to show *you*, Gary. Go look in the last room. You'll see… You'll see who wrote the message…" He laughed again, harder. Gary was barely reining in his temper when Todd went into convulsions, swallowing his own tongue. Gary tried to hold him down, shouting for someone to call 911.

It was too late. His eyes fixed on Gary's hairline, he just stopped. Gary set the kid down. Picked up his camera and flicked the screen on the back to review the pictures he took, to find out what the heck happened.

He wanted to drop it. Smash it and stomp on it. There could be no doubt, unless they were *both* losing their minds.

Todd had indeed been to Hell, and come back with pictures.

They were blurry, lit only by fire, rendering the capering silhouettes into literal devils, demons, monsters and witches. Amid the flames they reveled in and worshiped, bodies hung like rotisserie chickens just above the heads of the crowd, dangling from the lamppost in the parking lot out front of the Devil's Dungeon—

He dropped the camera. The floor squirmed underfoot and nearly missed him when he fell on his ass. He saw it watching him.

In the doorway of the Black Chapel. He saw a thing of black glass. Regal and rigid, a faceless pharaoh. Its skull opened like an orchid and a crown of mouths did say his name, and the sound of its wings was a voice like frigid mercury knives rasping between his teeth that did tell him the wicked would be winnowed away from the righteous, and he would be the instrument of their deliverance.

Nearly tearing his velvet-trimmed cape when he stood in his cloven-hoof boots, Gary unclipped the pepper spray off his belt and ran to the Black Chapel. He took no notice of the sound of a massive door slamming behind him, for he knew the Black Chapel, like every room in the haunt, had no door.

❖

"Gary, do you still believe that Todd's death was a sign from God?"

Gary blinked and resisted knuckling his eyes like a kindergartener at nap time. Lean back in the leather recliner, try not to make fart noises the microphone under your sweat-sticky shirt will pick up. "Nancy," he said, then remembered to look at the host, "I've asked myself so many times… Look… What happened to Todd was between him and God, but every one of us can draw our own conclusions."

It still rankled him that he had to answer these questions, but resisting the revisitation was all part of the act that had, in the twelve months since that fateful night, propelled him into the national spotlight.

Nancy dragged the bait back in front of him. "In your sermons, you still call him a casualty of war."

Gary shrugged and tried out a disarming smile that looked better on almost anyone else. "I know I should go off foaming at the mouth and giving you the soundbytes you need to throw more gas on this fire without ever teaching or convincing anyone… but here goes.

"I'm not afraid to say it. We're fighting a war against evil. And I still believe poor Todd Chicoine was struck down by a vision he had of the world to come, if we continue to lie to ourselves about the nature of evil, while we're all marinating in it."

The host simpered, "I think everybody's onboard in the fight against evil… but why *Halloween*, Gary? It's America's second most favorite holiday. It's about fun and fantasy, not Satanism."

He pivoted to mad-dog the host's eyeline, though she'd wandered off the set to refresh her drink. "People don't need to cut up black cats or listen to Judas Priest backwards to worship Satan, Nancy. They just have to sit back and please themselves. Halloween is the second most lucrative holiday for retailers, so speaking out is a threat to America's *real* religion. It mocks God and celebrates darkness and evil in the worst way possible, with a nod and a wink that says it's all a big joke."

Turn to look dead into the camera. "But it thrills the Devil to see folks who think they've outgrown faith wallowing in pagan idolatry, and giving in to their most self-destructive urges. It exalts him to see empty people playing at cartoon monsters while real monsters walk among us every day, because we all believe there's no plan, no God watching, no reason to be good."

Drink discreetly out of frame, Nancy cut him off and took Camera 2 for a tight close-up. "A lot of people are taking your message seriously, and they're saying this Halloween, they're not going to be silent. But a lot more people are pretty angry at you, Gary Horton."

Gary sipped water from a coffee cup, noticing he had white curds of foam in the corners of his mouth. These cable hosts were easier to work than a pro wrestling referee. Gary smiled, and said what he always said. "I'm not even the messenger, killing me won't stop what's coming. I'm just an envelope, containing the message. It's up to you folks out there to take it in, or stamp it RETURN TO SENDER."

It's never stopped feeling like a miracle, he thought as the segment cut to commercial, and the kids watching in the break room burst into wild applause. He shut off the TV, told them to get back to work and went to check the crowds.

If he didn't believe before that the Lord had a plan for him, then the last eleven months had made him a knower. Without setting his foot on the path, some force had not so much guided as pushed and prodded him up out of obscurity. Presidential and congressional candidates wanted photos with him, and knitted their brows seriously as they endorsed his crusade. Many authoritative voices on the national stage agreed that the seeds of this "innocent" children's holiday had blossomed into pernicious weeds of adult lawlessness and violence, and statistics showed ever-escalating acts of hostility towards the church and anyone who opposed vice and blasphemy, that would only worsen with every return of that cancer on the calendar.

With Todd's death, the Devil's Dungeon was shut down by the Sheriff last Halloween night, but the notoriety *of the hell house that scared a man to death,* fueled by the video of Gary railing at the deputies who dispersed the rowdy crowd, went viral. Most folks laughed at the wild-eyed hick ranting about the Devil in his cheap Devil costume, but god-fearing folks from all over reached out, telling him they felt his message, they saw the same signs he did, and they wanted to help.

Within three months, he bought the old Wal Mart and made the Devil's Dungeon into a radical new youth church. Their numbers were still small, but his web-sermons racked up a couple million views every week, tax-free donations rolled in, and people started to take notice. Within nine months, he had the mayor and town council on his side.

This year in the town of Shafter, celebrating Halloween was against the law.

And he was just getting warmed up.

Something like this would never fly in Sacramento, but his congressman had tried to force a floor vote on the Save America's Soul Act, which included, among other things, a national ban on children trick-or-treating, and restrictions on going masked or wearing lewd, provocative or blasphemous costumes in public.

But would it be enough, on the day of the vision that stopped Todd's heart?

Gary knew he should welcome their anger at his work, but weathering it took its toll. He had to flush them out in the open, had to make the good people see what was coming for them before it was too late.

Whenever he came away exhausted and angry from a TV appearance, he went straight to the mail pile and read letters until he felt grounded again.

Dear Pastor Gary, My son was killed by a drunk driver last Halloween night—Every year, they egg and TP my house, but THIS year—Our daughter overdosed on one of those club drugs at a Halloween party—Pentagrams and pentacles and "666" gouged into the front doors of our church—Said if I didn't "shut up and fork over the candy," I could move away or someone might burn my house down—Sometimes I see behind their faces, the sin that rots, the demons that possess—They don't put on masks at Halloween, they take them off—*Where will it end? Who will stand up?*

Who?

Facts were important. And the fact remained that the local authorities could find no evidence to discredit Gary Horton's account of what happened last Halloween night.

He told them he saw someone lurking in the haunt when he discovered Todd, but they escaped. He didn't tell them *what* he saw. He insisted it was one of the vandals who'd defaced the haunt, and let them conclude that they somehow caused Todd's death. The inquest concluded the cause of death was heart failure caused by an acute shock. The only evidence of trauma was mild abrasions and bruising around the photographer's throat and traces of skin under his fingernails, which proved to be his own.

It was just enough to set the public imagination on fire. The Devil's Dungeon was the only working haunt in America with an actual body count. Attention focused on Gary Horton and his hell house, opening only on Halloween night in the town that banned it, on the anniversary of Todd's death.

And it would be the only attraction in town tonight.

Outdated laws forbidding masks or facial coverings dating back to the days of bank-robbers on horseback were trotted out, and public nuisance laws were beefed up to cover the rest. No public events could represent or allude to Halloween unless they were affiliated with a church. The only other attraction in the whole county was a corn maze just outside town limits, which was supposedly attracting a big crowd with nowhere else to go.

A lot of people were out front of the Devil's Dungeon, though not many seemed to be on God's side. The crowd spilled out of the serpentine roped area into the parking lot, where a wall of angry protest signs chopped up the orange light from the street into a fitful, fiery glare. They looked defiant, rowdy, drunk and hateful, those who were recognizably human at all.

Leah came over and took him by the arm. "We're not going to open while there's people out there wearing masks, are we? Isn't it against the law now?"

Gary looked out where she was staring. "Nobody out there is wearing a mask, sister."

She grabbed Gary's arm and leaned on him. "C'mon hon, let's get you into makeup."

In the dressing room, he looked at himself in the mirror, and saw not his blunt, balding pate or lopsided mustache framing lipless mouth clenched between musclebound jaws, or the fire engine red greasepaint and goatee and rubber skullcap with droopy horns devised to make him a cartoon.

Instead, he saw the Real Thing, looking back at him, as it had in the Black Chapel.

He averted his eyes, feeling his blood turn to salt. First, he thought it must be a prank. How could he not? He knew not how, but nothing was impossible when smartass boys set out to make a fool of you.

The cold returned, a blade of frozen nitrogen stropping his brain and lightning frying his temporal lobes and his agony squealed, *brain tumor.*

If it was cancer, then let it be cancer... for this was what he prayed for, this was the divine hand touching his soul as it did the prophets in the gospels. *If it was just an epileptic fit that struck down Saul and turned him to Paul on the road to Damascus, then strike me down, too, Lord, shake me, make me your instrument—Let me show them the Way, let me* change *them—*

But answer there came none.

If he was slipping, it was long overdue. Seven years of year-round work on the Devil's Dungeon had finally broken him, and it would surprise nobody. He had already chalked it all up to a pending nervous breakdown and prayed for serenity, when he turned and witnessed a pulsating mound of flyblown entrails and offal whimpering at him to say if he liked how he looked or not.

Jolted by sheer terror, Gary laid hands upon the abomination, only to find it was Wenda, wailing at his feet. Wenda the haunt's den mother, the jovial spinster. Wenda the gossip. Wenda the glutton, the bloated husk of thwarted lust...

Worst of all was the look she gave when he apologized, the leer that turned to pus encrusting her doughy face as he stormed out of the dressing room.

The show must go on, he told himself. And it had, up until the passing strange moment at the opening prayer huddle. Some of the kids stared at him oddly as he went through the obligatory pep talk. It was easier if he didn't look right at them. Lice, earwigs and worms infested their scabbed and flaming features, and the fecal stench of unborn and aborted sin washed off them like the outgassing from rat carcasses.

It took Gary's breath away. Babies fresh from Sunday school, innocent kids, thoroughly screened, disqualified by the slightest sign of risky behavior, but not one among them was untouched by the vile parasites of sin in thought and wish, the ravages of a million petty transgressions.

And these were, Gary had to admit, the cream of the local crop, the kids who never really had the *chance* to sin, because they were fat, acne-scarred, spastic losers, or they never would've come to the haunt. Even in a town where possession of a single joint by a minor triggered asset forfeiture laws designed to knock down drug cartels, so many homeless families living under bridges because Junior snuck one of dad's PBR's when the deputies came about a noise complaint... Even here, there were plenty of parties, make-out spots and cool things to do that none of these kids ever had the opportunity to turn down.

When he looked them over, he saw only one face unblemished by the mark of sin... the stolid, back-of-a-shovel profile of his right hand, Burt Coughlin—who, everybody was pretty sure, was deeply mentally impaired—absently scrubbing his few remaining teeth with the toothbrush he always carried in his hip pocket.

He heard Wenda and some others buzzing about the news back east. In Fort Lauderdale, five kids were dead and nineteen hospitalized for strychnine poisoning. Police were conducting an extensive neighborhood search, and the mayor was ordering every household outside the suspect neighborhood to throw away its trick-or-treat candy.

A retired Sunday school teacher in Muncie was under arrest after a child bit into a candy apple with a razorblade in it, and similar foreign objects turned up in all the treats sold at a local elementary school Halloween fundraiser. Before lawyers retained by an anonymous donor took her away from the cameras, she claimed that the forces of darkness possessed little children at Halloween, and she couldn't abide it any longer. She cited the same passages from scripture that Gary had invoked again and again in the last year. She said she was just an envelope. Her Master had written the message for all with eyes to read it…

Just the envelope—

There were others, too many to keep track of. Rumors and instant urban legends ran amok, but this Halloween came after a hot, dry summer and two weeks before the ugliest, most divisive election in modern history. People were looking for any side in any argument as an excuse to fight, and the War on Halloween had come at a perfect time.

People all over America were throwing out their candy and keeping their children at home, trashing their slutty cheerleader costumes and Donald Trump masks and praying for God's forgiveness, if they knew what was good for them.

Two crying boys hugged and blessed him before he hit the stage. One of them wept into his ear, "I'm so sorry, I didn't believe you… but sweet Lord Jesus, I can *see* them…"

"You're spreading His message," a teen girl said before she kissed him full on the mouth, smearing his makeup. Another one he didn't recognize hugged him against her bosom until his manhood stirred, then pressed a box cutter into his hand. "Be safe," she said. "Be ready."

The prayer meeting with the cast had been an ugly revelation. Stepping out onto the stage and looking at the crowd was like cracking open a long-sealed casket. Expecting it didn't begin to prepare you for the overwhelming, septic stench of their sin.

Gary pinched the bridge of his nose, his earlobes, until his head stopped spinning. They'd spit on the message and cause trouble, but he saw news cameras out there too, so he rallied.

The opening was rocky, but he stayed calm, oddly disconnected from the nerves that seemed to extend out past his body like antennae, conducting bad luck and entropy into everything he touched when he was least able to cope. It was just another massive crowd, if he didn't look too closely, idly curious shading to openly hostile, frustrated young locals grudgingly checking out the hell house because it was the only show in town.

But he couldn't stop *seeing*, even as he whipped out his bullhorn and played the role. Looking out over the crowd, he pointed here and there and called out what he saw. He couldn't seem to stop egging them on. It was the reason his hell house was a national sensation, and angry money spent the same as the cold kind.

"I see a secret drunk," he witnessed, "and another who steals from his church to gamble every night. I see a righteous man who sponsors starving children around the world to assuage his guilt over the children here at home he's molested, and I see a beloved teacher who delights in sex tourism with little children overseas. I see faithless women and two-faced men, liars and shiftless idolators, drinkers and druggers and masturbators. I thought this was a god-fearing town, but just about all of you are bound for Hell without any help from *me!*"

The crowd was angry, churning and growling. Catcalls came thick and fast. Gary turned up the bullhorn. "What the hell did you rubes expect, I'm the *Devil*! You want to taste the fruit you're going to reap, then come ahead and buy a ticket. Maybe *this* Halloween, you'll be saved from ending up on *my* plate!"

Someone threw a pumpkin. Their aim was lousy, but the smallish jack o' lantern burst at Gary's cloven-hoof feet. A wave of nauseous rot splashed him. People laughed. Lit cigarettes and a few beercans followed. Gary tried to reclaim his self-control. He knew how to deal with hecklers.

"I hope you didn't sell your *soul* for that throwing arm!" A few laughed and he felt like he'd won them back. He reminded them not to touch the performers inside, or there'd be real hell to pay. He waved for Burt to start taking the tickets.

Someone threw a bottle.

It hit him in the back of the head. The glass and foamy backwash caromed off his skull in a thorny corona. The impact sent him down on one knee, like he was going to sing or propose marriage.

"Close the doors!" he shouted, but he restrained himself from diving for cover. Give them enough rope, let them show the world what they're really like. If the martyrs could walk into lions' dens and brave arrows and torture and the stake, he could stand for a little rough heckling.

More bottles, cans and pumpkins, candy and trash and rocks. "We're not going to sell a single ticket until you people move back," he said, and then he heard the sirens.

All over town, they howled like hollow dogs, but they seemed to come together at the far end of Main and fade to the east, where the fat orange harvest moon was obscured by a column of black smoke.

Gary ran off the stage to the doors. Without a word, Burt turned and ran away, the stinking coward. Leah had closed the ticket window, but the monsters in the crowd were burning trash and pushing it through the bars.

"Someone set fire to the corn maze," Wenda told him.

"Dear Lord," Gary said, but he felt only that insidious, seeping cold under his ribs.

"There were at least a couple hundred in that field, Gary," she said. "All of them dark-sided."

"I know, it's terrible," he said, but he didn't know anything. A couple hundred people in this town, it was like lopping off a limb. But a rotten, sick limb could only be amputated. "Did you know anyone who was there…? Do they know who… who did it?"

She shook her head. "God bless them, whoever it was. If those godless creatures were struck by lightning, it couldn't a clearer sign of God's anger." Her eyes bright, brimming with joyful tears. "All those idolators and arrogant unbelievers, they're gonna find out what *real* fire feels like…"

He could tell she saw it too, when she looked at them. Saw what they did, knew what they were… And once you saw it, how could you turn a blind eye?

The crowd simmered as the breaking news spread from their phones. Gary was thinking they could let things settle down for a half hour and then try to reopen, when the truck came.

The big old blue Ford Ranger jumped the curb, V-8 engine screaming, and pounced amid the thickest of the serpentine crowd. It bore down several dozen people, screeching wheels grabbing horrible traction on a road paved with bodies. They tried to run, but tripped over the ropes and turned to stacks of screaming meat.

Gary ran out onto the stage and screamed at Burt to stop, but he couldn't even hear himself.

The truck stalled, the axles choked with limbs, quivering on an unsteady terrain of dead and dying sinners.

The door flew open and Burt climbed out onto the bed of his old Ford with that stupid toothbrush in his scowling mouth and an AR-15 with an extended banana clip on his hip, and commenced firing into the sea of survivors.

"You're *monsters*," he kept shouting, "*You're* all monsters..."

Gary looked around for someone to help him stop it, to bring order and peace, to block the damned *cameras*—

Four kids dressed in hippie costumes came out onto the stage. One of them lit something in the hands of the other three, and they lobbed bottles with flaming rags stuffed in the necks into the crowd. Most of the people still in the lot were dead or wounded. Burt patrolled the perimeter, shooting anyone who still moved.

Gary ran in the only direction he could, back into the haunt. Something had gone horribly wrong, the message he sent was meant to unify people against the adversary, it wasn't meant to inspire hatred or violence.

He ran into the Black Chapel and collided with Todd.

"Hey, Pastor Gary," Todd mumbled in a cracked voice. His hair was shot through with white, his features drained, hollowed out by horror.

"It sure as hell works," Todd said, "this hell house of yours. Did you ever *really* experience it, do you know what it really does...? I went in and got lost... and then I got out, but I wasn't really *out*. It trapped me in something that looked like my life...

"The first room, I got sucked into a cult, and... we... sacrificed babies... and *worse*... We all committed suicide when the cops came, and then... oh, God... I died, and guess where I went? To Hell, right?

"Wrong! I woke up in the next fucking room!

"I was molested by a priest... It was like a false memory I couldn't make myself forget... and I didn't *want* to do it, but I was going insane with the nightmares, the wanting. I never touched them, I just took pictures... but people found out, and I went to jail, and they really, *really* don't like child molesters in jail…

"See, after the first four rooms,I realized the only way out, was to die… So I took the easy way out… but I'm still stuck… and here we both are, what a surprise!"

Gary shook his head, this was not just impossible, but *wrong*. "You don't understand, Todd. You *died* a year ago, and everything after that…"

"*No, you* don't understand, you *fucking idiot*! We're inside the hell house! We went into the Black Chapel last Halloween, and *we never left*! The last time I saw you, I was twenty-four, but I've lived *four* fucked-up lives since then, and I *still* can't find the exit…"

"Todd, get a hold of yourself. Things are a mess outside, but come with me. I can prove that God does miracles…"

"*Miracles*?" Todd cracked up. "You can't swing a dead cat without hitting a miracle, in here. *This* is a miracle, right now. How do you like it?" He pushed past Gary and ripped down a black curtain to bare a window overlooking the parking lot.

The survivors from the crowd were long gone, and the police and fire were still busy across town. The Devil's Dungeon cast and a big mob of the faithful had gathered the bodies into bonfires, and were stringing them up on the lampposts. The faces of the ones doing the burning were monstrous, things he thought must be cemons when he'd seen them before, on Todd's camera. They were singing a hymn he didn't recognize as they fed the fires.

Todd took pictures.

"Do you want to know the best thing I saw, in the Black Chapel?" Todd asked. "I saw God. No shit. I was an agnostic… I guess that's why I saw God… and heard Him… constantly. Telling me what was good and what was evil and making His miracles until I ate rat poison, just to shut Him up.

"God is just one of its masks, Pastor Gary. It never created anything but misery, but it sure likes to be called God… But you know what? The Devil isn't God's enemy. He's just the *garbageman*. And *we're* the garbage. Maybe behind our masks, we're all God, burning ourselves…."

"That's enough, Gary. I know you've been through a lot, but I won't hear your blasphemy—"

"You already know it, Gary! You didn't build this place to save people. You just want to rub their noses in where they're going. But where are *you* going, Gary?"

No more.

Gary punched out with his fist. The box cutter made a neat slot in Todd's neck just below his ear.

Blood sluiced down the front of his shirt. His voice was a relentless, breathless locust buzz. "God doesn't want our love… It just wants to watch us burn… and hear us say its name… Do you know God's true name, Gary?"

Gary stabbed him in the neck again.

Todd fell backwards, gasping, "You finally saved somebody." He staggered out of the corridor and collided with a man in a cheap devil costume, who screamed like a little girl and knocked him down.

Gary turned and ran, rushing to the empty crimson throne that loomed over the three chutes that exited the hell house, but he couldn't remember which was for the saved, which for the damned and which was the one for really *bad* kids. He dove into the middle one and closed his eyes and he was sliding and then he spilled out into darkness and kept *running*—

He was running, he was so scared he'd dropped his candy, somewhere back there, but he was never going back for it.

It was the first Halloween he was big enough to go trick-or-treating on his own. Dad helped him with his costume. The ones in the store were silly, he pointed out. The real Wolf Man would never run around in a rubber jumpsuit with a picture of himself on the front that said "The Wolfman" on it. He dressed Gary up in old torn up clothes, and swaddled his arms and legs in strips of an old, moth-eaten bearskin rug, painted his face with brown shoe polish.

Gary was beside himself with glee. He was scary! He was the Wolf Man! He'd never have a nightmare again, never wet the bed after watching monster movies on weekends. *He* was the monster, now. The world would cower in fear of *him*.

He went out with an old *Space: 1999* pillowcase, growling in the back of his throat. He told his dad he was meeting friends, but knew Dad wasn't fooled. Gary Horton had no friends. But the Wolf Man *needed* no friends.

The first house he came to, there was a garden party on the lawn. A bunch of people in funny costumes were drinking and carrying on over his costume, he was the most adorable werewolf of the night. They told him to go ring the doorbell for his treat.

He went up on the porch and pushed the button. The door opened. He looked up and wet his pants.

Its skull was a black orchid that opened and breathed mist in his face. A straight-razor claw unfolded from its radiator ribcage to hold out a box of Cracker Jacks.

Gary stumbled backwards on the porch, stepped in an overripe pumpkin and lost his balance. He fell on the ragged old couch on the porch, sank into it, felt the cushions tense underneath him like muscles, felt its arms wrap around him and clasp over his pounding heart—

He hurled himself off the couch, stumbled down the porch and across the lawn, explosively wailing and hot piss splashing down the insides of his legs.

Behind him, a big grown-up got up off the couch, wrapped in the old sheet covering it, and ran after him screaming, "Fucking kid *peed* on me!"

Gary ran to the edge of the property and turned around. The adults were all bent over with laughter, dropping drinks and swatting each other on the back. Dracula and Darth Vader and Wonder Woman and kids in stupid rubber costumes that said "Barbie" and "The Creature From The Black Lagoon" on the front laughed and pointed and laughed.

"Thanks for being a good sport, kid." An old man in a pirate outfit tried to give him a fistful of Tootsie Rolls, but Gary's terror had already turned to hot, righteous rage.

"All of you can go burn in Hell!" he shouted, and he ran, he was running, he was almost home, but he had no home, but next Halloween, *he'd show them all*—

Gary crashed through the turnstile at the exit to the Devil's Dungeon. Wenda and Leah were taking the tickets. Burt looked at him expectantly.

"Something wrong, boss?" Burt asked, toothbrush clamped in his teeth as he discreetly averted his eyes.

Gary pulled the cape across his velvet pants to hide the wet spot. His heart was still pounding, but—

None of it was real, it was just a vision. But not of the future, he knew that. It was just a vision to test his resolve.

"Nothing's wrong," he said, looking out over the crowd of monsters and mistakes and empty vessels waiting to see the light. Or at least the fire…

"Open the doors," said the Devil. And in his heart, he prayed for the strength to show them where they were going.

That Small, Furry, Sharp-toothed Thing

Paul Dale Anderson

Some smart marketing genius labeled the "new this year" Brown Jenkin Halloween Costume: "Howard Phillips Lovecraft's scariest character ever." Which wasn't exactly true, but one seldom expected truth in advertising.

Brown Jenkin appeared briefly as a minor fictional character in Lovecraft's "Dreams in the Witch House," published by *Weird Tales* in 1932. He was a small, furry, sharp-toothed witch's familiar, part king-sized rat and part tiny human that supposedly died at the end of the story. He was scary. But nowhere near as scary as most of Lovecraft's other creations.

Consisting of little more than a child-sized—one-size-fits-all-children ages three through ten—zippered synthetic-fiber bag with oval holes for arms, legs, and face to fit through, each Brown Jenkin costume came covered with what felt like real brown-colored human hair. The brown was an odd hue, like rust on nails or stains from dried blood.

Each cheaply-made costume sold for under twenty dollars. That coarse brown hair had to be fake fur. Although strands did look and feel like real human hair, there weren't enough heads in the whole world to provide all that hair.

The accompanying feral face-mask appeared human-shaped with two oversized plastic fangs, not unlike a vampire's, and those teeth also looked and felt incredibly sharp and real. The mask sold separately for an additional nine-ninety-five. Kids loved the costume because the combined effect was breathtakingly menacing. Few if any children, or even their parents, had ever read a word of H. P. Lovecraft's actual works. But the name itself—familiar from television, motion pictures, and derivative mythos tales—invoked an unexplained chill, as if Lovecraft and Halloween and inescapable horror were synonymous.

Those marketing gurus certainly picked a winner this year. Brown Jenkin costumes sold out within a week of initially going on sale. Orders continued to pour in by the truckload, and sweatshops in the Far East added multitudes of 24/7 shifts of child laborers to be worked to death to meet demand.

As evidenced by a man-sized mouse with big saucer-shaped black ears who greeted kids at fantasy theme parks, children worldwide possessed a natural fascination with anthropomorphized rodents. On the night of All-Hallows' Eve, they would eagerly don Brown Jenkin costumes to become little sharp-toothed furry things. I refused to allow my own two children to be among them.

You see, I'd actually read the entire *Necronomicon* as a graduate student in Massachusetts, back when I worked part-time as Library Assistant in the archives of Miskatonic University Library. I knew Brown Jenkin wasn't the Devil's pawn.

He was Cthulhu's.

I dared not permit my own children to dress and act as Nyarlathotep's messenger on a night when veils between worlds were thinnest. Although eight-year-old Davey and seven-year-old Julie pleaded and begged, cried and cajoled, and finally threatened, I steadfastly refused.

Linda, my blissfully ignorant wife, chided me for being overly harsh and rigid. "Why not let Davey and Julie enjoy a pagan holiday? What's the harm in it, John? Let them have fun while they're young. Heaven knows, they'll grow up soon enough."

"No," I said, remaining resolute.

Little did Linda know that I, in my own impressionable youth, became so enamored of Lovecraft's weird tales of elder gods and witchcraft I fervently sought out forbidden books—the dreaded *Necronomicon* of Abdul Alhazred, the fragmentary *Book of Eibon*, and the suppressed *Unaussprechlichen Kulten* of von Junz—to read first-hand in their original incantations at Arkham. My duties as a student Library Assistant required me to accompany scholars researching those ancient texts into the archive's vaults to assure they did not steal or damage priceless and irreplaceable artifacts. Many tried to do so. Therefore, I was required to leaf through each book or manuscript while wearing pristine white gloves before returning the work to its designated shelf. Of course, I read whenever possible.

By the time I graduated, I'd digested them all. I knew, for a fact, the fabled Lovecraftian mythos was not pure myth but hinted at a truth far beyond human understanding. There are indeed more things in heaven and earth, Horatio, than are dreamt of in your philosophies.

Lovecraft was, however, wrong about one essential. The oldest and strongest kind of fear was not fear of the unknown but fear of the known. Knowing what to expect and knowing there was nothing I, or anyone, could do to stop it from occurring, wasn't simply horrifying but utterly terrifying.

As Halloween approached, fear gripped me with icy tentacles. Incredible visions—daydreams and nightmares—filled my head, awakened weird memories in the back of my brain. I grew feverish. Linda complained I cried out often and talked nonsense in my sleep.

Only I was certain it was far from nonsense. It was prophecy.

Each trip to the local pharmacy, grocery, or department store brought me face to face with sold-out Brown Jenkin displays near the front of a store. "We can't keep them in stock," a harried clerk at checkout informed the young mother in line ahead of me. "As soon as we get a new shipment in, it sells out. Come back next week. We may have more then."

Television stations blasted Brown Jenkin commercials incessantly, at least every quarter hour, and my poor children were constantly bombarded with images of small, furry, sharp-toothed things toting bags overflowing with delicious treats on Halloween night. Davey and Julie wanted to be exactly like those kids in the commercials. They grew to hate me. I could feel resentment eating away at our already fragile parent-child relationship.

"You're being totally irrational," Linda said, repeatedly taking their side against me. "What harm is there, really, in dressing up for Halloween? Everyone does it, for Christ's sake! You're acting like a superstitious fool, John, making life miserable for all of us."

She didn't know what I knew. How could I tell her? How could I make her see what I saw?

"Too many fever dreams," she would say. "You're not well, John. You must see a doctor."

"A shrink? You think I'm crazy? You think I need a psychiatrist?"

"You need something. Something to help you sleep. Go see a regular doctor. Maybe a physician can give you a prescription. You haven't slept soundly for months, not since Halloween displays first appeared in stores. You toss and turn. You cry out. Sometimes you get out of bed to wander around like a zombie, and when you wake you have no memory of where you went or what you did. That's not good, John. You can't go on like this.

I can't go on like this. If you don't see a doctor, I'll take the kids and leave."

Reluctantly, I agreed to see a doctor. Not today, but soon. I promised. Scout's honor. "Hope to die if I lie," I told her.

As the days passed and each night became dark longer than the night before, I grew ever more anxious, more fearful. I was certain something cataclysmic was about to happen. Those Brown Jenkin costumes were but a portent of terrible things to come.

Visions of giant rats and bloodied children filled my feverish dreams. I swore my children would not be among those sacrificed on All Hallows' Eve. I would prevent it. Or I would die trying.

No matter how much they cajoled, pleaded, cried, or acted out, I stuck to my guns. No Brown Jenkin costumes for Davey and Julie. If they wanted to dress up for Halloween, they should dress like Count Dracula or Cinderella. I really didn't care if they celebrated Halloween this year or any other. All I cared about was keeping my children out of the clutches of Cthulhu and his minions.

For was it not written in those ancient texts that on certain nights like All Hallows' Eve, doors between worlds opened wide and the call of Great Cthulhu could be plainly heard by all creatures bearing the mark of the beast? In my visions, during my most fevered dreams, I saw children dressed as small, furry, sharp-toothed things responding to that call for sacrifice like rats dancing to the eerie tunes played by a fish-faced Pied Piper.

I dreaded Davey and Julie might be among them.

Linda kept insisting I see a doctor, and I finally relented and visited Doctor Jared Hornsby, our family physician. My boss told me to take a week of accrued vacation time to get well, because I sure as hell didn't look good. He said my work had recently plunged downhill, and if I didn't fix whatever was wrong, he'd be forced to fire me.

Doctor Hornsby determined my physical and mental health had rapidly deteriorated from recurrent panic attacks, diagnosed me as suffering from general anxiety and seasonal affective disorders, and prescribed powerful medications to help me relax and induce sleep. "Take two of these tiny tranquilizers in the morning and one of the huge horse pills every four hours." He wrote another script for sleeping aids. "Take one tablet an hour before bedtime. You need to sleep, John, if you want to get well. These should do the trick. If they don't, we'll simply adjust the dosage until they do."

I thanked the doctor and visited the local pharmacy to fill the three prescriptions. I couldn't help but notice the store's Brown Jenkin display had recently been replenished. When I came face to face with the object of my anxiety at checkout, the fear I felt threatened to consume me.

How could a child's Halloween costume drive a grown man mad?

I don't remember what I said. I don't remember what I did. Later, I do remember police snapping handcuffs on my wrists and leading me to a patrol car, then placing protective hands on the crown of my head so I didn't crack open my skull on a metal doorframe and sue the police department for brutality.

I was photographed, fingerprinted, and spent the night in jail. Linda bailed me out the next morning after she explained to authorities that I suffered from occasional panic attacks and I'd be fine once I began taking appropriate medication. In fact, I was in the pharmacy to pick up my prescriptions when I experienced another panic attack. I didn't know what I was doing when I smashed the Halloween display, tore dozens of costumes to shreds, and nearly torched the entire store. Since it was obvious I was indeed ill, and I had no previous police record, I was released into my loving wife's custody. Linda wrote a check for damages, and the pharmacy dropped all charges.

"What on earth got into you?" Linda demanded as she drove me home. "I swear, I don't know you anymore, John. You're not the man I married."

She made me take all my meds. Then she put me to bed and left for her job downtown. If my job were in peril, she said, she definitely needed to retain hers.

Fortunately, I had the rest of the week off from work. I followed the doctor's advice to the letter. I took my prescribed medications religiously, got plenty of sleep, and began to feel more like myself.

Until, alone in the house all day while Linda was at work and Julie and Davey were in school, I perceived furtive scrapings and scratchings within the walls.

It sounded as if something tried desperately to get inside the bedroom from outside, something that couldn't open doors but was nonetheless determined to reach and destroy me.

To tear me apart like I had torn those Brown Jenkin costumes apart.

One part of my mind said it was only my own overactive imagination while another part insisted the scratching noise was real. We lived in a nice, quiet middle-class neighborhood out in the landscaped suburbs, the house relatively new. Rats had never been a problem before. Why now? Why did I hear such noises only two days before Halloween?

I got out of bed and attempted to track those scraping and scratching sounds to their source. There! I heard it again! Scratching. Like tiny claws tearing away at drywall.

Our bedroom was on the second floor of a modern two-story Cape Cod. The children's rooms were directly across the hall. Did rats climb? Had they climbed up inside the walls to get to me? To get at my children? Was no one safe? Was no place, not even the marital bed, sacred?

Don't be silly, my rational brain coaxed. *Maybe it's time to take more meds. Double the dose. That's what*

Doctor Hornsby would recommend. No need to call him. No need to shell out another co-pay. Just do it.

Get an axe, the other part of my brain urged. *Rip into the walls and find the little bastards. Chop them up. Make mincemeat of them. Get them all before they get you.*

Torn between two minds, I did nothing as the scratching sounds continued from within the walls.

Those clawing noises became even more frantic when the kids came home from school. They ceased entirely, however, when Linda arrived home from work shortly afterwards. She found me standing in the bedroom staring at the wall. The room was unearthly quiet.

"What in the world are you doing out of bed? You need your rest, John. How can you expect to recover if you don't sleep? You're not sleepwalking again, are you?"

Her words snapped me out of the fugue I'd been in. "I hear strange noises and can't sleep," I responded. "The meds aren't strong enough."

"Then tell the doctor, not me," she said. "Have him phone a stronger prescription to the pharmacy. I'll pick it up for you. I don't want you anywhere near that pharmacy until after Halloween. Your last visit cost us over six hundred dollars."

"Six hundred dollars?"

"Your rampage destroyed or ruined their entire stock of two dozen costumes and masks. They'd just arrived that morning and a dozen were out on display with the rest stacked nearby in boxes. You ripped the display apart, tore up the costumes, and somehow set fire to the full boxes. They erupted in flames as if constructed of combustible material waiting for a spark to ignite and completely consume them."

"I told you those costumes were dangerous!"

"Oh, stop it! Stop being such an ass. It's not the costumes that are dangerous, John. It's you. You're a danger to yourself, to me, to our children. I'm certainly not scared of any silly Halloween costume. But I *am* scared of you, John. I'm scared of what you might do." She picked up the phone and handed it to me. "Call the doctor. Do it now. Tell him you need stronger medications. I'll get the kids ready and take them with me. We'll pick the pills up for you. I want you to get into that bed and stay there. Don't go anywhere or do anything."

I telephoned the doctor, got transferred to his answering service, left a message. Twenty minutes later, Doc Hornsby called back. I explained all that had happened since he saw me three days ago. Hornsby agreed to double the strength of my meds, adding two more prescriptions to the ones I already had. He also agreed to telephone them directly to the pharmacist.

After Linda and the children left to pick up my new pills, those weird scrapings and scratchings resumed behind the drywall. I remained in bed and tried to ignore them.

Despite the incessant noise, I fell deeply asleep. I suppose I could blame the sleeping pills Linda insisted I swallow before she departed, or perhaps the raging fever that suddenly came over me after she was gone, but I'm certain the real reason I fell asleep was because that repetitive noise lulled me to dreamland as surely as a lullaby, sung by my long-dead mother, had so often lulled me to sleep as an infant.

I dreamed, and my dreams were horrible nightmares. Like other fever dreams I'd recently experienced, these were crudely disjointed and made little logical sense. Surreal landscapes, houses with no doors and no windows, people with no faces, raced past as if I rode aboard a speeding train and they stood still.

And then my train derailed taking a curve atop a high cliff overlooking the ocean while proceeding ten times too fast to remain on the tracks, and I was falling, falling...

And down, sang my long-dead mother's voice, *will come cradle, baby and all!*

As the train plunged into the sea, tentacles of the same puke-green hue as the waves, reached out for me, wrapped suckers around both of my arms and legs, and dragged me deeper into the fathomless depths. Down, down, down into madness.

I couldn't breathe. My lungs threatened to burst within my chest. Darkness enveloped me like a shroud. Certainly, goodness and mercy had deserted me and only death waited for me at the bottom of the sea.

Only there was no bottom. I fell and fell, pulled ever-downward by gravity and those terrible tentacles.

Down into an ancient city that had existed on the floor of the ocean nearly forever, fabled Atlantis or lost Lemuria, I knew not which. There was an eerie green glow, some kind of bioluminescence, that illuminated tall spires on a foreboding castle where the ruler of this underground kingdom must reside. Off in the distance, mountain-like crags rose where shifting tectonic plates had buckled bedrock, beyond which seemingly-bottomless caverns yawned.

All kinds of aquatic creatures inhabited this land beneath the sea, including many with rows of teeth sharper than a shark's and some with eyes and hands that looked human.

As tentacle suckers deposited me on solid ground outside the castle walls and withdrew, releasing me to wander this strange place on my own, I found I could breathe again, almost as if I had grown gills, which I discovered I had.

Moving about in water of any depth is difficult. It's nearly impossible on the bottom of an ocean. Two-legged creatures weren't meant to walk on or under water, but I managed to make my way inside the castle as if drawn there by some invisible force like iron to a magnet. Once inside the castle walls, I no longer had to fight the currents.

My feet became flippers. Fins sprouted along my spine.

The stone edifice felt familiar to me. I had seen it often enough before, I suppose, not in my own dreams, but in the vivid imaginings of others. It looked a lot like the castle wherein Sleeping Beauty lay dreaming of Prince Charming, as depicted in illustrated books of children's fairy tales.

Now I could discern the odd shape of everything wasn't simply because water distorted and bent visual images but was really because the shapes I saw were unlike anything I'd previously witnessed anywhere. Walls appeared jointed at weird angles, doorways were misshapen, roofs peaked like a tall black witch's hat.

I was wrong. This place wasn't like castles pictured in fairy tales but more like the demented drawings of M. C. Escher.

It wasn't built for humans. Nor by humans. It was already ancient when Adam and Eve left Eden.

Some entranceways were quite huge, tall and wide enough for an elephant or whale to easily pass through. Others were minuscule, like mouse holes chewed in baseboards of old houses. Floors were slanted and made not of bricks nor wood nor cobblestones but of human bones piled together one atop another.

The castle was a charnel house, the bones picked clean of flesh.

If I could have fled, I would have run away as fast and as far as my legs would carry me. Everything about this place was repulsive to humans. Unfortunately, some obscure compulsion assured the only direction my feet would move was deeper into that unspeakable darkness at the heart of the castle where neither sunlight nor bioluminescence penetrated and a monstrous evil eagerly awaited my arrival.

Although no humanly-perceptible sound existed in such total darkness at the bottom of the sea, I swore I discerned scrapings and scratchings and titterings like those inside the walls of my own home. Surely, there were no rats this far under water.

Again, I was wrong.

Swarms of small, furry, sharp-toothed things emerged from the darkness calling my name.

"John!" I felt their paws upon me, shaking me, repeatedly slapping my face. "John! Wake up!"

I opened my eyes to find Linda, my wife, plus David and Julie, my two children, staring at me as if I were a stranger, an alien from another galaxy or different dimension, who had invaded their otherwise-normal world.

"We returned from the pharmacy to discover you wandering aimlessly around a neighbor's back yard in your pajamas, thoroughly soaked in salty-smelling sweat, as if your fever spiked and you didn't know where you were or what you were doing. You broke your promise, John. You promised me you'd stay in bed, and you didn't. I can't trust you anymore."

I saw I was indeed in the back yard adjacent to our own, my nightclothes drenched as if I'd been for a swim in the ocean. Since we lived a thousand miles from the nearest seaport, visiting an ocean was patently impossible in the brief time it took Linda and the kids to go to the pharmacy and back.

Linda insisted on moving me from the master bedroom I shared with her into the guest bedroom on the first floor. "Just until you get well," she said. "We'll both sleep better if we don't sleep together."

I changed into a fresh pair of pajamas, got into the twin-sized bed, and Linda pulled the covers up over me. She handed me two pills and a glass of water.

"Take these new sleeping pills Doctor Hornsby prescribed. I'll wake you in time for supper."

My hopes that a different room might be free of rats in the walls were shattered as soon as Linda left me alone. The furious scratchings and scrapings had followed me downstairs like stink follows excrement.

I was afraid of going to sleep, afraid I'd find myself

back in that castle under the sea. If Linda hadn't awakened me when she did, I'd have come face to face with the evil that resided therein.

I must have slept, though, because the next thing I knew, she was calling me to the dining room for supper. If I had dreamt, I could not remember about what.

Julie and Davey were already seated at the table. Linda brought individual salads from the kitchen, then baked tuna casserole in a serving dish. Our children hated green vegetables and fish, and the only way they would eat either was to hide them beneath layers of noodles and cheese. Tonight, however, they both ate their salads without complaint, and they dug into the casserole with an ardor I'd not seen before.

I, too, devoured a salad and consumed two large helpings of casserole. I was hungrier than I thought.

"Feeling better?" Linda asked.

"Those new sleeping pills really worked," I said. "I got the first decent sleep I've had in weeks."

We managed to get through an entire meal without Julie or Davey beseeching me to buy Brown Jenkin costumes for them. The children were unusually cheerful and complacent tonight.

Maybe I had been unreasonable, as Linda often accused me of being, to forbid our children to dress in such cursed costumes. How unfair it must seem to Davey and Julie that I didn't want them to be like all their friends. Should I relent at the last moment and allow them to dress like other kids?

I was beginning to see everything so much clearer now after just a few hours of uninterrupted sleep. Perhaps, by tomorrow, I'd have regained a proper perspective. There was still time. I could sleep on it and make a rational decision in the morning.

I told Linda what I was thinking. She smiled at me for the first time in weeks.

She wouldn't allow me to help with the dishes. "Julie

and Davey will do dishes," she said. "I want you back in bed. Take another sleeping pill. Get a full night's rest." She kissed my cheek. "Goodnight, John. Day after to-morrow is Halloween. Then all the nightmares will be over."

I took her advice, swallowed two more of the new pills, crawled beneath the covers, and fell asleep almost immediately. If I dreamed at all, I couldn't remember any of it when I awoke.

Bright sunlight streamed through the windows, I glanced at the digital alarm clock next to the bed. It read 10:05 AM.

Davey and Julie were attending school where they belonged. Linda was busy at her job downtown. The house was all mine. I could turn over and go back to sleep, if I wanted.

And then I heard the scratchings begin again inside the walls, and I knew I wasn't alone. I lay in bed and listened. How many rats were there in those four walls? How big were the rodents? How long would it take for them to claw or chew their way through the drywall to reach me?

Why me?

And then it dawned on me, as if the early morning fog had finally burned off my brain to reveal the bright-ness of naked truth: Whom the gods wish to destroy, they first make mad.

If Cthulhu's minions desired my children as sacri-fices to the Great Old Ones on All Hallows' Eve, they needed to get me out of the way first, either by killing me or by driving me crazy. I knew far too much, and my steadfast refusal to allow Julie and Davey to don Brown Jenkin costumes on Halloween, which provided the mark of the beast to identify suitable sacrifices, foiled their plans.

I was the fly in their ointment. I posed a threat and needed to be eliminated.

Those horrible scratching and scraping, clawing and chewing sounds seemed to grow louder and more frantic with each passing moment. The rats were coming to get me, to rip me apart with their razor-sharp claws and needle-pointed canines.

I decided I had to find a way to kill them before they killed me.

Throwing the covers aside, I leapt out of bed. If I had plenty of time, I'd set rat traps or call in an exterminator. But tomorrow was Halloween. I had to do something today. I needed a moment to think what to do.

I dressed in jeans and an old sweatshirt. Then I went to the kitchen to make coffee. Despite getting a full night's sleep, I was still drowsy. Those new sleeping pills were powerful, and I'd taken two tablets instead of the prescribed one. I'd think clearer after a cup or two of coffee.

While the coffee brewed, I glanced at today's paper Linda left for me on the kitchen table.

The date on the masthead read October 31. That had to be wrong.

I checked my cell phone. Then my computer. Then I phoned Linda at work.

"How can today be the thirty-first?"

"You slept for two entire days, John. I knew you need the sleep, so I didn't try to wake you."

"Tonight's Halloween?"

"It is."

"Shit!" I said and hung up.

There was no time to waste. I had to get rid of those damn rats before they got rid of me.

Get an axe, my brain urged. Rip into the walls and find the little bastards. Chop them up. Make mincemeat of them. Get them all before they get you.

I kept an old axe in the garage, along with other outdoor tools like rakes and shovels. I ran to the garage, found the rusted axe, and returned to the house.

I spent the rest of the day tearing the walls apart, beginning with the second-floor master bedroom and continuing to the children's rooms, and finally the downstairs bedroom. I found no rats, no evidence of rat droppings, no proof rats had ever existed anywhere in the entire house.

It was almost dark when I finally fell exhausted atop the bed, popped another sleeping pill, and allowed my eyes to close, my mind to go blank. Linda and the children should be home soon, and I didn't know how to face them. I'd destroyed the drywall in four rooms of the house, caused thousands of dollars of damage, and for what? To fend off something that existed only in fever dreams?

How could I have been wrong about so many things?

When next I woke, the house was completely dark. I switched on a bedside lamp and looked around. I was all alone in an empty house.

Linda and the kids should be home by now. The alarm showed 7:12 PM. Where were they? Why weren't they here?

Then the doorbell rang, and I heard children's voices singing, "Trick or treat."

I picked up the axe and moved into the living room, turned on the porch light, peeked through the peephole in the front door. I saw two small, furry, sharp-toothed things standing on the porch.

The rats were coming for me, and I was ready for them. I raised the axe. I opened the door.

I swung the axe.

One thing marketing geniuses knew that I didn't was humans, not unlike rats, were herd animals. No one wanted to be different, to feel left out. People, especially children, needed to be accepted as part of the pack, as "normal", to be essentially the same as everybody else. Of all the things human beings feared, being excluded or left out of the herd topped the list.

Davey and Julie devoutly desired to be among the thousands of children dressed as Brown Jenkin on Halloween. In my fevered state, I'd been oblivious to their pleas. But their mother hadn't. She'd outfitted them in remnants of the costumes I destroyed at the pharmacy and she'd paid for. On Halloween night, she took them trick or treating, and the children insisted on visiting their father to show me their costumes.

When I heard Linda scream, I knew the truth. After all, as Lovecraft once said, "the strangest and maddest of myths are often merely symbols or allegories based upon truth."

My children had been marked for sacrifice from the moment I'd read the forbidden *Necronomicon*. The true mark of the beast was the fevered dream that consumed me, not the singed man-made costumes Linda had salvaged from the remains of the pharmacy fire. If I hadn't been a true believer, none of this would have come to pass. I, the madman, not the fabled Brown Jenkin nor Nyarlathotep nor even Great Cthulhu caused this tragedy to occur. I, alone, am to blame.

For I *am* alone. From this moment forward, I shall always be alone, a true outsider.

I raised the axe and stilled Linda's screams.

And then I began hunting small, furry, sharp-toothed things wherever I might find them.

"Cthulhu fhtagn!" I shouted, as I hefted the bloodied axe onto one shoulder and disappeared into the darkness.

Waters Strangely Clear

Alan Baxter

Under grey skies threatening rain, Howard Bloch drove east. Behind the wheel for hours already and still Skye's voice echoed through his mind, biting, mocking him.

"So you're really going?"

"I have to!" Infuriated at her refusal to understand.

"A Halloween party? You're a grown man!"

"It's our conference. It's my *job*."

"The *conference*," disdain drooled from the word, "is a lame excuse for grown adults to act like children."

"I'm a regional sales manager. The year's targets and strategies are laid out over three days."

"As an excuse to then have the lame-ass party."

So much more hung off that phrase. Lame-ass job, lame-ass husband, lame-ass man. He had shrugged, no idea how to respond.

"You're really going? To talk about tacky Halloween decorations instead of staying to save us."

"Is there us any more?" he'd asked.

"I guess not."

Her eyes were wet with hurt and anger as she'd turned away. Without another word, he'd wheeled his suitcase out to the car and driven off.

On I-95 somewhere north of Boston, Howard's eyes were wet too. He loved Skye… Had loved her more than life itself. His breezy, beautiful songstress. She'd loved his stability after a childhood with commune-living parents who spent their days stoned, talking about permaculture farming and the spirits of the wind. But her spirit had been like the wind too and perhaps it was inevitable she would grow bored of him. But was that all it was? Boredom? Their life lacked adventure, that was one constant complaint from Skye. *You're so pragmatic, there's not an esoteric bone in your body!* Isn't that why she married him? Maybe they should have had kids, but that was something she resisted. Their slight misalignment on so many things seemed to have widened through the years until now all the gaps appeared insurmountable.

He took the Yankee Division Highway off I-95, squinted at his phone's GPS as it directed him towards Essex Bay. The leaden skies broke, rain bucketing over the windscreen as he finally spotted the sign directing him north: *Innsmouth, 6 Miles.*

"Backwater place for the conference," Howard muttered as the day grew unseasonably dark, even for the end of October.

Head Office had sung the virtues of the location, old world charm and a powerful sense of the macabre, like a town that time forgot. "This year is an auspicious one for the company," the memo had said. "And we're returning to the source for a very special conference." Perfect for the best Halloween party yet devised, apparently. Always in place of a Christmas celebration, Day & Gohn Inc. made its fortune from Halloween merchandise, so that holiday was its central focus. Until now the annual conference had always been in Pittsburgh, much nearer to Howard. Why the CEO, Geoffrey Day, had insisted on the change was a mystery.

Howard drove past Essex Bay, out of sight in the darkness somewhere east of him, and entered Innsmouth. He was exhausted, eyes red and gritty from the long journey, strained from staring through the downpour. All he wanted was a hot bath and a soft bed, tomorrow would be better. He missed Skye already.

The rain fell, hard and heavy, and he slowed, staring past the swiftly whipping wipers at a town of wide extent and dense construction. Everywhere seemed dark and still, though it was only just before seven o'clock. Few lights shone in the windows, chimney pots stood inert on sagging gambrel roofs. As the road descended towards the harbour, the sense of broken down decay became stronger, some roofs fallen in entirely, some walls missing windows like skulls with black, empty eye sockets. Other buildings were in better condition, Georgian houses with cupolas and widow's walks guarded by curlicued iron railings. Three tall steeples stood out against the ocean horizon, black against the dark of night. Howard drove past a factory built of brick, sturdier looking than most buildings he had seen, though the majority of the rest of the waterfront bore structures seemingly uninhabitable due to decay.

Not so much old world charm but a derelict, forgotten ghost town. Where was everyone? He passed the sand-clogged harbour surrounded by stone breaker walls and there, on a slight rise above the small port, was the Deepwater Hotel. That, at least, was well-lit, an air of vibrancy about it. He turned onto Maron Road to access the lot and parked, the hammer of rain the only sound after he killed the engine. Cold permeated the car, as though the turning of the key had swung wide some unseen refrigerator door behind him.

With a shiver, he got out, hunched against the rain, to smell a sharp, briny tang of saltwater and old seaweed on the icy breeze. He dragged his case from the trunk and ran to the hotel lobby. No one greeted him at the door, the reception desk unmanned. From somewhere distant he heard the quiet murmur of voices and the chink of glasses. He realised a stiff drink before his bath and bed would be most welcome, assuming it didn't involve too much socialising. He wasn't yet ready for people, Skye's disappointment still raw and smarting. Had she really finished with him right there by the front door? The chasm between them finally whole? Surely there was a way to find common ground again if they tried.

"Help you? Conference is it?"

Howard jumped, the disembodied voice sudden and sibilant. He turned, no one to be seen. When he returned his gaze to the desk he jumped again, a man waiting as if he had been there all along, looking with one eyebrow raised. Had he been there all along? Surely Howard would have noticed. The man's face was pale, almost grey, his mouth flat and wide, eyes too large as he stared.

"Yes, conference," Howard managed, unsettled by the cold perusal. "Howard Bloch," he added, and spelled out his surname. People always assumed a CK.

"Three-fifteen, third floor. No lift, broken. Stairs are that way." The pointing finger was greyer than the man's face, long and trembling slightly as it indicated dark wooden stairs, highly polished, with a thick bannister and intricate balusters like kelp weed twisting upwards.

Howard glanced down at his heavy case, fatigue sinking deeper into his bones. He opened his mouth to speak and the clerk said, "No bellboy. Finished for the day."

"Right." Howard took the offered key, careful not to touch the pale hand, and turned away.

"Dagon's eyes see you."

Howard turned back. "Pardon me?"

"I said have a nice stay." The man's expression was unchanged, without any apparent emotion.

"Right," Howard said again. "Thanks."

He wheeled his case towards the stairs but was intercepted by someone emerging from a pair of heavy wooden double doors to one side. "Howie Bloch!"

Howard winced, but couldn't help smiling. At last, some normalcy. Something familiar. "Dean Stringer.

How many times do I have to tell you not to call me Howie?" His mother had called him that, her soft voice plaintive as she mollified him after another of his father's alcoholic outbursts. His mother's own breath sour with bourbon and cigarettes and surrender. He'd always promised himself any marriage of his would never be like theirs. Instead he'd managed to make one so dull it had withered on the vine and died.

Dean Stringer smiled. "Howard, sorry. Good to see you, man!"

"You too."

They shook hands, Dean's grip firm and vigorous. "You believe this place? Like something from… I don't even know!"

"It's pretty weird."

"The boss man says it's important to be here this particular Halloween. Reckons it's a perfect time for company growth."

"Perfect time?"

"Alignment of stars or some shit." Stringer laughed, shrugged. "Great location for us, though, right? Try selling these people Halloween décor, that'd be like selling snow to the eskimoes, am I right? Really test your skills, Mr Regional Sales Manager of the Year."

Howard laughed. "That was last year."

"Maybe this year too! You'll find out in three days."

"We'll see." Honestly, Howard doubted he would qualify. He worked well, always had, but the slow dissolution of life with Skye, particularly over the last few months as the breakdown gained momentum, had certainly affected his performance. It must have affected his sales, even though he had met all his targets. Someone else would surely have exceeded theirs by more.

"Drink!" Dean exclaimed. "Come on."

"My bag," Howard said weakly. "I've only just driven in, I feel… rumpled."

"A drink first!"

The hotel bar was busy with Day & Gohn Inc. staff and the buzz of life and activity was like a bath in itself. Howard drank his first beer reluctantly, but soon relaxed and met others he knew well, new employees he hadn't met before. He felt isolated among the crowd, but bourbon followed beer and in an hour he was warm and laughing, not sparing a thought for life beyond the job.

Dizzy and staggering, he fumbled the key into the lock of 315, left his clothes on the floor as he fell into bed a little after midnight. The sheets were so cold they felt damp, the high ceiling with pressed metal edges spotted with blackened mould and rippled with water stains, but he didn't think much about it before sleep closed over him like a wave.

Howard woke from dreams of rolling seas and curdled stomachs. Of leaning over the sides of creaking boats with peeling paint, staring into gloomy depths where things unrecognisable looped and flew. His mouth was dry and furry, his head thick.

He staggered from bed, went into the small bathroom to piss, and winced at the yellow-stained toilet bowl, the rust streaked tub with its dripping shower head, lumpy with lime scale. But relieved, and revitalised with a long drink, though the water was bitter and hard, he returned to the room and its small window. His view looked south over the harbour. He smiled. The rain had eased, though the skies were still slate, and people milled in the street. Some buildings seemed to be shops with their doors open. Everything appeared more alive, more intact, than it had in the rain-soaked night before. Howard was glad of that. After a breakfast in the bustling hotel dining room – bustling only due to his fellow company staff – he headed into the main conference rooms and was soon lost in the business of sales districts, new products, electronic gadgets to hide around the house to turn it into a terrifying haunted experience. These were things he understood.

During lunch he was slapped hard on the back by Geoffrey Day, CEO. The man was tall and broad with a wide face and protuberant eyes. Not so pale as the desk clerk of the night before, Howard was nonetheless struck by their similarity.

"Good to see you, Bloch!" Day exclaimed. "All well?"

"Absolutely!" Howard lied, thoughts of Skye slipping back into the cracks between his thoughts, and hurried away.

By evening he was back in the bar, sampling the food and more of the booze. One day down, two to go, then the party. He began to relax. Dinner was ordinary, an uninspiring fish stew with hard, tasteless bread, but he and Dean had decided to go further afield the next day and explore the town, find restaurants to try. Thankful though he was to have Dean nearby, he had trouble connecting with anyone else, the faces all blurring into one seething mass. He shouldn't be here, not really. He was made remote by thoughts of home and Skye. And that made him tense and bitter, hurt by the thought their marriage was done. They should have had kids. He should have insisted. He smarted that now they never would. But it wasn't too late...

Avoiding conversation, Howard found himself on a weathered leather bench seat when a slim, dark-haired woman of young middle age sat beside him. He estimated she might be five or six years younger than his grizzled thirty-nine, and she retained an attractiveness that spoke of a youth turning eyes wherever she went. As general conversation lulled she smiled at him, held out a long-fingered, slim hand.

"Darya."

"Howard. Darya is a lovely name." He took her hand, glanced down at its icy coolness.

"I never could get used to New England winters. It's why I went away. I'm always cold!"

"It's barely autumn yet."

She gave a shrug. "Yet already freezing."

"And so damp here too," Howard said.

"Always. It means 'sea', by the way."

"What does?"

"Darya. It's Iranian."

"Oh, right. You're Iranian?"

"No, my parents just liked it. I'm New England born and bred."

Howard laughed. "Yet you never got used to the winters."

"No, that's why I went away."

A silence fell, a moment of awkward strangeness following the awkward conversation. Darya flickered another smile and Howard sucked in a quick breath, tried to rein in sudden disorientation. "Drink?" he said.

Darya visibly relaxed, eyes crinkling. "Yes! Vodka and soda?"

"You got it."

Dean stood at the bar, half a smile pulling up one side of his mouth like he'd been caught by a fisherman.

"What are you grinning about?"

Dean nodded back towards the table in the corner. "Chatting up the new girl, eh?"

"New is she?"

"I haven't seen her before. No one I spoke to has. Must be new."

Howard grunted. "And I'm not chatting her up."

"What, because you're married? What happens on tour, stays on tour, buddy. I won't tell your wife."

"Gee, thanks! How's your wife?"

Dean grimaced. "Honestly, I don't think we'll be together much longer. I'm feeling a bit lost, truth be told. Long story, I'll tell you later."

Howard nodded, unsure what to say. He was certainly the last person to offer advice. Dean gathered up four glasses in a tenuous two-handed grip and returned to his table where several employees sat laughing and talking over one another drunkenly.

Howard waited at the bar and eventually the woman serving turned her attention to him. He startled slightly, convinced for a moment it was the desk clerk from the night before wearing a straggly ash-blonde wig. Their resemblance to each other was uncanny, but the woman had a kind of fatty lump just below her bottom lip and eyes a pale grey where the man's had been sickly green. They must surely be related, though. Family business, Howard presumed. He ordered the drinks, bourbon and coke for himself, and returned to Darya.

Their conversation was messy, continued to be awkward, but they drank more and cared less. Darya moved closer, put a hand on his arm, his knee, his thigh. In her presence he felt dizzy and weirdly dislocated. He repeatedly pushed away thoughts of Skye, playing over and over in the back of his mind those last words.

Is there us any more?

I guess not.

The evening rolled on and the bar became ever less occupied, then Darya leaned forward, whispering. Her lips were cold against his ear, but the words heated him. "Shall we go upstairs?"

"My room?" he asked, trembling like a teenager.

She nodded, slipped her fingers around his, gently pulled him up and away. They climbed the stairs quickly, stumbling drunkenly and giggling. In his room they didn't speak again, plucked and fumbled with each other's clothes, kissing every newly revealed bit of skin. Her tongue was cold and brackish in his mouth, as though she had drunk vodka and seawater all night not vodka and soda, but the taste wasn't unpleasant. As they kissed he became dizzier still, lost in lust and booze.

She was cold all over, the poor thing not lying about

never getting warm. He gasped as she took his cock in her mouth, his shock as much from the icy chill of her tongue as the sharp sexual pleasure. They rolled onto the bed, he atop her, and inside she was as cold as out, and though the fact discomforted him, he was too drunk and too rampant to care. The booze made him clumsy, but gave him time and the sex was good. She bucked beneath him, staring up with wide eyes as though she couldn't believe her own orgasm, and that inflamed him and he was spent, explosively and totally. Still without words they rolled over and entwined. As sleep stole over him he realised she was still cold.

Howard dreamed of a city underwater. It's twisting spires stretched up through waters strangely clear, the surface of the ocean unseen far above. This was no earthly sea, that he knew without doubt, intrinsically. This place existed everywhere, just below the surface of real life. It could be entered from anywhere, go from it to anywhere else, like it flowed intertwined with the threads of the tapestry of reality.

Howard walked its streets, marvelling at serpentine architecture, rounded byways, the smoothness of every feature. Straps of kelp rose in clumps, undulating in soft currents. He came to a temple in the city's centre, a tower of intertwined columns winding upwards, surrounded by smaller spiralling towers buttressed to the middle with arcs of dark stone. Giant double doors, forty feet high, thirty feet wide, inscribed with disturbing symbols, swung silently open and he realised everywhere was silent. Inside the temple, rows of pews rose from the ground as if carved. Or as though they had been grown like intricately managed coral. Hundreds of people occupied them, rocking gently as if moved like the kelp by deep, gentle waves. All had hoods or long hair shadowing their faces, not a visage visible in the dimness. An altar at the end of the temple stood on a raised dais, impossibly tall figures stalking slowly around it. Whip-thin and angular in their movements, they reached long, stick-like arms towards the congregation. Those arms bent once about one-third along, the forearm too short. Then they bent again further up, double-elbows uncannily placed as they gestured complicated patterns, a silent sign-language Howard could not understand but yearned to know. He realised he was holding his breath, had been all along. For how long? Hours? He knew if he breathed in he would drown, but suddenly felt like he was drowning anyway. And part of him longed for that watery suffocation. Panicking, he gasped, ice cold salt water flooding his mouth and lungs.

He jerked awake, bounced on the cold bed, heart pounding, breath short. He tasted salt water, but realised that would be from kissing Darya, not from the dream. Wouldn't it? He rolled over and saw she was gone. Disappointment carved a hole in him. His brain was foggy with sleep, with drink, with the remains of the powerfully clear dream. He lurched from bed to piss, the air cold against his damp skin. His feet squidged against the hard, worn carpet as he walked, leaving a trail of wet footprints. Still drunk, confused, bereft, he ignored it, pissed, and fell back into bed and a restless, dreamless sleep.

"You're not the only one who got lucky last night!" Dean was enthusiastic over breakfast in the hotel dining room of dark wood and sallow serving staff. They looked a lot like each other. Just how big was the family running this business?

"What do you mean?" Howard had a headache from ruptured sleep and too much bourbon, his mood sullied by that and by guilt over what he had done. He and Skye weren't finished yet, and Darya hadn't even stayed the night, creeping out like it was nothing but a booty call. There had been a text message from Skye when he awoke: *Sweetheart, we really need to talk. When you get back, let's take a break somewhere. We need time together.*

She was prepared to attempt reconciliation. And so was he, desperate for it, in fact. But would he have to tell her about last night? Could he live with the guilt either way? He found himself questioning what the fuck he was doing about anything in his life, but knew one thing. He wanted Skye.

Dean was saying something.

"Sorry, what?"

"Man, you are out of it. Too much to drink, eh? I was saying that a few of us scored last night. That girl you took upstairs, she's not with the conference. She's local."

Howard frowned. Nodded dumbly. "She said something about that. But she moved away."

"There's a few of them, they came to hang out knowing we were in town." Dean leaned forward, conspiratorial. "You look at most people here and who can blame them? It's ugly central in this town, right?"

Howard tried to remember what he and Darya had talked about all evening but it was hazy. He couldn't remember much at all. "You scored too then?"

Dean beamed. "And it was good, man!"

"Was she…" Howard swallowed, shook his head. He had been about to say *Was she cold*, but that just seemed absurd.

"Was she what?"

"Doesn't matter. Good for you, man." He pushed his plate aside, appetite gone. "I gotta call my wife."

"Guilty conscience!" Dean grinned around a mouthful of toast, wagged a butter knife like an accusatory finger.

Howard walked around the harbour, talking to Skye about the future, and he felt encouraged. The conversation was uncomfortable, but she reiterated her desire for a break, he said he would like that. She told him to enjoy his conference and his party, and it sounded as though she meant it. He hung up wracked with guilt.

He looked around, wondering if he might see more of Innsmouth before day two of the conference but though the town wasn't nearly as dilapidated as he had thought that first night, it was still run down, dirty, uninviting. Pale, wide faces stared around door frames, as if wishing him away, hoping he wouldn't stray into their shop. One large building had a peeling sign, *Maron Shipping and Freight*. He'd seen that name in several places around town, for some reason that unsettled him. With a shiver he returned to the hotel.

❧

During lunch, after eating floury apples and damp sandwiches of fish paste, Howard went upstairs to nap, to catch up from his disturbed sleep of the night before. He dreamed again of the underwater city, walked to the high, wide doors, but paused, nervous. He thought of Darya, of Skye, and cried out in frustration. Ice water flooded his mouth and he startled awake. His clothes were wet, like the mother of all cold sweats. He changed and went back downstairs for the afternoon session. What he would give to be warm and dry.

❧

Rather than brave the unwelcoming streets with Dean, he ate the hotel stew again. The same lumpy casserole as before. The meat was tough for fish, odd lumps in places, the gravy waxy and thick. He would kill for a good old burger and chips, but didn't really care. He thought only of seeing the conference out, enjoying the party, then getting home to Skye. Even the party now seemed like a chore. Skye had been right, it was grown adults trying to recapture lost childhood and it was sad. The hotel had used the company's products to decorate in preparation and it all struck him as garish and tacky.

He promised himself he wouldn't drink again, but Dean returned and bought the first round and anything seemed better than sobriety at that point. By around ten o'clock he was warmly inebriated, relaxing, when Darya appeared beside him.

"I'm sorry I left without saying goodbye. You were sleeping. You were... very deep."

Howard licked suddenly dry lips. "I didn't expect..."

"You didn't expect me back? I had to work, but I came as soon as I finished." She raised a glass, clinked it against his. He opened his mouth to speak, to say something about Skye, about his life, but she silenced him with cold lips over his. Her briny tongue caressed his and dizziness swept through him. Over her shoulder he saw Dean entwined with another woman, similar looking to Darya. Dean gave a thumbs up, then returned all his attention to his new friend.

Howard tried to glance around the bar. So many other people there, but they were so many blank faces in a sea of weirdness. Only Darya appeared solid. Only she showed any detail for his eye to lock onto. He swallowed hard, wondered if he was more drunk than he had realised. Darya kissed him again, cold and salty, and it inflamed every fibre of him. She pulled back, handed him another drink. Where had that come from? It tasted strong, at least a double measure. With an internal sob of frustration he swallowed it down and let his mind swim.

Darya pulled him by the hand, led him to his room, where they repeated the night before, faster, harder, better than ever. As he frantically kissed along her neck, thrusting powerfully, his lips passed over a row of thin striations. He leaned back to look and saw three almost imperceptible slits in the skin at the side of her throat that quickly closed together as though they had never been. Darya pulled his face down between her breasts, bucking up into him desperately.

〄

Howard dreamed again of the serpentine temple, the tall, rangy priests exhorting the congregation with complicated signs. As he stared, he began to somehow understand the gestures, *He is ready to rise* and *He has slept for long enough.*

Something in the broken, truncated messages caused rills of terror to flood through Howard and he felt the intense pressure of his held breath. He wanted to breathe deeply and join the huddled masses and simultaneously wanted to run far away, to Skye, and feel the genuine warmth of her embrace.

The urge to run won out and he stumbled from the temple, along the softly winding streets. He remembered this ocean was not earthly, but a place in between, a place that flowed within all things. He kicked hard from the street and swam up, keeping only Skye in his mind, and found himself swimming over their shared bedroom, so far away. She slept there, alone in the bed, one arm thrown across where he should have been. Across her pillow was the shirt he had been wearing the day before he left, looking rumpled and unwashed. She must have it there for the scent of him. His heart ached.

He gasped, ice water rushed through him, and he woke.

Darya was gone.

〄

The mood in the dining room was sombre, faces dark. It took a moment to find out why, but Howard soon discovered there had been a tragedy. Dean Stringer was dead.

"What happened?" Howard asked of Sarah Cheeseman, taking a spare seat at the table she shared with two others.

"Drowned," Sarah told him.

"What?"

"But found in his bed!" Gary Clarke said, shaking his head.

"Drowned in his bed?"

Gary barked a laugh. "According to the authorities I overheard talking to the boss, he fell in the harbour and drowned late last night. A local carried him to bed, not realising he was dead, thinking he was just drunk."

Howard frowned. "Who does that?"

Gary shrugged. "No idea. But you can't actually drown in your bed, can you!"

"Geoff Day was here a moment before you arrived," Sarah said. "Despite the horrible event, we're to see through the conference and party."

"It's what Dean would have wanted, according to Day," Gary said, his face bleak.

Howard mechanically forked wet, thin scrambled eggs into his mouth, not really tasting them.

❦

Howard wanted to go home, but it was October 31, last day of the conference and Halloween. It was a long drive, he was prepared to make his excuses and leave, but Geoff Day opened proceedings with a request that everyone honour Dean Stringer by sticking together, considering the Day & Gohn Inc. family had meant so much to Dean. *Had it really?* Howard wondered. Haunted faces filled the auditorium, all wearing a mask of determination. He would look like a dick if he ran out now.

"Call me superstitious if you will," Day said in a strong voice, "but this Halloween sees a planetary conjunction that occurs only once every few hundred years. And it's happening on *our* day, on Halloween! That's why we're here, in this place, at this time. We'll see our numbers grow!"

Day went on to announce the year's best performers and Howard gasped when he was named again as Regional Sales Manager of the Year. Confused by the applause and faces that still bore shock under a veneer of celebration, he went to the stage, accepted his plaque and bonus cheque. How could he have outperformed everyone despite his crumbling life? Was his competition here that weak? He needed more from life than everything represented by this award. And he knew there was so much more to be experienced.

During lunch he called Skye and said how much he missed her, and he wasn't lying. But something else had occurred to him and he knew it would appeal to her esoteric mindset.

"I'm going to swim the sea of dreams tonight and come to you," he said, huddled for privacy in a corner under the polished stairs.

She laughed. "That right?"

"I'm serious. This place has been giving me crazy dreams. Last night I swam to you and watched you sleeping."

"That's a little creepy, love."

"No, it was beautiful."

"It sounds like a nice dream," she said, amending her opinion.

He took a deep breath, ready to test his theory. "You're sleeping with my blue shirt on your pillow."

Her gasp at the other end was quickly suppressed, then a moment of silence.

"Skye?"

"How could you know that?"

"I think it's wonderful."

"But how could you know?"

"I told you, I've been dreaming, deeper than you could imagine. I'll come tonight, in your dreams, and we'll swim together."

Skye laughed again, but there was an edge of nervousness to it. "You're kinda freaking me out, but okay. I'll look forward to that."

The conference wrapped and when they emerged from the meeting rooms back into the bar, it was dressed up like a funfair haunted house. Cobwebs everywhere, bats and pumpkins and witches on broomsticks swung from every available point. Among the regular Halloween décor were bizarre chitinous creatures, like plastic parodies of lobsters and crabs with uncannily articulated limbs, set as if they crept across every surface, hunting for something.

Music blared from the rig of a DJ in one corner, rotating lights with blue and green filters turned, casting flickering underwater shades across the walls and ceiling. Food and drinks were laid out on tables. Howard ignored it all, keen to be on his own. Darya came to him, her hips swaying like a soft tide, eyes hooded. He saw her now as cold and dangerous, the image of Dean with another woman disturbingly similar to Darya leapt through his mind and made his stomach churn.

She held out a drink, began to say something. Howard pushed the drink aside, shook his head. "Not tonight! No more, okay?"

Her face flashed fury and for a startling moment sharp teeth bristled behind her full lips, three slits either side of her throat gaped angrily, then flattened shut again. Howard's mouth fell open, fear trickled through his limbs. Darya's expression softened as she glanced past Howard's shoulder. He turned to see what she was looking at and saw Geoff Day gesture to the woman, his fingers mimicking the silent sermons he had witnessed in his dreams. *Enough.* Howard's eyes widened and he turned back to see Darya's reaction, but she had already turned away, offering his drink to another employee. Gary Clarke, he realised absently, who he had spoken to over breakfast.

Howard looked back to Geoff Day, but the boss was already deep in conversation with others, his face wide with laughter.

Howard hurried to this room. He locked the door and sighed with relief. All he wanted was to hold Skye. And he wanted to show her the wonders of the world he had discovered under reality. The peculiarity of people notwithstanding, that place called to him, cajoled him to fly in its endless depths, and he had to take Skye there. He would show her adventure. He could ignore the dark city. These people be damned, he and Skye had journeys to enjoy.

He watched the hours crawl by until he was sure Skye would be in bed, then fell into his cold, damp sheets and closed his eyes. He relaxed and breathed deeply, thinking only of sleep and the deeps of the ocean below the world. He smiled as he gently walked the streets of the serpentine city, supported by the salt waters of infinity. But not to be tempted, he kicked away and swam up, distancing himself from the temple, thinking only of Skye.

He saw the floral designs of the bed linen in the shadows beneath him and swam down to her. His held breath began to burn his lungs, but he knew he had held it for impossibly long periods before this dream, on previous nights. He could hold it longer still. Long enough to show her wonders.

He put a hand on Skye's shoulder and she startled awake, looked around herself with wide eyes. Then she looked up at Howard, her expression both impressed and full of disbelief. He nodded, pointed at the pillow below her, his shirt. *You're dreaming,* he said with complicated patterns of his fingers that suddenly came as naturally as blinking. *We're dreaming together in the oceans of infinity.*

He pushed aside his guilt at thoughts of what he had done with Darya, took Skye's hand. She let herself be lifted and they swam together. Unsure where to go, they drifted, and then there was the city below them. He was shocked to see the entire congregation in the streets outside the temple, looking up with wide, sad faces. The tall priests stalked among them, more than a dozen of them, then as one they turned their thin faces upwards too. Their wrongly jointed arms raised and together they spoke in sign, telling Howard and Skye to breathe, to let infinity in and feel the sacred blessing of the eternal Dagon.

Of course.

Howard laughed, knew that any resistance was pointless. The ocean was already in him, had been since his lips had first touched Darya's. This was inevitable. He turned Skye to him and her face was twisted in terror, eyes wide. She shook her head side to side, hair floating behind like a halo in the currents. She opened her mouth to scream, tried to pull away from him, but he held her tight, his hands around her upper arms. He opened his mouth and drew in a great breath of salty ice water and nodded at her to do the same. As her scream came to an end she had no choice but to do so and he refused to let her go. This was them together at last. Always together.

❦

Geoff Day, CEO of Day & Gohn Inc., stood with Cecil Maron, the Innsmouth Chief of Police, Geoff's cousin on his mother's side. Beside them stood Stanley Maron, Cecil's brother, the town's forensic examiner. They surrounded Howard Bloch's hotel bed, where Howard lay cold and wet. His blackened eyes stared unseeing at the mould-stained ceiling.

"You've filled in the paperwork?" Geoff Day asked his cousins.

Cecil nodded. "Drowned in the harbour. Hell of a thing."

Stanley signed off the sheets of paper on the battered clipboard, returned it to his cousin.

"The next of kin?" Day asked.

Cecil laughed, a clotted, wet sound. "Wife. Spoke to the local PD this morning. Says it's the damnedest thing, they found her dead in her bed at home. All signs point to drowning."

Day joined in the laughter as they left the room, allowing hotel staff in to tidy up. "Dagon's eyes see you," Day said to his cousins as they parted in the hotel lobby.

"And find you pious," they both replied in unison as they stepped out into the rain.

The House on Jimtown Road

Ran Cartwright

Two days and it would be Hallowe'en.
Falcon Point was in full spook mode as if the area wasn't already spooky enough. You'd think so with the tales of spooks, ghosts, shadows, rumors of *things* in the bay, the ruins of the old Enoch Conger place out on the Point (who the Hell knows what happened to old Enoch; a lot of silly tales were spread back in the day, but were largely discounted long ago). And, of course, across the bay to the north was that fish bait slime pit, Innsmouth. That place alone is enough to spook your drawers down around your ankles.

But the tikes and teens just love their Hallowe'en.

So, parents were running off to Kingsport with their happy laughing wild-eyed youngin's buying Hallowe'en decorations, costumes off the shelf, pumpkins to carve into Jack o'Lanterns, and bags and bags of candy to satisfy those wild-eyed youngin's that would be showing up on their doorsteps.

Jack o'Lanterns decorated porches and sidewalks. Fake cobwebs were strung across doorframes, windows, and front yard shrubs. Fake tombstones decorated yards, and dancing skeletons, witches with glowing eyes, zombies, and bed sheet ghosts were popping up everywhere. And there was the Jaycee's haunted house, decorated to thrill the older thrill seekers.

Yeah, Hallowe'en was just two days away.

And there were those late teens, early twenties folk looking for a good time, parties, pranks, and tricks.

Like Martin Gilford.

Martin was always looking for a good time, a prank, a trick, a laugh. Mostly at someone else's expense. Hallowe'en provided the perfect excuse. Yeah, at someone else's expense.

"I've got an idea," Martin said with a grin, leaning over the table in Falcon Point's Dockside Diner.

It was nigh on evening and the diner was mostly empty; most of those who frequented the joint had gone home to prep for the coming spooks and festivities.

"You always have some fool stunt of an idea," Billy Finley said from across the table, a blank expression on his face. "I'm almost afraid to ask."

The guys were sitting with their girls in that diner booth, Martin with that young hot blonde, Julie Harper, and Billy with that young hot brunette, Donna Wilson.

Martin's eyes danced from Julie to Donna then back to Billy. His smile widened to a full on mischievous grin. "TP and paraffin," he said.

Billy sat back in the booth with a sigh. "Who's place?" he said.

"The MaGee place over on Jimtown Road."

The girls suddenly glanced at Martin as though they had seen a certified genuine Hallowe'en spook while Billy sat bolt upright and glared across the table at Martin.

"Are you nuts?" Billy said.

"Why not?" Martin said.

Billy was indignant. "Well, first of all, they call that old dude The Shark and for good reason…"

"Yeah yeah, I know, they say the old dude eats people," Martin interrupted with a nod and a chuckle. "You believe that bull?"

Julie giggled. Apparently she didn't believe the stories about The Shark.

Billy ignored Martin's question. "Second of all, he's one of them."

"One of who?" Martin said.

"One of the Marsh clan," Billy said. "That old dude's uncle, James Marsh, founded Jimtown and his grandpap was Ezra Marsh, Obed's brother. That old dude is named after his grandpap."

"I don't need a history lesson," Martin smirked. "Besides, Jimtown is long gone and the old MaGee place stands alone out there with no neighbors for miles. Nobody is going to see us if we…"

"Nobody except that old MaGee dude and those two things that live with him," Billy interrupted. He sat back, tapping the fingers of one hand on the table top. "I ain't going and neither is Donna."

Martin sat back and sighed his disappointment. "Okay, Julie and I will go alone," he finally said, squeezing Julie's hand under the table. "Tomorrow we'll hook up and check out the Jaycee's haunted house over on First Street."

Donna and Billy remained silent, scowling, Billy still tapping his fingers on the table top as Martin and Julie slipped out of the booth. They walked away without another word.

"Billy…?" Donna said, looking up at her man after their friends had gone. There was concern in her voice.

Billy Finley just shook his head and stared at the table top. His thoughts were dark, ominous. The MaGee place. Nothing good could come of that.

"Foolish stunt," Billy suddenly muttered the thought.

The sun had long since set. It was cold; a heavy gray cloud cover hung over the eastern seaboard. Night was fast approaching.

Martin and Julie had gathered up a couple rolls of

toilet paper and a bar of paraffin at the corner market, eliciting a cross-eyed glare from the grocer. He knew what was up. Hallowe'en. Youngin's will be youngin's. The foolish stunts youngin's pulled, it happened every year. The grocer had shook his head, tallied the goodies, bagged them, and Martin and Julie were out the door and on their way.

By the time Martin and Julie had crossed the Alternate Route 1 Bridge, night had fallen. Two miles up the road Alternate Route 1 became Federal Street cutting into the heart of Innsmouth. One mile up Alternate Route 1 the Jimtown Road branched off to the northwest where it merged with Garrison Street at Bates before turning west, passing through the ruins of Jimtown five miles west of Innsmouth then turning southwest toward Ipswich.

A mile west of the Garrison/Bates intersection on Jimtown Road a lone three story house stood off the north side of the road. The MaGee house.

"I'm not so sure this is a good idea," Julie said softly, more out of concern for having to suffer the cold than TPing and paraffining that old dude's place.

Martin and Julie stood at the edge of the road, peering up at the old MaGee place. Just like the old dude, the place was creepy. A two foot high stone wall surrounded the property with an additional two foot high wrought iron fence and rail atop the wall. Centered in the front wall was a wrought iron gate, two steps up to a cracked and broken sidewalk that led to the front porch.

The grass looked as though it hadn't been cut in years. Shrubbery was dead and the few trees that dotted the property were bent and twisted with branches reaching for the ground as if they were trying to steady themselves from toppling over.

There was no street light out there on Jimtown Road, just a dim yellow light on a pole behind the house, backlighting a part of the third story casting an ominous black edifice against the night sky haloed in the dim yellow light, and highlighting the shadowed forms to two gibbets that had been erected on the west side of the house.

The place looked like something out an a Hollywood horror film. Martin stared, his heart racing. Two films had come to mine – *Rattlesnake Pit* and *The Death-trap Horror,* long time favorites. Martin hesitated and sighed out of momentary fear. Maybe Julie was right, he thought, maybe this wasn't such a good idea. But he chuckled softly and brushed the thought off.

"You TP the place and I'll get the porch windows," Martin whispered as he held up the bar of paraffin then started toward the gate, Julie hesitantly following behind.

He swung the gate open slowly, the gate protest whining on its hinges. They hadn't gone ten feet into the yard before a blinding white light suddenly erupted and shown in Martin's eyes. They stopped, Martin raising a hand to shield his eyes against the glare.

The light was coming from the porch. Something was there, on the porch, a form, a thing, and mad laughter. Then suddenly a shadow rose up from the tall overgrown grass next to the sidewalk.

Something cracked hard against the back of Martin's head and everything spiraled black as he pitched forward unconscious while Julie's sudden scream trailed down the long black corridor in his consciousness until silence and oblivion.

※

It was late afternoon on Hallowe'en day.

Billy and Donna sat opposite each other in a booth at the Dockside Diner. They were silent, staring into the drinks they had ordered, waiting for word from Martin and Julie. But there was no word. Martin and Julie hadn't shown. No one had seen them since they had left the diner the evening before.

Donna slowly raised her head and looked across the table at Billy. "What are we going to do?"

"We'll check out the MaGee place," he said softly, still staring into his drink.

A chill ran up Donna's back. "Then we'd better go before it gets dark," she said, none too thrilled at the idea.

Billy shook his head. "We'll wait until dark," he said, looking up at her.

She stared back at him, her eyes wide and fearful.

"Less a chance of us being seen or caught," he answered her fear.

⁂

Dusk had come to Falcon Point.

Festivities had already begun. Little Supermans and Batmans, Howdy Doodys and Buffalo Bobs, Cinderellas and Snow Whites, and bed sheet ghosts with their eye holes cut out were crisscrossing Falcon Point streets, their parents tagging along close behind, making sure pranking teens weren't going to rush out of the shadows and nab bags of Hallowe'en goodies from the expectant and happy little tikes.

No such festivities were going on across the bay in Innsmouth. It was mostly quiet there with a scattering of young Deep Ones in various stages of transformation hanging out on street corners or in alleys. Some had gathered in taverns, quietly sniffing and gurgling down drinks, and shuffling in and out of the shadows to mingle. Some were swimming in Innsmouth Sound, some hanging out on Devil Reef waiting for nightfall, some breeding with their own kind and humans alike in a couple of teetering dockside warehouses.

Billy and Donna had crossed the 1A bridge. Steering clear of Innsmouth, they had cut across open fields, moving northwest to Jimtown Road beyond Innsmouth's town limits. By the time they had made Jimtown Road, night had fallen.

They walked along the side of the road, Billy focusing his thoughts on the dim yellow glow from the pole light behind the MaGee house a half mile away. His apprehension and uncertainty were building.

Donna walked behind him. She was silent, lost in her own thoughts, her eyes turned to the ground as she walked. She was more and more convinced that they shouldn't have come. Martin and Julie hadn't been seen or heard from since the night before at Falcon Point's Dockside Diner. Something had happened to them, Donna was convinced, something terrible.

She raised her head, her eyes meeting the dim yellow glow of the pole light, the house black as a burial shroud against the sky as they approached.

Yeah, something had happened to them, she thought, there...at that place.

"That sure is one scary looking place," Billy said softly as they stood on the road, staring up at the old MaGee place.

"Yeah," Donna said, barely a whisper. "I don't like it. Let's go back to Falcon Point."

Billy ignored her comment. His eyes danced across the MaGee property, straining to cut through the shadows, see what he could see, deciding on a course of action. The house was dark but for the dim yellow glow of the pole light behind the house.

"If Martin and Julie are here, they'd be insi...," Billy said softly then fell silent. A subtle movement in the shadows cast by the dim yellow glow of the pole light had caught Billy's eye, something turning on a slight breeze.

"They'd be what?" Donna whispered.

But Billy had already started for the gate and the cracked and broken sidewalk that led to the front porch. He swung the creaking gate open. Half way up the sidewalk he turned into the tangle of overgrown grass and vegetation, making his way toward the west side of the house. His eyes were focused on the two shadowed gibbets that were backlit by the pole light behind the house.

Donna's eyes wandered, peering about the shadows, the brush, bushes, trees. No toilet paper, she thought, they didn't TP this old place.

Billy and Donna emerged from the shadows into the dim yellow glow of the pole light and stopped. Donna gasped, raising her fingertips to her lips. Her eyes were big, round, watery, and fearful. Billy stared as a sudden fear closed in around him, his mind suddenly invaded by images of things lurking in the shadows and high overgrowth, watching and waiting.

Two naked bodies hung by their bound feet from the gibbets, one male and one female. Their hands were bound behind their backs and their heads were missing. They had been gutted like ocean caught tuna, their bodies split open from pubic bone to severed necks.

Billy caught his breath as he slowly approached the gibbets. He knew instinctively that the two headless gutted bodies were those of Martin and Julie. His gut feeling was confirmed when he noticed in the dim yellow glow the mermaid tattoo on the upper left arm of the headless male body. Martin had such a tattoo.

"Billy, let's go home," Donna called out fearfully from the edge of shadow.

There was sudden movement in the high grass then three figures appeared in the dim yellow glow, old Ezra MaGee and his boy and girl, Joshua and Martha Jean.

Billy momentarily stared at each in turn. Old Ezra MaGee, what a piece of work. His hair was gray, frizzled, a beard hung to the middle of his chest, and he showed a perpetual scowl. The old dude looked like he'd been in the sun way too long. Weathered and leathered, lines crisscrossed his face looking like a road map to Helltown.

Joshua MaGee was a hulking brute with hunched shoulders, wildly disheveled black hair, a lopsided drooling sneer, and lazy left eye. He looked a few bricks short of a full load.

Martha Jean MaGee, the term blonde bombshell came to Billy's mind. No more needed to be said or thought.

"Well, looky what we have here," the old dude said, holding a shotgun pointed waist high at Billy. "A coupla fish come t'dinner!"

"Billy..." a sudden glare from old Ezra's narrowed eyes cut Donna off.

The two young MaGee siblings were smiling, Joshua making eyes at Donna while Martha Jean was making eyes at Billy.

"You the Shark?" Billy stammered.

"Some folks call me that," the old creep hissed as he approached Billy, the shotgun still leveled waist high. "But m'name's Ezra MaGee. It ain't no matter to no fish."

Ezra suddenly swung the shotgun around and buried the stock end into Billy's gut. Billy grunted, hissed air, and doubled over. A swing of the shotgun caught Billy under the chin and sent him out cold on his back at the foot of a gibbet.

"Joshua, bring it inside," old Ezra said, glancing over his shoulder at his boy.

"Sure pa," Joshua said, crossing the yard to where Billy lay and hoisting him over a shoulder.

Old Ezra turned to Donna. "You, fish bitch," he said, motioning with his shotgun, "around the back."

Martha Jean prodded Donna with a shove, Donna stifling back a sob while tears trickled down her cheeks.

It was nigh on 10:00 PM when Billy's eyes fluttered. He was disoriented, his thoughts fragmented. He winced and groaned. There was pain in his gut and jaw. Something hard was pressed against the side of his head and a bright light shown in his eyes. He tried to move his arms to raise and steady himself, but found he couldn't. His hands were bound behind his back with baler twine.

Piece by piece the surroundings became clearer. He was in a kitchen, seated at a kitchen table, leaning forward, his head laying on the table top. The bright kitchen light shown in his eyes. Suddenly, what had happened came flooding back. The MaGee house. The bodies hanging from the gibbets. The old creep and his two…

Billy's eyes shot open wide. Unsteady and nauseated, he forced himself to sit up and peer about the kitchen through squinted eyes.

Donna sat at the kitchen table opposite him, her hands also bound behind her back with baler twine. She was lost in horror, a blank stare at the table top, tracks of tears trailing down her cheeks. Old Ezra was leaning against the kitchen counter, still cradling the shotgun, Martha Jean and Joshua flanking him, the two MaGee youth still grinning and making eyes at Billy and Donna.

"So, the fish man has finally woke himself up," old Ezra said with a sneer.

"You're a Marsh," Billy stammered, fighting back the pain in his jaw.

"Yeah, I reckon so," old Ezra said, "My grandpap was Ezra Marsh, brother t'Obed. My ma Celia gave me Ezra's name."

"You're not one of us," Billy said.

"I don't cotton t'no tainted fish," old Ezra said. "We ain't got no truck with Obed's line. Theys tainted. I ain't havin' none o'that taint in my line."

Joshua suddenly pushed off the counter and rounded the kitchen table to where Donna was sitting. "Can I keep this one, Pa?" he said, leaning over and gently touching the side of Donna's neck with two fingers, "she got pretty little gills forming."

Donna didn't move.

"What you want with a fish, boy?" old Ezra said.

"I wanna have some fun, Pa."

"What kind o'fun you talkin 'bout?"

"You know, down in the basement," Joshua grinned.

"Ain't your sister good 'nough for that?"

"Pa…"

"Martha Jean's good 'nough for me," old Ezra interrupted, "Why ain't she good 'nough for you?"

"Pa, I ain't never had me no fish b'fore," Joshua said.

Old Ezra sighed and stared at the floor for a few seconds. "Ah'right, boy," old Ezra finally said then looked up at his son, "Take her down t'the basement an' have yur fun. But I'm warnin' you boy, I ain't havin' no fish babies in my house!"

"Don't you worry none, pa," Joshua said, his eyes lighting up.

"Billy!" Donna suddenly cried out as Joshua dragged her off the chair and out of the kitchen. Her screams trailed away as Joshua dragged her down the basement steps.

Martha Jean pushed off the counter and swaggered over to the kitchen table. "Pa, can I have him?" she said, sitting on the edge of the table next to Billy. She grinned as she leaned over and began to play with his damp hair.

"No!" Ezra glared at his daughter. "I ain't havin' m'daughter tainted with no fish man! Now git that outta yur head, girl!"

Angry, Martha Jean slammed a closed fist on the kitchen table, jumped to her feet, and stormed out the back door into the Hallowe'en night.

"Now you, fish man," old Ezra growled after Martha Jean had gone. He prodded Billy off the kitchen chair with the barrel of the shotgun. "You git outside t'the back of the house. We gonna have us a fish fry in the mornin'! Y'all make for good eatin'!"

Martha Jean had wandered around to the east side of the house and to the stone wall with the black wrought iron fence and railing. She leaned against the wall, mad and brooding, gazing across the open field. She was sick and tired of Pa MaGee telling her what to do. Her eyes narrowed and she frowned. I'm nineteen, an adult, she thought. I can do whatever I want.

The back door of the house suddenly slammed open, interrupting her thoughts. She glanced back over a shoulder. Under the dim yellow glow of the pole light, she saw Pa MaGee and the Deep One that called itself Billy leaving the house, saw Pa MaGee force that Deep One to its knees, saw Pa MaGee put the money end of the shotgun against the back of the Deep One's head and pull the trigger. The gunshot echoed through the night as the Deep One toppled over, Pa MaGee howling and laughing and waving the shotgun in the air before picking up an ax to cut off the Deep One's head before gutting the poor fish man.

She shook her head and turned her eyes away. It was cold and the jacket Martha Jean wore was thin. She wrapped her arms around herself and shivered. It didn't matter. Nothing much mattered to Martha Jean anymore. The dim street light in the distance caught her attention. It was nigh on a mile across the open field at the Bates and Garrison Streets intersection.

Innsmouth, Martha Jean thought.

On a whim, she suddenly climbed the stone wall, hopped over the wrought iron fence and railing, and jumped to the open field on the other side. She started across the field, heading for the corner of Bates and Garrison Streets.

As she neared the intersection, she spotted five male Deep Ones, early to mid-twenties, nearly transformed, nigh on tadpoles to a toad, standing on the corner under the street light. They were young and rebellious, dressed in jeans, jean jackets, cowboy hats and boots, their cowboy hats pulled down low over their brows.

And they were bored, looking for fun. It was Hallowe'en, but the holiday was foreign to them. They didn't celebrate; even the humans that lived in Innsmouth didn't celebrate. The humans were mostly an older lot, their kind dying out. The sooner the better as far as Innsmouth's Deep One populace was concerned.

Martha Jean suddenly appeared out of the shadows. The five Deep Ones turned, stared, gurgled and grunted, their big round watery eyes glistening in the street light. Here was a human female, young, blonde, stacked, and grinning. She approached the young Deep Ones and ran a hand over an arm. It was cold, clammy, and slick, like slime.

"Happy Hallowe'en boys," Martha Jean said, a sensuous taunt to her voice. "Any plans for the night?"

Well, it looked like fun had just arrived.

The young Deep Ones, all five of them, grinned and gurgled and grunted with excitement as they gathered around her, tugging at her jacket, toying with her hair, running cold and clammy webbed fingers over her face.

Fun had indeed arrived.

❈

It was a small abandoned shack just off Elliot Street on Innsmouth's southwest side. The wood was rotting, some roof tiles stripped away by Atlantic storms, some wall slats missing. The place contained a scattering of dust and cobwebs. A four legged table was pushed up against a wall. An oil lamp rested on the table; a small flickering flame cast dancing and writhing shadows on the walls.

Martha Jean lay on her back, her jacket and clothing piled in a corner of the shack while boots, cowboy hats, and jeans and jackets were scattered about. She smiled up into the large round watery eyes of a Deep One that was hovering over her. Her time had come, she had decided. The old man wasn't going to tell her what to do anymore.

Pa ain't gonna like it, she thought as she reached up for the Deep One, but it serves him right.

When the sun rose on All Saints Day, Martha Jean MaGee would be tainted.

Across the bay, all was quiet again in Falcon Point. It was late, nigh on midnight, and Hallowe'en had ended for the night. Jack o'Lanterns were dark, TP fluttered on a slight breeze, some windows were waxed. The Jaycee's haunted house had been a success. The streets were now deserted but for a few straglers shuffling along the Falcon Point wharf.

The little tikes and early teens had all gone home, prodded by their parents. Fat and happy, they had sampled their hordes of candy before slipping off to sleep the night away, eager to wake on All Saints Day to sample more.

Somewhere in town a lonely bell chimmed the mightnight hour while out on the Point a mist was rising off the ocean. Something was there, something dark in the mist, briefly returning to the old Enoch Conger place. It would be gone back to the ocean by morning.

Spider Wasp

Tim Curran

Moss pulled into town at 4:15, his anxiety spiking as he stepped from the car, a tall knife blade of a man with a face scraped hard by life. His flinty eyes sat in craggy draws, taking in the town, the festivities, the throngs of people that wriggled in the streets like spawning salmon. Place was called Possum Crawl, of all things, a lick of spit set in a bowl-like hollow high above Two-Finger Creek in the very shadow of Castle Mountain. Lots of pastures and trees, hicks towing hay wagons outside town.

This was where The Preacher had gone to ground and Moss was going to find him, drag him kicking and screaming out into the light.

Sighing, he stepped out on the board sidewalk, checking his watch and lighting a cigarette. He carried only a heavy silver case. What was inside it, would be for later.

"Festival," he muttered under his breath as he stepped down into the street and merged with the mulling crowds of the town. "Festival."

That's what they called Halloween up here in the yellow and gold hills of Appalachia. Maybe it was about tricks and treats other places, but here in this dead-end mountain town, it was serious business. Festival was not only a harvest celebration, but a time of seeding and renewal, a time of death and resurrection.

The streets were a whirlwind of people, a scattering of autumn leaves blowing down avenues and filling lanes and clogging cul-de-sacs with thronging bodies, conflicting currents, human riptides of chaos. No one sat still. It was almost as if no one dared to.

Moss could feel all those bodies and minds interlocking out there with grim purpose, a rising electrical field of negativity. One thing owned them, one thing drove them like cattle in a stockyard, and tonight they would meet it.

He walked down the main thoroughfare, beneath spreading striped awnings. Blank faces with sinister dark eyes watched him, studied him, burned holes through him. It made something inside him writhe with hate and he wanted to open the briefcase, show them what was inside it.

"No," he said under his breath. "Not yet, not just yet."

Not until they were gathered and not until he saw the face of The Preacher.

He avoided the herds as best as possible, taking in Festival. Vines of dangling electrical cords drooped down like snares to capture the unwary. Orange-and-black cardboard decorations leered in every window. Corn shocks and wheat sheaves smelled dry, crisp, and yellow like pages in ancient books. And the pumpkins. Oh yes, like a million decapitated heads, orange and waxy and grinning with dark pagan secrets.

As he passed huts that sold baked potatoes and popcorn and orange-glazed cupcakes, he was amazed at the harmless façade that was pasted over the celebration. What lie beneath was old and ugly, a pagan ritual of the darkest variety like slitting the throat of a fatted calf or burning people in wicker cages. But in Possum Crawl, it was not openly acknowledged. It was covered in candy floss and spun sugar and pink frosting.

This is what drew you in, Ginny. The carnival atmosphere. The merriment. The glee. The Halloween fun.

Your naivety wouldn't let you see the devil hiding in the shadows.

Moss blinked it all away. There was no time for remembrance and sentiment now; he was here for a purpose. He must see it through.

Now the evil face of Festival showed itself as parade lines of celebrants intermixed and became a common whole that crept forward like some immense caterpillar. They carried gigantic effigies aloft on sticks, grotesque papier-mâché representations of monstrous, impossible insects—things with dozens of spidery legs and black flaring wing cases, streamlined segmented bodies and stalk-like necks upon which sat triangular phallic heads with bulbous eyes. Antennae bounced as they marched, spurred limbs dangled, vermiform mouthparts seemed to squirm. Subjective personifications of an immense cosmic obscenity that the human mind literally could not comprehend.

And here, in this incestuous, godless backwater of ignorance where folk magic, root lore, and ancient malefic gods of harvest were intermixed like bones and meat and marrow in the same bubbling, fat-greased cauldron, the image was celebrated. Something that should have been crushed beneath a boot was venerated to the highest by deranged, twisted little minds.

But that was going to come to an end. Moss would see to it.

He walked on, a sense of dread coiling in his belly. Not only for what was to come, but what he carried in the case.

As he watched it all, he felt words filling his mouth, wanting to come out. Ginny had been fine and pure, a snow angel, eyes clear blue as a summer sky. He worshipped her. She was the altar he knelt at. She had been perfection and grace and he lived in her soul. Then she had come to Possum Crawl with that little girl's fascination of pageantry and spectacle and this place had ruined her. It had handled her with dirty hands, sucked the light from her soul and replaced it with black filth. Contaminated, she no longer walked, she crawled through gutters and wriggled in sewers.

She loved Halloween. The child in her could never get enough of it. That was how she heard about Possum Crawl's annual celebration, its arcane practices and mystical rituals. That's why she came to this awful place and why the best part of her never left.

But the child, Moss thought. *She should have thought of the child.*

As the shadows lengthened and a chill made itself felt in the air, he watched little girls in white gowns casting apple blossoms about. They wore garlands of flowers in their hair. Symbols of fertility. And everything was about fertility in Possum Crawl—fertility of the earth and fertility of the women who walked it and the men who seeded both. The crowds marched and whirled and cavorted, singing and chanting and crying out in pure joy or pure terror. It looked like pandemonium to the naked eye, but there was a pattern at work here, he knew, a rhythm, a ceremonial obsequience to something unnamable and unimaginable that was as much part of them as the good dark soil was part of the harvest fields.

Moss was shaking. His brain was strewn with shifting cobweb shadows, his eyesight blurring. For a moment, a slim and demented moment in which his lungs sucked air like dry leathery bags, Possum Crawl became something reflected in a funhouse mirror: a warped phantasmagoria of distorted faces and elongated, larval forms. The sky went the color of fresh pink mincemeat, the sun globular and oozing like a leaking egg yolk.

Barely able to stay on his feet, he turned away from the crowds that swarmed like midges, placing his hot, reddened face against the cool surface of a plate glass window. His lungs begged for air, sour-smelling sweat running from his pores in glistening beads. After a moment or two, the world stopped moving and he could breathe again. The plate glass window belonged to a café and the diners within—old ladies and old men—were hunched-over mole-like forms scraping their plates clean with sharp little fingers, watching him not suspiciously, but with great amusement in their unblinking, glassy eyes. They looked joyful at the sight of him.

"Ginny," he said, the very sound of the word making him weak in his chest.

He saw her reflection in the glass—she was striding out of the crowds, a swan cut from the whitest linen, her face ivory and her hair the color of afternoon sunshine. Her sapphire eyes sparkled. Then he turned, hopeful even though he knew it was impossible, and saw only the mulling forms of Festival: the dark and abhorrent faces shadowed with nameless secrets and mocking smiles. He could smell sweat and grubby hands, dark moist earth and steaming dung.

There was no Ginny, only a shriveled beldame with seamed steerhide skin, head draped in a colorless shawl, her withered face fly-specked and brown like a Halloween mask carved from coffin wood. She grinned with a puckered mouth, sunlight winking off a single angled tooth. "It was only a matter of time," she tittered. "Only a matter of time."

"Go away, you old hag," Moss heard his voice say.

His guts were laced with loose strings that tightened into knots and he nearly fell right over.

"Oh, but you're in a bad way," a voice said but it was not the scarecrow rasp of the old lady but a voice that was young and strong.

He blinked the tears from his eyes and saw a girl, maybe thirteen, standing there watching him with clear, bright eyes. Her hair was brown and her nose was pert, a sprinkling of freckles over her cheeks. She smiled with even white teeth.

"I will help you," she said.

"Go away," Moss told her. He didn't need any damn kids hanging around him and especially not some girl dressed in Halloween garb like the others: a jester in a green-and-yellow striped costume with a fool's cap of tinkling bells.

"I'm Squinny Ceecaw," she said and he nearly laughed at the cartoonish sound of it.

"Go away, kid," he told her again. "Go peddle it somewhere else, Squinny Seesaw."

"Ceecaw."

Her eyes flickered darkly. She looked wounded, as if he had called her the vilest of names.

Suddenly, he felt uneasy. It was as if he was being watched, studied, perhaps even manipulated like a puppet. A formless, unknown terror that seemed ancient and instinctual settled into his belly and filled his marrow with ice crystals. Again, his eyesight blurred, pixelated, and his head gonged like a bell, his body twisting in a rictus of pain as if his stomach and vital organs had become coiling, serpentine things winding around each other. Then the pain was gone, but loathsome images still paraded through his brain, a psychophysical delirium in which the horned mother parted infective black mists to spread membranous wings over the cadaver cities of men and peered down from the blazing fission of primal space with crystalline multifaceted eyes.

Then he came out of it and Squinny Ceecaw had him by the hand, towing him away he did not know where. He told her to go away, to get lost, but his voice did not carry. It seemed to sound only in his head. He gripped the silver case as if his fingers were welded to it. He felt weak and stunned.

"It's too early for Festival yet," she informed him.

She brought him through an alleyway and into an open courtyard. Then he was on his hands and knees, gulping air and swallowing a dipper of water she handed him from a well. It was cold and clean and revitalizing.

But seconds after he swallowed it, he had realized his terrible mistake—he had drank the water, the *blood,* of this terrible place.

"You've come for Festival?" the girl asked him.

"Sure, kid. That's why I'm here."

He realized he had set down the silver case. She reached for it, perhaps to hand it to him, and he cried out, "Don't touch that!"

She jumped back as if slapped. He shook his head, wanting to explain there were reasons she should not touch it. But in the end he did not speak. Perhaps, he could not speak.

"Do you live here?" he asked, mopping sweat from his face, pulling the case close to him so that it touched his knee.

"Yes."

"Do you know The Preacher?"

She looked at him for a long time. Her mouth did not smile and her pert nose did not crinkle up with sweetness. He sensed something old about her, something in the shadows behind her eyes, a forbidden knowledge. She studied him suspiciously as if he was playing an awful trick on her.

"Do you know The Preacher?" he asked again.

"Yes, yes, I do."

"Where can I find him?"

"You have come to Festival to meet The Preacher. Many do," she informed him. "Many, many come but they are not like you. You are special, I think. You are one of the few and not the many."

Tell her, he thought then. Tell her all about it so she'll know. Tell her about Ginny, about how fair and pure she was until she got stained dark by this awful place. Tell her how she came for Festival and stayed forever. How she left you with the baby. Tell her how you came after Ginny that night and dragged her back to the city. How she squirmed like a snake in the backseat until you had to tie her hands behind her back with your belt and gag her with your handkerchief so she'd quit screaming obscenities about the Great Mother who seeded the world, reaping and sowing. And how first chance she had gotten, she slit her wrists, dying in your arms and spewing madness about the Mother of Many Faces who was Gothra.

But he didn't tell her about that. Instead, he just said, "Tell me about Halloween. Tell me what it means to you."

The girl sat in the grass not far from him, a brooding look coming over her features as she began to speak. "It is not Halloween here. It is Festival, which is much older. It is a celebration of harvest, of leaf and soil and seed," she said as if by rote. "The Mother gives us these things as she gives us birth to begin and life to enjoy and death to take away our suffering. Once a year we gather for Festival. We celebrate and give back some of what we have been given. It is our way."

Although the degenerate truth of what she said was not lost on him, he refused to listen or accept any of it. He had heard it before and did not want to hear it again. "You should go home now, go to your parents."

She shook her head. "I can't. They disappeared last year playing festival."

"Get the hell away from me, kid."

Then he'd elbowed past her, making his way up the alley and to the main thoroughfare, whatever it was called in a pig run like Possum Crawl. He moved through the crowds like a snake, winding and sliding, until he found a bar. Inside, it was dim and crowded, a mist of blue smoke in the air. He could smell beer, hamburgers and onions that sizzled on a grill behind the bar. The tables were full, the stools taken. Men were shoulder to shoulder up there. But as he approached, two of them vacated their places.

Moss sat down and a beer was placed before him. Nice, that. Didn't even have to wait for service. It came in a frosted mug. It was good, ice-cold. He drained half of it in the first pull, noticing as he had outside that there were no women. Outside, there were old ladies, yes, and little girls, but no teenagers, no young women. And in here, not a one.

Funny.

As he sat there in the murky dimness, thinking about the silver case at his foot, he had the worst feeling that he was being watched again. That everyone in that smoky room had their eyes on him. Sweat ran from his pores until his face was wet with it. He caught sight of his reflection in the mirror behind the bar and didn't even recognize himself. He looked dirty and uncomfortable, rumpled like a castoff sheet, his face pale and blotchy, pouchy circles under his eyes that were the color of raw meat. There were sores on his face that he was certain had not been there the day before. His guts turned over. His hands shook. His head hurt and his gums ached. Again, he felt waves of nausea splashing around in his belly and he felt the need to vomit as if something inside him needed to cleanse itself.

Moaning, he grabbed the case and stumbled back out of the bar. The sun had set. Shadows bunched and flowed around him like pools of crude oil. Faces seemed to crowd him, pushing in, eyes bulging and hands reaching, fingers brushing him. The crowds surged and eddied, hundreds of pumpkins carried on shoulders like conjoined heads. Scratchy Halloween music played somewhere. High above the town, the mountains were dark and ancient and somehow malefic. Their conical spires seemed to brush the stars themselves.

He found a bench and fell into it, gasping for breath. The apprehension was on him again, the neurotic, skin-crawling feeling that there were things going on all around him that he could not comprehend. Possum Crawl, goddamn Possum Crawl. It was like onion, layer upon layer of secrets and esoteric activities that you could never know nor understand even if you did. The unease flowered into terror as the darkness and silence seemed to crowd him. The sense that he was in an alien place amplified and he heard voices muttering in tongues that were guttural and non-human. In the glow of streetlights, he saw rooflines that were jagged and surreal. Castle Mountain above seemed to shudder. Fear sweated out of him as his brain whirled and his stomach rolled over and over again. He shivered in the night as a delirium overwhelmed him, squeezing the guts out of him until he became confused, not sure where he was or even *who* he was. The night oozed around him, thick and almost gelid.

He stumbled away, cutting through the crowds, getting turned around and around, hearing a high, deranged wailing and then realizing it was coming from his own mouth.

He was propelled in conflicting directions, taken by the crowd and carried along by them until he fell free into a vacant lot strewn with the refuse of Festival: paper cups, streamers tangled in the bushes, dirty napkins and broken bottles and cast-aside ends of hot dog buns. He lay there, face in the grass, until he calmed and a voice in his head said, *I will not submit.*

He sat up, lit a cigarette, thinking about Ginny and the night he had taken her from this madhouse of a town. As fevers sweated from him, he was not even certain it had happened. He was no longer certain of anything. There was only this awful place. The night. The cigarette between his lips. He touched the silver shell of the case and his fingertips tingled as if his hand was asleep.

The Preacher. He had to find The Preacher and do what was right, do the thing he had come to do which was becoming steadily convoluted and obscure in his brain. He began to fear that his memories, his mind, his very thoughts were being stolen from him. Shaking with panic, his identity fragmenting in his head like ash on the wind, a stark image of Gothra floated in his brain, rising, filling the spaces he understood and those he did not—a great monstrous insect, a primeval horror that was part spider-wasp and part mantis and wholly something unknown his feeble brain could not describe even to itself. In his mind, he heard what he thought was the insect's voice, a buzzing/croaking chordal screech. *I am here. You are here. Together we shall bring evil and madness into this world and make it our own.*

No, no, no, that droning, wavering squeal…it could not be a voice. He was coming apart. His mind was failing. None of it was real. He heard maniacal laughter, the sound of sanity purging itself: his own. Running back out in the street, he was absorbed by the bustling crowds that carried horrible effigies of Gothra high above them. Faces were twisted masks. The stars blinked on and off like cheap bulbs in the sky. He could smell rotting hay and blood, manure and black earth. Voices jibbered and screamed and shrilled around him. Now the festival was reaching manic, hysterical heights as what he had been feeling for hours took hold of them, too, carrying them forward like a dark river seeking the sea.

"It is time," a voice said at his ear. "Time to meet The Preacher."

It was Squinny Ceecaw, yet it was not her at all. The voice was too mature, all velvet and spun silk, the sort of whispering smoothness one would acquaint with experience and sensuality. Certainly, this wasn't the kid, not Squinny. But it looked like Squinny and as her hand clasped his own, he was certain that it was. Her nearness wedged a seam of pure terror through him. He wanted to throw her off and run. But he didn't; he marched, he melded into the procession that carried pumpkins and flickering candles. It was happening, really happening. Festival was about to reach its terrible climax. The very thing he had anticipated and feared, was about to be realized.

Now no one was singing or crying out. They marched in orderly rows. Many carried pumpkins, but many carried other things—briskets of raw beef, pork loins, shanks of lambs, other primal cuts; dead animals such as rabbits and possum and coyote. Two boys led a massive hog on a rope. Some carried bags of what smelled like rotting vegetable matter.

All of it was so strange and alien, yet so uncomfortably familiar.

Moss knew many things at that moment and knew nothing at all. He walked with Squinny, his mind cluttered, his thoughts muddled. The town was a trap. He knew that much. It had been a trap meant to ensnare him from the moment he arrived and he had stepped willingly into it this afternoon. Possum Crawl owned him now. Festival owned him. Squinny owned him. The people that walked with him owned him. He belonged to them and he belonged to this night and the malevolent rituals that were about to take place. But mostly, oh yes, mostly he belonged to Gothra and the rising storm of anti-human evil he/she/it represented. Now he would become meat and now his mind would be laid bare.

They marched out to a secret grotto beyond the limits of Possum Crawl and up a trail into the high country until the face of the mountain was right before them. And even this opened for them. They passed through a gigantic cave-mouth and into the mountain itself.

Moss began to tremble, because he knew, he knew: the mountain was hollow. Hadn't it been this that he was trying to remember when he'd first drove into town? *The mountain is hollow, the mountain is hollow.* Yes, it was really just a sheath of rock and within, oh God yes, within…a high, craggy pyramidal structure of pale blue stone. It rose hundreds of feet above him, illuminated by its own pale, eerie lambency. Its surface was not smooth, but corrugated and carven with esoteric and blasphemous symbols, bas-reliefs of ancient words in some indecipherable language. The pyramid itself was old, old, seemingly fossilized by the passage of eons.

Now the procession moved inside and Moss heard what he knew he would hear—the wet, slobbering noises, the rustlings, the busy sounds of multiple legs, the chitterings and squealings, and, yes, rising above it all, that immense omnipotent buzzing, the unearthly droning of the great insect itself.

The pyramid was just as hollow as the mountain, its sloping walls honeycombed with chambers, many of which were sealed with mud caps. The women of Possum Crawl had gathered here. They accepted the gifts the men brought. No longer were they women as such, but hairless, pallid things that cared for the white, squirming grubs of the immense gelatinous insect, the Mother of Many Faces, the all-in-one, the progenitor that all in Possum Crawl worshipped for she brought life, she nurtured it, and filled the earth with crawling things and the skies with her primordial swarm.

Vermicular shapes squirmed at his feet, crawling about on their hands and knees, moving with a disturbing boneless sort of locomotion like human inchworms. He saw contorted faces and glistening eyes like frog spawn staring up at him. They touched him with flaccid, fungous hands.

And now Moss could see her—within the limits of the third dimension—surrounded by a veritable mountain of yeasty gray eggs that glistened wetly from her multiple ovipositors. She was a titanic, bloated white monstrosity, an elemental abomination that sutured time-space with her passing and whose origins were in some deranged cosm where the stars burned black. Her membranous wings spread like kites filling with wind, her thousand legs scraping together, her bulging compound eyes looking down at the offerings laid before her.

Her nest.

Yes, the Earth was her nest.

By then, Moss was on his knees, his sanity gone to a warm mush in his head. He had seen her before and she had erased his memories. Now he understood. He shivered there in her shadow. *Ginny, Ginny, Ginny.* Oh God, he had not stolen Ginny away from them after she was indoctrinated into the fertility cult of the Mother of Many Faces. No, no, she had escaped them and they called out to him, stealing his mind, and he had brought Ginny *back* to them. Yes, in the back of the car, tied and gagged, he had returned their acolyte to the hollow mountain.

But she was not what the Great Insect wanted.

No, Moss was spared, his memories subverted, his will possessed, so that he might bring that which the Mother Insect demanded, the expiation she hungered for.

And now his shaking hands were opening the silver case, fumbling at the locks, working the catches, and then it was in his hands, the reeking mass of meat in the shape of a shriveled infant. The fruit of his marital congress with Ginny. The offering the Great Insect anticipated from the beginning.

It was accepted and found pleasing by her servitors.

Then Moss waited there, his mind gone, his eyes glazed with terror, his stomach pulsing with revulsion. Squinny stepped before him and said, "Your place has always been here. Your destiny is to be meat because all meat has its purpose and all flesh is to be consumed."

The Preacher.

He did not fight when the yellow-eyed image of the girl came for him, the avatar of the Mother of Many Faces, when her barbed tongue took his eyes so that he would not look upon the holy rite of birth, the spawning and renewal. He did not even cry out when she jabbed her stinger up between his legs and into his body cavity. He squirmed, he writhed, but no more. Then gray waves of lethargy washed through him and there was only acceptance. He was tucked, not unlovingly, into one of the cell-shaped chambers and sealed in there as food. A flaccid, dreaming, unfeeling mass, he did not even flinch when the eggs began to hatch and the wriggling young of the Great Insect began to feed.

The Old Man Down the Road

Arinn Dembo

The night before they left for Tennessee, they slept in a double bed on Striver's Row. Traffic slashed through the autumn rain below as they wrestled in the sheets, chasing away anxiety with love-making. James drifted off with sweat drying on his belly, his lover's breath blowing warm on his shoulder.

Hours later he woke alone in the cold bed, his bare feet curled back to find shins that weren't there. For a panic-stricken, half-asleep moment he found himself thinking *he's gone.*

He sat up, white sheets pooling over dark thighs, and saw Tommy standing by the window. The rippling sodium light flowed down his pale skin like molten copper.

James reached for his glasses on the night table. Even in this surreal moment of broken sleep, he still could drink in the sight of his lover's body.

Thomas Newcombe Baird. The only white man he had ever seen naked, outside of a medical textbook or a muscle magazine. The curve of head and neck as Tommy stared down past the fire escape. His shoulder-length shag had been clipped just this morning; the fat man with the trimmer laughed about giving White Jesus a haircut. Tommy's shy little smile, eyes downcast as the brown silk fell like feathers from his Teutonic skull.

The angelic spread of his shoulders. The long, liquid muscles of his back and legs. The way his chin and chest lifted as he ran down the gravel paths in the park, stride extending into effortless thoroughbred speed. The sculpted line of his spine, the dimples just below his lean waist.

Tommy turned his head, a skull with two eye-pits of shadow. "You should sleep." He spoke softly. "It's hours 'til dawn."

"Me? You're the one who has to drive."

Tommy turned and pointed his chin at the storm sweeping the gutters below. "He's back again."

James felt a chill. "At this hour?" He stood up, wrapping the sheets around his waist and throwing the tail over his shoulder like a toga. He went to the window and saw the ominous figure on the corner, water streaming down the dome of a black umbrella. "Is it the same guy...?"

"Hard to tell, with the coat and hat. I reckon they dress that way so you can't tell 'em apart."

James hugged himself with a shiver. "I've never been 'staked out' before. I don't like it."

Tommy put a bare arm around his shoulders and drew him close. As always, his skin seemed to radiate an envelope of seductive heat; James leaned into him like a sparrow huddled in the glow of a street lamp.

"You must be important." Tommy's voice was low, half-amused. "The FBI doesn't follow nobodies, right?"

"They follow nobodies just fine," James replied acidly. "The somebodies get shot."

He felt the silent wave that passed through Tommy, the quickening of the heart, the tightening of the arm around his shoulder. "They're going to have to go through me first. That's all I can say."

James shook his head sadly. "Is that why you're coming on this trip? Because you think they won't 'go through you'?"

"No." The arm was tighter now. "I grew up down there, hon. Ran away from that place a long time ago. I know what happens to folk who get in the way."

James turned, letting his chest and belly flatten against Tommy, reaching up to touch his cheek with a cupped hand. "You know I have to go. Lena and Walt are counting on me to help with voter registration. They're covering three counties this year. There's no way they can do it on their own—and they're my friends. I can't let them down."

Tommy closed his eyes, tilting his head to let his cheek lie in the palm of his lover's hand.

"But really, Tom…there's no reason you have to come." He spoke as gently as he could as he dropped his hand. "I know you don't want to go back."

Tommy shivered. "I might still have….family, down in Carolina. Looking for me."

James nodded. "Abel and I can manage."

Tommy snorted. "Abel and you will do what, exactly? Hitch-hike to Tennessee?"

James drew in a long breath. "We could get bus tickets. I can afford it."

"Money can't always buy safe passage, hon."

James rolled his eyes. "We wouldn't even have to sit together. We could ride down quietly and pretend not to know each other. Like perfectly respectable folks."

It was Tommy's turn to unsheathe the edge of his tongue. "With you sitting in the back of the bus? Like 'respectable folks'?"

James stiffened. "If need be. Yes." He raised his chin defiantly. "I choose my battles. You know that."

"I do." Tommy shook his head. "I'm sorry, James. I don't want to go down South. I'd do anything if you'd stay with me. But if you're going…I just…can't let you leave me behind."

"I wasn't! Tom, I would never—"

"You would. You were going to try." The words shook as he spoke. "And I cannot bear it, James." Tommy opened his arms, still perfectly nude, palms open. A gesture of surrender. "Please don't leave me here alone."

James looked up and saw light follow the tracks of silent tears. "Tom... come on, now..." He was moving forward, the sheets forgotten and tangling around his legs.

Tommy's arms closed around him. The bigger man was shaking now, crushing him close. "I'm scared." A high boyish whisper. "What if something happens down there?"

James swallowed twice before he could speak. "If something happens...? Then you'd be safe. Tom..."

"No. You can't leave me, James. If anything happens to you...it has to happen to me. It has to." His voice broke. "I cannot live if you're gone."

"Tom. Tommy." He murmured the name over and over again, stroking the smooth back and shoulders, punctuating his caresses with "It's all right" as if the words were a mantra.

I know you love me. I love you back, he wanted to say. *I won't ever leave you.* But those words would not come.

In two years, he had never said anything like that aloud.

He opened the door at dawn to find Abel Feinman standing on the front step with his suitcase. Feinman was wearing Moroccan brown slacks and a green Paisley shirt...and still hadn't cut his hair.

James looked him up and down, silently disapproving of his rabbinical beard and luxuriant mane of oily black curls. He held the silence so long that Abel pushed up the bridge of his glasses and cracked a nervous smile. "What, am I at the wrong house or something? Let me in already."

James invited him in with a sarcastic wave of his hand. "You couldn't find a barber, man?"

Abel set down the suitcase in the foyer. "Sorry, James. Couldn't go through with it."

James rolled his eyes. "Yeah, I bet. What did Joanie say, exactly?"

Abel had the grace to look down at his loafers. "Aaaaah…she said something about Samson and Delilah. And told me I was going to look like a baby-faced narc…."

"Who's a narc, now?" Tommy came around the bend of the curving stairs, a suitcase in each hand. He was already wearing his Sherpa jacket and aviator glasses. "Better not be talking about me."

Abel looked up and laughed out loud. "Jesus, Tom. What'd you do, enlist?"

Tommy smiled and stepped out the open door. "I'll just bring the car around."

James gave Abel another look over the golden rims of his glasses. When he had full eye contact, he deliberately dropped his gaze to the avocado-green suitcase on the floor. Then back up into Abel's eyes, lips pursed.

"Anything I need to *worry* about in there?"

The beatnik could read his mind. "Aawww, c'mon James…"

"C'mon my *ass*. You already proved you can't listen to instructions. I told you to clean yourself up."

"I did!" Abel flapped a hand defensively up and down, indicating his new JC Penney ensemble. "This is all brand new! Everything in my suitcase too! I spent twenty dollars, man!"

"That's not what I meant. And you damn well know it." James cocked a fist on one hip, and put out the other hand palm up, making a "gimme" gesture. "You look like Phineas Freak, Abel. Nothing I can do about that now, but I'll be *damned* if I'm riding with your dope."

Feinman rolled his eyes. "For Christ's sake…"

"Don't you go bringing Him into this. Hand it over now, before I get mad."

Abel gave a long-suffering groan and opened his suitcase. The marijuana was "cleverly" hidden in a pair of socks—and if those socks were brand new, James was Nancy Sinatra. Abel handed the dime bag over with a show of reluctance, and James shook his head in disgust.

"Mmm-hmm. Now give me the other one."

Feinman looked up into his eyes, startled. James gave his head a long, slow shake.

"Do. Not. Even. Try." He made the "gimme" gesture again. "I am not playing with you."

Abel hesitated, and James saw a flicker behind his eyes—try to bluff? But it was gone just as quickly, and without another word he reached into the Samsonite bag again and pulled out a Gideon Bible. Inside the book, a hole had been cut through a hundred pages of onionskin paper to make a nest for a meerschaum pipe and another bag of green herb.

"Yeah. Real smart." James shook his head, turned on his heel, went to the credenza in the foyer, and un-locked the top drawer. He dropped Abel's things into it, re-locked the drawer firmly, and then made a show of leaving the key on the moulding above the front door. "It'll be right here for you when we get back. You can do without that stuff for a few days."

Abel rolled his eyes. "Whatever, man."

Tommy appeared at the doorway, his smile a lit-tle uncertain. Over his shoulder, James could see the brown Chevy Bel-Air double-parked in the street. "Y'all ready?"

"Ready as we'll ever be." As the two white boys clat-tered down his steps, James locked his front door behind him and spared a final glance at the man who sat at the bus stop, watching them over the top of his morning pa-per.

James raised a hand and waved.

The man did not wave back.

Tommy took the George Washington Bridge out of the city and followed the New Jersey Turnpike to connect to I-95. The freeway led them south through Pennsylvania, the motorway ablaze with autumn color in late October. It was a pleasant ride, and James kept the Negro Motorist Green Book in his lap, guiding them unerringly to safe gas stations and diners. At nearly every stop, Abel had to find a lavatory or a pay phone, but he was equally quick about calls of nature and calls to his mother.

That night they arrived in Richmond late and rented rooms at Slaughter's Hotel. They ordered sandwiches and ginger ale from room service and ate in Tommy's room, watching Bonanza on the black-and-white television.

Despite the pleasant weather and the ease of travel, there was an unspoken tension in the air, and Abel seemed to pick up on it with fine-tuned antennae. He kept silent for most of the trip, reading the books he'd brought in his suitcase, rolling and smoking tobacco cigarettes or folding his arms over his beard for a cat nap when he was bored. Tommy didn't try to make conversation. Instead he spun the dial on the radio back and forth as he drove, occasionally picking up a snatch of Paul Harvey or hillbilly country songs, dialing it in more slowly when he found black music or a black DJ speaking. He'd looked over at James for a nod of approval when the signal finally came in clear, and sometimes, if Abel's eyes were closed, James would answer by reaching out to lay a hand on his blue-jeaned thigh.

On the last night of the trip they listened to Chattie Hattie from WGIV, following a narrow strip of highway up into the Blue Ridge mountains. Solomon Burke sang about sweet lips coming closer to a phone, his mellow croon dissolving more and more frequently into bursts of static with every curve of the road.

Just as the last of the radio signal was lost, a siren whooped behind them, and the cherry lights of a police car started to flash in the rearview mirror.

Tommy stiffened and cringed, hands locked on the wheel. He looked down at the speedometer, guilty—no, he had not been speeding—and then gave James a pained look. The Adam's apple jumped in his throat like a frog on a string as he hit the blinker and pulled over at the side of the road.

The silence when the engine cut out was deafening. James kept still, his shoulders hunched in the passenger seat, as the doors of the sedan behind them opened and slammed. The crunch of approaching boots was slow and ominous.

"Get out the car."

The highway patrolman stood in the middle of the road, already in a firing position—his pistol drawn, both hands on the grip. James shivered at the sound of that voice, already shaking on the verge of panic.

White.

Southern.

Angry.

The man raised his voice. Louder now. "Get out the car, boy! Ain't going to tell you again!"

Tommy Baird turned in slow motion toward the open window. The black unblinking eye of a .38 met his blue gaze.

"Whatever you say, Officer." Tommy's tone was mild as milk. "We don't want any trouble." His hands were parked on the steering wheel at ten and two; now they rose into the air like moths and fluttered gently to the handle of the door. He opened it with exaggerated care and stepped out into the night air. Those same long-fingered hands rose to chest height, offering open palms to the gun.

James glanced over his shoulder. The second cop was an armed silhouette in the headlights, also holding a pistol—the weapon was pointed down at his side, not at Tommy.

Abel Feinman slid lower in the back seat, eyes floating behind his thick lenses like pickled eggs. His acne-scarred cheeks were pale as the moon in the strobing blue light. "This is it," he muttered. "This is it."

"This is nothing," James hissed back. "Hush up."

"Turn around and bend over. Right now."

"Yes sir." Tommy was working with the script he'd been given—he and James had rehearsed it a hundred times. He turned slowly, hands in the air. "May I ask what this is about?" His intonation stayed calm and slow, but James could read the fear in his knotted jaw, the set of his shoulders, the way he breathed.

Fast movement in the dark. Tommy's torso slammed into the hood, a reverberating boom of meat and bone on Detroit steel. Despite himself he cried out in surprise, and James felt the pain in his chest, as if that cry had pierced him through.

You can't protect him. He can't protect you either.

"Shut up." The cop snapped Tommy's wrists into handcuffs. "Y'all think you can just come down here and—"

"Careful, Andrew. You are not to damage him." The second policeman spoke, cutting through his partner's snarl like a scalpel. It was a very different voice—cool, aristocratic, commanding. A Southern gentleman. The ring of it sent the skin crawling over James in a wave.

Tommy reacted immediately as well, standing bolt upright, his hands pinioned behind his back.

"No." His eyes were wide with horror as he turned toward the glare of the headlights behind them, the shape of the second policeman. "No!"

Officer Andrew turned his head and nodded. James saw the gun spin and swing back.

"Tommy—!" He started to cry a warning, but butt of the pistol struck Tommy's head with a heavy thud. Tommy crumpled into the gravel.

The gun was pointed at him now.

"Your turn, nigger. Get out the car."

James froze. He moved slowly, as Tommy had, eyes on the cop, hands inching toward the door handle.

At the last minute he tore his eyes away from the gun and turned to look out the window. It was after midnight. Tommy's Bel Air was parked on the side of a lonely mountain road, somewhere in the thick woods between Tennessee and North Carolina. If they'd been coming the other way, back toward New York… the passenger side door would have opened onto the guard rail and the depths of a steep gorge.

Then he might have made a break for it.

He could see it in his mind. Throw himself out the door. Pray the cop would miss a clear shot at his back. Jump the rail. Throw himself into the abyss below.

But the passenger door opened onto a wall of solid Appalachian rock, slick with October dew. There was nowhere to run. He stood up, turning back toward the road like a man facing a firing squad, raising his hands up to his chest.

"Come around. Nice and slow."

James walked. His mind had gone numb. Someone pushed him face down onto the Chevy. The heat of the engine soaked through his shirt as the cop wrestled his wrists into the cuffs. He thought wildly of Tommy's radiant warmth in the moment before he was slammed to his knees in the road.

Tommy was lying beside him. He rolled his face up toward the stars and for a moment their eyes met, but Tommy's gaze slid away, unfocused and confused. *Possible concussion.*

"The third gentleman too, Deputy. If you please."

James heard rather than saw Abel pulled out of the back seat. "You can't do this!" he brayed. There was a hollow thump as he was thrown back against the door. "We're human beings! We have rights!"

"Shut up." The cop turned to his partner. "What now? We all done here?"

There was silence for a moment, and then a chilling chuckle from Officer Shadow. "Yes, I do believe our business is almost concluded."

"Good. What you want to do with these other two?"

"An excellent question." The man in the shadows paused in deliberation. "A Negro is always useful, of course. If only for brute labor. But I have no use for a Jew. Especially one with poor vision."

The pistol cracked in the cold mountain air. Tommy rolled himself up and screamed. And his scream went on, cracking up into sobs as he floundered forward on his belly and knees, arms still buckled behind his back, across the broken asphalt to Abel.

James was moving forward himself, dragging his knees over the rocks, until he felt a stinging pain in his shoulder. He turned his head and saw a needle flicker away like a sliver of blue light, quick as a dragonfly.

He looked up directly into the cop's sallow face in the blazing headlights of the police car. A lumpy white man in his forties, cheeks and jowls decked with stubble, blue eyes rimmed with red.

"Your name is Andrew," James told him solemnly. He looked back toward his friends, his vision swimming. Tommy was still crying. Abel Feinman stared up into Appalachian night, his glasses askew and speckled with red. His last three breaths came in tiny quick pants, and the rich bloom of ruptured bowels and blood filled the air.

James Aaron Locke toppled forward into blackness, listening for a fourth breath that never came.

⁂

He woke again to voices raised in an adjoining room. "You said you'd let him go."

James breathed in the thick smell of disinfectant and rubber. His throat hurt. He tried to rise, but there was a tremendous weight bearing down on him. Paper crackled under his back.

I'm naked.

He opened his eyes in a pitch black room. His head was pounding, his mouth cotton-dry.

"I done everything you said." He recognized Officer Andrew. There a sulky note of protest when he spoke—a boy complaining that adults were unfair. "You told me you'd leave him be if I—"

"And indeed I shall, Deputy. But your Sheriff weighs over two hundred pounds, and you're in no condition to carry him far. We wouldn't want to aggravate that hernia, would we?" Officer Shadow sounded playful—enjoying himself cruelly, a cat toying with a bird.

"No sir."

"I'll walk him to your car, if it's all the same to you."

"Yes sir."

James swallowed and felt a spasm of agony in his throat. He winced and listened to the heavy boots moving away, the whine and wheeze of a door opening and then slowly swinging shut. The rattle of iron and the moan of a hydraulic lift soon followed.

He tried to sit up again, fighting back a surge of nausea and disorientation, but he was held fast. There was a leather strap across his forehead. Another pulled tight and buckled across his chest. When he tried to flex his hands, he could feel the soft cuffs on his bare wrists and arms as well. More straps and cuffs below, when he tried to kick his feet.

"Help." The attempt to use his vocal chords was agony, and the word came out a ragged whisper. Somewhere to his right, he heard a gasp.

"Aaaaezz…?" Tommy's questioning voice, broken and shapeless, followed by a wet, gagging cough. He heard Tommy panting for breath and another crackle of paper. "Aaaeez…? Iiizh aa ooo…?"

"Tommy." Something was wrong with Tommy's

mouth. Something was wrong with his own throat as well—it hurt terribly, and now he tasted a little blood. He twisted his head toward the right. Tommy was across the room on a long table, naked and strapped down with medical restraints. James could see the glitter of steel, the shine of wet teeth.

Tommy tried to speak again, tongue flapping helplessly in his gaping mouth. There was machinery holding his jaws open--a dental gag strapped around the back of his head. "Aaez, ai eeeah…"

"I understand." He rasped the words out painfully, trying not to swallow too much. Oddly enough, he did understand. He was the son of Aaron Medgers Locke, the finest dentist in Harlem, and he had earned his allowance for years mopping the floor and replacing the lollipops in his father's office. It was no trouble at all to understand English spoken by someone who couldn't close his mouth.

James? Is that you?

James, I'm here…

He tried to turn his head the other way. "Where are we…?"

For answer, Tommy started to cry.

"Ai oh awe ee…Aaez…" *I'm so sorry…James…*

"Don't be a fool." James wheezed the words out angrily, despite the pain. "These people are crazy. We have to get out of here."

There was a sudden noise in the next room, a wet gurgling like a sink full of sludge pouring down a narrow drain. It was followed by a spastic thump, rattle and squeak—like an animal struggling in a cage, or someone having a three-second seizure.

A moment of silence.

The unmistakable noise of someone passing wind, long and slow.

A scuffle and scratch. Wheels creaked. To his left, beyond his field of vision, a door opened, and a shaft of light sliced across his torso. Someone had thrown an ivory sheet over him like a shroud.

Tommy huffed silent tears beside him. "—Oooh…" he moaned softly.

No.

"Good evening, gentlemen."

James jumped. The tone, the accent was unmistakable—it was Officer Shadow. But the vocal chords were no longer those of a strong, middle-aged man. This vocalization came from a much older person--someone whose throat creaked with age, lungs rattling with every breath.

"Thomas, since you are unable to make a proper introduction, I will have to do the honors myself." The wheels rolled forward, and fluorescent tubes overhead buzzed and blazed into blinding light.

James clenched his eyes shut, stabbed with twin spears of new pain. When he could open them a crack, he found himself looking up at a mummy—a human head wrapped in brittle crepe, bald pate sporting a few random strands of grey. The old man had a pug nose, swollen to a red carbuncle with two ugly nostril slits. The eye sockets were mottled with brown bruises, the skin covered with liver spots and lesions. The eyes were milky blue and veined with blood.

The skull smiled at him, chapped lips peeling back over yellow tusks.

"How d'you do, Mister Locke?"

James kept his mouth clamped shut. *He stripped us buck naked. Of course he's seen our wallets and all the cards…*

"My name is Ezekiel Baird." The skull was speaking in that aristocratic drawl, the one that made his stomach clench. "Ezekiel Abadiah Baird. It's a pleasure to make your acquaintance."

The skull made a show of waiting for his reply, mock-listening for words that did not come. The old man cackled merrily. "Cat's got your tongue, I see! Understandable. You've come such a long way. I will confess, it has been many years since I visited New Amsterdam—I hear it is much changed. Harlem Village is now home to the cream of Negro society!" Another chuckle. "I've never met a Harlemite of such substantial means before. You must forgive us, Mister Locke, if our country manners here in Carolina seem rough and quaint by comparison."

The wheelchair squealed and the skull retreated from view, moving along the length of the table.

"Where are we?" James grated out the words as the old mummy rolled away, teeth clenched with pain. "Where have you taken us?"

"Why, this is my home, Mister Locke!" The wheels rolled on toward Tommy. "You may not know it, but the Baird family has run the finest funeral home in Buncombe County since before the Civil War."

James turned his head, trying to look over to Tommy. *The Baird family? Is this person related to you?*

"This old place was once my residence and my place of business. I have not practiced the mortuary arts since the turn of the century, of course, but… these old rooms still have their uses!"

Tommy tried to speak. "Eeaz, zuh. Eeeaz zeh ick oh." *Please sir. Please let him go.*

The old man laughed again. "I'm afraid that's out of the question, young Thomas! But I'll tell you what. If you're fond of this one, we'll keep him. You'll need a place to stay, after all, when you take me in!"

Tommy gagged in a deep breath and wailed in denial, flexing and twisting on the table. There was something crazed and mindless about his struggle, like a fish flopping in the dry leaves.

"Wait," James rasped, trying to distract the old man. He knew instinctively that whatever he was about to do to Tommy would be horrible. "My family has money. I'll pay you." He coughed blood, swallowed it grimly, and tried again. "I'll give you a thousand dollars to let us go."

"Will you now?" The skull wheeled about, leering over the humped shoulder like a Halloween mask. "Is that what your life is worth, Mister Locke? Your body, your soul? Ransomed for a few portraits of Benjamin Franklin on cheap green paper?"

Confused, he tried again. "What do you want? Whatever it is, I'll give it to you."

The skull grinned. "Why, yes. I believe you will, Mister Locke. Young Thomas certainly gave me everything I asked, and more! I've missed him since he ran away, more than I can say."

The old man turned back toward Tommy's table. "I cannot thank you enough for returning my beloved nephew to the fold, Mister Locke. If not for you, I don't believe he would have come within a hundred miles of here. Why, without your very special relationship... I might well have *died*."

A withered hand reached out toward Tommy's face. The old man ran a palsied fingertip over the drool-slick chin and trailed it along Tommy's lower lip. He bent forward, bringing his face in close to Tommy's, shoulders hunched.

"Stop it! Don't touch him." James felt his mouth fill with red copper as he struggled against the straps, trying to work his arms free.

The old man ignored him. "Now then," he crooned to Tommy. "Let's get reacquainted, shall we?"

Tommy shuddered and squirmed at every touch, desperately trying to prevent contact with his skin, but it was no use. One gaunt hand closed around his throat, the other stroked his sweating, weeping face tenderly. "There's a lad." He sounded almost gentle. "You remember. Breathing in... breathing out."

Tommy's eyes rolled up into his head, the whites showing stark as his muscles locked into rigor and began to shake. His whole body trembled, an earthquake ripping through muscle and bone. His breath roared in and out of his chest in huge gusts, like a bellows.

"Stop it!" His shout was an agonized gasp. He was crying now himself. "You're killing him!"

Tommy lay flat on his back on the table, his chest rising and falling, the blood visibly pounding in his temples. The old man unbuckled one of his wrists and tilted his head back, like a doctor trying to clear the airway of a patient having a fit.

The horrible liquid gurgling sound began, coming now from Tommy's open mouth, as if some invisible thick slime was pouring down his throat. His tremors increased in strength one last time, his heels drumming the table top like fists on a tin roof. Then he was quiet— his breath had stopped.

James held his own breath, paralyzed with horror, until Tommy's lungs filled with a sudden clear whoop of air. The old man slumped back in his wheelchair as Tommy breathed in deep.

"Tommy?" James whispered. "Are you… okay…?"

Tommy answered with a low, deep groan of pleasure.

One hand had been unbuckled from the leather cuff. He reached up now with that free hand, slipped the retaining band of the dental gag up over the back of his head, and carefully removed the appliance from his face. When he had teased it out of his mouth, he tossed it casually on the metal tray beside the table.

"Woo! God Almighty, what a thrill. It never pales."

James felt his breath catch in his throat, going shallow and rough. *Tommy always had a Southern accent. He's playing with you. Doing an impression.*

Tommy's movements were swift and sure as he unbuckled the strap around his chest, then rolled to free his right hand, and sat up to unbuckle his legs.

He tried again. "Tommy?"

Tommy looked over at him, his eyes blazing brilliant blue as he swung his bare legs off the side of the table. "Never fear, Mister Locke! Tommy Baird is right as *rain*." He ran his hands over his naked anatomy with almost gluttonous delight. "Tommy Baird...will do very nicely *indeed*."

He hopped down lightly, stood on his tiptoes, and threw up his arms in a long, balletic stretch. At the peak of the movement he laughed out loud, so full of triumph and joy that James almost wanted to smile with him—he had never seen Tommy this happy before.

"Tom..." James hesitated. "Can you help me with these cuffs?"

Tommy dropped his arms to his sides and smirked. "No...I'm afraid you'll have to sit tight for a bit longer, Mister Locke. I have some business to attend to."

"What...?" James flexed his hands into fists. "Are you kidding? Let me out of these straps, Tom!"

Tommy chuckled. "Might do, yes." He spoke lightly. "Eventually. But not before I've applied myself to a fine steak, a bottle of brandy, a pitcher of good cream and a nice, big slice of pecan pie." He licked his lips and smiled. "One must have priorities!"

He strode to the door, confident and careless in his nudity as a Greek statue. "Be a peach and wait patiently, won't you?" He turned to look back over his shoulder. "If you need something to occupy your mind, Mister Locke, I'll tell you a secret. The rats in this basement get mighty bold, when the lights are out. Back in my undertaker days, I used to keep a nigger down here at night to guard the bodies. Keep them from *chewing* on my clientele." His eyes danced with humor. "Those coloured boys carried a broom and a coal shovel, but they were *always* getting bit."

Then he flipped the light switch and closed the door, leaving James in darkness.

He waited a full minute before he closed his eyes, and let the tears of rage flow freely. Even in the midst of those tears he struggled for control, breath hissing between his teeth, trying to calm himself and think, damnit. Think.

Tommy is gone.

It was a barbed thought, a crown of thorns laced around the inside of his skull. Every time he tried to touch the idea, it hurt, and he could feel himself tearing inside. It was the mental equivalent of trying to swallow with his torn throat.

Some part of him was being ripped to shreds--maybe the part that believed the world made any kind of sense.

One half of him knew the truth: that Tommy Baird, the man he loved, had gotten up off the examination table, laughed in his face, and left him here to die.

The other side of him knew another truth: that the man who walked out that door was no more Tommy Baird than the Man in the Moon. He was someone else entirely, looking out of Tommy's eyes, talking out of Tommy's mouth, and joy-riding in Tommy Baird's beautiful body like a thief in a stolen car.

James clenched his fists and rotated his feet in their cuffs, listening to the clink of the chains that secured his ankles and wrists to the table. He could keep working them, but the odds of breaking free of medical restraints were low. They were designed to hold violent patients in place for many hours.

Tommy—or whoever it was passing for Tommy— had left him alone. That would normally be a foolish thing to do, if a person could scream and call for help. But he felt a cold certainty that his power of speech was gone for a reason. They had done something to him, while he was unconscious.

Will I ever be able to speak again?

No. Not a good thought. Think something else.

As it stood, he was likely to remain alone down in

this basement until Tommy (*Ezekiel... his name was Ezekiel*) came back.

Alone except for the rats.

And the old man in the wheelchair.

Speaking of the old man...was he still breathing?

James tried to be still, to slow down his own shaking breath, to quiet the heartbeat that pounded like thunder in his ears. The wheelchair should be off to his right, next to the table where Tommy was strapped down. Was it still there?

Had he heard the creak of a wheel? A wheeze of labored breath?

Something soft, wet and cold touched his hand in the dark, and he jerked away, moving so fast and hard that the chain rang against the table like a bell. He began thrashing and fighting with all his might, hoping to frighten away whatever had come nosing around looking for a mouthful of meat.

"James." The sound was like a rusty hinge. "Be still, hon. I'll try to get you loose."

Tears once again flooded his eyes. "Tom." The instrument was wrong, weak and reedy, but there was no mistaking the music. He would know that voice anywhere.

"I'm here." James heard the trembling hiss and felt the cold wet touch again, this time on his wrist. Chilly fingers fumbled with the buckles of his cuff. "Try not to move. These hands don't work so good."

"How...?" His questions swarmed up into his mouth, all of them too crazy to ask. Finally he settled on, "How did this happen...?"

"I can't explain what he does, James. He's always done it." The shaking hands finally seemed to conquer one buckle. They crawled on, reaching for the next one. "There's a trick to it—some of him has to be inside you. I saw him take a man once by spitting in his eye. That wasn't the way he took my father, though. Or my mother. Or me."

James swallowed hard, grimacing as he did. "Your father…?"

The fingers shook as they worked, cold and clumsy. "Yes. After the War. I told you once that he shot himself… I didn't tell you why." The tongue of the buckle resisted, and Tommy cursed it quietly.

"What happened to him?"

"There was a lynching, down in Hendersonville." The hands went still for a moment, then back to work more slowly. "My Daddy didn't hold with the Klan, especially after he come back from France, but someone slipped an envelope under the door of his office in town. It was a picture of the necktie party, with the two black boys hanging from a pole. And somehow my father was there in the photograph, standing in the front row looking right at the camera with a big ol' grin on his face." A deep breath. "I found him in the parlor that night, just sitting with that picture in his lap and crying." Another moment of silence, broken only by the whistle of bad lungs. "The next day he drove over to my Uncle Ezekiel's house and rang his door bell. When the old man answered the door, he blew his brains out right then and there."

The second buckle gave way, and James felt the cuff on his wrist relax.

"I wish I had done the same," Tommy said quietly. "I wish you had never met me, James."

James wriggled out of the cuff, flexing his free hand…and then reached toward the hand that freed him. It was a gnarled, elderly claw, every joint a swollen and misshapen knob of bone. The owner of that hand could only be in constant pain—he had seen rheumatoid arthritis before.

The hand pulled away from him after a moment, trembling, and he heard a strangled hitch of breath. "I'm sorry…" The squeaky old hinge wheezed laughter. "I'm afraid I'm not myself right now."

James reached up to the strap across his forehead. His own fingers were still nimble and swift, and he was almost free by the time Tommy could roll the chair across the room and find the light switch.

"Cover your eyes, hon."

James lowered his head and closed his eyes, then opened them slowly. He was in a room with a floor of stained tile, sitting on a high table of cold steel. There were glass fronted cabinets and trays of instruments along the wall. A room for the preparation of bodies.

He put a shaking hand to his throat, found the bandage and gauze that covered it. He took a deep breath and slid off the table carefully, extending his foot to catch himself—it was a long drop to the floor.

He crept to the door, holding his genitals cupped in a protective hand. Outside there was a wide silent hall, leading to an old-fashioned Otis freight elevator. The room next door was a wood-paneled office, lit with banker's lamps of brass and green glass. Through the open door he could see the bent figure in the wheelchair.

"Tommy?" He put a hand to his throat and winced, moving into the room.

The figure in the chair cringed lower, and did not face him. "Just trying to find your clothes. He'll have them in a gunny sack somewhere. Ready to dress you again, if need be. Or to throw into the furnace, if..."

He didn't seem able to finish the thought. Instead he put his hands to the wheels and struggled forward a few more inches. "Soon as we find your clothes, you can slip out the old coal chute in the back. If you listen for the sound of water you'll find Smith Mill Creek. And if you follow the stream downhill, it'll take you all the way to the French Broad River. The black folks live around Burton Street. I reckon you'll know it when you see it."

He would have continued rolling toward the wardrobe in the corner, but James stepped up around the chair, planted his hands on the armrests to stop it, and crouched low to look directly into his lover's eyes.

The man in the chair was not just old. He was ancient. James looked him up and down slowly. The ruined head was resting atop a scrawny chicken neck, all bone and wattled folds of leather. The starved frame was only loosely dressed, a thin robe belted at the waist and open to reveal slotted ribs and a shrunken belly. The skin was scaly grey and sick, covered with vivid purple spots and red, raw sores.

He looked up into blue eyes milky with cataracts, and saw Tommy Baird looking back at him.

"I used to love the way you looked at me," the old man said. "Like I was everything good in the world." He raised his gnarled hands to cover his face, bending his head to avoid his lover's gaze. "I did wonder sometimes…'Could he keep looking at me like that? When I'm old and grey?'" The chest hitched with something like laughter or tears. "Could anyone look at me like that forever?" He sucked in a hissing breath. "I guess now I know."

James reached out and pulled the tortured hands away from the old man's face. The fingers were freezing cold, still damp, swollen with ague. Even touching them made Tommy's face twist with pain.

Slowly, holding the Tommy's eyes with his own, James raised those hands to his mouth and kissed them.

"I still see you." His whisper was hoarse and painful. "You still hear me?"

There was a long moment of silence, and then Tommy shook his head. "Damn. I can't even cry. The old bastard's got no tears--he's dry as a popcorn fart." He looked away. "Get dressed, hon."

James went to the wardrobe. He found his clothing, wallet, watch and glasses in a burlap sack, along with the Green Book and the notebook and pencil he'd been keeping in his coat pocket. The socks and shirt were missing, but he put on his coat and stuffed his bare feet into his shoes with a grimace.

There was a cracked mirror on the inside of the door, and he looked into it warily. A short, muscular black man with gold-rimmed glasses, his throat wrapped in cotton bandages showing a tell-tale splotch of red. He buttoned up the coat as high as it would go, hoping it would look more as if he was wearing a turtleneck sweater, and then turned toward the door.

Tommy sat in the wheelchair, a massive pistol in his lap.

"I'm ready. Just push me into the hall before you go. When he comes back down the elevator...I'll be waiting."

James froze. "What?"

"I'll take care of him." Tommy patted the gun. "Like my Daddy should have done."

"No." James shook his head in slow disbelief. "You can't..."

"I'm dying, hon." He put his free hand to his sunken chest. "I can feel it. This body...it's so weak I have to *think* to keep the heart beating. And the only reason I'm not already dead is money, most likely. He probably needs a lawyer to sign papers, make sure he keeps his property."

James stepped forward. "Come with me. Forget him. Forget this."

Tommy smiled with genuine tenderness. "Tried that before, hon. And look where that got us." He shook his head. "Just go. Leave me here. Let me do...what I have left to do."

James clenched his teeth and shook his head stubbornly.

"I love you." The words were painful, and tasted of blood. "I won't ever leave you."

In the end, they waited in the dark for three hours before the Otis elevator returned to the basement. Dawn was just starting to break, the first lark singing in the woods behind the house, when the door swung open.

The report of the pistol was thunderous in the enclosed space. James held his head in his hands as it crashed three times, four…and looked up through the smoke to see a bleeding form still crawling in the hallway, dragging itself with a shattered spine toward the open lift door.

He took the pistol from Tommy's shaking hand and walked into the hall, aimed the gun at the back of a familiar head, and pulled the trigger twice more. The spray of blood and bone formed a halo around the ruined skull—he pulled the trigger again to be sure, but there was no more thunder. Only a dry click.

James threw the gun away, turned his back on the mess, and walked back to Tommy's side. The azure eyes looked up at him, warm and alive.

"I love you," Tommy whispered.

James bent and gathered the frail limbs in his arms. He carried Tommy over the mess and into the study, settled him into the old wheelchair as gently as he could, and wrapped a sheet around his shoulders. Then he rolled the chair down the hall without looking back. He held the Dead Man's switch as they rode up in the freight elevator to the ground floor, pushed Tommy out onto the front porch and down the ramp to the driveway.

Tommy's Bel Air was parked in the grass behind the house, the keys still in the ignition. James opened the passenger door and settled Tommy unto the seat, got behind the wheel, and mouthed a silent prayer as he turned the key.

The car roared to life without hesitation. He put it in gear and drove through the grass and out into a rutted country road.

"Which way?" he asked.

"There." Crushed by exhaustion, the bony hand twitched toward the left. James put an arm around Tommy's shoulders and drew him close, pulling him into the warmth of his side as he drove.

He went as fast as he could without bottoming out the car, following the lane as it turned from dirt to gravel. The pink glow of sunrise in the east was getting stronger, filtering through pines and the golden beech that crowded the lane on either side. Around a final curve, James saw an intersection with a paved road. He looked down at Tommy for further directions, but the head was nodding now, the rheumy eyes closed.

"Tommy?" He squeezed a bit tighter. "Which way do we...?"

The sudden shriek of rubber was his only warning. He looked up at the last moment, in time to see the grille of the police car bearing down on them, coming at impossible speed down the highway. He reached for the gearshift just before impact, the crash and crunch and scream of two cars shattering.

Just a few feet away, through the storm of exploding glass, he saw the blazing blue gaze of the man in the uniform. His red face was lit up like a Jack-o'-lantern in the early morning light, on fire with a familiar madness, the mouth wide open and twisted ugly with rage.

James closed his eyes and turned his face away from his enemy as the car tumbled, clutching the man in his arms with all his strength.

Until the very last moment, he held love close.

The Immortician

Andre E. Harewood

I: Talitha Cumi
6:56 PM, Friday October 30, 2020: Devil's Night

"Sorry. I thought an old woman died in here."

The young doctor wandered back out of Room 11 and walked next door to watch an orderly cart out a human-sized blue box to the elevators.

With the minor interruption over, Anaea Robinson went back to the conversation the police detective and the hospital administrator were trying to have with her. The two women talked at her about what had happened to her grandfather a few hours before: Buchanan Robinson was murdered via lethal injection in this hospital room by a nurse at the age of one hundred and twenty years and seven months. Anaea had been at work when it happened, where she always was when all the important things in her life happened. Her daughter's last three birthdays, her last three boyfriends breaking up with her, now her grandfather's death all went by while she was running around being a good and overworked guest liaison manager at the most expensive hotel on the Caribbean island. Quay Way was frequented by anonymous billionaires, loud musicians, sloppy starlets, unfaithful footballers, incontinent Counts, and the occasional doomsday cult out for some fun in the sun before committing mass suicide in the hotel's fifty room private villa. Cleaning up that mess took her staff the better part of last week and killed her latest boyfriend's patience and interest.

The women continued to talk at her but Anaea just stared at and stroked the edge of the soiled blue sheet her Papa Buck died on.

"Your grandfather put up a fight and shouted for help, Ms. Robinson," the detective said. "That's how we found out about all this. The nurse… responsible is in custody. Doctor Greaves?"

"Thank you, detective Bosch. The hospital will be working closely with the police to…"

She paused, scoffed, and continued, "Fuck it. We're going to make sure that sick bastard gets exactly what he deserves, Ms. Robinson. I've spoken with the police, the prosecutor's office, and our board… and we have a unique proposition for you."

Anaea finally looked the administrator in the eyes, a turn that shook her curly black hair.

"What could you people possibly offer me?"

The look of shock on Dr. Greaves' face quickly turned to resignation. "Mr. Robinson was here under observation for his persistent cough… and one of our people murdered him. There would be nothing we could do beyond paying millions in a pre-emptive settlement but, as you already know, there may be more victims. Hallowmas starts tomorrow, Ms. Robinson. After our pathologists finish his autopsy, we can send him to an immortician."

"I don't have money for resurrection," Anaea said angrily. "Buck was a boxer but there hasn't been any money left since before I was born."

"As I said, the hospital would end up paying you millions anyway, Ms. Robinson. The unique timing and nature of Mr. Robinson's… passing doubled with the police and prosecutors wanting at least one first-hand account equals a chance for you to say goodbye to him. It's literally the least we can offer you."

"But you said Papa Buck was dead, mom," Vanessa stated in confusion.

And Anaea thought the next difficult thing she had to explain to her eight year old daughter would be sex.

The living room looked pristine, straight out of a housekeeping digest, because no one did any living in it. Anaea was always at work or in her backyard gym, Vanessa was always at school or extracurriculars or bouncing between friends' homes, and Buck was usually either in his room or the garden or the kitchen. Mostly murder happened in the living room since Jack Marsh, Anaea's best friend and Vanessa's godfather and Buck's nurse, played hours of violent video games on the wall screen TV. There was no running over prostitutes who owed him money with his '67 Chevy Impala hardtop tonight, though. Jack sat on the large blue couch beside Vanessa and Anaea being a responsible adult, not a drug-addicted ex-con on a virtual rampage.

"He is, Van," Jack explained, "but being dead is more complicated than it used to be."

Anaea closed her eyes and sighed silently, thanking him for taking the lead.

"Everybody dies, Van," he continued. "Some people come back. It doesn't happen often, sweetie, but it's what'll happen with Papa Buck. We all have something in us. Some people call them souls. I don't know what they really are. I… Anaea, the immortician should be the one to explain it to her."

"The immortician can explain it to me, too," Anaea replied.

"Uncle Jack told me that babies come from sex, then people live, then they die," Vanessa stated, much to her mother's horror.

"You told her about sex, Jack?!"

"Only age appropriate information. She asked, I'm

a medical professional, and you tense up every time she mentions it."

"Jesus, Jack."

"What's an immortician, mom?"

"Like Uncle Jack said," Anaea happily got the derailed conversation back on track, "people can sometimes come back from the dead, and the immortician helps."

"Come back like zombies?"

"No, honey. Not like zombies."

"But Uncle Jack's always killing zombie hookers."

Anaea shot Jack another stern look to which he replied with a shrug.

"Zombies aren't real, Van," Jack explained. "They're just made up monsters in video games and movies."

"I thought people coming back to life was made up, too," the girl countered.

"We all did until a few years ago," he explained. "If the timing of someone's death is right and their soul wants to come back…"

"And if their family has enough money…" Anaea grumbled.

"…and a few other conditions are met," Jack continued while shooting Anaea his own dirty look, "the dead person can come back to life for three special days starting on Halloween morning."

"And Papa Buck will come back tomorrow morning?"

"We hope so, Van. He can help make sure the bad nurse who hurt him never hurts anyone else ever again… and we and Papa Buck can say our goodbyes to each other."

"Will he be all rotten?"

"No, he won't be rotting. He'll look just like he did when we last saw him, maybe even a bit stronger."

"You're sure he won't try to eat my brains?"

"Positive, Van."

"You should bring a console controller along to protect us, Jack," Anaea joked. Neither Jack nor Vanessa laughed.

"Can I watch Papa Buck come back to life with you and Uncle Jack, mom?"

"I don't think children are allowed, sweetie."

"I'm almost nine!"

"I'll call the immortuary and see if they'll make an exception in this case," Jack offered.

"We should all be there for him, mom. We should all be there when Papa Buck comes back."

Jack and Anaea were still on the couch a while later talking and occasionally looking into the kitchen where Vanessa had been suitably distracted with a kids show on her tablet and some pre-Halloween candy after a very early dinner.

"She'll need you a lot more now without me and Buck here," he said.

"You'll still be around."

"As long as you have that wall screen and surround sound."

"Thank God for you, godfather."

"My goddaughter barely sees her mother."

"If she saw me more, she'd be seeing food less."

"Anaea…"

"I'll excuse you. You've got to call the immortuary."

"That isn't how you speak to someone doing you a favour."

"No. It's how I speak to family doing their job. Later, godfather. I've got things to kick."

The garden shed she'd converted into a gym was Anaea's sanctuary. Gloves and shin guards were the armour she put on every day, weights were every burden she had to bear, the skipping rope was every obstacle she had to overcome, the free-standing black punching bag was everyone she wanted to kill. She jabbed her right fist forward, threw a left hook, ducked, brought her right knee up, then kicked the dark obelisk with her left foot. She kept her hands up, ducking, squatting, lunging across the fluorescent bright interior of the gym. It took an hour before she realized what she kept wiping from her eyes wasn't only sweat.

"I put Van to bed," Jack announced from the plastic door. "You've been out here awhile. I'm not coming in so you can kick me in the nuts...."

"It was an accident."

"...again. I'll stick to the shooting range."

"I'm not going to break down, Jack. I've been prepared for this since before Vanessa was born, since before my parents died and Buck moved to the island to live with me."

She uppercut empty air.

"He was old, Jack, as old as people can get. He couldn't live forever!"

She grabbed the back of an imaginary opponent's head, bringing it down onto her rapidly rising left knee.

"He just had a cough."

She stopped fighting, fists still raised and ready, knees apart and slightly bent, redistributing her weight from side to side as she looked at Jack.

"He just had a fucking cough..."

They stood in silence for a bit.

"Phil called a few minutes ago, Anaea. He wants me to come over, thinks I need a hug."

"He should know by now you're not a hugger."

"Neither are you," Jack said as he walked in and hugged Anaea who reluctantly and sweatily hugged him back, "and we're not big criers, either. Old Buck was like family to me, too. I'll be back in the morning around four to help you and Van get ready for the rising."

"You cared for us almost as much as you cared for Buck."

"Just family doing their job."

Jack released his embrace but Anaea held on for a few extra seconds.

"Get off me, MILF. I love you but I've got a boyfriend to go special hug."

"I can't believe *you* told my daughter about sex." They laughed.

"See you at four, Jack."

"See you, budget Ronda Rousey."

She raised her right knee dangerously close to his groin, causing him to deflect it with his hands.

"You're learning," she said with a smile.

II: The Green Treatment
5:45 AM, Saturday October 31, 2020: Halloween

In daylight, the infinity pool deck of the Coal Ridge Immortuary had a breathtaking view of the island's rugged and mostly undeveloped east coast. In the early morning, however, darkness extended from the somber lights of the immortuary over the dense tropical forest and rocky promontories jutting up through the rough Atlantic Ocean to the stars and full moon above. Now that it was approaching six, the sky brightened considerably, and the sounds of animal life grew louder.

"I'm still surprised work gave you time off," Jack whispered to Anaea.

"My grandfather was murdered and he's about to be resurrected. Work didn't have much choice. And I think that's my cue," she replied while adjusting the flowing white robe she wore for the ceremony then walked to the water's edge.

Jack, Vanessa, and representatives from the hospital, police, and prosecutor's office sat in wicker chairs at mahogany tables arranged in an arc around the large circular pool's near edge. Rising ceremonies were all essentially the same, varying only in the amount of money you wanted to invest to make sure they actually worked. Most were lavishly catered affairs like this one with incense, exotic sweets, expensive alcohols, and cooked meats in abundance to entice the recently released spirit temporarily back to its former carcass prison. There was no need for this extravagance, though. The centuries-old original way with participants smoking tobacco while eating raw sugar, drinking cheap rum, and slaughtering livestock worked just as well sometimes if the spirit was truly eager to return. And the spirit had to be willing. There were reports of souls being dragged back to their corpses and trapped there, but immorticians denounced such tales as malicious rumours.

Two attendants in black wetsuits helped immortician Yewande Ayodele bring the white shroud-covered body of Buchanan Robinson through the small crowd and down a ramp into the pool. Ayodele, a middle aged, thin woman with light brown skin, wore a top hat and a well-tailored tuxedo into the pool where Anaea joined her. The mistress of ceremonies' watch vibrated with her two minutes to sunrise warning, and the attendants left her and Anaea holding Buchanan's body in the water.

"The souls of the departed can always hear us but today, All Hallows' Eve, when the walls between the living and the dead become fluid," immortician Ayodele pronounced, "we can also hear them. There are many words that can be said to the dead, and none will move them except words from those they loved."

Anaea leaned down and whispered in her dead grandfather's ear, "Come back to us, Papa Buck. Just for a little while. Please."

As dawn threatened, the two women submerged and surfaced his body once, then again. On the third submersion, immortician Ayodele let go of the body, leaving Anaea alone holding him. As the sun broke over the Atlantic with a green flash at 5:52 AM, Anaea saw a similar tongue of green fire appear on Buchanan's head underwater, then his eyes and mouth opened to show verdant energies burning within. Steam rose and the infinity pool's water bubbled and roiled as Anaea raised Buchanan's head and shoulders into the light of a new day. The young man in her arms who had seconds before been a supercentenarian shouted his last words first, "Keep that damned needle away from me!"

"Papa Buck! What does that mean, Uncle Jack?" Vanessa asked.

Jack remembered his distant Sunday school lessons, furiously made the sign of the cross, and mumbled, "He's had too much wine."

III: Harlem Smoke
2:00 PM, Saturday October 31, 2020: Halloween

"How did he die?"

Seated in the living room, detective Bosch cleared her throat before answering Anaea's question.

"We found Herb Easterman dead in his cell two hours after your grandfather identified him as the nurse who caused his fatal cardiac event. You know Easterman confessed to using an ajmaline and lidocaine cocktail."

"*How did he die?*"

"Easterman had brain hemorrhaging, bits of his glasses embedded in three skull fractures, a shattered eye socket, multiple cracked ribs, a punctured lung, ruptured spleen, bruised kidneys, and a broken collarbone."

"Someone beat the shit out of him."

"Someone beat the *life* out of him. He looks like he went ten rounds with Mike Tyson but the irony is the coroner thinks Easterman died of cardiac arrhythmia."

"And Buck used to be a boxer."

"Yes, a world champion nicknamed the Harlem Smoke, and you're one of this island's best amateur mixed martial artists."

"We went with you to the hospital and the police station after the ceremony, then you made sure we got back here safely."

"Can anyone vouch for you after I left?"

"It was just me, Buck, Jack, and Vanessa here for hours. Buck's been following the immortician's orders: meditating and contemplating and all that."

"I've heard of risings where paraplegics come back able to walk again, Ms. Robinson. No one has ever heard of one where the dead returned a century younger."

"Immortician Ayodele is just as shocked as the rest of us, detective, and she's researching it right now. If she can look up the esoteric stuff, why can't you just look at video to see who killed that pale bastard?"

"Our cameras in that part of central station haven't worked in weeks. We're fully staffed so security hasn't been a problem... until now."

"The regular police beatings were fine but this one got out of hand? The thirty six murders Easterman confessed to were too many?"

"Stop that 'arrest and molest' foolishness. We don't abuse our prisoners, Ms. Robinson," detective Bosch said sternly, "despite what people may think. Look, we have no idea how someone could have gotten into the station, slipped past a dozen officers, beat the nurse to death, then escaped without anyone seeing or hearing anything."

"Sounds like you're here trying to find a way to blame this on anyone but fellow officers," Anaea said as she got up and opened to the front door. "If you have any more questions or accusations, we can speak in the presence of the most expensive lawyer the hospital's blood money can summon. Until then, please leave."

The unmarked police car backed out of the driveway, and Anaea watched it disappear down the palm tree-lined avenue. Plastic skeletons and papier-mâché gravestones decorated the house across the street, a sign of the more Americanized tastes of her upper middle class area. The neighbourhood children would be trick or treating in a few hours so Anaea had a jack o'lantern bucket filled with candy by the front door to be neighbourly even though she wouldn't allow Vanessa to go door to door begging almost strangers for confectionery. She unwrapped and munched on a mini-Uranus bar as she walked to the backyard gym. Some local priests decried anything to do with Halloween as pagan but most people simply saw it as another opportunity to get drunk and dress up provocatively.

Buck was wearing nothing but one of Jack's borrowed sweat pants as he bareknuckle jabbed in basic one-two combinations at a punching bag suspended from the shed's ceiling. She had known him all her life as thin and frail, not the six feet tall, two hundred pounds of sweaty, brown muscle expertly pummeling her equipment with his powerful fists. Buck's dark arms were slightly longer than normal for someone his height, giving him an increased range that provided an advantage he ruthlessly exploited. He had been a world heavyweight champion, one of the best boxers of the early twentieth century, a man who had three of his fights dubbed 'the fight of the century'. She could see some of that in his movements now though he was taking things relatively easy. Buck looked just like he did in old pictures and news reel footage: tall and handsome, built like he could break through skulls with a single punch or hearts with a single smile.

"That's not meditating," she said.

"It is for me, girl."

He added some footwork, moving around the bag on his bare soles as his simple strikes continued.

"All these years in this house and the closest I ever got to out here was gardening and cooking in that fucking kitchen."

Anaea flinched. She had never heard her grandfather curse in all her forty years.

"You… Uh… You baked some great ham… and you never showed any interest."

"I did this shit hours a day for thirty years. I should never have given it up."

"After the accident…"

Buck stopped, his hands falling to his sides as he pulled himself up to his full height.

"I took punches to the head for decades but one car accident turned me into a retard. Ain't life fucked?"

Anaea's grandfather had been a sweet man who cared for his third and final wife and their son by working numerous menial jobs up and down the Carolinas. Her grandmother never talked about what Buck had been like before he crashed his car in 1946 but there were more than enough articles and tabloid gossip from the time to piece together that he wasn't the nicest person. Drinking, cheating, spending all his prize money on everything but his family… That young Buchanan Robinson was a terror Anaea was happy to have never known, and she realized she might not to be happy knowing this young Buck, either.

"Nice setup in here, girl. I got a good workout."

"Glad you enjoyed it. We need to talk, Papa Buck. It's about that nurse."

"Easterman? The scrawny cunt who killed me?"

"He's dead."

"Can't say I'm broken up. Who offed him?"

"The police aren't sure."

"At least I got to look him in his blue four eyes this morning and let him know I'd be the one sending *him* for lethal injection this time around. Hhh. I guess someone who knew other people he killed got him first. Remember what he said in that weak voice? About killing people because he got off on trying to save them? Sick fuck had it coming."

Buck took a towel from a weight bench and wiped his sweaty face and muscular chest. As she watched, Anaea had to remind herself this gorgeous man barely in his twenties was her supercentenarian grandfather.

"You stopped him."

"He still stuck me and killed me. It's the best thing that could've happened, though."

"What?"

"I'd rather spend three days like this, being myself again, than fuck knows how much time I had left in that hospital bed."

"The doctors said you were getting better."

"There ain't much to look forward to when you're a hundred and twenty, girl. I'll take these three days, thanks."

"Papa Buck…"

"Just call me Buck, yeah."

"Buck… Do you remember dying? Do you remember anything about the other side?"

Anaea had never seen anyone with the look on Buck's face before. She couldn't identify it, either, beyond being possibly an otherwise impossible mélange of disparate emotions.

"The immortician said not to talk about that. Breaks the spell early."

"I didn't know, sorry."

"It's OK, girl. I'm going for a shower. Have some of those little Lazarus cakes for me when I get out."

The immortuary provided Lazarákia since the spicy-sweet breads were part of the ongoing ritual to keep this old yet new him, this renewed him alive.

"OK, Papa…" Anaea stopped and corrected herself. "OK, Buck."

"Good girl."

Buck squeezed her shoulder with his free hand, looked into her eyes, smiled, then went into the house. It was all Anaea could do not to pull away. As the punching bag slowly swung, Anaea wondered how much of the old Buck had returned and how much of the true Buck she had ever really known.

IV: Deep Taint
5:00 PM, Saturday October 31, 2020: Halloween

"These aren't the kind of damages I was expecting you to discuss, Dr. Greaves," Anaea said to the woman seated across the desk from her and immortician Ayodele. The hospital administrator's room was cozy, filled with books and family pictures and plants, its view took in the hospital garden and the river that ran through the heart of the capital along which a few tourists kayaked.

"With the unprecedented return of your grandfather's youth, we're taking special note of abnormalities and anything of interest, Ms. Robinson," Greaves began. "We have his MRI results and a preliminary genetic analysis."

The doctor tapped a few buttons on a keyboard, and a holographic screen appeared between her and the other two women. Greaves reached into the blue light and enhanced a slowly rotating three dimensional brain scan with her fingers.

"Mr. Robinson's brain as seen in his full body scan taken when he was admitted last week. As his doctor discussed with you, there was severe chronic traumatic encephalopathy common to people who fight and play football and other contact sports. Violent behavioural and destructive mood disorders are almost universally present at this level of traumatic brain injury... but everyone describes Mr. Robinson as a sweet, gentle soul perhaps a bit below average on the IQ scale."

"That sounds right. And what about his scan from today?"

Greaves reached into the hologram again, enhancing and rotating a second brain scan.

"Instead of being shrunken and withered, his brain is now, just like the rest of his body, perfectly healthy... except for here," Greaves said while pointing at an area highlighted in yellow near the center of the second brain scan. "There is greatly reduced activity in his orbital cortex which regulates emotions, impulses, morality, and aggression. With everything around it suffering from a degenerative disease, it was impossible to see this. All that damage most likely also mitigated against the sociopathic tendencies many with this condition exhibit. Has he done anything strange since you took him home?"

The boxing, the cursing, the way her skin crawled when he touched her shoulder and smiled at her...

"No... I... don't think so."

"Watch for them. His preliminary genetic screening showed the MAOA-L gene variant as well as at least two other mutations linked to impulsive behavior, sleep disorders, mood swings, hypersexuality, and violent tendencies. This is very serious."

Greaves sighed, took a deep breath, and continued.

"I'm sorry for throwing so many terms at you, Ms. Robinson."

"No kidding," Anaea replied, not even trying to appear unflustered, "since you're telling me Buck is insane."

"Sociopathy manifests itself as egotism, persistent antisocial behavior, and impaired empathy and remorse... and I promise I'm done listing pathologies now. Some incredibly successful and non-violent people have these traits to varying degrees. Ruthlessness in business and sport can be an asset, and Mr. Robinson was an incredibly successful boxer. He was described as fearless and unflappable according to my research."

"Detective Bosch already called you."

"She asked me what the tests had found so far, and I told her only you or Mr. Robinson can divulge his medical information. She didn't say why she was so interested. Is there something I should know about?"

"I... don't think so, no."

Immortician Ayodele touched Anaea's shoulder, causing her to flinch.

"I don't believe that's entirely true, Anaea," Ayodele commented, "but you must decide. *I* decided to perform Buchanan's rising because his soul was… very eager to return, the most eager of all those whose families vied for their return today. It spoke to me even before the ceremony, saying it would no longer die, that it was immovable. I've never felt such force before in my forty years of performing the rising."

"Did that… force have anything to do with him becoming young again?" Anaea asked.

"That has more to do," Dr. Greaves interjected, "with the unique gene mutations governing his Wnt and telomerase proteins."

"Even with resurrection as an undeniable fact," immortician Ayodele countered, "scientists still refuse to believe in the spirit's true power."

"You can resurrect the dead for three days with magic," Dr. Greaves replied. "I want to keep people alive forever with science."

"Stop it!" Anaea shouted as she stood, pushing her chair back and toppling it over with a loud thud. "Fight on your own time!"

"I'm sorry, Anaea," Ayodele apologized. "These arguments are for another place and time. I asked to be here because I am afraid for you and your family. I should have refused such a supremely assertive soul access to the living world again, and hearing now about its body's tendencies toward violence only strengthens that fear. You should leave him alone or let the police watch over him, anything but remain with him in your home."

"We agree on that, at least," Dr. Greaves concurred.

"There is nothing I can do to help you, Anaea. Only the arisen can break the resurrection spell before the triduum…"

"I think you're all overreacting," Anaea cut the immortician off as she righted the chair. "Thank you both for the information, and I remember that immorticians are bound by a code similar to doctor-patient confidentiality. I'm going to enjoy every minute of his brief time with us. I'll see you Tuesday morning, Ayodele."

Anaea walked to the door, opened it, and closed it firmly behind her.

"I wonder what *her* brain and DNA look like," Dr. Greaves mused to herself as Ayodele bowed her head in prayer to the benevolent orishas.

V: Slow Perdition
9:00 PM, Monday November 2, 2020: All Souls' Day

Apart from a persistent distant cousin of Buck's who kept calling to get some of the supposed hospital settlement windfall, the rest of Hallowmas passed uneventfully. The young old man spent most of his time alone either in his room or training in the backyard gym. Vanessa wanted to spend time with her great grandfather but Anaea sent her to play with friends or stay longer at swimming and ballet classes. Jack wasn't around the house much, either, due perhaps to something Anaea hadn't witnessed but could clearly see in the cold way Buck looked at him and the resultant unease in Jack's face.

With the end of Buck's time almost upon them, Anaea invited a few friends over to celebrate his life before the katabasis ceremony. The guest of honour remained silent most of the night, only tersely answering questions about what it was like boxing and winning in early twentieth-century America as a black man.

"Sure as fuck wasn't easy but I beat everyone stupid enough to get in that ring with the Harlem Smoke. No matter what colour you are, you still cry the same when I beat your ass."

His secret to longevity was just as eloquent.

"Get knocked too stupid to die."

He not so politely declined requests to see his fighting technique.

When dirty plates and glasses and bottles were randomly left around the house and those who abandoned them were long gone, only two guests remained along with the immediate family. Dionne and Makeba both worked in accounts at Quay Way, and both looked far older than their forty-five years. They helped Anaea clean up while Jack put Vanessa to bed. Buck slipped out of the proceedings half hour earlier to train in the gym one last time.

"I should go, Ann," Dionne said after they'd brought everything into the kitchen. "I was at church early on Sunday to get a good parking spot, and you know how Mondays at that hotel can drain you. I need a good night's sleep or I'll be useless to myself."

"Pushing fifty, no husband or kids, buried in work and the church..." a shirtless, sweaty Buck said from the back door, "I bet you're still a virgin, too. Sounds like you're already useless, Dionne. You don't need God. You need fucking."

He smiled broadly at her shocked face.

"I can help you with that. I saw you looking at me like I'm communion you want to swallow."

Dionne put down the two empty bottles of wine on the cluttered counter, turned, and walked briskly to the living room to get her bag.

"Jesus, Buck!" Anaea shouted.

"What do I care? I'm dying again in the morning... for good this time. Didn't even get any pussy while I was young again."

The stack of dirty plates in Makeba's hands was liable to fall to the floor and shatter. Buck walked over, took the plates from her, and put them in the sink. He grabbed a half empty bottle of Extra Old rum from beside her, had a swig, and continued smiling.

"You should probably go with your friend... unless you want to stay and help me with my problem. Or are you and her together? I haven't had that in a while, either."

"I'll see you at work next week, Ann!" Makeba blurted out and followed Dionne into the living room and out the front door.

"Anaea? Are you alright?" a tall, blonde man asked as Makeba rushed past him.

"Phil?!" Anaea exclaimed, "Jack'll be ready in a few minutes! Why don't you wait out in your car, please?!"

"Phil, huh?" Buck asked after taking a gulp of rum. "You're the batty boy's other half, right?"

All Anaea could do was stand by the refrigerator in stunned silence.

"Yeah, we're a fudge package deal," Phil explained, "and you're the asshole who punched my man in the stomach."

"You hit Jack?!" Anaea shouted at Buck.

"Little fag tried coming in my room when I was changing. He might have helped bathe and dress me when I was ancient but that shit won't work now."

"I thought you should know but Jack didn't want to tell you, Anaea, so I kept quiet."

"I still didn't want her to know," Jack said. He stood next to Phil and put a hand on his boyfriend's shoulder. "We should do like everyone else and get the hell out of here."

"Jack, please…" Anaea began before Buck cut her off as he walked slowly toward the men.

"Yeah, get the fuck out of here before I tell her you're in the living room watching 'Open Rearlationship' and 'Net Dicks' and 'The Little Hermaid' on the big screen when the girls are out and you think I'm sleep…"

It was Buck's turn to fall silent as Vanessa pushed her way past the two men and into the kitchen in her pajamas.

"Why's everybody shouting?" she asked. "Papa Buck needs to sleep before his kitty basics."

"Katabasis," he corrected her then scooped her up in one muscular arm.

Anaea went numb.

"They'll put me back to sleep, Vanessa. At least you got to know me in my prime."

He gave her a kiss. She laughed and tried to push his face away.

"You're stinky, Papa Buck!" she said through her giggles.

"And you're beautiful just like your mama and your grandma. Now go back to bed. I'll see you in the morning."

"OK, Papa Buck. G'night!" she said as she weaved her way between Jack and Phil again and back to her bedroom.

Anaea hadn't realized she'd been holding her breath for the last minute until the pain in her chest became almost unbearable. She inhaled sharply, felt a bit light-headed, and held the refrigerator door for balance.

"I'll take this baby with me so I'm not alone in bed again," Buck said, raised the rum bottle for emphasis, and pushed past the men. "Excuse me, ladies."

Buck disappeared down a corridor with the slamming of his bedroom door punctuating his exit. Anaea slumped down the side of the refrigerator and sat on the kitchen floor.

"Who is that?" she asked no one in particular. "That isn't the man I grew up with. That isn't the man I loved and took care of for twenty years. I need you to take Vanessa with you and Phil tonight, Jack. I… I don't want her here and I don't want her at the ceremony tomorrow."

"OK," Jack agreed. "I'll pack a bag and get her… quietly."

"Whoever that is," Phil reasoned, "that *isn't* your Buck."

Anaea sat outside Buck's door for the rest of the night and into the early morning. There was nothing to do but watch and wait in the silent darkness.

VI: A Dust Full Of Hand
5:50 AM, Tuesday November 3, 2020

Buchanan Robinson said nothing during his last meal of Lazarákia and a bitter drink made from tree bark called mauby. The ride to the island's east coast was another half hour of silence between him and Anaea, a silence unbroken even after arriving at the immortuary to Yewande Ayodele's barely restrained concern in her greeting. Buck didn't ask where Jack or Vanessa were or if there would be anyone else but him and the two women on the immortuary's pool deck for the ceremony. The only emotion Buck showed was when he stripped naked before following the two women in white robes into the infinity pool. He liked that their eyes took in all of his magnificent body, and he took special notice of how uncomfortable his bare flesh made his granddaughter. Buck, naked as he was reborn, floated between the women with Anaea's hand on the back of his head.

"Conduct life gently that you may die a good death…" immortician Ayodele began.

Buck's almost unblinking eyes stared right into Anaea's as her shaking hand closed them with only minor resistance from him.

"…that your children may stretch their hands over your body in burial," Anaea completed the prayer.

The sun's rising green flash flared at 5:53 AM. Buck lay still in the water, and Anaea's sigh of relief was cut short when he reopened his glowing green eyes.

"Iná l'ọmọ aráyé lè pa kò s'ẹ́ni tó lè pa èéfín!" Buck said in a voice that startled both women and rumbled through the early morning air. "You can put the fire out but you won't get rid of the smoke!"

He grabbed immortician Ayodele by the throat then threw her with inhuman strength out of the pool and into a section of the tables and chairs arranged around it. She lay unmoving amidst the upturned furniture. His

other hand wrapped around Anaea's throat. He effort-
lessly lifted her while he walked out of the pool, glistening water dripping from his nakedness in the rising sun.

"You know what I used to do, girl? I used to raise the
dead. I was an immortician, a babalawo of Orunmila for
almost a hundred years. I got older and older until I realized I was terrified of dying… so I didn't. My body just
started getting younger, aging backwards."

Anaea tried everything she could to break free, every move to break an arm, every kick to his body or head
but none worked. She began to see spots but could still
hear Buck's booming voice.

"Columbus was pretending to discover America
when I was discovering myself and what I could do.
Worst thing was when I got thrown in a slave ship heading for the U.S. a lifetime later. Fuck, it wasn't even the
United *States* back then. I did what I had to do to sur-
vive. You've got to be cold to live forever. All that love
and compassion shit doesn't work when you hit the
middle of your second century and everyone you love
is dead, when people only know you as an old man. You
forget about your wives, and your kids're just meat you
make and leave behind. I can't tell you how many of my
kids and grandkids I've fucked but most of them weren't
as pretty as…"

There was a click behind him as Jack shouted, "You
sick fuck!"

Buck didn't flinch as Jack unloaded six rounds from
his Glock pistol into the immortal man's chest. Buck
merely turned around to face Jack, reaching out with his
free hand wreathed in green flame.

"None of that shit!" Jack shouted as he fired two bul-
lets through Buck's head. "I play video games!"

Anaea gasped for breath when she and Buck's body
fell to the wood deck, and she scrambled to Jack's side.

"What? How?" were the only words she could manage through her bruised throat.

"Detective Bosch called me when she couldn't reach you."

"Turned phone... off..."

"Your idiot cousin in South Carolina? Dan? Police found him beaten to death last night. His last call was to you trying to get some of the hospital settlement. They called Bosch. She's on her way here now."

"Why... you... here?"

"When do I ever listen to *you*? I was already coming to make sure you were alright and that son of a bitch died for good this..."

An invisible force bashed in Jack's nose. Blood spewed all over his shirt and Anaea's wet white dress. It hit him twice more, lifted him into the air, and threw his body and his gun over the edge of the infinity pool into the deep, wooded gully beyond.

"Jack!"

"Cudn't... mmmgm... do dat.... gggh... fore I died," Buck slurred. A bloody scalp flap attached to a chunk of skull swayed as he shambled toward Anaea, the green energy beneath working to heal his gunshot wounds.

Anaea crouched, clenched her fists, and rushed him. Buck smiled crookedly, his brain still rewiring itself, and tried to take a defensive stance. The world heavyweight boxing champion from eighty years ago wasn't prepared for the swift kick to his exposed testicles that was her specialty. When he hunched over in crippling pain, Anaea pulled his head down and shattered his nose with her rising knee, sending him crashing to the floor. She wanted to snap his neck but something unseen punched her in the stomach then forced her to her knees.

The Buck that approached her was a smiling, bloody mess.

"If I'd known I could do *this* just by thinking about it, I would've died the first time around and let another babalawo bring me back on Halloween. We called this the Season of Souls back then, and an adamant soul reborn in an immortal body? Power from the other side is *bleeding* through me!"

Anaea struggled helplessly against the invisible grip.

"After I kill you, I'll go find Vanessa. I'll have her calling her Papa Buck 'daddy'."

"Did you always know?" Anaea asked in a strained whisper.

"What?"

"That you were afraid to die because you were going to burn in Hell?"

Now fully healed, Buck crouched beside Anaea. He wasn't smiling anymore.

"When I was first young, our people believed in reincarnation through your bloodline... but some souls were too evil for that, some souls would only know torment forever. I brought back one like that by force, a woman whose family was happy she died. She told me about the absence of light and hope, the nothing, the pain... and she told me she'd see me there soon. We had nothing like it in our religion, no place where the dead were punished! The truth was too horrible, too unimaginable! You can't fathom getting older, feeling the dread getting worse and worse, knowing there was only horror on the other side of life!"

"But you beat it. Your genes..."

"Genes, blasphemous prayers, who fucking knows?! I reveled in everything *this life* had to offer for centuries. Drinking, fighting, fucking... but that car accident must have been too much for my already addled brain. I turned into an invalid who forgot he could become young again, a fool who let himself get killed. I have to thank you for bringing me back, Anaea."

"So you could kill the nurse and Dan?"

"Worthless little shits deserved it, and I'm sure a lot more will, too."

"You'll stay alive and keep murdering, sending souls where you're afraid to go?"

"Those few hours I was dead were an eternity of being broken over and over again into smaller and smaller pieces that screamed louder and louder! And there was something there, girl, something… something *happy*. I'm *never* going back to the devil of the shards!"

"But you have called it by name, Buchanan Robinson," immortician Ayodele said from her unmoving position amidst the disarrayed furniture in a voice unlike anything Anaea had ever heard before, "and you have spoken of your fate in its realm. Now say 'yes' to the pit of shards, Buchanan Robinson, and break for all eternity!"

The grip on Anaea slackened, and she uppercut the terrified Buck away from her into the infinity pool which immediately started to boil. He screamed unintelligibly before there was a flash and the superheated water disappeared in a burst of annihilating steam.

Anaea crawled to immortician Ayodele's unconscious side. Whatever said those words, it wasn't her. With as much strength as she could muster, Anaea got to her feet and looked over the edge at the now empty pool, its spotless white tiles, and the brown fingers that clung to the outer edge of the pool's glass back wall.

"I knew… you'd kick him… in the nuts," a hoarse voice croaked.

Anaea gasped in surprise and happiness, and rushed to pull a traumatized Jack back from the other side of infinity.

Nyarlahotep Came Down
to Georgia

Nancy Holder

I *l arrive.*
    He's coming.

Three more nights until All Soul's Day and the drums were flapping their yaps.

Bone fingers snapped *alors alors zut alors.* Fireflies and gators winked, blinked, scooted away through the murk and the muck of the bayou. Things was about to go bad, *sha.*

Spanish moss tugged at Evangeline's hair as she cried and swept the alleys between the tombs with a twig broom she'd wrapped herself, every twist counted three-three-three. *Go home, sha, get out of here, ain't no place for you. This the battleground. Go, go, go.*

She kept sweeping, gaze locked on the mound of bricks where she had buried a lock of her *maman*'s hair. A spiral of shiny black curls was all she'd had. Her *mere* was planted in a different place far away. Her cousin Beau had a picture on his phone of a mound with a wooden cross marked *Marie Belle Chevalier September 25, 1992–September 30, 2018* he said that someday he would take her there to lay down flowers. But not today. Not next week. It had been a month since Evangeline got the news and everyone else had stopped crying but she wasn't even sure that her *maman* was dead. Maybe they were just making it up because her mother was so wild, such a trial, and so her gramma told Evangeline that her *maman* was never, ever coming back to the bayou. It done, it over, life is like that. You move on.

Her heart hurt; it ballooned inside her chest and bobbed against her ribs. Bee sting tears prickled her cheeks. She shook all over as she swept, tears and dust on her beaded flats. Gramma was going crazy. *Folle.* She said godlessness had stolen Evangeline's *maman* away and if Evangeline wanted to make it to twenty-one herself, she had to give herself in all honesty up to Jesus Christ. Evangeline had said it over and over, Yes, Gramma, yes, I am saved. The blood of the lamb done washed me clean.

But the truth was, when she had buried that little pinch of shiny black hair, Evangeline had tiptoed out to the walls of this very graveyard with a chicken and a knife and no idea what to do but ask for some help. Ask for someone to tell her where her *maman* was now.

Her brush made a swishing sound, *chaka, chaka, chaka.* Shotgun tombs in rows, walls all around, tombs losing their roofs and stoving in. There were renovation efforts in some of the more historical New Orleans graveyards but this one was old and neglected. No-account. Graffiti decorated walls and steps, nasty words voodoo signs. Weeping angels with shiny green faces perched on tombs of brick and plaster; stones and the statues shimmered with the drumbeats.

Evangeline was eleven. Her hair was a dark brown cloud as she kept her head down and swept. She was trembling all over as if the spirit had filled her. She *knew* something bad was coming. The drums zummed the warning inside all her bones.

Dust kicked up in the dying sunshine; the world was purple-green like Mardi Gras, a fuzzy blowsy yellow-brown like dried-up chickweed. Beyond the cemetery walls, New Orleans was gearing up for Halloween,

Day of the Dead, All Soul's, *bontemps*. For weeks there had been ghost walks and voodoo tours for the tourists and a *fais-do-do* in every shack and plantation mansion still standing. Her *grand-mere* was not so strict that they didn't celebrate; she had no idea that chicken they were missing was the one Evangeline had snitched so she could open up a conversation with the *loa* of the dead.

Shake-a shake-a shake-a; she was trembling hard; spirit possession maybe, or just pure silvery fear; something was changing in the air; the drums and the nutria *ca-woo ca-woo* and the swaying cypresses; a wind—

And there *she* was.

Evangeline dropped the broom and sank to her knees.

She glimmered in and out of sight; shrouded in black lace, seated on a tumbled-down pile of bricks and blurring. Wearing a top hat rimmed with roses and crow feathers, the rest of her a secret, a mystery. One arm extended from the black lace shroud; it was covered in ebony silk that glittered as she crooked her finger at Evangeline. Evangeline tried to rise but she was too awe-stricken, only just now aware that she was drenched in sweat and had been ever since she started cleaning the charnel streets. Now her sweat was a flood, and there were fresh tears, too, dripping down her nose to across her lips to her chin.

"*Ma sha, ma belle*," the figure murmured softly, maybe not even a whisper. "Why you so frightened? Not on account of me."

She gestured again for Evangeline to come to her, top hat, lace, a ghostly presence perched on some family's ruined bonehouse. Evangeline still wasn't sure she was truly there. The drums, the chattering drums … then Evangeline forced herself to stand, ran to her, and clambered up the bricks like a baby goat; then she was enfolded in a bouquet of jasmine and rum and scratchy lace and for a moment, smooth bone; then a lady with soft white skin and big green eyes and long shiny red hair curled around her in the most loving of embraces. Maman Brigitte.

Maman Brigitte was a *loa,* a goddess, the Queen of Graveyards and the wife of Baron Samedi, who was the King of Death. It was to summon her that Evangeline had swept the streets of one of Maman Brigitte's domains today. This was the third time the lady had appeared to her.

"*Bonjour, ma petite,*" Maman Brigitte said. The beautiful *loa* spoke French even though she had originally come from Ireland. "How the fuck you doin', Evangeline?"

Evangeline giggled in spite of everything. Maman Brigitte also swore a blue streak.

"I'm sad and scared, *Maman*, is how I'm doing," Evangeline said, and Maman Brigitte pulled aside her veil to let Evangeline snuggle inside, then drew it back over her. She had turquoise eyelids and long black eyelashes, crimson lipstick on her bone lips. The crown of her wavy red hair was clustered with roses like a Day of the Dead sugar skull. "All I was doing was listening for my mother's heartbeat. But then I heard the drums. They say a bad man is coming. They say the bayou is shaking."

"How do you know the drum language?" Maman Brigitte asked, and Evangeline blinked, thinking the question over.

"I don't know. I didn't know it was a language. I thought it was just what they said."

Maman Brigitte brushed springy coils of hair away from Evangeline's forehead. She had cigarette breath. She said, "It's a gift then, *sha.* You gotta a knowledge other living folks don't." Her teeth clacked. She had lots of them and they were very white. "The drums are right. He's gonna show up in three nights. On Halloween night. And you can't be anywhere around here when he does."

Evangeline's heart did a little leapfrog. "Why not? Who is he?"

"The Black Man." Her words were a whisper of a whisper. "Old Pharaoh come out of Egypt's land. He gonna turn the bayou red and the moon green, *m'enfante*. He's bringing his army. You gotta steer clear. You gotta swear to me that you let us dead folk take care of it."

"He's got an *army?*" Evangeline cried.

"Ssh, ssh, Evangeline," Maman Brigitte cautioned. "The Evil One has good ears. C'mere, *sha*." She eased Evangeline out of her lap and stood. Then she took Evangeline's hand and together they climbed off the pile of red bricks. Maman Brigitte's black skirts flared out, a triangle, as she took Evangeline's hand. Sometimes skin, sometimes bone.

Together they walked down the dead road toward the saddest part of the graveyard, where none of the graves were intact and weeds tangled one over the other over another like kudzu. Marble angels lay in mud with their wings broken off, bricks were sinking; a fragment that read ROBICHAUX was drowning in a rain puddle.

And Maman Brigitte's husband Baron Samedi, King of the Dead, was sitting on a big chunk of plaster, legs crossed, top hat tilted, smoking a cigar. His skin was dark and his eyes were soulful and deep-set. His eyebrows and eyelashes were thick. His nose was hooked and elegant. He wore a black suit with narrow white stripes and a blood-red rose was pinned to his lapel. Or maybe it just grew there from out of his heart. Evangeline wasn't sure. But she had seen him two times before, and that same rose was always there, but it was real.

"*Bonjour, bell'enfante,*" he said. "*Ça va?*"

"She knows," Maman Brigitte cut in. "Knows the whole thing."

"Not the whole thing," Evangeline said, and Baron Samedi chuckled.

"I'm guessing she don't know much." He tapped his

cigar; a chunk of ash fluttered toward the rain puddle. "There's going to be a war between folks like us, *sha*. Dead folks. You need to stay outta the way."

"I already fucking said that," Maman Brigitte informed him.

"Who is the Black Man?" Evangeline asked. Most of the folks she knew were black.

The baron looked at his queen and she shook her head. "She's too young for this," Maman Brigitte said.

"From where I sit, she's nearly grown up," Baron Samedi replied.

"*Tais toi*. She's a human," Maman Brigitte said. King Death puffed smoke out of his cheeks and fished a piece of tobacco from between his teeth. "I'm telling you, little one. This is not your affair."

"Affair," Baron Samedi said. "Yes, an affair." He gestured with his cigar. "Tell your little girl there, Brigitte. This living *bebe* who adores you. Tell her that's why her precious new *maman* is bringing hell out our way."

Maman Brigitte put her arm around Evangeline and squatted down, coming nose to nose with her. Her ghost eyes darted; she licked her lips. She gave Evangeline a little squeeze and said, "The Black Man is in love with me."

"Oh," Evangeline said. Her voice was very small. She was a little lost. *Was* Maman Brigitte her new *maman* now? A queen? Could she have more than mother? She didn't really know what to say. "Do you love him?"

Baron Samedi broke into peals of laughter that clanged like church bells. He rocked back and forth like a bell, too. Maman Brigitte huffed.

"Of course I don't. How could I, when I got a man like this?" She waved her fingerbones at the baron.

What about the two mothers, then? She loved her *maman*. She didn't remember her very well, but if she didn't love her, she wouldn't be crying over her, right? Was it all right to get a new one?

"Well, it could be like children. My gramma has seven grandchildren but she loves each one of us the same," Evangeline said. "And I think my old *maman* loved more than one man."

The baron roared with glee and Maman Brigitte smiled and kissed Evangeline on the forehead. Maybe she had lips now but maybe they were still bone. Everything drifted in and out, then snapped into focus, then blurred again.

"This one understands the complexities of life, her," Baron Samedi chortled. "Told you she was grown up."

Maman Brigitte narrowed her eyes. "You stay away from my little girl. She ain't got folk and she misses her human *maman*."

"She got plenty of folk," the baron said. "Some of 'em here and some of 'em down below with us."

"Down below? Do you know my cousin Jimmy?" Evangeline asked. Jimmy had been shot in an alley last year. Folks said it was over a woman. There was a lot of that going around.

"Jimmy Chevalier? *Oui,* I do," Baron Samedi informed her. "He's in my army. He's got a bazooka made of hexes. He gonna shoot it at Nyarlahotep. That's my wife's boyfriend's name."

Baron Samedi's smile shifted as he looked over at Maman Brigitte and pulled the brim of his top hat even with his eyes. His cigar smoke rose lazily in the damp, gray air. Maybe it formed the shape of a skull.

"Are my other dead people in your army?" she asked, crossing her fingers behind her back for luck.

"*Oui, sha,* they sure are," he said. "Got more cousins of yours. And they are gonna rise in three nights to kill that ol' black man."

Evangeline's balloon-heart filled with more air. The air whooshed into her throat and made it impossible for her to swallow. Finally she ground out the words: "Is my real *maman* in your army?"

"Oh, *ma sha, non* she is not," Maman Brigitte said

softly, and Evangeline burst into tears. Loving bone-arms slid around Evangeline and pulled her into an embrace. "Dear little darling girl." The lady-god rocked her back and forth, back and forth, and Evangeline held onto her like someone sinking below the surface of the bayou.

"Her grave is too far away," Baron Samedi said.

"I want her to come up." Evangeline's voice shook. Maman Brigitte, I called you because I don't know where she's buried. And she doesn't have a headstone, or flowers. But if she can come up…"

"Someday, when you're older, you can go," Maman Brigitte said. "I'll tell you where—"

"Now! I want her now! I'll do hexes! I'll be in the army! I'll-I'll *kill* someone if you want me to. I'll kill Nyarlahotep!"

Maman Brigitte kissed her forehead. "No. This war is for dead folks. Nyarlahotep, he's a god, like us. He can zap you to a cinder with a look if he wants. Or make you fall in love with him."

Baron Samedi spit out his cigar with a guffaw. "Don't give him powers he don't have, Brigitte," he said. He gazed at Evangeline, then put a hand on top of her head. Felt like an ice cube seeping into her brain. "This is who he is, *sha*. Listen and stay away." He crossed his legs and took a fresh cigar from his breast pocket, rolling it between his bone fingers.

"Nyarlahotep is an ancient god," the baron said. "Some call him the Crawling Chaos, and see him with bat wings and tentacles. But my wife sees a tall, thin black man with an angel's smile. He's got tricks, lots of tricks"—the baron reached into his coat pocket again and this time drew out four playing cards, all aces, fanning them into the air, where they floated "—tricks that make you fall all over him in a swoon. His own army's standing—that means it's always ready. We been building ours, sweet-talking our dead into joining this battle."

"He could capture them, take them away to his kingdom. His hell," Maman Brigitte said. "You don't want that for your *maman*."

Evangeline shifted uneasily. She didn't want bad things for her mother, but oh, what it would be to see her again, even if she was dead. Even if her face was a painted skull. She thought about that a moment. How much could change before her *maman* was not her *maman*?

"How could you love someone who can take dead folks to hell? Someone with tentacles?" she asked Maman Brigitte.

Maman Brigitte shrugged. "I never loved him, *sha*. Me and the baron, we step out now and then. We live forever. If all you ate every day was donuts, wouldn't you get tired of them, maybe want a piece of chicken?"

"Is that why you showed up when I brought you a chicken?"

Both the *loa* chuckled. Then Maman Brigitte stopped smiling and touched Evangeline's cheek. She said, "Honey, I gave that chicken to my hungry dead children. Dead folks are the same as living folks—they need food and love."

"Is my *maman* hungry?" Maman Brigitte cocked her head. "Don't be so worried about her, *sha*. When this is over I'll go check on her. I promise."

"Unless Nyarlahotep's army beats your army," Evangeline said. "*Then* what happens?"

"It won't happen," Baron Samedi said.

Evangeline's balloon-heart swelled, ready to pop. Her forehead beaded with sweat and she looked at Maman Brigitte, so pretty. "But what if it does?" She grabbed Maman Brigitte's fingertips and held them tight. "I want to fight. I can fight!"

"He take one look at you, he eat you up," Maman Brigitte said, and Baron Samedi nodded.

"*C'est vrais*, sure enough," he concurred. He pushed back his top hat. "I'm thinking you best go home now and stay away. In three nights, it'll be over."

Two nights left:

The drums chanting: *Crawling Chaos, Lord of Infinity, King of Madness, he come from the power, he come from the glorious kingdom. Baron and Maman, give up now!*

"There's bad stuff in the air," Evangeline's cousin Beau said to someone in the back yard, a man she couldn't see and didn't know. It was dark out; the fireflies buzzed around. Frogs croaked. "I don't understand it all, but—"

"It's a devil coming, Beau," the other man said. "I brought you a hex to keep your family safe. Put it over your door. It'll keep that devil away."

"*Merci*, my friend," her cousin said. "Hey, so how's your sister?"

"You stay away from her," the stranger said. "She's engaged."

"So?" Beau asked.

The two men laughed.

One night:

The hex was a circle of straw with a tiny stuffed doll stuck with sewing pins stretched across the center. When no one was looking, Evangeline got the rickety wooden step-ladder out of the shed where they kept the pirogue. Once, twice, three times she raised up on her toes and flailed her arm to grab it. When her fingers wrapped around it, lightning sizzled down her arm. She cried out and dropped it. Smoke fluttered upward and she crouched on the ladder, rubbing her arm as tears sprang, watching the smoke as it traced a thin line in the sunshine, then faded away.

"Evangeline, honey? Can you go to the store for me?" her gramma asked from inside the house. "I got the list."

Catching her breath, Evangeline clambered off the stool, grabbed up the hex, and stuffed it in the pocket of her jeans. It burned. Burned bad. She jumped in a little circle, then checked to see if there was smoke or if her pants were on fire, but no; she dashed inside and saw her grandmother with her straightened hair and grabbed up the list.

"Going!" she ground out, and she flew down the path and ran for all she was worth to the graveyard.

"Maman Brigitte!" she shouted, whirling in a circle. "Please come! I got something for you!"

Between the tombs, dusty weeds baked; her hand throbbed and suddenly—

Immediately—

Without warning—

A horrible fear washed over her like the river water at her baptism. Washed right over her, clogged her throat; there was a pin-prick stabbing against the walls of her balloon heart.

Danger.

Terror.

She was rooted.

Il arrive.

Farther down in the City of the Dead, a shadow hovered. Her eyes watered as it stretched upwards, sideways, floating and undulating like something underneath the bayou water; she thought *tentacles* and then she forced herself not to think at all because if this was who she thought it was, she didn't want to call him to her.

I got the hex, she reminded herself. But she didn't know if it would work.

The shadow thickened, darkened. Blacker than black.

She blinked, and the next thing she knew, a tall, thin black man in a robe and a cloth wrapped around his head stared at her with purple-black eyes from atop the pile of bricks where her mother's hair was buried. Dizzying sickness clutched at her stomach and she staggered one step to the left. The hex burned a mark on her thigh—she was sure of it—but she pressed her hand against it; her head pounded with warning drumbeats. Or maybe it was just her heart, ready to explode.

"Hello, lovely one," said the man. His smile was as pleasant as Baron Samedi's. He raised a hand and pointed at her. His whole arm seemed to stretch like a garden hose. "What do you have there on this fine afternoon?"

The ground under her feet shifted and rumbled. He looked startled. Was it the *loas'* army of the dead? Then his face kind of closed in on itself. Blurry and hard to see, the crackling air waved around him. *Tentacles.*

"I got something to keep you away," she said, raising her chin. She was shaking so hard she thought she might throw up. This was Nyarlahotep, the devil-god who might kill Maman Brigitte and her husband and their army. And she was just one skinny little human girl.

And then all the blurriness was gone. She stared hard at him; at dark brows and heavy lashes, deep, dark-brown eyes and a pleasant smile. He was actually pretty good-looking, which was a shock, because he was evil.

"Why do you want to keep me away?" he asked and his voice lulled on a breeze, soft and gentle. He tilted his head. He couldn't be more than eighteen.

Before she could answer, a tear spilled down his left cheek and spattered in the dust. He dropped to his knees and reached down, raised up his hand and showed her a single red rose petal—had to be one of Maman Brigitte's.

"I love her," he murmured. "I love that beautiful coffin queen."

She stared at him. She didn't know what to say. Another tear coursed down his face and he raised the petal to his lips. He kissed it. "She is my lady, my life."

"She's no one's life," Evangeline said. "She's dead."

"Where I come from, what I am, there are so many variations on that theme. There's not just dead and alive.

There are worlds…" he trailed off. Then he said, "You don't need to worry about your mother, dear one. The only thing wrong with her is that she misses you."

Evangeline's mouth dropped open. He nodded. "Yes, she and I have talked."

Her legs went out from underneath her. She fell hard onto the dusty ground and the hex burned into her thigh. She cried out.

He stayed where he was but knelt on one knee like a prince and reached one hand out to her. "*Sha?*"

"I'm fine," she said, but tears coursed down her cheeks. "Can you make her come up? My *maman?*"

He paused. "Maybe."

And then she remembered about the war. The Crawling Chaos. The tentacles. He wanted to kill Maman Brigitte.

"No," he said. "I do not want to kill her. I love her."

Her eyes widened. "Can you read my mind?"

She turned and ran all the way home, swearing to herself that she would stay away.

But the night of the war, the night, *la nuit*:

Beau took her to the Krewe of Boo Halloween parade because some girl he liked was jiggling her stuff on the Frankenstein float. Hundreds of people with skull faces danced and marched down the streets while thousands of people cheered, and the glowing floats towered into the sky like the Egyptian pyramids—mummies plus werewolves, ghosts, vampires, skeletons. Beau kept hold of her hand while he waved at his girl. The drums were screaming, shrieking, and she told Beau over and over that she was not a little kid and she wanted to go trick-or-treating, not stand there looking stupid in her witch costume. She had a pumpkin-shaped trick-or-treat bag. The hex was lying at the bottom of it and she could smell stinky burning felt. She wished she had made a costume to look like Maman Brigitte, but she hadn't known the *loa* then, and anyway, Maman Brigitte was beautiful.

"I'll come back and meet you here," Evangeline told Beau, but he wasn't even listening to her. The drums shouted and her ears pounded and her balloon-heart threatened to lift her up into the sky—up—

She gasped. The sky was pitch black; there were no stars. Not a one. She tugged at Beau's hand until he looked down at her and said, "*What?*" in an irritated tone of voice. She pointed upward and he looked, huffed, and started back down at her again. "*What?*" he said again.

"There are no stars." Her head was *thundering* with the drum-talk. *Nyarlahotep, Nyarlahotep. Il arrive!*

Beau scoffed. "What are you talking about, girl?'

He didn't—couldn't—see it. Didn't understand the drums. Evangeline looked up again, looked hard, hoping that she had imagined it. In the bleak black sky, something blacker swirled and moved, crawling across a field of ebony; tentacles and talons pulsated in and out of existence. Something as big as the moon threw back its head and teeth towering at a height beyond her ability to understand dripped with blood.

"Beau, *Beau!*" she shouted.

But her cries were lost in the chaos of the parade, and Beau's attention was riveted on the beautiful Frankenstein girl who sauntered toward him in a tiny black-and-red top and a spangly black skirt. Evangeline yanked his hand. He didn't even notice. The girl was skakin' her boobs and telling Beau that she had to be careful because Antoine might see them.

The drums were screaming, shrieking. *It gange! He is winning!* Nyarlahotep was going to kill Maman Brigitte!

"No!" Evangeline cried, and she dropped to the ground, breaking Beau's grip. He might have shouted but she didn't hear him; she scrambled to her feet and ran out of the crowd, arms failing, shouting, "Out of my way! Get out of my way!" She went wild, baring her teeth and hitting and pushing; she would have bitten someone to get them to move if she'd had to. Lots of folks were drunk and they laughed as they wobbled and stepped aside.

Someone shouted, "It's all just pretend, honey!"

And then she was running for all she was worth to the graveyard, rolled by the drums—

La guerre Maman Brigitte Baron Samedi the war the war the war

—falling and struggling to get back up as the ground buckled. The entire world was pitch dark; green light blazed down from the sky, *shoot-shoot-shoot* like falling stars; a thousand skeletons charged forward, scrambling over the tombs in the city of the dead; the earth broke and spewed into the air, bringing bones and grinning skulls that assembled into skeletons as they plummeted back against the dirt. They charged forward; she gaped as her cousin Jimmy flew past. In their midst, Baron Samedi rode a sort of float drawn by skeletal horses with black plumes in their manes of smoke.

Then strange, luminous *things* shambled from the direction opposite the skeletons. They were human-shaped, their faces elongated; they sharpened and became people she could see through: ghosts. Phantoms. And carried on the shoulders of two of them, Maman Brigitte was urging the horde of boogies toward the skeletons.

"Maman Brigitte! Baron Samedi! I have a hex! I can help!" she shouted. She pulled it from her pumpkin-shaped trick-or-treat bag and lifted it up.

A roar exploded the tombs nearest her, *blam-blam-blam*; the sky broke apart and pieces careened and cartwheeled, slicing away more of the starless night. Skeletons and ghosts dervished and whirled; the Crawling Chaos blared out a sound that threw Evangeline to the ground and made her throw up. Darkness ground down on her like a falling marble angel. Then someone's hand brushed hers, cold and hard and bony. Whoever it was took her hex. She tried to look up, but it was too much for her. Pain, swirling, vomiting, fainting.

Her eyes closed.

Heat.

Heat.

On her eyelids.

Evangeline groaned and opened her eyes. Golden dawn shone down on her. The air was still. Her witch costume was thick with red dirt.

She rose up on her elbows. All around her, blood-soaked bones were heaped like haystacks—legs, arms, spines, skulls. Crimson. Inert. And on the tallest heap, Baron Samedi was stretched out on his back, arms and legs spread-eagled, head tipped. His mouth was open; his eyes were closed. His suit was soaked in blood. His red rose was missing.

Farther back in the graveyard, a man in a robe with a cloth around his head was trudging away, his back to Evangeline. Head bowed, shuffling through the weeds and dusty dirt. He turned and looked at her. The Black Man, Old Pharaoh. He looked old now, not eighteen. He looked like he had given up, shot his dog, and doused his truck with gasoline.

"*Ma sha.*"

Maman Brigitte appeared, standing over Baron Samedi, dipping her hands into his chest, her fingerbones scooping up thick, viscous blood, and covering her face with the gore of her husband. *"Ma petite, ma belle."* She smiled down at Evangeline and gestured for her come closer. "*Merci.* Thank you."

Evangeline could not find her voice. It had floated

away. All she could do was stare as Maman Brigitte, white face blood red, descended from the bone pyramid with her arms outstretched. The bones beneath her feet cracked and shattered. Evangeline shrank back, and then Maman Brigitte laughed and wiped her own cheeks with the hem of her black lace shroud. The blood was still there, smeared all around.

"Your hex," Maman Brigitte said.

Evangeline cleared her throat. A chunk of sheer terror loosened and plopped into her stomach. She said, "My hex saved you?"

"Fuck, *mais non*," the loa replied. "But it showed me that you loved me. And that is so sweet." She reached out her bone fingers and wrapped them around Evangeline's arm. They were cold as marble.

As death.

"The baron," Evangeline said. "Is he—"

"*Mort.* Dead." She shrugged.

"But he's already dead," Evangeline blurted.

"Not when it's the kind of death the Pharaoh dishes out. He got hexes we haven't even dreamed of." When she smiled, her white teeth split her red face like a wound. "I let the Black Man put his hands on me. Then those two god-men locked horns, like I knew they would, and Nyarlahotep got rid of my man for me. Then *my* army swooped in and shut *him* down." She pointed in the direction that the Black Man had trudged away.

"But *how*?" Evangeline asked. "Did you get a hex?"

Lady Death sighed happily and arched her back. "Never underestimate your powers, Evangeline. You can wear a man out if he wants you to. And most of 'em want you to, sure enough." She planted a kiss on Evangeline's forehead, and it was like a hex mark, Evangeline was sure. The hex of her womanly power. "Do you want to go see you *maman* now?"

"Oh, *oui!*" Evangeline cried, and she threw her arms around the *loa*. "Thank you! Thank you!"

"Then let's get going." Maman Brigitte smiled. Her face was bloody, but her teeth were white.

Very, very white.

"Okay, *maman*," Evangeline said.

The blood was wet on her forehead. The drums sounded with her footfalls as beside Maman Brigitte, she crushed man bones. The drums said:

Elles partent.

They leave.

A Night for Masks

Brian M. Sammons

A ndy fumed as he watched his little brother, Devon, run up the barely lit path to the stranger's door. Andy was sixteen, his brother was eleven, and the two boys could not be more unalike as brothers. *Check that, half-brothers*, Andy reminded himself. Andy was skinny, sullen, red-haired, brown-eyed, and with a face speckled with freckles that thankfully did a pretty good job at hiding the pock marks of adolescent acne. Devon was short for is age and a bit pudgy thanks to too many video games and bad eating habits, which in turn was thanks to the boy's mom being single, working two jobs, and not having enough time to cook the kids decent meals. *Bitch*, Andy thought as he saw Devon met up with a trio of other kids at the closed door to the house, under the lit porchlight. Devon was also almost always happy, the dimwit, and had blond hair and blue eyes that matched the cheap plastic Thor mask he wore.

"Trick or treat!" the impromptu quartet yelled out.

"Twick or tweet," Andy said under his breath with mock syrupiness. He brought his right hand up and used his thumb and forefinger to smooth out his wispy, vernal mustache. He watched the kids shift around, one foot to the other, bobbing and jostling, like they all had to take a leak or something. Clad in bright costumes, except for one kid that went as the Grim Reaper, they looked like the assclowns they were as the door stayed shut and no one replied to their initial challenge.

Come on, shitnugget, ring the damn doorbell or something, Andy thought as he dug his phone out of his pocket for the eighth time that evening and checked the time. 6:48 PM. Goddamnit, he was missing the whole thing. He still had to drag Devon to Ford Street and then back home or else his little brother would no doubt tell mom when she got home from work later tonight and she would have his ass.

"Hey, Devon, come on," Andy yelled and that caused Thor to turn around and give him a literal blank-eyed stare. Then all of a sudden the house's door whipped open, there was a cheap, speaker-straining shriek, probably off some Haunted House Sound Effects ripped off of YouTube, and a guy in a rubber and fake fur werewolf mask jumped out of the darkness beyond the door, growling and howling. The kids all jumped, especially Devon who was caught looking the other way, and their legit fright caused Andy to smile in spite of himself. *Good, I hope you pissed your pants*, he thought.

As the werewolf started pawing out candy to the now giggling kids, Andy looked up at the starless sky and the bulky black clouds that had been promising rain all day but had yet to deliver. *Come on, rain already*, Andy wished for the umpteenth time that day. Rain would have brought this Halloween bullshit to an early close, and that meant he could run Devon back home and then go off to Ashley Donner's costume party. That was where he wanted to be, not out here shepherding his little brother as he loaded up on more future diabetes fuel. But while the eleven-year-old was old enough to stay home by himself for a few hours at a time, mom thought he was still too young to go out at night by himself.

Hell, he's too damn old for tricks and treats, Andy thought, purposely ignoring the little voice in the back of his mind that spoke up to remind him that he had only stopped trick or treating three years ago.

I really don't care about Ashley's party, his mom had said, *your little brother has waited all year for Halloween, and I have to work, so please, help me out a little will you? After you take him down to Ford you can bring him home and then go to your precious party, okay?*

Slap, slap, slap, Devon's sneakers sounded on the path back towards Andy. "Hey did you see that guy?" He said, lifting the plastic visage of the Asgardian up to reveal his sweaty face beneath. "He was really scary."

"Uh-huh, come on," Andy mumbled, as he looked across the street at the next block up. One block closer to the Ford Street finish and then freedom. He placed his hand on Devon's shoulder and started briskly walking in that direction, hoping that the kid wouldn't spot the little ranch style house, pushed back from the street and shrouded by pine trees, with the lit Jack-o'-lantern and the porch light on.

Of course he wasn't that lucky.

"Hey, Andy, there's a lit house!" Devon cried, spying the house.

Andy dropped his hand from Thor's plastic shoulder as he dropped his head in resignation. *Shit.* He knew trying to talk to his half-brother would only waste time as the goddamn crybaby would just play the trump card of 'telling mom' after any debate. So he just sighed and mumbled, "Go ahead but make it fucking fast."

Devon's mouth made a comical O as that F-word was a word no one in their small family was allowed to say.

Andy gritted his teeth, pushed the thin plastic mask down over his brother's (*half-brother*) face and hissed out, "Shut up and just go." And then for added emphasis he barked out, "Run!"

The mini-Avenger turned without saying a word and ran like he was told for the lit door and the flickering pumpkin.

Andy straightened up, jammed both his hands into the pockets of his jeans, and wished he smoked. He had never tried, but right now he felt would be an appropriate time to start. He took his eyes off his fleeing brother to examine some of the other Happy Hallow-wieners about him. There weren't that many. There was one kid in the lamest of all costumes: normal street clothes but with a cheap, blank white hockey mask. *Knockoff Jason. Way to put in the effort, kid.* There was a band of four, all of them as tall or taller than Andy, dressed as Spider-Man, a kind of cute chick as Little Red Riding Hood, a guy as Wonder Woman (*hairy legs and all, nice*), and president Donald Trump, complete with an exaggerated orange face and bad blond toupee. *Oh come on, you all are way too old for this.* There was a young couple, maybe in their early twenties, not dressed up in any way, but they were pushing a baby carriage with a little…something (boy or girl, Andy couldn't tell) in it dressed as a tiny yellow and black bumble bee with an orange plastic pumpkin pail sitting in its lap. *Oh come on, that kid is way too young for this.* Lastly, about midway down the block that they had just come up, was a tall man in a bright yellow sheet and nothing else. Like an old fashioned sheet-ghost-costume. *What a yellow ghost? You piss-ghost or something?*

"Hey, that old lady was nice," Devon said as he came charging back, "she gave me a full-sized candy!"

Andy looked at his brother, then at the already bulging pillow case he was using to hold his haul. "Give me something out of there."

"Nu-uh, this is mine." Devon said, comically clutching his bag to his chest.

Andy cuffed his brother upside the head, not hard but hard enough to show he wasn't fooling, and said, "Come on, give it."

Devon sighed, stuck a pudgy hand into the pastel blue sack, fished around, and then handed his older brother a mini Three Musketeers bar.

Andy smiled, "Good kid, now come on." And walked him across Freedmont Street to the next block.

The next block was even worse than the last. Over half the houses were lit up and had grinning and candle-lit Jack-o'-lanterns out front. This made Devon squee with happiness, and Andy to mutter, "Shit," under his breath again. The Ford deadline was still four blocks away. "Shit, shit," Andy repeated. He resisted the urge to check the time on his phone again, that would not help speed this along, and instead pointed Devon at the first lit up house and said, "Go on, and hurry!"

For the next god-only-knows how long, Andy shambled down the sidewalk that ran parallel with the street as Devon ran back and forth from the sidewalk, along driveways and walkways to the houses, and then back. Andy's latest ruminations to keep him from going crazy with boredom were once again about Ashley Donner's party. Specifically the fact that he knew Tommy Jenkins, who had no kid brother or sister to make him late, was going to the party, too. Tommy and Andy were best friends, but Andy knew that wouldn't matter when it came to Ashley Donner. Both of them had a major hard-on for the girl, and how could they not? She was fine as hell. In Andy's mind's eye he could see Tommy, one hand leaning against a wall, red Solo cup in the other hand, talking with Ashley, and sneaking closer and closer to the girl in the most nonobvious way the dickhead could pull off. Until the two were very close. Too damn close. Then Tommy would drop his oh-so tired arm right around Ashley's shoulders. She would give him a cute, awkward smile, he would return it with a shit-eating one of his own. Then he would lean in, licking his thin lizard-like lips, and –

"Fuck it!" Andy said, his hand going darting in his pocket for the phone again. It was only with Herculean effort that he was able to pull his hand back out of his pocket sans phone. *Man I wish I smoked or something.*

He turned back to studying the people around him to take his mind off such things as Devon was at the new house, screaming, "Trick or treat!" One girl dashed past him dressed as one of the princesses from Frozen, the icy one, but Andy didn't know her name. An Optimus Prime came running from the other side of the street, toward the door where Devon still was. And then there was...*what the hell*?

It was another old timey sheet ghost, this one white with the two eye holes cut out. A cartoon classic. But it was all just...wrong. First it was short, like under three feet. *Okay, small kid, no big deal,* Andy rationalized. But the little "tyke" was nearly as wide as it was tall, like there were three little kids clustered together under that sheet instead of one. Then there was the sheet itself, it was greasy, filthy, like the kid (kids?) had been dumpster diving in it or wallowing around in pig shit. *Who the hell would wear that?* And as the dirty sheet spook waddled past him, the stench of it was pure backed up sewer line, and the little freak wheezed and slurped as it walked.

Get the fuck back! Andy's mind screamed and he leapt off the sidewalk, stepping up onto the lawn to get out of the nasty thing's way. He turned his head over his left shoulder and saw Devon still at the house, now talking to some other costumed kids that looked about his age. He turned his head back, and that's when he saw the yellow piss-ghost again. It was just about five houses down, in the middle of the street, and it was staring at him. Now that it was closer (*you've called him 'it' three times now, he's just some guy in a yellow sheet*) Andy could see it wasn't a yellow sheet he wore, but a yellow robe. One with a hood that the stranger had up. But the guy was faceless, for under that hood was nothing. Only blackness and nothing more. That's how Andy could tell that the weirdo was staring at him, that empty black hole of nothing was pointed right at him.

Come on, he's just got his face blacked out with make up to make it look like an empty hood. That's all it is. Andy said to himself, but it did nothing to stop the shiver that ran down his spine. *Damn I wish I had my knife.*

The knife in question was one of Andy's prized possessions. Or at least it had been. He had bought it from Tommy Jenkins three years ago, who had stolen it from his older brother, Jensin, once he went into the army. Andy loved that badass knife right up until the time his mom found it under his bed and confiscated it about two years back. He still missed it at times. Like right now. It was so damn sweet, with a curved blade that had a jagged, serrated edge along its back. The best thing about it was that it had a nasty-ass trick. In its handle was a little button that if you pressed it, it caused the blade to fold in, but not all the way. Once it folded in ninety degrees it would lock in place making a T with the handle and the blade. Then it became a push dagger, and man, that could do some damage. Locked in that position you wouldn't slice or even stab with it, but punch with it, and that would mess anyone up.

Yeah but you don't have that knife anymore, so just quit it, he scolded himself. Then he jumped and yipped like a sissy when he heard someone shout his name from right behind him.

It was Devon, back at last from the house and the other kids.

Devon laughed, lifted up his Thor face and said, "Did I scare you?"

Andy turned, grabbed his little brother by the hand, and started speed walking down the sidewalk, literally dragging the kid along.

"Wha – Andy, stop. Ow, you're hurting me – "

But Andy wasn't listening to his kid brother, he was listening to himself. *Man, settle down, what got you so scared?*

I'm not scared.

"Come on, Andy, lemme go. There's more houses over there with—"

Bullshit you're not scared. Thinking about your knife, what you going to do with it if you had it?

I don't know...something...

Dude, it was just some guy in a yellow bathrobe with his face painted black. That's it.

"I'm gonna tell mom!"

No, I felt it.

Felt what?

Felt it—

Him.

Whatever, felt him staring at me.

So?

It felt cold. His gaze was ice fucking cold.

That's crazy.

No, it felt like—

"Ow!" Andy screamed as pain flared in his right calf. He looked back at his wide-eyed little brother, at the kid's sneakered foot, then down at his leg as his brain put two and two together. "You kicked me, you little shit."

"Well you were ripping my arm out of my socket," Devon said and with a twist and a yank, pulled his left hand out of Andy's sweaty grip. "What got into you? What's wrong?"

Andy looked back down the block at where Mr. Yellow Robe had stood, and saw nothing. The freaky guy had vanished.

Devon followed Andy's gaze and also saw nothing. "So, what was it?" the child asked.

"Nothing..."

"No you weren't running like it was nothing."

"I wasn't running," Andy began to protest.

Yes you were.

"Yes you were," Devon said, "Like you were scared of something."

"Shut up, forget it," Andy said a little too forcefully.

Are you talking to yourself or your brother? Andy chuckled at that, looked to both sides of the street to make sure the yellow guy was really gone, and then turned back to Devon. "Look it's getting late—"

"Nu-uh, it's only—"

"So get a move on." Andy spun him around again and this time gave him a little kick in the pants to get him going. Devon rubbed his backside with one hand as he looked back at his big brother, still confused. Then he heard a merry chorus of "Trick or treat!" behind him, and he turned and ran off, putting his mask back in place as he went.

Things went back to normal for the rest of the block and most of the next one, too. Andy kept an eye to his back for a time, but there was no sign of the yellow-robed man. Just normal folks doing the normal Halloween stuff. The tightness in his chest that he hadn't noticed before, but upon retrospect he guessed started when he saw that black face-hole in the yellow hood staring at him, loosened up and went away. He felt relieved, stupid for having scared himself over nothing, but mostly relieved. Snagging another piece of candy from him protesting little brother helped. And hey, he hadn't even thought of the time or the party at Ashley's place since –

The growing smile that was blooming on his face froze then disappeared altogether as he spotted another… *something.* This one wore another white sheet with two black eye holes, but it was a very big sheet. A long sheet. The sheet-ghost's head was maybe four feet high, but it was very long, like Chinese dragon long. Andy pictured four or five kids under there, bent over after the first child, head to ass. *Who would do that? Got to be uncomfortable as hell.* But Andy knew that wasn't it. He wished that's all it was, but somehow he just knew it wasn't; the last part of the thing was dragging thick and heavy on the ground. *So if that's a train of kids, then the last one is dead. So how are the rest dragging him? And why?*

He turned to see where Devon was in his latest candy begging session, and his bladder let go. Just a little, he stopped himself by grabbing his crotch and squeezing, but he felt a warm trickle run down his left leg. Devon and three kids were at the door. Two were waiting anxiously for the candy giver to answer their summons, the third had its back to the door. It was staring back at him. It held no bag or plastic pumpkin to hold candy. It of course was dressed in a white sheet, one with a single eye hole on its lumpy, far-too-large shape of a head. And the white sheet was splattered, no, covered in red. Blood. Not fake blood, Andy could smell, he could taste the copper in it from where he stood.

Then there was a rustle of fabric and a flash of yellow to his left.

He turned to see what it was.

His bladder finished what it had started moments ago.

The Yellow man stood before him, over seven feet tall if he was an inch. He looked taller still, for he wore a spiked and spired crown of gold on his hooded head. Standing this close, Andy could see that the robe was in tatters but was immaculately clean, and that the copper stench of blood radiated from this crowned king in yellow. He could also see inside the folds on the hood. The king wore a cracked and pitted pale mask. It looked dull, like bone. *Was it ivory?* Its only feature was two eye holes and the two eyes beneath…

…*Pain. Wounds. Blood. Loss. Tears. Sickness. Infection. Futility. Hopelessness. Meaninglessness. Despair. Desire. Time. Age. Rot. Rust. Decay. Stink. Entropy. Entirety. Cruelty. Savagery. Blackness. Void. War. Slaughter. Death. Death. Death…Truth.*

Somehow Andy managed to tear his gaze away, his eyes blurry, wet, and leaking. The King reached out with a tawny-bandaged hand, yellowed and crusted, log-nailed and dripping, and oh so gently took Andy's trembling hand. He spread the fingers and placed something it his palm: his knife, already locked in the T punch dagger position. The robed one then carefully closed Andy's hand, making a fist, and patted his white knuckles. He then leaned in and whispered something in a voice of rusty coffin nails pulled free and the unsheathing of misericordes.

"Andy, you peed your pants!"

Andy turned around to a voice both familiar and not. He expected to see…something…someone? Instead he saw another sheet-clad monster, all lopsided and lumpy. Filthy, reeking, and… it wore a cheap, plastic, kiddy Halloween mask. Some superhero, blond hair, blue eyes, helmet…what was his name?

Andy turned to ask The King, he would know, he knew *everything*, but he was gone.

"Andy?" He felt a tug on his sleeve.

Andy turned and roared at the sheet-ghost-thing that clutched at his arm. Not with fear, not to frighten, it was communication at its most primal: raw, savage, and so *right*. It felt so *good*. It felt *true*.

He knew what he had to do. What you always had to do with monsters. He punched out with his already clenched fist. And again. And again. And when the figure fell, he went down with it, mounted it, and punched and punched and punched…

Andy heard screams. He heard shouts of both fear and anger. He heard an "Oh my God!" and a "Stop it!" and a "…just a kid!" and laugher. That last sound came from him. And as he rose and looked at a half-dozen sheet-covered monsters, most running away, some staring at him, one filming him with an iPhone, he knew why he laughed. He knew why he was so filled with joy despite all the monsters in the world. At last, long, long last, his mask was off. This was him, the real him, his true face, and killing was as natural as breathing, blinking, or pissing. So he withdrew his fist from the warm, sticky mess beneath him, pulled his splattered arm back, ready to punch out again and again, and with a laugh he charged the nearest monster.

No Other God but Me

Adrian Cole

O ctober's a weird month. Sometimes you get an Indian summer, and days are more like the good ones in August. Other years it's like November's come early, with high winds, seas fuming and a deep chill settling under clouds that never disperse. Here on the north coast of South Western England, where the villages jut out into the Celtic Sea before it merges with the open Atlantic, we notice the cold. Our climate is pretty mild, even in the autumn. Maybe this change they keep talking about had something to do with events two years back. When all hell woke and came visiting.

People think it began with the vicar, Martin Shute. The way he died and all. They found his body one morning, down on the beach. It was a mess: the gulls had already flocked in to feast on it. They eat anything, not just fish: food waste, chips they can pinch off tourists, even human flesh if it's available. The police reckoned it was the birds who'd picked Shute clean, but I don't see how they could have leeched all his blood and flown off with half his bones. Maybe they knew there was something nastier at work, but they couldn't figure it out. They did admit it was unusual – their word – for so much religious stuff to be scattered around the priest's remains. A number of small crucifixes, a Bible and a prayer book, both badly torn up, a couple of silver salvers from the church, crumpled like paper and a miniature Jesus statue.

It didn't need a genius to know someone was taking the piss out of Shute's Christianity. It was an act of violation, coupled with the killing. Someone suggested sacrifice, but the police were prepared to consider it religious mania, the work of nutters. They combed our village, Rooksands, but found nothing, no clues. The national press had a wonderful time and we suffered TV people milling around, as bad as the gulls, but once the trail went cold with nothing new to add, they all took off back to look for something else to gorge on.

The Reverend Shute was found at 5:00 AM on October 1. Three weeks later, Rooksands was almost back to normal. The police maintained a watch, an 'incident room' in the Parish Hall, so they could continue their investigations, but the fact was, they were going backwards.

Like I said, people think it began with the vicar. Me and most of the villagers knew otherwise, but we weren't about to blab to the police. They'd have taken us for lunatics if we had. Mind you, Shute's death was the last straw for us. I'd been saying for a long time we needed to take action ourselves. No one liked that, or my suggestions, but the death of the holy man broke the camel's back, so to speak. Maybe it did some good, though I'd not have seen Shute slaughtered like he was. He'd been a good man. Naïve, but kind.

So where did this nightmare begin? I'd say two years ago. I was one of the first people to know about it, because I spend a lot of time at sea. I don't make my living as a fisherman, like a lot of the Rooksands men, but I have a small boat and I like to go out into the bay for mackerel, or sometimes I'll go for something much bigger. I'm fifty and I retired early. Drove big trucks for most of my working life, never married (came close twice) and put enough money aside to keep me going. Bought an old cottage in Rooksands, where I grew up, and modernised it. I like the simple life.

Only life in Rooksands wasn't so simple. Not once the killings started. Make no mistake, they were killings. I know they were seen as accidents and at first it seemed like they were – people lost at sea in storms, others carelessly falling from the local cliffs. Easy to dismiss them as freakish. The coast and sea here are a harsh environment. There's an old village further along the coast, Trewithick Hole that was almost dragged off the shore and flattened in a horrendous storm back in 1922. All that was left was a few broken-down houses, like huge gravestones. Tourists like to visit the place and I know Tom Kellow makes a bob or two taking his Ghost Walks along there.

So a handful of local deaths – with no trace of any of the bodies – could be attributed to freak weather. Some of us in the village suspected something worse. Trouble was, the things we saw weren't credible. I mean, this land is stiff with legends. Down in Cornwall they have the Beast of Bodmin, a big cat or something that chews up sheep and the like. Never been caught. I know people who've seen the thing, but as far as the world is concerned, it's a myth, a night shadow.

The things out in our bay are the same. Like the night Davey Smale and I was out fishing for shark. Thought we'd hooked a big one, but when we got it into the boat, we had a shock. At first I thought it was an oversize squid, almost as big as me, only we don't get them here. It must've come up from beyond the Atlantic shelf. We had a hard time killing it and Davey suffered nasty damage to his arm from the thing's suckers. We got it back to my place and stuck it in one of my small outbuildings. Covered it with a tarpaulin. Next morning the door was ripped off its hinges and the thing was gone. Tarpaulin was shredded. Worse than all that, Maurice Tiddy, a neighbour, had lost two dogs. We found enough blood to suggest foul play.

Davey Smale and I described the thing we'd brought

ashore to the police, but it didn't help them. Soon after that the so-called accidents began. Five people lost,
two local and three holiday-makers. All in bad weather,
in some cases in the middle of summer. I'd found some
weird tracks along the narrow beaches, leading into the
sea, and the villagers complained about a stench that
hung over the water, like something huge had died out
there, a whale maybe. But there was no carcass washed
up. I don't reckon anyone would have suspected what I
did. They might be superstitious, but the world isn't so
small any more. They like practical explanations.

My trucking days had taken me all over Europe. I'd
heard some strange tales. I'd met sailors and travellers
who'd picked up word of things at sea, things they said
explained what I'd dragged out of the deeps that time.
Creatures that lived out in the ocean and worshipped
gods most of us never heard of. Mostly it had struck me
as rubbish, the booze talking, or just someone spinning a
good yarn to entertain us on the long nights on the road.

It struck me, though, that Rooksands needed to
defend itself from whatever was out in the bay. At first
everyone laughed it off. The nasty death of the vicar
brought the village to its senses. While the police were
nosing around, trying to make sense of things, I had
a small posse visit me. Tom Kellow, Davey Smale and
Kelvin Dobbs, spokesmen for the rest. They were good,
honest men, hard workers all. They'd put their necks on
the line to help you if need arose.

"You were right," Davey told me. "About fetching
help. The police are stumped."

"They will be," I said, "as long as they're looking for
answers on land. You boys know where the real problem
lies. It's out there in the bay."

Tom nodded. "My ghost stories are based on legends
and the like, though I don't believe in ghosts myself.
You're right, though. Whatever did that to the vicar, isn't
normal."

"It was a warning," I told them. "Martin thought he could use his Christianity to ward off those things. It took a lot of guts for him to recognise the problem and stand up to it. You saw what they did to him. His God wasn't strong enough to defend him."

Before Shute's death, the three men would have been appalled by that kind of comment, but not now. They were frightened, and none of us was sleeping well.

"The whole village has been talking," said Kelvin, who'd been radically opposed to bringing in any outside help. He'd changed his tune, big time. He really was scared. "I don't mind admitting I was against it, but what sort of help can we get?"

"This is something outside normal bounds. That's why Martin's religion didn't work. This goes way, way back. Primitive, you know?"

They were all nodding.

"We have to fight fire with fire. We have to bring in someone who really knows about this stuff."

Tom scowled. "You're talking about witchcraft?"

"In a way. But not the twisted medieval version. Wicca craft, the craft of the wise. Maybe even older stuff. We need a shaman."

Again, they would have scoffed at the idea once, but not now. "Any port in a storm," said Tom, trying to make light of it, but the others were as serious as they could be.

"You know one?" asked Kelvin. He'd always been impressed by my tales of wandering and the world outside, not having travelled much himself.

"I think so. There's someone on the edge of Dartmoor. She's not a freak, or a hermit, or anything like that—"

"She?" said Davey. "Then you *are* talking about a witch?"

"Morgana wouldn't call herself that, but she does have that old kind of wisdom. She's no fool. I reckon she'd be able to help."

"How soon can you get her?" said Tom.

"As soon as I can. We need to act quickly. I reckon whatever is out there in the bay will be coming at us soon."

Davey swore. "What – an invasion?"

"Something like that. No one will be safe."

I spoke to her on the telephone. I'd never met her, though I'd seen her on local television. She wrote books on the occult as well as herbal stuff, and had done well for herself. She must have been about forty, and from what I'd seen of her, looked like she spent a lot of time outdoors, probably on the Moors. She spoke with a cultured but natural voice, very assured and easily deflected some of the more sceptical questions her interviewers like to taunt her with. My initial awkwardness at contacting her dissipated quickly: it was almost like she'd been expecting my call.

"Rooksands?" she said. "That's not far from Trewithick Hole, right? I know the place. Can we meet there? Given what you've told me, we better make it soon."

Two days later I drove along the winding cliff road to the open area above the cove where the remains of Trewithick Hole poked up like huge tombstones above the rocks. The road was narrow, pitted and in places overgrown, ending in an open area that had been fenced off. The fencing was dilapidated and dangerous, though few people came here unsupervised.

Morgana was already here, her four-wheel drive parked close to the winding path down into the cove. She was dressed in a thick woollen jumper and jeans, her raven hair piled up and pinned. Her face was all angles, too sharp to be pretty, but she was an attractive woman. Her eyes were mesmeric, a steely gray. We shook hands and I was surprised at the strength of her grip.

"Thanks for coming," I said.

"I've been here before." She looked down at the sea as it rolled into the cove, for once subdued, although I knew how treacherous those currents would be.

We exchanged a few pleasantries, but she was obviously eager to get on with the business and led us down the path. Some attempts had been made to shore up its worst sections, and we said little as we concentrated on getting down to the crumbling village. There was a quay, which was also in danger of disintegrating, and the curved sweep of a narrow jetty. We walked out on to it.

She studied the swirling waters inside the miniature breakwater it made. I was looking at the ruined houses. Not much left of them now, just a wall here and there, or a shed or two. All the roofs had long fallen in and much of the debris had been swept out to sea.

"What's happened at Rooksands," said Morgana. "Also happened here, at the time of the 1922 storm. It wasn't a natural one, although that's how it was reported and recorded. The cliffs here have been collapsing for years. It's a notorious stretch of coast. That night the village finally succumbed was part of something else." She indicated the sea beyond the jetty. Its waves today were gentle, undulating almost invitingly.

"The things inhabiting the deep waters came." She was cool, almost casual. "They took many of the villagers back into the deeps. The records show people were caught by the unusually high tide. Some fell into the sea when chunks of the land fell away like sand. It was far more sinister than that."

She stared down at the waters below us, her body statuesque for a moment, then she suddenly drew back as if she'd seen something, watching the waters more closely. I couldn't see anything other than shadows, but her perception of things was more acute than mine.

"It's the seventeenth," she said. "We don't have a lot

of time. They're here. They don't usual risk exposure by day. Tell your villagers to keep away from the sea."

"I doubt I'll be able to keep the fishermen from going out."

"It'll be Samhain in just over two weeks." She pronounced it 'Sah-when'. "They've already discredited the Christian god. And they'll know I'm here. I've fought them before. They'd like to discredit the Old Magic. Samhain would suit them as a testing time. We have to prepare, and quickly. Take me to the village."

Her extraordinary presence and that total belief in what she was doing, coupled with my anxieties for the village brushed aside any lingering doubts I might have had about this business. I told her about the police.

She smiled. "They know me. I'm a crank. Harmless. They won't bother about what I get up to. They'll be glad of me when this is over."

"You can rid Rooksands of this…intrusion?"

"I've been expecting something. It'll be tough. But if we don't make a stand, it'll get far worse."

Back at the village, I showed her around and introduced her to some of my friends. Her presence made them uneasy and I got the impression Kelvin thought she was a bit maze, but they were committed. The death of the vicar had shaken everyone up. Ironically, when she drove off, there was a strange vacuum, as if we'd become a little more vulnerable.

She'd given several of us some strict instructions about preparing the village, protecting it. There were certain charms and spells we could use. So we cut branches from elder, hawthorn and rowan among others and gave them sharp points, digging them into the ground so their tips faced the sea. Morgana had also given us a notepad in which she'd scribbled sigils and weird doodles.

"Carve them into your doors," she said. "Take the bigger pebbles from the beach and create the signs at its edge." She also gave me a number of small wooden figurines that looked like variants on the piskies of Cornish legend. "Hang these in the trees." My companions surprised me by their sudden faith, and got on with the job industriously, almost like children, absorbed by their activities. No laughter now, this was deadly serious.

By evening we'd made a thorough job of setting out the first wave of protection. A few of the villagers, particularly the ones who'd come here most recently, wondered what the hell we were doing, but we said it was part of the early planning for the Halloween festival, coming up soon. Most of them took it in good spirits and asked if there was anything they could do. No one mentioned the shadow lying over the village.

I spoke to some of the fishermen and told them up front what we'd been about. Normally they would have rejected the suggestion they stay out of the water, but I could see the fear in them. Some of them were tight-lipped, but I knew they'd seen worse things out in the bay than the thing I'd brought ashore. They knew something evil was stirring. Old superstitions die hard in these parts. In the end I had a compromise. They'd stop fishing a week before the festival.

❈

The following day Morgana returned, her big vehicle towing a long trailer. I helped her undo the tarpaulin and gazed in surprise at what was revealed. She smiled at my expression.

"Pumpkins?" I said. "There must be dozens of them. Is this for the festival?"

"Powerful magic. Yesterday you showed me some fields backing on to the village, overlooking the beach."

"Riddick's Farm."

"We must set these in the soil. Get the farmer to plough it."

I frowned. Jed Riddick was an ornery type. Very protective of his land. The fields in question had been fallow for years. They were reedy and the soil wanted too much doing to it to make it much use other than for grazing Riddick's sheep.

"And I mean now," Morgana added.

Kelvin Dobbs was Riddick's cousin, so we gave him the job of twisting the farmer's arm. Surprisingly Kelvin came back from his visit promptly. "He's getting his plough out."

"That quickly?" I said. "What did you say, mate? You hold a shotgun to him?"

Kelvin shook his head grimly. "He's lost a lot of sheep. Found remains down along the waterline. He said if ploughing the land will help, so be it."

The words sobered all of us and Morgana pointed to the trailer. "There are two hundred pumpkins in there. As the land is ploughed, put them into the soil, cut end down. Twenty rows of ten, each row three feet apart."

None of us asked her what for. If she was working magic, it was fine by us and we set to with a will. Jed Riddick was as good as his word and had the ploughing done in no time. He and the rest of us seemed to be reaching back to a far past, something atavistic, in all of us, and up there on the slopes of the fields we were like men of a different age. Morgana walked among us as we set out the rows of pumpkins. Tom Kellow asked with a grin if we should have carved eyes, nose and mouth out of them, but Morgana shook her head.

"Once they've rooted in," she said, her face completely straight, "it won't matter."

By the time we'd done, it was late afternoon, but we had our twenty rows of pumpkins, all partially buried in the clinging loam. Morgana had fetched several buckets from the front of the trailer. She set them down and we watched in fascination as she peeled off their plastic lids. We reeled back at the stench.

"Blood and bone, and a few other things besides," said Morgana, smiling at our revulsion. "Very potent. Come on, we need to feed the plants."

Again we did as bidden and emptied the disgusting contents of the buckets evenly among the pumpkins, the soil soaking up the liquid mess. We all stood back, mopping our brows, after it was done and Morgana said she was satisfied.

"Good work. You've earned your beer. And the drinks will be on me. Mind you, you've one more job. These plants need to be watched. From tonight and every night, set at least two men to watch them right through till dawn. With shotguns."

Tom glanced at her uneasily. "Expecting trouble?"

"Possibly. I don't want the plants harmed, but the deep dwellers will be curious. If they come, use the guns."

"And the police?" I asked.

"Say you were scaring off poachers. Tell them there's been a bit of sheep rustling going on. The guns are just for effect. They'll buy that." She was right, I thought. Sheep rustling across the country had become a problem these days. It would make a good cover.

I shared guard duty with Davey on the third night. The other guys reckoned on having heard something down on the beach the first couple of nights, and that ripe sea smell stank a few times, otherwise things were quiet. They livened up when I was there. It was long gone midnight when that familiar foul stink permeated the air. I'd taken one end of the pumpkin rows, Davey the other. It was very dark: apart from a few street lights on in the village there was nothing to see by, other than our flashlights. It was a wild night, clouds blotting out any potential moonlight and a blustery off-sea wind racing up through the fields.

Davey's flashlight was on. I heard him moving across the bottom of the field, nearing the beach. He shouted something but a gust clouted the words away. I saw a flash and heard the shotgun go off, two distinct blasts. Quickly I got to him. He was reloading, his flashlight at his feet. I swept my own beam in an arc across the beach and something was moving at the water's edge, maybe thirty feet away. I couldn't make out what it was, so didn't fire.

"Kill it!" shouted Davey, face twisted with fear.

I heard the splash as whatever it had been went into the sea and although I shone my flashlight, it was too quick. Davey rushed past me and fired off another two cartridges, pausing close to the water's edge.

"What was it?" I called.

"It must have crawled up the beach. It was almost on me, going for the rows of pumpkins. Had some kind of weapon. I think it dropped it. I saw its head…its face. Christ, it was revolting. Long hair, more like weed, so I only got a glimpse. Mouth like a big sucker…like a lamprey's, you know?"

"You must have hit it," I said, bending down to the sand. "See, what's this stuff? Blood?" I shone my flashlight on a patch of sticky muck that could have been from the wounded creature. We walked back up the beach, following the scuffed sand. There were no footprints, just deep scores, as if a turtle had struggled back to the sea, or a huge slug. Further up we found more of the blood stuff and with it a chunk of something flesh-like. It reeked and we knew this was the source of the stench from the sea.

"Looks like you hit the bastard," I said. "Blew part of it off. Don't touch it."

Davey knelt down and shone the flashlight on the mess. I heard movements nearby and saw another beam. One of the policemen had come to investigate.

"Bury it – quick," I told Davey.

He wasted no time and used the stock of his gun

to scoop out a hole in the sand. He prodded the chunk of meat into it, burying it, roughly smoothing the sand over it.

"What's the problem?" said the copper. "Why the shooting?"

"Bloody poachers," said Davey. "Don't worry, I only fired into the air. Scared 'em off, though. They sneak up through the fields and set traps for rabbits. They'll likely damage the pumpkins."

The copper, a young lad of about twenty-two nodded uneasily. "Right."

"Festival's coming up soon," I said. "We don't want the pumpkins ruined this close. Can't replace them."

"No," he said. He hadn't noticed the scuffed sand. If he caught the foul whiff from the sea, he didn't mention it.

Later Davey and I found the dropped weapon. It was a thin length of old beam, twisted and maybe carved into a shape like a digging tool, primitive but effective. We didn't show the copper. He'd gone back into the village to a mug of hot tea.

There were no other sightings in the last few days up to the end of the month. Morgana said the sea dwellers had learned all they needed to know. Halloween came and that night Morgana stood with me and a couple of the other guys down at the tiny harbour, watching the waves snarling in on what had become a blustery night. The moon was full, the clouds sparse, so the sea had a brilliant tinge to it, heaving and tossing out in the bay. High tide was just after midnight, and with this wind, it would roll right up along the harbour. Everywhere was battened down. Behind us, in the higher village, around its small square, the festival was in full swing, with numerous lanterns and candles, other pumpkins, these carved, brandished on poles, or set in numerous windows. People were singing, cheering, and generally having a good time.

We'd warned them all to get inside their houses and lock everything down tight after midnight. They knew the storm was going to be a really bad one. Many had already retired, especially those with young children, but there were still plenty of revellers, and the endless supply of hot dogs and grilled burgers filled the buffeting air with their unmistakable reek.

"They're out there," said Morgana. "I can feel the hatred of the sea god. It knows me, and the things we've set here against it. Its servants will come. Nothing will prevent that now."

She was right. The bigger waves that battered their way in along the narrow harbour clawed at the buildings, whipped up by the ferocity of the wind. Lightning forked over the bay in dazzling displays and thunder rolled over us, almost drowned out by the roar of the waves. Small ships bobbed up and down at their moorings, tossed dangerously high. Several smaller craft were flipped over and dashed to pieces on the quay. I saw something emerging from the sea, a shadowy mass, like one wave had formed itself out of thick, glutinous tar. It wrapped itself around the bow of a trawler and I realised what it was – seaweed. Tons of the stuff, mangled up and balled into a massive web by the madness of the sea.

In that flickering light it extended several tendrils; they snagged the back of the trawler. Davey cried a warning. The boat belonged to his cousin. He could see it was in danger of being wrecked. Already the weed had tangled itself around the wheelhouse. Another huge wave tore along the harbour and as it hit the trawler, the weed mass was flung completely over it like a black blanket. Moments later it subsided, dragging the craft under the water.

Davey howled in fury, but there had been nothing

any of us could have done. We raced along the harbour side, opposite the maelstrom where the trawler had gone down, but there was no sign of it.

"Get the last of the revellers inside!" Morgana yelled, heading back to her vehicle, which was parked up one of the narrow side roads.

As I started for the village square, the air writhed with shapes, debris perhaps, ripped from buildings, fences, anything loose. Ahead of me, one of the villagers was coming to see what was happening: something hit him in the face and chest. His hands tore frantically at it and I almost choked in revulsion as I recognised it. A jellyfish whipped up from the sea and hurled like a missile. We'd often had plagues of these creatures, but they were smaller than the palm of your hand and relatively harmless. This thing was three feet across, a sickly transparent colour, its long fronds barbed and deadly. They swung like lashes and cocooned the upper body of the villager, flinging him to the ground.

Before I could react the air was filled with more of the things, blown into the village like a wave of mutant bats or aerial manta rays. I wove my way to the side street where Morgana had disappeared and barely reached its sanctuary in time to evade the whipping tendrils of another of the creatures. I could see the square. Most of its lights were out, the people having made for their homes now that the storm had erupted so violently.

Morgana had pulled from the boot of her vehicle a long canvas bag. She hastily undid it and another bolt of lightning was reflected on what she revealed. Swords. A half dozen of them. At first I thought they were samurai blades, as they had that slight curve and were their typical length. But as she gave me one I realised it was something different, maybe from another time, an ancient weapon, although beautifully preserved.

My other companions had all made it to the side street and each of us took a blade, unsheathing it to reveal a silvery blade on which unusual runes had been carved. Morgana waved to us to follow her. She was dressed in clinging dark clothes, a black assassin, a tight mask hiding all but her eyes. In the constant flicker of lightning she moved like a huge insect, occasionally swinging her blade at the air, slicing into the things that were gusting past us like missiles. We did the same, slicing the horrors apart in thick spatters of fluid.

At the edge of the village, higher up, we could see the tide's edge where the frothing white insanity of the waves disgorged more shapes. Things hopped ashore like giant fleas, and man-like beings shambled out of the water, apparently not damaged by it, as at home in its turmoil as seals. They were entering the village but I couldn't see any of the villagers. The storm had thankfully driven them inside. Doors had been doubled locked and windows boarded up in preparation for this mayhem.

Morgana shouted something about a black god's army, intent on driving home his will. "They'll want to reduce Rooksands to rubble, as they did with other villages. This time they'll be weakened by the relics and the charms you set as protection the place. If we can divert their attention to us," she added, but the wind tore the rest of her words away.

I stood with Davey, Kelvin and Tom and in a minute we saw another figure coming down from the fields beyond us. Jan Riddick. He carried a shotgun, though Morgana tossed him the last of the swords. He gripped it uneasily but nodded. We were exposed up here, the storm raging around us, and it was all we could do to keep on our feet. We could see the edge of the sea, where waves larger than any we'd seen before uncurled and crashed down on to the beach, churning the sand and flinging it back up onto the edge of the field.

Beyond us, out of reach of the waves, the lines of pumpkins stretched away into the darkness. I had seen them grow daily, the bloated shapes emerging from the ground at an extraordinary rate. Whatever foul concoction Morgana had fed them had done its work well.

"There!" cried Tom, pointing with his blade.

They were coming for us, knowing we were the key to the success of their invasion. The seas spewed forth another wave and it burst and reassembled itself into more skulking shapes. Tens, dozens, scores, a whole mass of them. The sea dwellers. The frightful, misshapen creatures that had been out in the ocean since before our own race walked the land. I tried to see their faces, but they were hidden under frond-like tresses, though their mouths gaped, ringed around with those lamprey-suckers. Their arms were elongated, ending in long, spatulate fingers. All carried a weapon, something resembling short spars of wood – ocean debris, perhaps, they'd shaped into killing tools.

Neither I nor my mates spoke the one thing we feared – we hadn't got a cat in hell's chance against this huge mob. And there was nowhere to run. We were just going to have to use our swords and protect ourselves as best we could. Jan Riddick thrust his blade into the ground and levelled his shotgun at the front ranks of the sea things. He shot at them twice, and two of the creatures exploded like sacks of treacle, collapsing. But it was like killing two flies in a swarm.

Morgana raised her sword. "Stand aside for a moment!" she shouted and the five of us fanned out away from her. She spoke strange words, which I took to be ancient Celtic lines, probably from the Old Magic she swore by. It was like she was conversing with the raging storm. To my amazement – and I admit, terror – she stretched upward and a crackling bolt of pure white light sizzled down from overhead and hit the end of her blade. The weapon went incandescent and I gasped, thinking Morgana would be roasted where she stood.

However, she seemed unharmed. Instead she swung the blade down to the earth and drove it home. The five of us watched in amazement as the white light poured from the blade down into the soil. More than that, it spread out like a huge stain, back towards the rows of pumpkins. It was like fire, only it didn't consume. *It empowered.* The pumpkins shook.

For a moment the ranks of sea dwellers had paused, perhaps smitten by the dazzling lightning. They liked the darkness.

On the upper slopes, all two hundred bloated pumpkin heads were shaking. I saw one begin to rise up, tearing itself from the ground, something from a nightmare. Shoulders, arms, a trunk – an entire body. Deep green, rounded, unfinished, but a body. Those arms unfurled, twice the length of human arms, and for hands there were roots, thick and gnarled, curling fingers of filament. And the faces!

If there are such things as demons, they would have such faces. Blazing eyes, jagged mouths, the scarlet light of hell itself pouring *from within*!

Morgana waved us back and the lines of earth creatures moved forward, down the slope, to meet head on with the sea creatures. Overhead the clouds boiled, like the two gods from remote antiquity watched as their servants tore each other apart. Chaos burst out on the slope as the conflict began. As for me and my companions, we were caught up in that lunatic affray, rushing down on the sea things, possessed by I don't know what, certainly a kind of ancient madness. I felt it coursing through my veins as I shrieked with the utter joy of it. We used our blades, spurred on by Morgana, who had become like some fantastic elemental warrior, clothed in the stormglow. I heard a deep, gurgling sound, the combined voice of the sea creatures, calling out the name of their god, indecipherable yet somehow unnerving. Morgana's curses crashed against the sound like those ragged waves below, equally as potent.

Somewhere deep within me, something stirred, a

memory of life long gone, a primeval striving, a power as dreadful as anything the sea had disgorged. It fed on Morgana's words, on the vivid light in her blade and our combined mental resistance. Our god had a name, and it formed in the air like a blast of anger.

The dreadful contest, the mangling of bodies on either side, the tearing apart of sea thing and pumpkin monster, ensued in a sudden grotesque silence, other than the shriek of the wind and the continuing blasts of thunder and crackle of lightning. It must have gone on for an hour, although we fought in a timeless vacuum. In the end I sagged down, exhausted, expecting to be swamped, but the world had gone still.

Morgana stood over me, her mask removed. Her face looked almost human. She gripped my shoulder, her hand and arm slick with the mess of battle. "They're beaten," she said.

I staggered to my feet and looked down at the beach. Through the littered dead sea things and the smashed remains of many pumpkin creatures, I saw the last of the enemy slinking back to the water. A wave unrolled like a boiling carpet and embraced them, dragging them beyond sight. My companions had all survived, though they were spent, their arms like lead, their bodies coated in the muck of battle. Each of us shook our heads, not quite able to credit what we'd been through.

Morgana raised her blade and kissed the runes. "It will be a long time before they come again. When dawn comes, all traces of these horrors will have been swept clean. Your people will remember Halloween and its storm, but no more than that. What lies out in the deeps will subside and lick its wounds. The Old Magic endures. And preserves."

Inheritance

Ann K. Schwader

This part of the country has too many trees. Too many, too close, and even the last of those famous fall colors isn't helping. Fighting claustrophobia, Zill stares out the window of Thali's Mercedes.

"So, did my mother tell you why she really wants me here?"

Here. Not *home.* Zill has learned to be careful with words, which unlike numbers harbor feelings. She is brilliant with numbers. She is not good at feelings. Her father told her this often when she was growing up, especially when he was drunk.

Which was also often. Toward the end, continually.

Thali shrugs, concentrating on the twisting seaside road towards town. "Only that she was sending you a ticket. And that you'd better use it."

There are breaks in the trees now, but that's not helping either. All Zill can see through those breaks are waves, gray and opaque in the failing light. She can't smell them yet, but her memory fills in: slime and fish guts from her father's last boat, gone from her life for over a decade. There's another scent underneath, but it doesn't bear thinking about. Not this time of year.

She drags herself back to the conversation. "Did she tell you it wasn't round trip?"

Thali keeps her eyes forward. They've been friends

forever, but she's a few years older—and her mother and Zill's are friends, too. Or were.

"Not that it matters,"Zill finally admits. "I owe so much already."

Inheritance. Another word with feelings. Very complicated feelings, and one Zill's mother has been using a lot lately. She has some sort of inheritance here, and if coming home is the only way to claim it—

Thali smiles grimly. "I hear you!"

She's got an MBA, Zill remembers. Those don't come cheap, though she's been doing all right since she moved back last year—a few months after her mother went. She's heading up the Chamber of Commerce, with two businesses of her own.

No wonder she looks so tired. Or at least older than Zill was expecting, when Thali met her at the… *Oops.*

"I'm really grateful you made time for an airport run. Grad school's done a number on my social skills." She hesitates. "Mom was so dead set on me coming, I'm surprised she didn't pick me up herself."

"Your mom's… not getting out much," says Thali. "Nothing wrong with her, I don't think, but she doesn't feel comfortable driving."

Which does not sound at all like the woman Zill's been talking to—every week—for these past couple of years. Shrike Harbor may be a classic small pond, but her mother has always made the biggest splash. Committee meetings, school board, library council: you name it, she's chaired it.

She and her friends have, anyway. Her father used to call them the Seven Pushy Broads.

On a good day.

"Probably just drama." She shrugs. "Like the damn ticket."

Mouth tight with grimly suppressed curiosity, Thali turns back to her driving, sliding the Mercedes into the last long stretch. Zill holds out for almost five minutes.

"It's not like I have much to go back to. That grant I won last year probably won't be renewed." Her hands fist in her lap. "My work isn't going well."

At the quantum level. Literally.

Physics plus math plus magic—that's what she's always called it. And until this fall, the magic still played nice with the math. The physics didn't twist into broken equations that had nothing to do with the shining patterns she revolved in her mind.

Now her dissertation is going nowhere, and the department's losing patience. She can still *see* the answers her advisor wants—from multiple angles at once—but the crude vocabulary of symbols and numbers is failing her.

Every time she almost breaks through, he shoves chalk in her hand and points at the old-school blackboard covering one wall of his office.

"Don't talk. Calculate."

Language for him is worse than useless, a tangle of imprecision. Only the purity of formulae will do. And there are no two-dimensional formulae for what happens—or might be made to happen—in the unseen dimensions beyond. The ones she has always sensed like shadows, behind the tedious three or four every idiot learns in school.

Thali's lip curls. "What a useless piece of—"

"Yeah, but he's still my advisor."

Zill's stomach clenches. *How much of that actually came out my mouth?* Thali's always been able to read her, but either she's gotten scarily better or her own subliminal whining is out of control.

Deep breath time. "And it's not like I can explain any of it to Mom."

"Probably not. Not one of them went to college." Thali's hands tighten on the steering wheel. "Or needed to."

This stark truth silences them both for the next couple of miles, to the first outlying houses. Then Zill feels a sigh rising.

"I still have to try. And you know how she gets this time of year." Another nasty thought strikes her. "She's going to expect me to attend services tomorrow, isn't she?"

In the deepening dusk outside, Shrike Harbor is tidy and well-preserved, not rundown like most fishing villages on this part of the coast. People still bring in good catches, and there's a little light industry. Doesn't look like the refinery's operating right now, but later this fall—

"Have you still got my number in your phone?" Thali asks.

Relieved to have her train of thought derailed, Zill digs in one jacket pocket and checks. Nods.

"Call me later, OK? After you've gotten unpacked and talked to your mother—"

"You think I'll need to?"

Thali looks conspiratorial. "I think you'll need a drink."

※

The house is nearly dark as she walks in. It smells as though it's been closed up a long time, or... *No, that's all it is. Stale air.* Flickering light and indistinct voices guide her back to the living room, where her mother sits wrapped in afghans on the couch. The big television her father bought last year is on as usual; some fake court-room show.

And not another light on in the whole house.

"Well, finally!"

Unfiltered by long distance, her mother's voice grates. Zill steps closer anyhow. "You were just lucky Thali could pick me up. If I'd had to find my own way out here—"

"Athaliah Bishop is certainly not her mother." A slow head-shake reveals thinning white hair. "The girl tries, I suppose, but she's just not."

Thank God. Zill reaches for the table lamp. Bad enough to start arguing with her mother the minute she gets in, without arguing in the dark—not that she hasn't been doing that her whole life.

But when she twists the knob, she wishes she hadn't.

It's not just the hair. It's the eyes—well, mostly the eyes—and the lipsticked line of a once-generous mouth, grown both too narrow and too wide. And the changes may not stop there: even these afghans conceal ankle-length skirts rather than pants.

Why didn't you tell me?

She stifles the question. When you don't come home for over two years, you should expect a few changes. The kind nobody bothers to warn you about, because you really should have been around.

Zill exhales slowly and starts over.

"At least I'm here now." She clutches the handle of her rolling suitcase. "Do you know when Dad's lawyer wants to meet?"

Her mother just blinks. Zill feels a cold sickness: she has misunderstood, or been helped to misunderstand. There is nothing in that will for her. She has been dragged cross-country and forced to buy a return ticket she can't afford, just to satisfy her mother's urge to see her. *Or something*

"I'm only here until November second, Mom." She takes another breath. "If we don't have an appointment yet, maybe you ought to call and—"

"Oh, your father left you something, right enough." Her mother's mouth quirks. "You're a Mason clear through, direct line back. Been proving it half your life. Why else you think I married the man?"

Her… smile…? widens at Zill's confusion. "We'll talk about it tomorrow," she says. "After services."

Driving in with Thali, Zill had glanced away as they passed the old meeting hall, its front porch crowded with corn shocks and pumpkins. Festive it might be, but no decorations could cover so many shadows.

Zill's earliest memories are of this hall crowded to overflowing, lit only by memorial candles set into niches in every wall. One for each community member departed; lost to the sea or industrial accident, to sickness or war. Yet the promise of eternity remains, so long as the people are strong. So long as the chant is raised in its seasons, and the communion Between is maintained—

Not by me, it's not!

Two years, she realizes, has not been long enough. "Sorry," she finally says. "I won't be going."

Tipping her suitcase forward, she starts towing it towards the staircase. Her mother unsnarls herself from the afghans and struggles to her feet.

"Zillah…!"

Zill bumps her luggage up the stairs, drowning out the rest of her mother's protests. The moment she reaches her bedroom door, she's pulling out her phone.

Thali's always been able to read her.

As they pull away from the house, Zill feels a rush of relief. It's a little high school, but that doesn't stop her from checking Thali's glove compartment for the bottle. Pre-party, they used to call it. Jack and Coke in Dixie cups on their way to wherever, just enough to take the edge off.

Looks like Thali's ahead of her tonight. The pint's already unsealed. Zill sneaks a sip before looking around for the soda and cups.

"Sorry," her friend says. "Pretty much nothing in this town stays open late, grocery stores included."

"But not liquor stores. Or bars." Zill rolls her eyes. "Gee, I wonder why."

It takes her another few sips to start talking, but after that she can't stop. The whole weird confrontation with her mother was both more and less than she'd been expecting, and nothing she'd been prepared for.

Though she should have been, after Thali's mom last year.

Staring into the night, Zill hears her own voice at a distance as the shock and disappointment sink in. Maybe it was stupid of her, but she really had believed her father left her something. That she'd have one more semester if her grant didn't get renewed—

"But why wouldn't it?"

Zill blinks back into focus. She's answered this question before, but Thali sounds a lot more interested in the details now. *Physics plus math plus magic.*

It's the last term that's widening the rift with her advisor. The man's blackboard mind cannot stretch into those dimensions. Cannot see that the answers he wants are such a miniscule part of what *is*—and not even the most interesting part. Not the part she's known about all her life, taken all the math she could trying to get close to.

And what, she wonders after another sip, *would he do if he* did *see?*

"He couldn't take it," Thali murmurs. Her windshield reflection looks pleased, though Zill can't think why.

The night outside is total now: no house lights or streetlights or anything to indicate they're heading for a bar in town. Shrike Harbor hasn't got that much town. Maybe Thali's found a roadhouse to do her drinking in since she moved back home?

When she tries to ask, though, something's wrong with her mouth. It's not moving right. There's a slick bitterness at the back of her throat that wasn't there a minute ago.

And the taste is getting worse and the night is getting deeper and no words are coming out—

Thali catches the pint as it slips from her fingers. "I'm so damn sorry, Zill."

Blackout.

※

It isn't the voices upstairs that rouse her. It's the rhythm beneath them, tidal ebb and flow of the Samhain-rite. As it has been conducted every year since Shrike Harbor's founding, and before that in another town laid waste by intolerance and ignorance.

As it must be conducted to maintain communion with those beneath the eternal waters sheltering Y'ha-nthlei, which the government believes destroyed—

"Zill!"

Thali's voice is too far away for her to care. Entangled in the dreams (*the nightmares*) of her childhood, of the old meeting hall overfilled with worshippers and the strange deep ocean scent (*visitors, you must call them visitors*) from the back pews, she whimpers and tries to roll over.

"Fool girl." An older woman's voice, this time. "You gave her too much, and if she—"

Zill's aching head thumps the floor as someone begins shaking her. That someone has grabbed a handful of fabric at her shoulder, though she can't remember what she was wearing last, or how there could possibly be that much to grab.

But she's going to puke if the shaking doesn't stop, so she finally opens her eyes.

Zill doesn't recognize her surroundings immediately. She has only been here once before, on her sixteenth birthday. Sweet sixteen and never been freaked so thoroughly in her life. She'd never looked at her mother and the other six Pushy Broads the same way again.

And that had been only the *first* Oath of Hydra.

Zill blinks once, twice, and the blur above her re-solves into Thali's worried features. She's got some twisty gold thing (*diadem, Zillah*) around her forehead, holding back her dark hair. The rest of her is swathed in ceremonial draperies—just like the ones she's wearing.

"Come on." Thali offers a hand up. " We don't have much time. The service is almost over."

Confusion washes over her as she stumbles to her feet, tripping on folds of heavy fabric. Upstairs, she can hear the last rising choruses of the Samhain-rite. It's been over two years since she last joined in—almost long enough to heal from a language never meant for human throats. Or minds.

But that's not where she is tonight.

The private chapel (*Hydra Mother's fane*) under the meeting hall is smallish, barely large enough for a few plain benches and an altar. She still remembers to glance away from the altar. Candles flicker in iron sconces along the walls, revealing seven robed women—including Thali—waiting for her to clear her head.

The seventh, still half in shadow, is her mother. Her mother as she has only seen her once before, with the high-spiked diadem of primacy settled on her white hair. First of the Seven.

Eldest of the Seven, too. Even candlelight is unkind, and Zill finally sees what she has struggled to ignore: marks of change in every feature, from protuberant eyes to lipless mouth to neck folds disappearing into fabric. Her mother's form underneath is bent and subtly twist-ed, already becoming something *other*—

"I know." Thali grips her shoulder. "I wasn't pre-pared, either."

With her free hand, she passes Zill a goblet. It's made of sea-gold, the same metal shining all around her in the diadems and ornaments of the Seven. Another gift of the communion being celebrated overhead, on this night when barriers between worlds and dimensions flicker.

Zill's fingers clench around the stem.

"Sometimes it helps," says Thali. "But you've got to drink it now." Her voice drops. "Your mother... she can't weave the gate any more. And it only opens out from this side."

Something clicks in Zill's mind at last.

It had happened last winter, though Shrike Harbor's only hospital hadn't called her immediately. A ministroke, they'd said. Her mother had come into the emergency room on her own, been evaluated and treated, and left on her own a few hours later. Against advice, but nobody in town would have stopped her.

What this has to do with weaving—or gates—Zill has no clue.

But Thali's expression makes her drain the goblet in three bitter gulps.

By the time she hands it back, all the candles have greenish halos. Her breathing is ragged, and her heartbeat makes it hard to hear the women around her as they escort her through an open door (*was it open before? was it even there?*) to the right of the altar.

Just beyond that door, the space expands into a cavern. Or a sea cave—though it can't be, this far from the ocean.

Her ears say otherwise. The salt air resonates to the same gray waves she noticed on her way into town yesterday. She and the others are walking over water-smoothed stone now, their bare feet damp. There's a lingering scent, too, one her memory skitters away from.

Then she sees the mouth of the cave.

The roiling translucence that fills it is less sea mist than hallucination: there are no waves beyond it, no rocky shoreline. Only the ocean's depths. A few spikes (*spires? towers?*) of unknown architecture rising from even deeper lend a dim fluorescence—

"Y'ha-nthlei."

Her voice, or Thali's? Either way, it is not a question. As the goblet slips from her fingers, Zill turns to face her friend.

"I still don't understand why I'm here. Whatever Mom did… with *that*… she never mentioned it to me."

In the dimness behind Thali, the diadem of primacy flashes as her mother shuffles forward.

"You already know what you need to. It's in your blood." The corners of her lipless mouth twitch up. "Your Mason blood."

She gestures left and right at the cave walls. As Zill struggles to focus, thin lines of light manifest and begin twisting themselves into half-familiar symbols. Diagrams. Patterns that reach into places she could never make her advisor understand even existed—

"The Keziah formulae." Her mother's hushed voice. Then Thali's, and all the others.

Zill sways on her feet, reaching out with both hands for the patterns now detaching from the stone, shedding symbols in their wake. *Physics plus math plus magic.* They make more sense than any blackboard equation, pure and certain. Obvious. So damn obvious how they run between here and *elsewhere*—

"Yes." Seven voices in the shadows.

Unimpeded by chalk, Zill's hands move freely through the shining patterns, weaving and revolving them. Helping them synchronize with unseen counterparts. *Quantum entanglement*, but there are no tangles here. No flaws or knots in the pattern now opening before her in the mouth of the cave.

At first, she barely hears the footfalls at her back.

Then their scent (*deep ocean strangeness turn your eyes away now*) washes over her, and her fingers move faster. As she feels the last of this pattern (*this gate*) mesh with its partner on the other side, her blurred gaze drops to the cave floor. She keeps it there as the visitors pass through, still chanting some phrase of the evening's rite. A reminder of their communion with the congregation; that all here are of one blood and one destiny, deathless.

After the last has crossed, she is still staring down at the wet stone when a hand fastens on her shoulder.

"Turn around, Zillah. Lift your eyes."

When she does not, cannot, comply, the grip tightens to pain. "Turn around, daughter. See me."

Her mother's features have changed beyond words— almost beyond recognition. Below the sea-gold diadem, eyes clouded with more years than she ever suspected meet hers. Zill struggles not to turn away, even when her mother lifts the diadem from her half-bald scalp and extends it towards her.

Those hands against her own are damp and cold and slippery. *And webbed?* Zill's fingers curl back reflexively, but her mother lifts the diadem higher.

Glittering in the cave's watery light, the object suspended above her head is distinctly misshapen. Oblong. Unlikely to fit any human skull, let alone hers. Yet her mother is lowering it now, clamping it onto her forehead with a strength she never—

White agony blossoms behind her eyes.

Momentarily blinded, dazed with the contents of Thali's goblet, she hears rather than sees her mother's robes slide to the floor. Then flat-footed, claw-scraping steps head for the cave mouth, and the pattern-gate through.

"Keep watching if you can." Thali's voice catches. "I didn't."

Her vision is already shattering, but Zill tries to hold on. There are swimmers on the other side of that gate, now, reaching through dark water to touch the shimmering lines. Her mother stretches out her own arms and leans forward. No one breathes.

Then, with a single splash, she is gone.

Daylight seeps through her eyelids like cold acid. Zill curses, rolls over, and shoves her face into her pillow, wincing at the pain this simple action brings.

Pain and remorse. No matter what she'd been trying to escape, going drinking with Thali last night (*last night?*) was her worst idea ever. Jack and Coke minus the Coke, not even a decent bitch session, and now she's got the mother of all hangovers—

Mother.

The word trips a trigger in her head—or a floodgate for nightmares she's had too little night for. Zill's hands clutch her blankets as the image-torrent rises, sweeping her back into memory, half-lit black waters and shards of a city drowned before Pangaea broke apart. Shining swimmers with gill-fringed throats stare out at her with her mother's face. With the face of Thali's mother, gone last year—

Gasping, she claws herself up into the light of waking. Her bed is a disaster.

As she struggles to pull the quilt straight, her hand closes on cold metal: some fragment of dreaming, sharp-spiked and impossible. Zill lifts it up with bloodied fingers, then carefully lowers it onto her matted hair. Into the fire still encircling her forehead.

It fits perfectly.

Hum—Hurt You. Hum—Hurt You. Hum—Hurt You.

John Shirley

Elwin McGrue was not ready for Halloween. He had not set up his sprinklers, to spray the bastards T.P.-ing his lawn. He hadn't bought the novelty store candy—super sour and super-hot and a few with ants in it—to drop in the bags of any who persisted in tormenting him. He hadn't yet received the mail-order recording of a vicious dog snarling and brutishly barking, which would trigger when anyone came up the walk…

It was already October 30, and he wasn't ready. Something else was troubling him more. The new house, a hundred feet from his, across the circle at the dead end of this street—the brand-new house that no one would ever live in. It bothered him. Indeed, it seemed to target him.

"Sometimes I think you like fighting with the kids on Halloween," said His neighbor Mary Sue.

"I don't relish the conflict, Mary Sue", he said, as he stood on his lawn in the morning mist.

"Certainly, you do, Elwin," she said, locking eyes with him, matching him frown for frown as they faced each other over the wooden fence—the decaying fence she said was on his property and he said was on hers.

Mary Sue was sixty-five, about seven years younger

than him, but just as stubborn. She stood there with her arms crossed, the wind stirring her long, white hair. It was a hair style she'd kept from being a damned hippy in the 1960s, he supposed. Her blue eyes were fading but could be just as chilly as ever. Secretly, he had always admired her.

"No," he said. "It's what happened to Andy."

It was true. McGrue had turned his back on Halloween, long ago, because of what had happened to his grandson, and he wasn't going to have it forced on him.

Her eyes softened at the reminder.

"He was a sweet little boy, Irwin."

"He isn't dead, Mary Sue."

"I know. Sorry."

"These kids now…they're no better than the ones who hurt him…"

And one of those kids, McGrue realized then, was riding down the street on a bike, without his hands on the handle bars. Lon Kimble. Maybe fourteen by now, Elwin thought. Acting like a drunk teenager just to mock him and Mary Sue.

Lon had his hands up in the air, and was whooping, steering by leaning this way and that as he came to the circular cul-de-sac at the end of Skellon.

Skellon Way, with its prominent Dead End sign, followed the top of a small branching ridge, right where the road ended in an ivy grown cliff. The cul-de-sac overlooked another neighborhood street below. Some of the Skellon kids last Halloween had gotten in the half-finished new house—the house where no one was ever intended to live—and stood on the raw wood planks of the second floor throwing bric-a-brac down onto the roofs below.

This kid—Lon was his name— was one the chief culprits, making twisted faces at Elwin as he circled on his bike, look-no-hands, around in the end of the road.

"Hon, I wish you wouldn't ride in a circle, with no

hands," Mary Sue called to him. "You're gonna fall and break something!"

But Lon handily completed the turn, still no hands, giggling out, "Oooh, look I'm gonna fall off the bike and break my ass! Yahhhh!"

McGrue watched in hope, but unfortunately the kid didn't take a header. Off he went, peddling and chortling down the street.

"Disrespectful little bastard," McGrue said. "Behaving like that toward you."

"Oh, I'm an old veteran," she said. "I've got a skin like a rhino by now." She was referring to having been a schoolteacher. She had taught Jr. High English for thirty-seven years before retiring. Teaching was something they had in common. He had taught at the same school, though he'd retired the year after she'd transferred in. He'd taught shop class before the District, in its infinite wisdom, decided that shop class was a waste of money.

He remembered a lot of good kids who spoke respectfully to him, in the early days, called him "Mr. McGrue". He'd liked most of them.

But something was screwing kids up now. Was it cellphones? Videogames? Parents more interested in social media than their kids?

Whatever it was, the kids around here, anyway, were worse than ever.

He couldn't afford to move away. He'd have to sell his house, which wasn't worth much, and live in some old folks' home, no other option. So, he stuck around, clinging like a barnacle to the ridgetop, working on little home repair projects, doing maintenance jobs part time. But now, at the end of the street, was the house not intended to be lived in, the house that buzzed and hummed and kept him awake at night. Sometimes he could feel it, the powerful field put out by the house. Microwaves, electromagnetics? Both? He wasn't sure.

"Mary Sue—your television working okay? Mine's

getting interference from that thing." He nodded toward the buzzing house.

"I don't watch television much. I like to read." She looked at the billowing fog below the ridge. "But I'm having trouble concentrating lately."

"Me too. And it started when they turned that damn thing on, up there."

"We were canvassed, the whole neighborhood was, Elwin. We had hearings about it."

"I was there. But they threw me out."

"You were unruly, Elwin."

"There were going to put in that big cell tower a hundred feet from my house!"

"The whole valley voted against that tower."

"So, what'd they do? They installed that camouflaged monstrosity!"

She sighed. "It looks like a house, it's cosmetic, I guess. I don't like it either. All the people with cell phones voted for it."

"You?" McGrue asked, looking at her with a scowl and narrowed eyes.

The expression on his face made her laugh. "No, Elwin. I've got a cell phone but service before this thing was good enough for me. I guess they all wanted to get all the internet all the time on their phones, or…And there they go."

She nodded toward a young couple pushing a stroller, each with one hand on the stroller and one hand holding up a cell phone. They gazed fixedly at their cell phones as they walked along. Occasionally the woman giggled.

"God help that child," Mary Sue muttered, as the couple pushed the stroller around the circular sidewalk, past the faux house, without looking up from their phones or speaking to one another.

McGrue noticed someone else coming down the sidewalk. "And who's that?"

The stranger wore a shabby gray suit, had noticeably muddy shoes, and toted a largish brown suitcase that looked to be heavy, judging from the way he carried it. McGrue could see the man had a scrappy short white beard, but his face looked fairly young. He wore a gray tweed cap, and had a long nose, a narrow face, red pouting lips.

The stranger paused by the fence and looked over at them. "Good afternoon," he said, touching his hat. Some kind of northeastern accent, McGrue judged, maybe some place like Rhode Island or Connecticut. He set down his suitcase and rubbed his arm. "I'm looking for a house that was built last year—a decorative shell for transmitters…"

"That's it," McGrue said, pointing. "Are you here to burn it down? I'll get you a match."

"Elwin!" Mary Sue hissed. "For heaven's sake!"

The stranger tilted his head and gave him a crooked smile. "The structure is, I take it, problematic?"

"It sure as hell is! You can hear it buzzing and throbbing—you can even feel it! Keeps me awake at night and gives me nightmares. Screws up my television so I can't see the Home Repair Show! Is that problem enough?"

"I see." The stranger looked at the house and said, just loud enough to hear, "Very good."

"Very good, that what you said?" McGrue snorted. "Is misery good?"

The stranger looked back at him and pursed his lips. "No sir. Misery is not good. I hope to end some of mine, here." He flexed his fingers. "Rather too much equipment for one suitcase."

"You're a technician, then? They send you to work on that thing?"

"Ah, well, as to that—I do intend to work on it, yes. I can make certain adjustments." He looked at McGrue quizzically. "I am missing my usual assistant today. You look like a fellow who might be handy? I wonder if I could trouble you to assist me, for just a few minutes. When all is done, I may be able to…modify the device, so it doesn't trouble you. I can even recompense you."

"That right?" Maybe this fellow could make the damned thing less obnoxious. "Why not!"

Mary Sue cleared her throat. "Mr. uh—Could I ask your name?"

"Oh, yes, forgive me, Ma'am. My name is Tillinghast. Oswald Tillinghast."

"I'm Mary Sue Ellsworth, this is Mr. McGrue. Don't you have a company truck, of some kind? I'd think whoever was tasked to work on that thing would be, you know, in an official vehicle…"

"Ah yes, that too is absented along with my assistant. It's a long story. And now I must get to work." He turned to McGrue. "No time like the present, do you agree sir?"

"Sure, let's have a look at the damned thing," McGrue said, stepping out to the sidewalk. "Let me help you with this." He picked up the suitcase.

"Very good of you, Mr. McGrue."

"Elwin—are you sure you should be going into that place?" Mary Sue called after him. "We're not supposed to get near it!"

Who does she think she is, my wife? McGrue thought. "I'll be fine, fine…"

He led the way around the circle at the end of the street, to the final house on Skellon Way. The house where machines lived.

"Really quite extraordinary, their choosing this exact site for the transmitters," Tillinghast said.

"Why's that?" McGrue asked, breathing raspily, beginning to regret offering to carry the suitcase. It was damned heavy.

"It's at the exact convergence of the sympathetic and disharmonious waves from a number of other transmission sources," said Tillinghast, the words tripping lightly off his tongue. "One is a cell phone tower, one is a satellite. The third is a signal bounced from the ionosphere—a signal that started at the HAARP array, thousands of miles north. And then the additional electromagnetic field created by intense microwave transmission from within the house…"

"Seems to me those microwaves are dangerous, down at this level, close to the people living on this street. They said those transmitters were aimed away from us, but I'm not so sure…And look at that!"

They had reached the house, and in front of it, at the foot of the steps, were several dead animals. A dead blue jay was half covered by the body of a striped tabby cat, and, nearby, facing away from the house, lay a dead racoon. All of the animals, McGrue saw now, had no eyes. Only little pockets of dried blood where eyes should be.

McGrue put the suitcase down and pointed at the dead animals. "You see that? I noticed the dead bird the other day…"

"Ah, most disturbing," Tillinghast muttered. "It appears there's already been a preliminary resonance wave."

"A what?"

"Resonance wave—ah, an unfortunate radiation leak as a result of the convergence of several resonation sources. It can be lethal. It's not typical of these cellular telephonic devices. Extraordinary conditions here. And yet, contained and controlled, it can…it can be useful. But it seems there has been an uncontrolled resonance wave here recently, perhaps over several hours. The bird died, the cat investigated and died, and the racoon investigated the first two dead creatures and died itself, trying to get away."

McGrue took a step back from the house. "So—how do you know it's not firing up that way right now?"

"Oh, I would sense it, if it was. I've become quite… attuned to it."

"Sense it?" That sounded kind of nutty. Could be Mary Sue was right? Maybe he shouldn't be here with this guy.

"However, I will check for you..." Tillinghast partly unzipped the suitcase, reached in, rummaged around, and took out what looked like a modified EMR meter. "Now... let me see..." He peered at the instrument. "No, you see, it's in the green range, here. No resonance waves. And I wouldn't expect another for some time— we won't have the full convergence here till tomorrow evening. Shall we go in?"

"You have a key to this place? That door's double locked."

"A key? Of a sort, come along, if you're coming, Mr. McGrue," Tillinghast said briskly. He picked up the suitcase, lugged it up the stairs, then took a tool from his pocket and did something to the front door locks that McGrue couldn't see. He heard a humming sound—and the front door popped open.

McGrue hesitated, looking up at the house—or the faux house, really. It was the equivalent of a cell phone tower disguised as a tree. The microwave transmitters were inside the shell of the house, which at a glance looked like a new, two-story tract home, its dormer windows tinted dark, and four dead junipers in the front yard. The house was eyeless, and empty of soul, and yet it hummed with an unnatural life. He could hear it; feel it in his back teeth. To McGrue it stood for the stupefying excesses of civilization in the twenty-first century.

Should he go in? No. But then again, this guy said he could turn the damn thing down some, and he needed help doing it.

McGrue growled to himself and shook his head, but he went up the stairs.

Inside, he found that Tillinghast had already unpacked the bag in a space behind two humming, circular microwave transmission drums, facing the front windows. There were three metal "drums", each ten feet across. Tillinghast was setting up a tripod.

"Hand me that thing that looks a bit like a small movie projector, if you please, Mr. McGrue…very good." He fitted it onto the top of the tripod, and tightened wingnuts to hold it in place. "This is my own new variation of my grandfather's resonance manipulator. I will be testing it shortly…Ha ha, can you feel the intense electromagnetic field here? Even Tesla would have been impressed. Grandfather knew Tesla, you know, they corresponded…"

"Nikolai Tesla! And your grandfather?"

"Yes. My grandfather was Crawford Tillinghast." He adjusted the manipulator and swiveled it. "You have perhaps heard of him?"

"I don't believe so. This humming…this place is giving me a headache…Smells like something's burning…"

"Crawford Tillinghast was a great scientific genius. His work was suppressed, by the usual bumpkins. I managed to find a way to adapt his system in a more… what is the contemporary expression? Ah! A more 'user friendly' way, ha ha! I will induce a localized resonance wave with this device. But it will be limited to a small area in front of the projector. Hand me that octagonal crystal there, please…"

That peculiarly giddy look on Tillinghast's face, and his odd tendency to articulate each syllable in a burst of laughter—it made McGrue uneasy. "You say your grandfather developed the, um, the prototype of what you have here? It's kinda funny, you working for the cell phone transmission company, and using something in the job that was developed by your grandfather…"

"Funny? Yes! Ha ha!" He clapped his hands together once and wrung them in quiet delight. "Now, I've got the booster ready—and we have the proper convergence of wave-transmissions. I believe we can run a short test, Mr. McGrue!"

McGrue's mouth felt dry. He felt hot and unsteady. "You feel kind of nauseated? Headachy?"

"Oh, that's merely the radiation. We'll soon be done here, for today and the effect will pass. Please be good enough to hold this attenuator…"

He passed McGrue a device that looked like a microphone with two crystal spikes sticking to the sides at the top. "Now, Mr. McGrue, if you will hold that device out at arm's length…Just take a step back…a foot more…that's it…and…hold it steady, a trifle higher…" Tillinghast looked through an eyepiece atop the device that resembled a little movie projector. "Ah ha! It's coming…"

A translucent shimmer emitted from the "projector". A loud repetitive thudding sound shook the walls, followed by a hum that filled the world. Then, over the floor near the front door an oval shape glimmered, rippled, and formed what looked like a window…

Through the vertical oval, McGrue could see a squirming thing resembling a giant centipede with a human head. Above it fluttered a baby with batwings flashing a long black tongue at another creature that was something like a jellyfish with legs. The odd tableau was lit by a sickly green luminosity.

McGrue was coming to the conclusion that Tillinghast was definitely not a cell phone tower repairman.

Something squished into view, within the oval. It was like a giant slug, big as a bear. It reared up, its front end opened and it inhaled the flying baby, swallowed it down, and then galumphed off.

"Oh, my dear God," McGrue said. Surely this was an illusion, a video projection, something unreal…

Flying, transparent, wormlike creatures, long as a man's arm, whipped through the green air in the other world. They squirmed in the air, spitting sparks. Beyond the flying worms was a mist the dull-green of mold—the mist parted, then, to reveal a faintly glowing metal cage.

Standing in the cage was a young man, quite human, waving frantically at them…

"There he is!" Tillinghast crowed. "My assistant! I am relieved to see he's safe. The repulsor cage is holding up! I'm coming, Syl! I'll be there soon! Hold on!"

Then something that looked like a reptilian goat standing on its hind legs stepped up, within the oval, and blocked the view. It was a goat, a man, a snake all at once. It turned to look through the oval with the wickedest eyes McGrue had ever seen. It hissed and bounded forward, then stopped to sniff the air, squatted as if preparing to leap through…It thrust out a scaly hand red and yellow hand, reaching through the oval, into the room with McGrue and Tillinghast.

McGrue, paralyzed with shock, shouted wordlessly.

Tillinghast said, "Don't worry, I'll shut it off, it won't get through! I hope…"

"The Hell with this!" McGrue forced himself to move. He dropped the attenuator and turned to stagger toward the rail-less staircase leading to the second floor. He pounded up the creaking wooden steps, feeling as if that thing with the murderous look on its face was going to pounce on him from behind at any moment. He reached the second floor where another set of microwave drums aimed at the front windows. A dormer window looked out on the weedy backyard. He kicked at the glass, it shattered, he knocked out the ragged bits with an elbow and climbed through, in his hurry moving as lithely as a young man. There was a ladder from the roof line under the window. He scrambled down it to the overgrown grass, and ran, puffing like a locomotive, for his own house.

❈

The next night.
Halloween was barely less boring than any other

damn night, Brian thought. It was cold up here, it was dark, the crickets were calling, some owl was hooting. Whatever. He wanted to be somewhere else, where there was light, and music, maybe dancing. But all he had was this place, and these guys.

He and the new kid Terry and that older kid Lon and his cousin Bud, and little Rudy who trailed after Bud, were all staring at Old Man McGrue's house hoping he'd come outside to get egged. That's what they had in mind this year.

Lon especially liked to go after McGrue, because a few years ago the old guy had tried to get Lon arrested after he chased Andy McGrue off the top of the hill. Brian hadn't been there, but he'd heard about it. Andy was eight years old, dressed like a fairy—his mom had put fairy wings on him for some reason—and that got Lon and the others making fun of him and Andy'd told them to shut up and they'd chased him, throwing rocks at him, and he'd fallen down a steep hillside, cracked into a rock and....*boom*, brain damage. So now he had to wear a special helmet and go to a special school and McGrue blamed Lon, calling him the ringleader. Which actually sounded like Lon. So, Lon had been taken to court and his attorney got him off, saying Lon was just a rambunctious eleven-year-old kid.

So here they were, three years later, with a lot of old eggs. They crouched near the weird house with the machine guts in it, and Brian just did not like to be here. He felt the house putting off pulsations, waves, or something. Whatever it was, it was making him feel kind of sick to his stomach.

And he could hear it. Hum. Hum. Hum. Hum. And then would come HUM HUM HUM and then back to Hum. Hum. Hum....

Maybe it was the pot he'd smoked with his Lon's brother Tommy, but it sure seemed like the hums had another sound in them. Like...*Hum—hurt you. Hum—hurt you. Hum—hurt you.*

Imagination, that part. Right? But the humming itself was something everyone heard. That's why Bud thought it was funny to call the place the Hummer.

"I'm sicka hanging here," he said. "Lon—let's go around behind his house, throw the eggs at his window!"

"Naw, he's got it all fenced really good, hard to get over, barb wire along the top. Too high to see over." Lon spat some of the smokeless tobacco he swiped from his dad. It was already making his teeth brown. "He'd hear us. Probably got a shotgun."

"He totally has a shotgun," Bud said.

"Oooh, a shotgun, cooooool," said young Rudy.

"You'll think it's 'cool' when it blasts your nuts off," said Terry, the tall, goopy looking new kid.

Rudy just looked at him with his mouth open, his big eyes goggling. Brian had to laugh at that.

"I got another idea," Lon said. "There's a ladder out back of the Hummer. We go up on the roof of the Hummer, we pitch the eggs high, so they hit his roof. He'll come outside to see what the hell, then we pepper him with 'em!"

"I don't wanna go up on this thing," Brian said. He heard a new sound, then, from the house—a clattering metal sound. Was someone in there? "I heard something…"

"You're being all scared little bitch on Halloween?" Lon sneered, showing his big mouthful of huge brown teeth with braces on them and too much gums. "'Oh, there's ghosts in the scary house!'"

"Fuck off!"

Lon looked at him, teeth bared in a different way now. "You want to get your ass kicked?"

Brian, who was thirteen, was almost as big as Lon, and not bad in a fight. "Don't be so sure how that'd turn out, dude."

"Oh, come on, Brian," Terry said. "Let's do it. Then

we can put on the stupid masks and get our goddamn candy and see if Dee's having a party."

"I don't think we're invited to that. But whatever." It was some kind of a plan. And he was no fan of McGrue, who'd yelled at him for skateboarding around a supermarket parking lot.

"Goddamn candy, hells-yeah," said little Rudy, making them all laugh.

Some people thought Brian and Lon were too old to trick-or-treat, but dude, free candy is free candy, especially good after a hit on a bong, and Brian had a mask in his coat pocket of Donald Trump with fangs.

"Come on," Lon said, and led the way around back. There was a ladder fixed to the back of the house, so workers could go up to that big metal utility box on the backside of the roof. It was tricky getting the four cartons of eggs up, and one fell, busting most of the shells.

But they managed to get three cartons up, and then Lon said, "Whoa! The windows busted out!"

It was true, the back-dormer window had been shattered, and there was broken glass on the roof.

"I think I heard someone in there, before," Brian said.

"This shit was probably done a long fucking time ago," Lon said. He had his cheap rubber Scream mask hanging from its rubber band down his back, till it was time for trick or treating, and Brian felt a clutching feeling in his gut from the way the mask was looking at him. Like some evil face just lived on Lon's back. "They're gone," Lon went on, looking inside. "Let's check it out. Might be some stuff we can sell. My uncle sells metal stuff. Leave the egg cartons on the roof."

Caught up in a sense of adventure made sharper by Halloween, the others followed Lon inside. Brian hesitated—then decided he had to go along or he'd never hear the end of it.

Inside, those big humming metal drums that pointed out over the valley. And there was another row of them downstairs. "Man, that shit is loud tonight," Terry said.

Hum. Hum. Hum. Hum. HUM HUM HUM HUM.

They looked around, saw nothing but stuff they were afraid to touch. Lon led them to the exposed-wood stairs going down to the first floor—and they all stared down at the man in the funny old suit.

He had a short white beard, a gray cap, and muddy shoes, and he was adjusting something that looked like an old movie projector on a tripod. A little ways away a microphone-type thing with something like crystals on it hung from a string. It was glowing…

"I told you somebody was in here!" Brian burst out, louder than he intended.

The character tinkering with the gizmo turned and looked up at them. "It's ready to go!" he called, shouting over the rising hum. "I must open the way! Get out, the way you came! Get out! Stay away! It'll shut soon and you'll be all right if you just *go!*"

"Fucking burglar telling us to get out!" Lon shouted. There was something strange about Lon's voice. And there was something strange about Lon's face. It was twitching. And his eyes seemed like an animal's, and he was breathing really hard.

"That guy might have a gun!" Terry yelled.

Lon was putting his mask on, maybe thinking of scaring the burglar away so he could take all his stuff.…

He started down the stairs.

But now Brian was looking at the space in front of the tripod machine. It was glowing. It was an oval kind of picture of something hanging in space in front of the closed front door. Through it, Brian could see another place,

"It's one of those Halloween gimmicks people put up to scare you!" Bud yelled. "It's bullshit! It's like a video!"

But Brian plain did not believe that. It didn't just

look real, it *felt* real—he could feel that place from here. It was like he could touch those things from a distance. And they felt nasty.

It was some other...real...*place*—where electric snakes flew around, and a giant slug wriggled by—and a little way further in, there was a man in a cage, waving.

Hum. Hum. Hum. Hum—HURT YOU. HUM-HURT YOU. HUM. HURT YOU.

"I'm coming, Syl!" the burglar yelled. "I'm coming! Open the repulsor!" He rushed at the oval...and jumped through. He was there, in the place beyond, dodging a flying giant worm, sprinting to the cage—which opened up to receive him. The cage floated upward, carrying the two figures away from the portal.

But something was coming at the portal—like it was outside a window and about to break through to Brian and the other kids. It was reptilian goatish thing saying, *"HUM. HURT YOU. HUM. HURT YOU."*

And now it was leaping through, and other things came with it, and Little Rudy was screaming as Lon picked Rudy up and carried him like a sack of potatoes under his arm down the stairs toward the portal...

Was Lon insane going down there?

Brian forced himself to look away and scrambled up the stairs, yelling, "Come on, you guys!"

He heard Bud and Terry and Rudy screaming. But he couldn't go back. The look on that thing's face...that much pure evil, that much rage, that much lust for killing...You see something like that, you ran.

In seconds Brian was through the window, down the ladder and sprinting to find the nearest help.

⁂

McGrue called Mary Sue again, and again she didn't answer, and then he remembered that last year she'd taken her grand nieces to a Halloween party for kids at the YWCA and that's probably where she was tonight. He only had her land-line number, didn't know her cell. Dammit. She might listen to him—she knew him well enough to know he wasn't crazy. Cranky, sure. Crazy, no.

He was having a hard time thinking things through right now. He needed to talk to someone. That hum seemed to get louder and louder. McGrue had barely slept the night before. And when he had slept—nothing but nightmares.

If he could talk to Mary Sue…

He hadn't gone out since he'd seen those things in Tillinghast's window. He just felt like he was too shaken up. He needed to process what he'd seen. Some kind of trick photography? A prank? But somehow, he knew…it just wasn't that.

For the dozenth time he thought about calling the cops. And again, he told himself they'd only laugh at him, or they'd investigate and find nothing, because Tillinghast had shut the thing down and gone away.

But Tillinghast was coming back.

McGrue figured he could drive away somewhere. But he had lived next to Mary Sue for years, he liked her, and he couldn't leave her with that door into hell going on within spitting distance of her house.

So, he lay huddled in his bed, in his bedroom, listening, thinking. The house lights were out except for a lamp in the back bedroom. No trick or treaters bothering him so far.

Then—he heard faint screams. Kids yelling for the hell of it? Or something else?

It seemed to him the humming from the fake house was getting louder…and louder still. The windows began to softly vibrate in their frames.

And a knock came at the door. Someone was yelling out there.

"Mr. McGrue!"

This was something he could deal with—a Halloween prank. He'd open the door, keeping the screen closed, and tell them the cops were coming, and then he'd point the unloaded shotgun to scare them away.

Energized by having something solid to confront, McGrue grabbed the 12-gauge from the closet, and went to the front door.

He hefted the shotgun in his most threatening manner, opened the door

—and saw Brian Worth, that kid with the skateboard he'd given a talking to, standing on the porch, panting, mouth and eyes wide open.

Beyond him were some kind of Halloween costumed kids or...

No.

Those weren't costumes. That thing that was like a boneless human being moving across the grass like a snake, rippling its way to his house—that thing with the face of a boy he'd seen on the street, glowing a faint sickly green.

And the flying creature, the size of a large owl, an infant with large batwings of human flesh, its face contorted—another child's face. It was flying in a zig-zag moth way toward his window.

And that one, a slug with a human face, glowing from within in purple-green coruscations. That was not a costumed child.

Tillinghast was at it again. He'd made an error. He'd let them through...

And there, the goat-headed lizard man McGrue had seen through the portal—head of a snake-skinned goat, body of a nude scaly man, hooves...loping toward McGrue's house. And on its chest, fused there, was a mask from that movie Scream, and as Brian turned to look the mask's mouth opened and showed big teeth and big gums and braces. The boy Lon—melded with the mask.

"Oh fucking shit shit *shit*, it's got Lon inside it!—"

The snake-skinned goat-headed creature, the giant

slug with a boy's face, the snake-thing, coming across his lawn. And over them the flying child flashed by, shrieking, "Mamaaaaa!", then circled to come around again. McGrue opened the screen door and shouted, "Brian get in here!"

McGrue ran to the armoire he kept his shotgun shells in, as Brian rushed in to the house, slammed and locked the front door. McGrue filled his jacket pocket with shotgun shells, cursing to himself and not even sure what profanities he was using.

With trembling fingers he loaded the gun as something shrieked in agony and hate just outside the front door. There was a crash from the living room window, and the flying infant flew in—it had a face of a child about seven but the body of an infant, the legs of a giant fly, and it swished back and forth shrieking for its mother.

Instinctively, McGrue aimed at the flying infant—and then Brian yelled, "No, it's Rudy!" and knocked the gun muzzle up just as McGrue squeezed the trigger. One shell fired and knocked a hole in the ceiling, so that the room choked with a cloud of plaster. The flying infant flew shrieking out the window

—just as the door crashed inward, splintering, and then the snake boy was there, the size of an anaconda swaying in the doorway.

At the broken window the goat-headed lizard man with the cackling Scream-face in its chest was climbing through, snarling, the goat hissing, *"HUM. HURT YOU. HUM. HURT YOU. HUM—"*

McGrue pushed Brian aside and fired the second shell almost point blank into the Scream face.

Lon's mask face vanished in a welter of blood and yellow effluvia, and the goat-thing staggered back. McGrue thumbed in another shell and fired again.

The thing threw its head back and howled, the howl combining with a roaringly loud background hum; a hum and a howl and a bellow of rage…

McGrue reloaded the gun and the thing turned and fled across the lawn.

Brian was throwing a brass vase at the snake. "Get out of here, Terry! He'll kill you!"

The snake turned and rippled into the shadows out front.

Heart pounding, McGrue, ran through the door. Time seemed to move in staccato flashes. From somewhere, a siren screamed, seamless with the sound from the goat-headed thing rushing into the fake house. And McGrue heard, *"HUM. HURT YOU. HUM. HURT YOU. YOU. YOU..."*

McGrue ran across the lawn, through the gate, and it seemed to take forever for him to reach the house. His lungs and knees ached. He just knew he had to kill that thing, had to send it definitely away from this world forever...

The front door of the false house was open, waves of energy rolled through it, invisible but palpable, like a current trying to press McGrue back. But he pushed upstream, climbed the stairs, entered the house—and saw the goat-headed thing turn toward him, hissing, in front of the shimmering portal.

"You're the one changed those kids!" McGrue shouted, even as the realization came to him. He fired one barrel from the hip and the thing was knocked off its hooved feet, backwards through the portal. The second shot he aimed at the projector.

It shattered, in a coruscation of sparks, and the portal vanished. Then the projector burst into flame—and the flame seemed to feed on the very air, spreading out, coming at McGrue in a wall of fire.

He turned, stumbled out the door, almost fell down the steps. Brian was there, now, steadying him, helping him down.

The light of the fire made the circular street area as bright as day, and McGrue felt the heat on the back of his neck.

Brian helped him back to the house…and he saw three kids curled up in the grass. They were moving, but shaking, weeping. But back to human again.

Brian went to kneel by the smallest one—Rudy, was it?—and McGrue found his way into the house, tossed his shotgun on the sofa, and sank down beside it, gasping.

Four days later. McGrue woke up groggy, the sleeping pill still with him. What was that sound?

Hammering, from the front of the house.

He pulled on his pants, and came out into the living room, to find plywood over the front window, someone nailing it in place from the outside.

McGrue went to the front porch and found Brian, nails in his mouth, a stepladder set up, nailing up the last corner of the plywood.

"Kid, what the hell?"

Brian climbed off the stepladder and took the nails from his mouth. He shrugged ruefully. "I…um…you had flies and stuff getting into your house. Mary Sue said it'd be okay. She loaned me the ladder."

"Oh, she did, did she." He went to look. Was surprised. "You did a good job. Not a crooked nail. The whole thing's squared. Nailed minimally because…temporary. Where'd you learn that?"

"My dad was a construction guy. He taught me some. I always thought I might want…"

"What?"

"To be a carpenter. Or something. Maybe make cabinets."

"No kidding?" McGrue rubbed his forehead. "Damn I need coffee. Well—thanks, Brian. I should've done that myself. And you did a good job, I gotta admit."

"That's okay, Mr. McGrue." The kid beamed at the compliment.

Mary Sue came to the gate, and, despite his pajama top, pants with no shoes, and rumpled hair, McGrue walked out through the crisp November morning to join her. They looked at the burned-out shell of the cellphone transmitter house.

"The police been back?" she asked.

"Naw, they went with the kids smoking pot and seeing things and an electrical fire. That's the official line. And that Lon kid vandalizing my house."

"He still hasn't turned up."

McGrue thought, *And he never will.* But he didn't say it. He and Brian had decided, that night, they shouldn't tell anyone what had happened. Neither wanted to be ridiculed. And neither wanted to think about that night any more than they had to. The three other boys didn't remember much of anything.

"Looks like the boy did a good job blocking up your window."

"Yeah. I guess...I could teach him some stuff. He's got talent. Maybe want to learn more about woodworking..."

"McGrue—is that icy heart of yours melting? It's going to run down onto your shoes."

He laughed softly. "I don't know." He smoothed down his hair with a hand. "I must look like a bum. I should go in and clean up. Maybe you and the kid could come over for, I don't know, hot chocolate."

A teenage couple was walking down the sidewalk together, hand in hand, their other hands occupied by their cell phones. They gazed fixedly at the cell phone screens. They passed McGrue and Mary Sue, never looking up from their phones.

And as they passed, McGrue heard a sound from the phone speakers. The same from both phones...

"HUM. HURT YOU. HUM. HURT YOU."

Cosmic Cola

Lucy A. Snyder

Millie leaned her forehead against the back window of her stepfather's new Toyota van, morosely watching the weather-beaten, navy-on-white "Welcome to Marsh Landing!" sign approach and recede. Welcome to what? There was little but some bone-white dunes and shuttered, peeling bait shacks so far. Nothing she'd learned about the isolated coastal town in her school's library made her feel any better about moving here. Population: twenty thousand. Primary export: fish and Cosmic Cola. Total Dullsville. It was probably one of those stuffy communities that forbade trick-or-treat at Halloween. Marsh Middle School was barely half the size of her old school and didn't have any Girl Scouts troops she could join. It didn't even have an orchestra. She'd only just started playing violin and already she was going to have to quit, probably.

Quitters never got anywhere in life. That's what her grandfather Ernest always used to tell her anyhow, before he had a stroke and quit living. In the months before he died, he'd argue about physics when he was alone in his room, as if the empty walls were his audience. She could play her violin in her room and pretend she had an audience, she supposed, but her bedroom walls wouldn't tell her if she dropped a note, or if her bowing was scratchy, or if her phrasing was awkward. So even if she kept going on her own, she wasn't sure she'd get anywhere anyway.

If she was honest with herself, giving up violin didn't bother her nearly as much as the notion of giving up Halloween. It was her favorite holiday, even better than Christmas, though she could never say that out loud. Her mom would say it wasn't *ladylike* to prefer Halloween over Jesus' birthday. And her love for it wasn't just because of trick-or-treating. It was the one night when all the things she dreamed of seemed like they could actually become real. The one night when she didn't have to always be nice and demure and could be something besides a girl from a little town in a flyover state. She could be a ghost. A witch. A werewolf. Something mythical, something to be feared and respected. Running down the street in her costume, she could close her eyes in the frosty fall air and just for a moment imagine that plastic teeth and waxy paints were enamel and skin, and she could go anywhere at all that she wanted on her own. What was Christmas compared to the chilly frisson of *becoming*?

"Gimme!" On the middle seat, her little half-brother Travis reached for his twin sister's Cabbage Patch doll.

"Nooo!" Tiffany hugged the doll to her chest and turned away from her brother's grabby hands. "Mooom!"

"Leave your sister's toys alone." Their mother's tone was one of utter exhaustion. Was exhaustion an emotion, or the lack of it? Millie wasn't sure. "Play with your Star Wars figures."

"Fifty," Millie announced.

"What?" Her mother turned in her seat and squinted at her tiredly.

"That's the fiftieth time you've said those exact words on this trip."

Her mother's lips twitched into a half-smile. "You counted?"

"I did." Millie couldn't keep the satisfaction out of her voice. She was *very* good at counting. Last year she'd won a fifty-dollar gift certificate in a contest at Harmon's

Grocery to guess how many jellybeans were in a big jar, and was a little sad afterward when she found out that since she won once she couldn't compete again. She'd missed the count by two hundred and forty eight, and was sure she could have done even better the next time.

Her stepfather cleared his throat, obviously annoyed. "Doesn't Madame Curie have a book to read?"

Her mother shot him a dirty look but didn't say anything. Millie felt her face grow hot. Her stepfather had started calling her "Madame Curie" after she won the school science fair with her homemade electrolysis set. And at first it had seemed like a nice thing, as if after five years of being her stepfather he was starting to like her a little bit and to be proud of her accomplishments, like he was proud of Tiffany and Travis. After all, Marie Curie was the only person in history to win Nobel Prizes in two different sciences! So calling her Madame Curie couldn't really be a bad thing, could it? But the way he started saying it after the first couple of times … it tasted like a razor blade inside a Tootsie Roll. But if she said anything, he'd just accuse her of not being able to take a compliment. Of not having a sense of humor. Of being a brat.

"I *had* a book to read," she said, trying to keep her voice steady, "and I read it."

"Then you should have brought more." His tone was hard as the pavement beneath his van's black tires.

"I brought *four*. And I read them all." Her heart was beating so fast her vision was starting to twitch.

The twins had gone silent in the seat in front of her, like nest-bound fledglings beneath the shadow of a hawk.

"You did *not* read four books in the past six hours." He stared at her in the rearview mirror, his gaze as steady as any raptor's.

"Did, too." She grabbed her library book sale copies of *Bunnicula, Superfudge, Blubber*, and *From the Mixed-Up Files of Mrs. Basil E. Frankweiler* and held them up so he could see them. "I read them cover to cover. Ask me about them. Ask me *anything.*"

She wasn't lying, and she knew that he hadn't enough of a clue about any of the books to even begin to question her about them. He'd made it clear he considered them to be kids' books, *girl* books, and he was a man. A man with a brand-new van and a fancy important job. Nothing in the books could interest him, so why bother? The idea of seeking a subject to discuss with his stepdaughter was so far from his orbit it could take him millennia to discover it.

"If you were so busy reading back there, how could you possibly know what your mother said to the twins?" There was a talon of warning in his tone: she had better stop challenging him, or else.

Or else what? she wondered bitterly. *Or else you'll take me away from everything I care about and drop me in some dumpy awful town that probably stinks of fish? Just because you got a job at some stupid soft drink company?*

Why couldn't he have gone away to work and left them where they were? Other dads did that to keep from uprooting their families. But her half-siblings weren't in school yet, so she was the only one being uprooted. Her real father had brought her mother to Greensburg so they could be closer to his father, and Mom hadn't liked it there since Grandpa Ernest died. She said that seeing his old room every day made her feel sad. And Millie wanted her mom to be happy. She *did*. But … ugh.

"I can count and read at the same time," she replied defiantly.

"Hey, look, it's our street," her mother exclaimed in the loud, overly cheery tone she used when she was trying to distract her stepfather.

"Craftsman Lane!" She patted his hand on the steering wheel. "This is so exciting, isn't it honey? Our first real house together!"

Millie glared down at her lap, feeling a spike of irritation at her mom's comment. The old house had been real enough, but Millie's father bought it before he died, and so it wasn't *their* house. But now they could move someplace new and pretend that Millie's real father had never even existed. It wasn't fair.

"Oh, what a lovely hibiscus!" her mother said.

Millie finally looked out the window and blinked in surprise. They had gone from dunes and bait shacks to a proper town with tree-shaded neighborhood streets. Teen boys were kicking a soccer ball around on a well-kept corner field. This place didn't look *too* bad, she had to admit. Maybe there would be some kids her age in the neighborhood? She hadn't had a lot of friends at her old school. She and Chrissy Romano were pretty tight, at least until Chrissy started having eyes for Mike Walhgren. Millie walked to school with Jeff Laramie for years and had thought of him as a friend until he joined Little League and decided he was too cool to hang out with girls. Sixth grade was confusing; everybody wanted to be with the boys and nobody wanted to spend time with Millie.

So, maybe seventh grade would be better? Maybe meeting new kids would be the one good thing about having to leave everything she knew behind?

Her stepfather slowed in front of a three-story white Victorian with a wraparound porch. "And here's our new home!"

Millie couldn't take her eyes off the amazing porch. It had steps wide enough for pumpkins on each side, and a railing that was begging to be decorated. "That's the perfect Halloween porch!"

"Aren't you getting a little old for Halloween?" her stepfather said.

"Not yet," Millie suddenly felt anxious. She couldn't tell from his tone if he was being serious.

"I think you are." He pulled the van into the driveway and parked. "I think you're getting much too old for things like Halloween and trick-or-treating."

"You said *teenagers* are too old. I'm not a teenager. Not until next April." She turned to her mother, her stomach churning. She *couldn't* be too old for Halloween. Not yet. "You said I could still trick-or-treat this year."

"Oh, honey, that's a whole three months away," her mother said. "Let's go in and see our new home!"

🏵

The house was fine. Millie's new room got too much sun in the mornings, but as her mother pointed out, at least she wasn't running late for school any more. Her stepfather was frequently gone on Cosmic Cola business—he bought her mother a Honda Civic so they wouldn't have to share his van—and frankly his absence was a relief. And Marsh Middle School was fine, too, at least as far as her classes went.

The kids were weird, though. She was used to the cliques at Wendover: orchestra kids, theatre kids, rich kids, poor kids. Pretty kids from wealthy families who were good at sports were at the top, and the special ed kids and the immigrant kids from poor families were at the bottom. It wasn't fair but it made sense. But at Marsh, it was mostly about whose families had been around the longest. Even the kid with crooked, discolored teeth and a limp got to sit with the popular kids at lunch because he was a real Marsh. So did the kid with the threadbare clothes. Sure, they had a hierarchy within their hierarchy, but nobody who was "new blood" got let into that club no matter how cool they were. And apparently you could still be new blood even if your family had lived in the town for several generations ... but meanwhile some of the other kids were considered old blood even though they'd moved to town just a few years before. The situation wasn't any fairer than at Wendover, and Millie couldn't quite make sense of it, not entirely.

The old blood kids were actually friendlier to Millie than they were to some of the new blood kids they'd grown up with, simply because when the teachers introduced her, they made sure to mention that her father was the new Vice President of Operations for Cosmic Cola. Millie never would have guessed that being the daughter of an executive at the soda company would be such a big deal. It was nearly as good as being a featured soloist in the choir! She didn't make new friends, not like Chrissy had been, anyway, but she always had a place to sit at lunch and people to talk to and nobody picked on her.

Once she realized the social advantage she had, she could never let on that she didn't even *like* Cosmic Cola. It was sickly sweet, and it had an unpleasant licorice aftertaste. And the bubbles seemed too harsh and made her sneeze. Everybody in town seemed to drink gallons of the stuff. Whenever someone offered her a bottle, she'd politely pretend to sip it and then pour it out first chance she got.

Late summer cooled to fall, and at the end of September the janitors festooned the school in black-and-orange streamers and grinning paper Jack-o-Lanterns, black cats, and green-faced witches. Millie was thrilled! Marsh Middle School was far more keen on Halloween than her old school was. And not only did the town have an official trick-or-treat planned from 6:00 to 8:00 PM on Halloween, they had special Devil's Night parties planned for older kids and teens on the days leading up to Halloween to prevent pranks and other mischief in town.

The biggest Devil's Night party—or at least the most *important* party as far as her classmates were concerned—was the Cosmic Cola Party at Marsh Mansion up on the cliff above the ocean. None of the Marsh family lived there anymore; old Jeremiah Marsh had donated it to the soda company for charity events and executive retreats. They'd get to ride in a chartered bus up the winding road to the mansion, and at the party they'd dance and drink Cosmic Cola and eat pizza and play games. All that, on the face of it, didn't seem so impressive to Millie, but the old blood kids all talked about how their parents had said that the company was bringing in a super-secret special guest to play at the party. Some said it might be Aerosmith ... others claimed it was Duran Duran or even Michael Jackson.

Millie's mother said she was far too young to go to a rock concert, so to think that she might be able to see someone as famous as Michael Jackson ... that was *most* impressive. And even better, because the party ran so late, all the kids who attended would be excused from class the next day.

The catch was that only thirty kids from Marsh Middle School could attend the party, and they'd be chosen in a special lottery in mid-October. Everyone got one ticket, but students could earn extra tickets by making As, volunteering to help out around the school, and other such things. By October seventh, she'd earned seven lottery tickets thanks to her good grades in math, English and history and a couple afternoons picking up trash. Seven was more than most kids, but she guessed that there were probably nine hundred tickets total for the three hundred kids in the school, which meant that her efforts had earned her only of a fraction of a percent of a chance.

And then she had a worrisome thought.

"Papa, I was wondering about something," she said that night at dinner. Her mother and stepfather preferred that she called him Papa, rather than Steve or Mr. Gibbs. Calling him that almost didn't seem unnatural anymore.

"Yes?" He took a bite of meatloaf. "What is it?"

"The Cosmic Cola party ... you work for the company. I won't be excluded from the lottery, will I?"

"No, not at all," he replied cheerfully. "You've got as much of a chance as any other kid. Better, I expect, since you got all those extra tickets."

Her mother suddenly looked anxious. "You shouldn't get your hopes up, dear. So few kids get picked. But don't worry; there are plenty of other parties that evening. There'll be a sock hop party at DiLouie's Pizza; that sounds like fun, don't you think?"

Millie shrugged and ate her mashed potatoes. The pizza parlor wouldn't have Michael Jackson except on the jukebox.

Her stepfather fixed a sharp gaze on her mother. "But if she *is* chosen, it's an honor to go."

He turned back to Millie and smiled. "Cosmic Cola is putting a lot of effort and money into this party for you kids. If you're chosen, you'll be representing our whole family, so you need to be on your best behavior. Can I count on you?"

His words made Millie feel uneasy; how could a party for a bunch of middle schoolers really be such a big deal? But she knew what he wanted to hear. "Yes, sir. You can count on me."

She looked at her mother; Mrs. Gibbs' face had gone white and she was staring down at her half-eaten plate. Her expression was carefully blank but her eyes shimmered as if she were holding back tears. It was then that Millie realized that her mother was not happy, and something was happening here that Millie could but dimly grasp. She wanted to go around the table to give her mother a hug, but she knew that would break some unwritten, unspoken rule; her mother would be embarrassed and her stepfather would be angry, but neither adult would tell her what was wrong. Millie felt as though she were on a boat adrift far from shore beneath storm-gathering skies.

The school's portly vice principal reached into the clear plastic raffle tumbler full of names on folded white notecards. He picked one out and opened it with a theatrical flourish.

"Millie Flynn," he announced into his microphone.

Millie sat in shock on the wooden gymnasium bleacher at hearing her name called. The girl beside her started shrieking in excitement and shaking her shoulder, and soon Millie was whooping and high-fiving the other kids near her who'd been chosen for the party, too.

After the school assembly was over, Millie had study hall, and her excitement faded into curiosity. She and twenty-one other new blood kids and eight old blood kids had been picked. Why had so few kids from established families won seats on the bus? The kid with the limp and the crooked, discolored teeth was one of them. She still wasn't sure what his name was. But, she reasoned, the old blood kids hadn't tried very hard. They hadn't been the ones volunteering for chores to earn extra tickets. They hadn't studied late trying to earn straight As. They weren't the ones who had to prove they belonged in Marsh Landing.

When she got home and told her parents the news, her stepfather seemed pleased and her mother smiled and congratulated her. Millie could see something like panic behind her eyes. That night after dinner, her father went to his Cosmic Cola bowling league, and her mother put the twins to bed.

As Millie was helping her mother wash and dry the dishes, her mother asked, "Have you thought about the costume you'll wear to the party?"

Millie considered. "A little. I liked being a witch last year, but my dress and stockings are too small now."

Her mother smiled, her eyes still dark with worry. "You've shot up like a weed this past year. You're nearly as tall as I am, now."

"Maybe I could be a werewolf this year? I saw a cool mask in the window of the costume shop."

"I had an idea," her mother said, looking around as if she was making sure that her stepfather wasn't still in the house. "Why don't you go as a pirate queen?"

Millie blinked. "A pirate queen?"

"They probably didn't tell you this in school, but a lot of women were very fierce pirates back in the day. Jacquotte Delahaye was a Caribbean pirate in the 1600s. They called her 'Back from the Dead Red' after she faked her own death to escape the British Navy. She became a pirate after her father died and eventually she became a master swordswoman and commanded a fleet of hundreds of pirates. She ruled over her own island. I think ruling your own island makes you a proper queen, don't you think?"

"Whoa," Millie said. Already in her mind she was swashbuckling on a beach, protecting a loot-laden chest from scowling English redcoats in pompous white wigs. "Yeah, for sure!"

Her mother dried the last dish and put it away in the cupboard. Her hand shook just a little as she set it down. "I was out shopping at the thrift store the other day, and I found some things some things in your size that I think would make a good pirate costume. Would you like to see them?"

"Ooh, yes!" Millie clapped her hands.

Her mother led her down into her sewing room in the finished basement.

"I found this." Her mother reached into a white plastic shopping bag and pulled out a gorgeous wig of long, thickly ringleted red hair. It looked like something from a fancy salon and not a cheap dimestore Halloween wig.

"It's so pretty!" Millie breathed.

Her mother looked pleased, but the fearful shadows hadn't left her eyes. "Well, Back From the Dead Red needs proper red hair!" She pulled out another shopping bag and laid out a rakish blue scarf, a poofy-sleeved white shirt with laces instead of buttons, a black leatherette vest, tan pants, a thick black belt, black knee-high boots, and a bunch of golden bangles. And a real genuine brass compass! It was so much nicer than the ones they'd learned to read in Girl Scouts, and it looked like something a real pirate would own.

Millie threw her arms around her mother's neck. "This is great! Thank you sooo much!"

Trembling, her mother returned the hug, rubbing Millie's back in gentle circles. "It's your last Halloween, and you're going to a very important party, so I wanted you to feel proud of your costume."

Millie hugged her mother more tightly. "You're the best."

Her mother began to cry and shake.

Millie pulled back and gazed at her mother, worried. "What's the matter, Mom?"

"Nothing, nothing." Her mother quickly wiped her red eyes and smiled widely. Unconvincingly. "I … you're just growing up so quickly. It makes me sad sometimes."

Her mother glanced at the compass lying beside the costume on the sewing table. "You remember how to use a compass, don't you?"

"Oh, yes, absolutely. It was my favorite part of camp craft!" That was a little lie; really Millie had liked building fires best, but she knew that didn't sound ladylike.

Her mother was still blinking back tears. "I think having a compass is a good idea in case they take you out someplace and you get separated from the rest of the kids. It's easy to get lost in an unfamiliar town, you know?"

Millie didn't, but she nodded anyway.

"Marsh Mansion is due southeast of here. If you had

to get back here on your own, go north on Oceanside Highway and follow it to Sixth Street, go left, and then take a left on Craftsman Lane. And you'll find us!"

That sounded like a whole lot of walking. "If I got lost, couldn't I just find a payphone and call you?"

"Oh, honey, that's a smart idea but not on Devil's Night," her mother replied quickly. "Your stepfather's concerned about prank callers and he's planning to leave the phone off the hook. So if something happens, just try to get back here, okay? I'll stay up waiting for you; just knock quietly and I'll know it's you. If it's late, we don't want to wake the twins or your stepfather. He hasn't been sleeping well and you know what a terrible mood he gets in when something wakes him suddenly."

Millie did. "Okay, I'll just come back and knock quietly if something happens."

"But nothing will! This is all just for contingency's sake. I'm sure you'll have a wonderful time."

"Okay."

A flash of remembering crossed her mother's face. "Oh! And I forgot the most important part of your costume." She went to the closet and retrieved a long white cardboard box. Inside was a cutlass with a tarnished brass basket guard in a worn leather scabbard. When she pulled the blade out a few inches, it gleamed steely and cold.

Millie could barely believe her eyes. "Whoa, is that a real sword?"

"It's a costume sword, but it's still pretty sharp, so don't go waving it around. Can you believe that this was actually cheaper at the thrift store than a plastic pirate's cutlass at the toy shop? Prices these days! Anyhow, this looks better with your costume, and you're mature enough to leave it sheathed so nobody knows it's dangerous, aren't you?"

Millie nodded vigorously. Her own real sword! "I'll just tell people it's wooden."

Her mother smiled again, looking relieved. "Good

girl. I have one more thing."

From the pocket of her apron, she pulled out a silvery flask, the kind Old West gamblers and gangsters put liquor in. "I know you don't really like Cosmic Cola, and that's practically the only thing they'll be serving at the party. This way, you can take something else to drink. Just, try not to let anybody see you with it, or they might think you have something you shouldn't. And that would have … consequences." She paused, rubbing her throat lightly. "Don't tell your stepfather about the flask. Or the sword. He wouldn't approve."

"I won't." Inside, Millie glowed with pleasure at her mother taking her into such confidence. Her own sword *and* a flask? This wasn't just the kind of cool boy stuff she'd previously been forbidden from on the grounds it wasn't ladylike; this was actual grown-up stuff! She was treating Millie like she was an adult! *Finally*!

Her mother smiled. "Well, it's an hour until your bedtime … want to go outside and carve a pumpkin or two?"

"Ooh, yes!" This was going to be the best Halloween *ever*!

❈

On Devil's Night, Millie's stepfather had some kind of meeting he had to go to, so he wasn't around when her mother helped her get dressed in her pirate costume for the party.

"There." Her mother adjusted the red wig, which was much heavier than Millie had expected, as was the lemonade-filled flask in the inside pocket of her vest. Even the brass compass rested more heavily than she expected in her right hip pocket. And the brass-hilted sword hanging against her left hip—Millie had spray-painted it in brown Rustoleum so it looked a little less suspiciously real—was heaviest of all. "Perfect. Turn around and take a look."

Millie did. The wig and her mother's makeup job to give her a proper Caribbean tan made her look much older, but more important, she looked like a real pirate!

"This is so cool! Thank you!" She hugged her mom.

Her mom hugged her back tightly. "You know I love you, right?"

"Of course," Millie mumbled into her mom's shoulder.

"I love you bunches and bunches. I know that, sometimes, I do things that don't seem fair, and I'm sorry about that. I just can't change how some things are. Steve and I have to worry about what's best for the twins, and … well, let's get you to the party."

By the time Millie's mother dropped her off at the school stadium parking lot, the twenty-nine other kids were clustered under a tall light, giggling and horsing around as they waited for the Cosmic Cola chartered bus to pick them up. Fifteen boys, and fifteen girls. Seven of the girls were dressed up as different kinds of witches; three were fairy princesses, three were black cats, and one was dressed as Princess Leia. The boys had a more diverse set of costumes; Millie figured it was because they had more movie characters to pick from. There was a Han Solo, an Indiana Jones, a cop, two Karate Kids, a Captain Kirk, three Ghostbusters, a Rocky Balboa, a Batman, a Superman, a solider, a masked slasher … and a pirate captain, who she was dismayed to realize was the old blood kid with the limp and crooked teeth. It made her feel weird that they'd chosen similar costumes. She felt her cheeks heat with embarrassment when he looked up at her and grinned and waved.

The Cosmic Cola bus rolled up, and a pretty woman in a mini-skirted black-tie magician's costume stepped out onto the pavement. The boys whispered she was dressed like a character named Zatanna from the comics, and once again Millie was annoyed that her parents had forbidden comic books, because she hated knowing less than the others.

"Hey, kids!" Zatanna beamed at them all. "Are you ready for the party?"

The crowd exploded in "Yeah!" and "Woo!"

"Well, everybody get on! Your party awaits!"

Millie was swept up in the boiling wave of seventh graders and shoved onto the bus. She stumbled into a row and plopped down on the plush red velvet window seat ... and her heart dropped when the weird kid sat down beside her.

"Hey." He extended his hand. "My name's Hubert."

She awkwardly took his hand and shook it. "I'm Millie."

"Yes, I know. Your father's the new executive. He must be so proud that you got chosen."

Millie squirmed in her seat; Hubert was looking at her so intently, and ... it was all just so weird. "Yeah, I mean, I guess."

"*My* father's *super* proud." Hubert gave her a snaggle-toothed smile. "He was always so disappointed that I was born with my legs messed up, and the doctors couldn't really fix them, but now I get to do something really good for the whole family tonight."

"Why is this party such a big deal?"

"Well, it's the thirty year, and ..." He paused, wincing a little, seeming to realize that maybe he'd said something he shouldn't. "Well, it's just going to be something special. You'll see."

Zatanna went up and down the aisle with a narrow serving cart laden with apple cider donuts, popcorn balls, bags of chips, frosted Halloween cookies, and of course cans of Cosmic Cola.

"They'll have pizza at the party, too." Hubert grabbed

double-fistfuls of donuts. "You want something?"

"No, thank you; I'm saving room for pizza." Feeling unsettled, Millie turned away to watch the Marsh Landing Lighthouse and the rest of the dark landscape pass outside the bus windows.

⁂

They reached Marsh Mansion just before 9:00 PM. It was a huge old place, built on a low cliff above the ocean, all covered in Victorian gingerbread and wrought iron balconies and railings.

Zatanna and the bus driver—a gruff, heavyset man who'd been silent the entire trip—ushered them all off the bus and into the mansion's vaulted foyer.

"Last year, we had the party in the second-floor ballroom, but there was a leak and some of the ceiling came down last week," Zatanna said brightly. "So this year, the party is in the downstairs grotto."

She opened up a pair of double doors at the side of the foyer that revealed wide stone steps with a wrought iron wall railing that coiled downward. The bass line of Michael Jackson's "Thriller" boomed faintly from below. "Everybody, follow me!"

The kids all jostled down the stairs. Millie gripped the iron railing, partly to avoid getting knocked over, but partly to still her nerves, which had been jangling ever since Hubert's comment. She felt badly for judging the boy on his looks, but it wasn't just his looks that made her recoil, and her instincts told her that anything he liked, she should be wary of. But that was silly; everyone said this party was a huge honor. Everyone. Her stepfather, her mother, the vice principal, the other kids. It wasn't possible that everyone could be wrong.

The railing was very cold, and slick from condensation. The air grew colder and damper and the music got louder as they went down, down at least three stories into the earth. She was glad for the cover of her vest. The widely spiraling stairs were at first lit with electric lights, but those changed to guttering, Medieval-looking torches in iron sconces.

"Mind the open flames!" Zatanna called up over the music. "Don't get burned!"

Just as the music switched to Duran Duran's "Hungry Like The Wolf," the stairs opened up into a big natural cave whose walls were strung with white-and-orange string lights. Along the left side was a big buffet line with a half-dozen pizzas from DiLouie's in white cardboard boxes and few steel banquet serving bins atop flickering Sterno cans. At the end of the long table beyond the food were plastic tubs of different flavors of Cosmic Colas on ice. There wasn't even any water. Millie was glad she brought her flask.

On the right side of the cave were some big heavy steel barn doors which had either corroded or were painted a rust brown. A bit of water puddled beneath them, and Millie wondered where they led.

The side of the cave directly opposite the stairs held a raised stage with a few big speakers and some sound equipment but no instruments. A DJ in a black turtleneck and jeans and a pair of huge headphones sat at a sound panel with a couple of turntables and reel-to-reel deck beside the stage. He gave her a little wave when he noticed her staring at him, and that made her flush with embarrassment and look away. And when she looked away, she noticed four other men—Chaperones? Security guards?—standing quietly in alcoves carved into the limestone walls. They were also dressed in black, and at first glance she thought they were statues or decorative dummies, but then one scratched his nose.

"Dig in, kids!" Zatanna shouted over the booming music. "Our very special musical guest will be out in a little while!"

The seventh graders swarmed to the food line, chattering and pogoing with excitement as they flopped pizza onto paper plates with greasy fingers. The other kids had gotten increasingly rambunctious as they'd drunk more soda and eaten more sweets, and the louder they all got, the more Millie lost her appetite and wished she could be someplace that wasn't so noisy. And that frustrated her. She was finally someplace cool with the cool kids; why couldn't she enjoy it? Why couldn't she just join in like everybody else?

Was this what getting old was like? To feel isolated in the middle of huge crowd and want to be someplace quiet? To feel oppressed rather than privileged to be in the middle of something everybody said was cool?

The DJ cued up Madonna's "Holiday" and a bunch of the kids started dancing, Cosmic Cola cans sloshing in their hands.

"You should get some pizza!" Hubert yelled at her elbow.

She turned toward him, startled. His eyes were glassy, and he had an enormous grin on his sweaty, flushed face. He gripped what had to be his third or fourth Cosmic Cola of the evening.

"I will," she yelled back. "In a minute or two!"

"Okay," he replied. "I'm not trying to boss you. It's just you should enjoy yourself! You earned it!"

I should, she thought. *I should stop being a stick in the mud and get some pizza, at least.*

Just as she made her way to the back of the buffet line, she saw a group of men and women in strange hooded robes come down the stairs in single file. Startled kids stopped dancing and let them pass as they made their way to the stage. When the last hooded figure—the thirteenth—had emerged from the stairway, two of the silent men in black suits pulled an iron gate Millie hadn't noticed over the entry to the stairs and chained it shut. The girl's stomach dropped and she lost any and all interest in pizza.

The DJ stopped the music and turned on the stage lights. Zatanna stepped up and approached the microphone.

"And here's our special musical guests tonight, direct from Innsmouth," she announced. "The Esoteric Order of Dagon Choir! Let's all give them a hand!"

Some of the new blood kids started golf-clapping uncertainly, but Hubert and the other old blood kids started cheering and whistling and stomping their feet and chanting like they were at a football game: "*FAA-ther DAA-gon! FAA-ther DAA-gon!*"

Millie blinked, feeling profoundly confused and unsettled. This didn't make any sense. Was Father Dagon the lead singer? Or was it the name of a song? What was going on here?

Zatanna hopped offstage. The leader of the group pushed his hood back and stepped regally to the microphone. The old, thin, white-bearded man scanned the crowd of kids. He wore a strange golden crown that was all high, asymmetrical spires in front with some coralline flourishes around the headband. It both looked like something someone found at the bottom of the sea and something she'd expect to see floating in outer space.

"You are the Chosen," he intoned into the microphone. "You are the Promised. You are the Honored. Tonight you ascend as you descend, and the gift of your lives ensures that Father Dagon smiles kindly upon your families and communities for the next generation. Those of you whose families are outsiders, rejoice! From this night forward, your sacrifice ensures that your bloodlines flow with ours. Your kin will be joined with the host, and you will all be profoundly blessed."

Millie felt her heart flutter in her chest and she took a step back, bumping into Hubert. The gift of their lives? *Sacrifice*?

"Father Dagon, take me first!" Hubert screamed behind her.

Millie frantically looked around for some other exit, or a place to hide, but there was none. Just the heavy metal barn doors that led someplace dark and watery, and the chained gate to the stairs.

The man with the crown took a deep breath, as did the twelve choir members behind him, and they began to sing. It was loud, like opera, but there was no melody and the voices of the chorus ground against each other like glass in disharmony. Millie whole body broke out in goosebumps and her heart pounded in her chest and she plugged her fingers in her ears, but there was no getting away from this strange, horrible, atonal music, no way to keep it from pounding into her skull like hurricane waves smashing against the beach, no way to keep from feeling like someone was reaching inside her skull and twisting her brains until up was down and down was up, and it was all so terrible that she just wanted to laugh and laugh and never stop ….

And the other children around her were laughing, laughing 'til they shrieked, laughing 'til they vomited up pizza and sweets and Cosmic Cola. The still-sane part of Millie's mind noticed that Zatanna and the men had gotten out hard-shelled ear muffs like her stepfather wore when he went to the gun range. And they just stood there on the margins, wearing their ear protection, impassively watching and waiting … for what?

Hubert finished puking behind her and gasped, "It's happening! It's happening! Praise Father Dagon, I am Becoming!"

She turned. The boy's whole head was swelling up like a grotesque balloon, his eyes bulging, his mouth widening impossibly. His back and shoulders hunched spasmodically, and she heard the crack of breaking bone. He yawned, making a terrible retching sound, and Millie watched in horror as his crooked white incisors, bicuspids and molars popped bloodily from his jaw, jumping free like popcorn kernels, only to be followed by the sharp grey irregular jags of brand-new teeth erupting through his raw gums, teeth like a shark's or a barracuda's. His eyes had bulged so much she was sure they'd pop right out of his head, the whites turning black, his blue irises turning a mottled golden like a frog's.

His skin split over his swollen flesh and he started furiously scratching himself with newly-clawed paws, tearing his clothing and pale skin away to reveal mottled, moist scales beneath. He threw the last rags of his captain's costume aside and crouched naked on muscular frog's legs, croaking hoarsely at her.

The awful sight of Hubert's transformation sent adrenaline surging through Millie's blood, and that broke the spell of the eldritch choir. She stepped away from the hopping abomination that Hubert had become and looked all around her, again seeking escape when she knew there was none. All the other kids were turning into monstrous fish-frogs. Everybody changing into something mythical and terrifying. Everyone but her.

The sane, calm part of her mind made note that while the dark part of her mind had long dreamed of being able to become something feared and respected, something that could send all the kids who'd ever bullied her and all the adults who'd ever belittled her screaming for the safety of locked doors … she most certainly did not want to become one of these god-awful things. They *stank*. Sweet lord, they stank like fish and vomit and blood. And one look in their bulging eyes and she just knew that they weren't in control of their own minds. They were slaves to Father Dagon.

If Millie ever became a monster, she wanted it to be on her own terms.

"Children, rejoice!" The leader of the choir shouted over the abominable song. "You are remade in your Father's image, and now you shall meet him!"

Two of the men from the alcoves pulled open the huge metal barn doors, and suddenly the grotto was filled with the smell of seawater and the sound of crashing surf. Immediately, the gibbering, baying, croaking fish-frogs swarmed toward the water, and Millie was carried along with them. She managed to take a deep breath right before they all plunged into the dark, surging waves.

Immediately, she lost her gorgeous red wig amongst the thrashing, splashing limbs. Millie had never been a fast swimmer, but she had always been a strong one. It was hard to swim in her boots and poofy-sleeved shirt, hard to keep her head above water with the brass sword weighing her down in the croaking throng surging out to sea, but she did it.

The throng thinned, and Millie distantly glimpsed the sweeping spotlight in the lighthouse, which she remembered the bus passing. That way was town, and her parents' house. Safety.

She started to awkwardly breast-stroke toward the lighthouse, but something grabbed the hem of her blouse. Hubert's awful croaking face loomed beside hers, his bulging eyes gleaming with mindless hunger.

Millie shrieked and scrabbled her pirate's cutlass out of its scabbard and jabbed it at him. She felt the blade sink into something soft. Hubert let out an inhuman barking cry and released her. She gave the sword another shove and let it go, too, splashing away as fast as she could.

He didn't follow.

Millie staggered to shore on the rocky beach a few hundred yards north of the mansion. Her arms and legs were numb with cold. She was so exhausted she wanted to lie down and sleep, but she knew she couldn't. The people from the mansion could find her here, and she wasn't convinced that some of the fish-frogs wouldn't track her down. Besides, she'd learned about hypothermia in Girl Scouts, and if she didn't keep moving she might get so cold she'd die. She sat down on a rock to pour the seawater out of her boots and wring out her socks as best she could. Her feet were wrinkled from her swim, and she had no doubt they'd be covered in the worst blisters she'd ever had by the time she got home.

The compass had stayed in her back pocket, and when she pulled it out, she was surprised to find that it had been waterproofed and still worked fine. She put her damp socks and boots back on and kept going down the beach, hoping that the rocky cliffs would end soon so she could get back onto the highway like her mother had told her.

"Like my mother told me," she repeated aloud to herself.

The sudden shock of realization made her stop and stand very still, shivering. Her mother had known this was going to happen. Maybe not *exactly* what had happened, but she knew *something* bad would happen. Why had she sent her to the party if she knew? Had her own mother betrayed her? Millie felt a new surge of terror and anger. If her mother was in on this, could she still go home?

But no. She shook her head, scolding herself. Her mom loved her. She *did*. She'd given Millie a real sword! And a flask so she wouldn't have to drink the hateful Cosmic Cola. She'd given her the tools she needed to escape. Millie couldn't understand why her mom would send her into the mouth of horror when her entire life she'd kept Millie away from anything and everything that seemed even slightly dangerous. But, she had … and Millie figured her mother had some explaining to do. At *least*.

Further, even if Millie did want to run away, where could she go? She didn't know how to contact any of her other relatives, and she didn't have any money for a bus or even for a pay phone. Millie had seen enough thrillers to suspect a conspiracy, and she didn't know who could be trusted. If she couldn't trust her own mom, she certainly couldn't trust neighbors or teachers she'd only known for a few months, could she? There wasn't much choice except to go home.

Shivering in the fitful wind, Millie plodded along the dark beach, eyes downcast, until she smelled burning gasoline and glimpsed the flicker of flames in her peripheral vision. She looked up. The Cosmic Cola bus had crashed over the guardrail onto its side and was burning. The whole thing was engulfed. Two firetrucks were vainly trying to put the flames out, and the local news van was filming a reporter a safe distance away.

This was how they were going to explain the kids' disappearance, she realized. A big tragic bus crash that people would forget in a decade or two. Probably if she looked in the town records, she'd find that some other terrible accident had befallen the kids picked for the big Devil's Night party thirty years before.

Left with no doubt whatsoever that this was a conspiracy, Millie crept onward, making sure that she wouldn't be seen as she passed the crash.

❦

She finally made it back to her parents' house in the early grey dawn when the sun was just a rumor below the horizon. Exhaustion had dissolved her rage and terror into a disbelieving numbness. Her mother was sitting on the front steps, dozing against a porch pillar, one of the jack-o-lanterns she'd helped Millie carve sitting in her lap. Its candle had gone out. A wine glass and an empty bottle of merlot lay on the white-washed wooden planks beside her.

Millie shrugged off the blanket she'd pilfered from a beach house clothesline and shook her mother's shoulder. "Mom."

Mrs. Gibbs woke with a start, looked around, and then pressed a finger to her lips. Her eyes were very red, as if she'd been crying a long time that night. "We have to be quiet. If anyone knows you're alive, they'll come after you again. I won't be able to do anything. I'm so sorry about all of this, honey."

"What the hell is going on?" Millie whispered, then flinched, expecting her mother to scold her for using a swear word.

But her mother didn't even seem to notice. "There's a cult here, and it's real, and Steve was a part of it long before I met him. And now we're all sucked in. I'm so sorry."

Millie felt her anger rise again. "Why didn't you tell me?"

Fresh tears welled in her mother's eyes. "I couldn't, honey. If you had known, you would have been so scared, and they'd have known that I told you. We'd both be dead now, and there would be nobody to protect your little brother and sister. I did the best I could think to do."

Millie wanted to scream at her, so she took care to speak as clearly and quietly as she could. "If you knew, why didn't you just take us and leave while he was away at work?"

Her mother's gaze turned distant, and when she spoke, her voice was hollow. "There was a ritual. I thought Steve and I were just going to lunch … but we weren't. They forced me. I'm bound here. I will literally die if I try to leave here with you or the twins. Steve had to promise a child to Dagon so he could rise in the ranks of the Order. He promised you. And you're still promised."

God. This was even more awful than she had imagined. "What happens now?"

"You have to leave here, tonight, and never come back. If they think you drowned in the ocean, the Order considers the promise fulfilled even though Dagon didn't get another child. But if they find out you're alive, they'll try to get you. And if they can't get you, they'll demand that Steve give them a different child. And then he'll hand over your little brother or little sister."

Millie felt a shock run from her skull to the soles of her aching feet. "He wouldn't. He loves them."

Her mother gave a short, quiet, bitter laugh. She looked terrified. "He would. He'd hand over all of us if they asked him to. And he'd get married and start a new family with another woman he does his Prince Charming act for. He's not all the man I thought he was. He's not even the man *you* think he is, and I know you never liked him much."

"He's a *monster*," Millie whispered.

Another quiet, bitter laugh. "This whole town is a monster factory, and it has been for a long, long time. But if you leave before they know you're alive, you and I and the twins stay safe. You can't call or write after you go; they read our mail, and they've tapped our phone. I wish it didn't have to be this way, but it does."

Millie felt completely lost. "Where do I go?"

"You're going to live with my cousin Penny in Fensmere, Mississippi. She knows a lot about monsters and cults and she can keep you safe."

"Cousin Penny?" Millie blinked. "You never mentioned her before, and now I'm supposed to go live with her?"

"It's not ideal. She's sort of a hermit. Not many people in the family really know her. I think she works as a private investigator? She tried to warn me about Steve, but I thought she was a lunatic." Her mother looked sad and deeply embarrassed. "I should have listened; everything she told me turned out to be true. She also told me that if any of my children were in danger, she would help. I called her from a payphone in Surfton the other night, and she said she'd send someone up here to collect you if you lived. And you did."

Her mother reached into her pocket for a lighter, re-ignited the candle in the jack-o-lantern. She stood and carefully set the pumpkin up on the broad porch railing beside their other jack-o-lantern and lit it, too.

At that, a car that Millie hadn't even noticed that was parked on the street a few houses down turned on its lights, flashed them three times, and turned them off again.

"And there's your ride." Her mother knelt to reach for something under the porch swing. When she stood up, she was holding Millie's old backpack—one she thought her mother had donated to Goodwill—and her violin case. "I packed essentials. Things Steve won't notice being gone. And a little money. I'll try to mail things from another town later."

The gravity of the situation finally hit Millie full-force. She was going to leave, maybe forever, and she might never see her mother again. She started to tear up. "I have to go now?"

"Yes. I'm sorry." Her mother set the luggage down and gave her a long hug. "Be good. A day won't pass where I don't think of you. I love you so much."

Tears flowed down Millie's cheeks in hot rivulets. "I love you, too."

"Go." Her mother helped her put on her backpack and gave her a gentle push.

Millie hurried across the lawns to the sedan. Someone inside flung the rear driver's side door open.

A black girl in pigtails who looked a little younger than Millie beckoned her excitedly. "Get in!"

Millie handed her the violin case. The girl grabbed it and scooted over on the seat so Millie could get in and shut the door behind her.

"Oh, cool, I play violin, too!" The girl exclaimed. "We could do duets later! Can you fiddle? I'm taking fiddle lessons from Miz Greene next year when she gets back –"

"Lena." The driver, a thirty-something woman with a short Afro haircut and hoop earrings, turned and gave the pigtailed girl a look. "What did I tell you?"

"Wash my hands?"

The woman rolled her eyes. "Context."

Lena brightened. "Oh. Right. Introduce myself first?"

"Yes."

The grinning girl turned back to Millie and stuck out her hand. "Hi, I'm Lena, and this is my mom Bess. Cousin Penny sent us to get you away from this terrible place. Cultists *suck*."

Millie shook her offered hand, feeling a bit like she'd fallen down a rabbit hole and this cheerful child was standing in for the Mad Hatter. "Hi. Good to meet you."

"Perfect!" Lena's mother started the car and pulled away from the curb. "As she says, I'm Bess. I'm Penny's investigative partner. She sends her regrets that she couldn't come get you herself, but she's got a distance vision problem that limits her driving. You'll meet her probably day after tomorrow. It's a really long drive to Fensmere, so I was thinking we could stop outside Harrisburg and get a hotel room. Your mom told Penny you love Halloween, and there are some good neighborhoods in the suburbs where I can take the two of you trick-or-treating. You up for that, Millie?"

Lena started excitedly whispering, "Say yes, say yes, say yes!"

"Sweet pea, don't pester her," Bess said. "She's been through a whole lot tonight. She might rather sleep, and we're not going to leave her by herself,"

"I'd like that," Millie said. "But my pirate costume is all gross, and I lost my wig and my sword besides."

"It's okay! I brought a whole suitcase full of costumes, just in case!" Lena replied.

"But on that note," Bess said, "once we're out of cult territory, I'll find a truck stop where you can get a shower and change into fresh clothes if you like. Folks gonna think we tried to drown you if I drive around with you like this."

"I'd *definitely* like that," Millie said.

"Consider it done," said Bess.

Millie looked out the window just in time to see the "Welcome to Marsh Landing!" sign flash past and felt a wash of relief and sadness at the realization that she might never see it ever again.

Lena nudged her. "Hey. You know what today is? Besides it being Wednesday and Halloween, I mean."

Millie shook her head.

"It's the first day of the rest of your life!" Lena grinned excitedly.

Millie couldn't help but smile back. "Yeah, it sure is."

Hell Among the Yearlings

Chet Williamson

It wasn't scary at all. Michael was playing it well enough, that wasn't the problem. Michael Wilkins always played great. It was just that everyone had heard the tune too many times. "Jerusalem Ridge" was one of those rare minor-key tunes that were in most fiddlers' repertoires. It was bouncy and moved along nicely, and made a nice variation, since the vast majority of fiddle tunes were written in upbeat major keys. But scary? No. Elmer would show them scary.

He glanced around to see the effect the tune was having on the crowd. Daisy Kreider, who was accompanying on her guitar, was smiling and watching Michael intently, the way she always did when she backed up another musician. That was one more thing he loved about Daisy, as though her looks and personality weren't enough.

Michael played on, having left the melody for the improvisation at which he excelled. With the crowd's attention fixed on Michael, Elmer used the moment to hold his own fiddle to his left ear and quietly check to see if the alternate tuning had held. It had, and he put the fiddle back on his lap on top of the dry, aged sheets of music he'd been studying, and listened to Michael finish his tune. Let him have his moment of glory. Elmer was going to cook him and serve him on cornbread. Elmer's music was going to be scary as hell.

✿

He found it in the attic, in a battered cardboard box full of music that his mother had gotten from an old violinist just before his death. He'd remembered the box when he was thinking about where he might find a new tune with eerie qualities for the contest. To his disappointment, the box was filled with formal violin exercises, classical sonatas, and dozens of Victorian era solos with piano accompaniment.

Still, he dug to the bottom, hoping to find a collection of folk tunes or Appalachian ballads, something previously unheard by the other kids and the judges. All the way at the bottom of the box, underneath a small pile of chipped and brittle Bach sonatas and partitas, was an even more time-ravaged piece of music. The paper, if paper it was, was cracked and yellow, torn in many places, and he saw immediately that the music was written by hand in black ink, as were the somewhat uneven staff lines. There was no title, nor was there a name of any composer, but what he found of immediate interest was that at the top left of the first of the two pages were four capital letters separated by vertical lines, reading "F|E|A|R."

✿

When Michael Wilkins played the final bars of "Jerusalem Ridge," he put everything he had into it, ending with an improvised cadenza that made his bow a blur and caused the strings to howl. The audience, in turn, howled their approval, clapping and cheering as Michael took a small bow and nodded to Daisy in recognition. From the way she smiled back at him, he knew she'd been mightily impressed with his performance.

More so than Elmer Zook, that was for sure. That big old farm boy was clapping hard enough, but the smile on his face said to Michael, *I'm gonna get you now, town boy.*

There it was, wasn't it? Farm Boy and Town Boy. When it came to bluegrass music, street cred didn't matter. What mattered was cowshit cred. It mattered to Ken Groff anyway. A former tractor jockey himself, Ken always seemed to favor the hicks, the ones who had old-time music, not only in their blood, but also symbolized in brown on the bottoms of their boots. And as head of the Smoketown Bluegrass School, Ken had his favorites, of which Elmer Zook was number one.

Michael had to admit that Elmer was a helluva natural musician. The kid had chops. His sight reading was impeccable, and he could spend a minute reading a new tune on paper, and then play it from memory. On top of that, his technique was impressive and his ear was sharp, and he could recreate old Kenny Baker solos note for note.

His sole failing was creativity. Michael left him in the shade as an improviser, but Ken Groff wasn't bothered by it. Ken's instruments were banjo and guitar, so he was easy to impress when it came to fiddle.

Now Ken stood up, still applauding, and faced the small audience of about two dozen people – students, parents, and a few friends. "All right, let's hear it for Michael and 'Jerusalem Ridge!' Really good! But the question is, was it *scary?* Remember, this is the night of the Halloween jam, and we're lookin' for the scariest fiddle tune ever heard! So far we've heard 'The Devil Went Down To Georgia,' 'Little Sadie,' and now 'Jerusalem Ridge.' Those raise a few goosebumps?"

Most in the audience chuckled, and there were a few shouted out *yeahs* and *nos.* Michael had put his fiddle back in its case, and now sat next to Daisy in the second row. "You playing for Elmer?" he whispered.

She shook her head. "He's playing alone," she whispered back.

Michael looked at her closely, trying to figure out whether she was pleased or displeased about not playing with Elmer. Their rivalry over Daisy was an established fact at the bluegrass school, though neither had yet gotten up enough nerve to ask her out. Ken alluded to it now and then, sometimes subtly, sometimes less so. One of his more blatant comments, offered when Michael and Elmer collided trying to open a door for Daisy, was that the two boys should do a duet on "Hell Among the Yearlings." Both Ken and Frank Withers, the fiddle and mandolin teacher, laughed hard at that one.

When Michael looked up the title on Google, he found that, besides being the name of a Gillian Welch album, it was a fiddle tune he hadn't been aware of, and that the title referred to young, rambunctious cattle. He wasn't flattered.

"All right now!" Ken said. "Our next fiddler is our old buddy, Elmer Zook! What are you going to play for us, Elmer?"

"It doesn't have a title," Elmer said softly, as he stood up, tucked some sheets of music into his case, and closed it.

"Well, you gotta call it something," said Ken.

"I, uh… I guess just 'Halloween Tune,' maybe?"

"Okay then, 'Halloween Tune' it is. Is it *scary?*"

❈

It was awful. He had taken the music down to his room, closed the door behind him, and tried to play the handwritten notes, but they made no sense. He figured that a piece of music entitled "FEAR" would sound weird, but he didn't think it would be altogether crazy, like this was. If a tune ever sounded like pure cacophony, this was it.

He sat down on his bed and looked closely at the brittle old sheets of music. There were no other notes, no name of any composer, just the four letters, separated by lines, at the top of the page:

F|E|A|R

Then it occurred to him that the lines themselves might have some significance. Instead of the letters indicating the title, maybe the lines meant the letters were something more than just letters in a name.

A tuning.

Guitarists used alternate tunings all the time, tuning their strings up or down to create an entirely different tonal sound. He'd never heard of anyone doing it on a fiddle, but that didn't mean it wasn't possible.

He picked up his fiddle and looked at the letters, "FEAR," again. Then he tuned his G string down a full tone to F, his D string up a tone to E, and left his A string as it was. But what, he wondered, was the R? Notes on the scale went from A through G – there was no note R.

But as he looked closer at the handwritten R, he saw that the looped upper part was larger than the straight lines that made up the bottom half, and he realized that if he ignored those lines he had a letter D. So was the composer making a wise-ass joke of some kind? Giving the piece a title while slightly hiding the proper tuning?

He tuned the highest string, the E, down a full step to D, then picked up his bow and drew it over the four strings. The D-E-F, three notes side-by-side, made for a strange dissonance, but one that brought a twisted smile to his face. Then he stood up, put the music back on the stand, and played the first few notes, fingering on the altered strings exactly as he would have on the standard tuning.

It took only a few notes for him to know that this one was scary.

※

"Is it?" Ken asked again.

Elmer Zook gave a little shrug. "Yeah. I think so anyway."

"Well, we'll be the judge of that," Ken said with a laugh as he went to sit down. "Take it away, Elmer!"

Elmer raised his fiddle to his chin, then flexed his bowing arm twice. He took a deep breath, and let the bow rest on the retuned strings. In his mind he saw the black, handwritten notes on the brittle old paper, and he began to play.

When the first notes tore into the fabric of the air, a change came over the attitudes of the listeners. The slouchers began to straighten up, and the heads of those already sitting straight began to lift like hounds on scent. Their gazes, initially fixed on Elmer, slowly rose until they were focused on something just above his head, something that wavered in the suddenly thick air of the room, shimmered in strands of red and gold and silver and black, and, as one phrase led to the next, the black began to predominate, subsuming the other, brighter colors, and finally taking even the deep, dark red into it, like blood turning black in starlight.

❦

The boy continued to play in the privacy of his bed-room, in the solitude of the empty house. This will work, he thought. This will be perfect. Damn, but it was weird. It was beyond just minor key, though it had that quality to it. There were scoops and leaps and jagged staccato passages that were enormously challenging, yet he was some-how able to negotiate the demanding maze of notes. His sudden ability surprised him. He knew he was good, but he hadn't realized he was this *good.*

But as the torrent of tones surged out of his violin, he saw on the page a flashing, shimmering light, and he thought, oh no, not again. He'd been troubled with ocu-lar migraines since eighth grade, painless but bothersome neurological illusions in both eyes at once, visions of a jagged-edged oval, as though something in his brain had shattered a glass sheet spread across his vision and shards glimmered across the landscape of his sight. It was annoying, but always went away within a half hour.

However, he soon realized that this ocular migraine was different from the dozens he'd had before. The area around the torn edges, showing the real world he had always continued to see during even the worst of these events, was changing, was becoming filled with bizarre colors merging with a lack *of color, and the jagged oval at the center of his vision was different too. Never before had anything begun to come through it.*

Elmer played on, as if unable to stop. His eyes seemed to have rolled up so that the pupils were hidden behind his eyelids, showing only the whites, but his right arm continued to saw at the strings, and his left held the fiddle under his chin, while his fingers raced and spasmed on the black fingerboard.

Except for the shrieking fiddle, the only sounds heard in the room were soft moans, whimpers, and deep, ragged sighs. Nearly everyone was looking into the space in the air above Elmer's head. Nearly everyone was seeing the same thing there, but each saw something different as well, something meaningful to him or her alone, something terrifying, something heartbreaking, something fearsome.

Midge Butler saw her father looming over her late at night.

Perry Crawford saw his mother on the bathroom floor, her head half gone, her pink .45 caliber handgun still clenched in her fist.

Eight-year-old Tim Keebler held his cat Pluff in his arms, panicked as to why she wasn't moving, why her hind legs just hung there as if there were no bones in them.

Abe Peters shivered over an open grave deep in his cornfield, a shovel in his hands, the body of his wife Esther at his feet, her neck twisted so that she was looking over her right shoulder, up at the stars.

And Esther Peters saw her best meat knife sliding in and out of her husband's stomach, just below his breastbone, over and over, her hand with her late mother's signet ring, the only piece of jewelry she owned, holding it with white knuckles. And she heard him grunt with every shove, and heard her own terrified breaths whistling in and out of her tight throat.

Everyone who heard saw something, events real, events imagined, things that still might be and things that never would. They saw these terrors in the space in the air over Elmer Zook's head, that space to which the music rose and then spread out over them all like a dark blanket of sound. They sobbed and trembled and wailed at what they heard and what they saw, and the boy continued to play. It was not music. It was not a tune. It was a surge of sound that gave them all a glimpse of a world they had not imagined, a world where fear and terror ruled, where there was no light nor joy nor love, only loss and pain and savagery, and they could do nothing to make it stop.

Ken Groff tried. He was the closest to Elmer, and he pushed himself to his feet, where he wavered for a moment before a flood of repeated, falling triplets drove him to his knees, and he grabbed his head in his hands and wept. And Elmer played on.

※

The boy played on, all alone, in his bedroom. He wanted to stop, but he couldn't. Even as more and more of those unformed, shapeless creatures undulated through the gap that had been torn in his vision, he knew he had to stop. He was beginning to have thoughts, bad ones, far worse than even the darkest fantasies he'd ever imagined in the blackness of midnight.

He began to cry, and thought he could feel his bladder start to empty itself in panic, wet heat like blood trickling down his thigh. He was gasping, barely able to breathe, thinking that soon, soon, he must surely pass out, fall unconscious while those creatures continued to pour into his sight, his room, his mind, and then—

Something took the bow from his hand, wrenched it away, and his right arm dropped, and the sound ceased all at once, the roar subsiding, his vision clearing, and standing there in front of him was his younger brother, looking at him in confusion and disgust, the plastic buds in his ears blaring hip-hop so loudly that the boy could hear it.

"What the hell are you doing?" his brother asked him, gesturing with the bow he was holding toward the growing dark, wet spot on the front of the boy's jeans.

"An accident," the boy said huskily. "Don't say anything to Mom and Dad about this," he added, with as threatening a look as he could muster under the circumstances. "Or I'll tell them you're listening to that hardcore crap." The threat, along with the fact that he was a head taller than his brother, seemed to be sufficient, as the younger boy nodded, handed back the bow, and left the room.

The boy changed his jeans and underwear, and washed the soiled ones, hoping they would dry before his parents got home. Then he sat on his bed and looked at the music that had affected him so strongly and unpredictably. If the music had had such an effect on him when he played it, what might it do to those who listened? Even if he managed to stay sane, the listeners to such musical blasphemy might never forgive him...

He thought some more. He thought about what he might do with the tune. Despite its power, and because of it, there was no way he could play it in the Halloween contest.

But it might be just right for someone else.

❊

It had gone on long enough. The effect the tune had produced was far more than he had intended. The music had to stop now.

Michael stood up and ran to where Elmer stood, his bow still slashing at the strings. As Michael tried to grab his fiddle, Elmer twisted away, right arm lashing out so that the bow ripped across Michael's face, making him stagger backwards, then fell upon the strings once more. Enraged and desperate, Michael tackled the other boy, and he and Elmer fell together, their combined weight upon the fragile instrument, which shattered with a crisp, treble cracking of maple and spruce.

Though his violin was now nothing more than a splintered box of wood held loosely together by twisted strings, Elmer tried to keep playing. He still held the bow, now broken in half, and moved the wood, devoid of horsehair, across the ruin of an instrument. When no sound resulted, he increased his efforts, and thrashed about on the floor, grunting with the effort, his eyes wild.

Michael tried to restrain him so that he wouldn't hurt himself or others, but it was difficult. Elmer seemed imbued with maniacal energy, and it wasn't until Ken and Frank Withers came to Michael's aid that they were finally able to hold the boy still.

Michael was surprised and relieved at the assistance, for it meant that Ken and Frank, at least, had regained their own emotional stability. As he looked around the room, he saw that the others were also coming out of whatever spell the music had placed upon them. Some were trembling, some were crying, but all seemed rational, more rational than Elmer Zook, at any rate.

When Ken and Frank's attention shifted from Elmer to his concerned and sobbing parents, and while the others in the room were assuring and comforting each other, Michael surreptitiously slipped the wax earplugs out of his ears and into his pocket.

⁂

When Michael came into the old firehouse that the Smoketown Bluegrass School rented for their lessons and gatherings, everyone was in the banquet room and kitchen in the back eating Halloween snacks and drinking punch and soda. Here in the big room where the fire trucks had been parked, the chairs were set up for the competition and jam session afterwards. Everyone had put their instruments along the side wall, which is what he had been counting on.

He carried his violin case over and put it near El-mer's. Then, glancing up to make sure no one else was in the room, he took from his case the brittle, folded music sheets and a small note, opened Elmer's case, slipped them inside, and closed it again. Then he joined the others in the back.

Elmer was talking to Daisy, of course, but she smiled when she saw Michael, and he joined them. None of them mentioned the contest. When Ken finally announced that the competition would start in ten minutes, Elmer went into the main room right away, while Daisy remained and chatted with Michael.

When, five minutes later, they went into the big room, Michael saw that Elmer was crouching in a far corner, turning his tuning pegs to try and get them to hold in an unaccustomed position. The old music sheets were on the floor, and Elmer was looking at them, playing very softly so no one could hear.

He'd taken the bait all right. Michael had written the note in what he thought of as a feminine hand, with loops and spirals and little hearts to dot the i's. It had read:

"Tune to F-E-A-R and kick Michael's bee-hind! A Friend"

Michael thought the "bee-hind" was a cute touch. And there was a bigger heart over the "i" in "Friend."

From the corner of his eye, Michael watched Elmer hold the music close and examine it carefully. He was sight reading sure enough, and memorizing as he went. Gullible hick or not, the kid really had a gift. He was going to ride this tune bareback.

As Michael tuned, Elmer, still holding the music, went over to Daisy. He couldn't hear them, but he figured Elmer was telling her that he wouldn't need her to accompany him after all.

Michael smiled. If that tune screwed up Elmer's head just half the way it had done to his, it was going to be a real spectacle. He nearly laughed aloud at the prospect of watching Elmer pee himself in front of Daisy.

It might even screw up the heads of some of the listeners, and that sure wasn't going to endear Elmer to folks either. Nope, Elmer Zook's name was going to be a dirty word from tonight on. Yep, I'm gonna get you now, farm boy.

Michael patted the pair of earplugs in his right pocket, and did a quick, soft run-through of "Jerusalem Ridge" once again. Winning the contest mattered, but what mattered most was that he played the best that he could. After all, it was getting to the point where, even as young as he was, music was his life.

※

Michael looked through the windows into the large, empty room. A lot could change in six months, and it had. He'd finally gotten his driver's license, and could drive on his own now. Sometimes he'd drive over to the old fire station, now empty and for rent once again, and look through the windows and think about making music.

Nobody did anymore. Nobody who was there that

night could even *listen* to music, let alone play it. Shopping malls, doctor's offices, stores that played background and elevator music were all off-limits to the students, parents, and friends of the Smoketown Bluegrass School who had come to the party that Halloween night.

And nobody knew why. In the ruckus and confusion afterwards, Michael had taken the music and note out of Elmer's case, balled them up, stuck them in his pocket, and burned them when he got home. So nobody knew why Elmer had played what he played, and nobody knew where in the world he got that tune in the first place. There were all sorts of theories, more about the reaction to the tune than the provenance of the music itself. They examined all the leftover treats and punch for food poisoning, and even inspected the building top to bottom for mold, but didn't find anything.

Ken and Frank stopped giving lessons right away, and Ken officially closed the school a couple weeks later. Though Michael hadn't actually heard Elmer's performance, he didn't play anymore, because there wasn't anyone around to play *with*. Daisy went to another high school, so he didn't see her either. And Elmer? Well, nobody saw Elmer. Michael heard that he'd been put in a "special" school, but was afraid to ask what "special" meant.

Michael looked through the windows one last time, then turned and walked down the street to his folks' car. He got in and figured he'd give it another try. He pushed the "AUX" switch on the dashboard, brought up Spotify on his phone, and from his playlist he chose Dirk Powell's version of "Lonesome John," a fiddle tune he'd always liked.

As he pulled out onto the street, the fiddle began playing in double-stops, and after a few bars the banjo joined in. He felt no sense of torment, but the music sounded ugly to him. He found no pleasure in it, and he turned it off and drove in silence.

Summer's End

Erica Ruppert

"It's not much of a town," Josh said.

Dana shrugged, watching the landscape rise and fall around them as Josh sped north on Route 41. Through the windshield, late October sun fell warm across her face.

"Up here, it's all these little spread out towns. The main businesses were the lodges, fishing, hunting, family stuff, but most of those are gone now too."

She turned to watch his profile.

"I haven't seen my mother's family for years," he said. "But it's time."

He slowed as they approached another of the tiny villages that clung to the edge of the highway.

The plain blue road sign said "Newbrook", but the mosaic of brown woods and fields continued. Then they passed a few widely-set houses, and were suddenly in the center of the town.

Dana looked around as they passed a low-slung motel set back in the trees, a small apartment block, a bank. At a T-intersection marked by a stoplight was an IGA, a dollar store, and a shuttered pizzeria. Past the light on 41 was a beer store and a medical clinic, then a few more houses on narrow strips of lawn.

Josh pulled into the driveway of one faded ranch house and turned off the engine. He sat for a moment, then reached over and squeezed Dana's hand.

"Are you ready for this?" he asked.

Dana watched the impassive front of the house. The porch was decorated for Halloween, with corn stalks and fat yellow gourds, and what looked like a goat's skull hanging on the door with a tufted beard on its jaw. She glanced away, up at the clean blue sky.

"Sure," she said.

As they climbed from the car and stretched, a young woman came out and stood on the porch, waiting for them to climb the steps to reach her.

"Hey, Claire, you look good," Josh said. "This is Dana." He nudged her forward.

"It's nice to meet you," Dana said, and held out her hand. Claire hesitated before she took it, as if making up her mind.

"Claire and I used to play back in the swamp behind the airport when we were little," Josh said.

"Airport's been gone a long time. No one wants to fly in or out of here any more," Claire said, looking past Dana with moony grey eyes. "Nursing home is out there now. But there's still Airport Road, and swamp."

Dana looked from Josh to Claire for any other details, but Claire kept her eyes on Josh, and Josh looked up at the curtained windows.

"You're just in time for winter," Claire said. "Year's almost done. And Dad, well."

"Worse?" Josh said.

"It's chilly out here. Let's go in" Claire said, and ushered Dana and Josh into the entryway.

"Dad's in there," she said, gesturing toward the living room.

Dana followed the line of Claire's outstretched arm to where a man slumped in a rocking chair beside the television set. His face was slack, and moist, without any expression. A blanket spread across his misshapen legs looked spotted and damp, almost moldy, and his feet jutted out at broken angles from beneath the stained cloth.

"Hi, Joe," Josh said.

Dana took Josh's hand. "Can he hear us?" she asked him softly.

"Maybe," Claire said. She herded them out of the room again.

"Our family originally came up from Massachusetts, after the witch trials," she whispered, leaning close to Dana's cheek. Dana held still. Josh looked disgusted, but Claire ignored him. "We bred like flies. Now the whole province is full of Masons and Mason cousins. And they say there's a weakness in the blood."

Claire straightened and raised her voice. "A weakness that lingers. So I'm surprised you came back, Josh, after your mother got away."

He looked over her shoulder to where Joe drowsed. "You knew I would," he said.

"What's with Claire?" Dana asked him as she put her clothes into the dresser.

"She's always been a little off," Josh said. "But she's okay. I mean she's friendly, but she will say strange things at times. You just have to ignore it."

"Did you tell her my family is from Massachusetts, too?"

"No," he said.

Dana closed the drawer and stuffed her bag under the bed.

"What did she mean about your mother, and you coming back?"

Josh sighed. "Family stuff she still follows. The end of October, all Samhain and Halloween stuff, ending summer and letting winter in. My mother left it behind and never came back. Uncle Joe held that grudge a long time."

Dana watched him.

"She makes you nervous," she said.

"Yeah," he said. "Sometimes."

He made sure the door was fully closed.

"Family can do that to you," he said.

❖

Dana woke before Josh did, and padded out of their room in search of coffee. The quiet in the house was broken only by cars passing on the highway.

She went into the cold, bright kitchen and looked around. The coffeemaker had been set up already. She turned it on and leaned against the counter while she waited for the carafe to fill.

Hung above the door was a dark wooden figure. She thought it might be some rustic crucifix. She reached up and took it down from its hook and found it wasn't a cross after all. It was a damp clump of woody roots about the size of her hand, still spotted with clots of dirt, wound to form a loose nest. Two straight sticks stuck up at angles from the top of it.

Claire came out of her room, and saw Dana standing there holding it.

"The Mother Root," she said, strolling into the kitchen. "The Lord of the Woods."

"Is it for good luck?" Dana asked.

Claire smiled and moved past her. "Sure," she said. "Something like that."

❖

In the afternoon Josh and Claire went out together. Dana stayed behind, not sure if she had wanted to. She drifted around the house, avoiding the living room where Joe sat in his slow decay. He disturbed her, not for his infirmity but because she had a primitive feeling that his helplessness was a lie.

At last she slipped on her coat, and headed out the kitchen door and around to the front of the house. The car was gone. She followed the road, kicking rocks along the pavement for a few hundred yards until the asphalt sidewalk began. The slanting sun fell over her head and back, driving her shadow ahead of her. There were a few people about, mainly going in and out of the supermarket driveway.

She reached the intersection in front of the IGA, and crossed the road to the wooden barn that was Davey's Variety Store. The front was decorated with pumpkins and faded plastic masks, and a bin of bundled firewood. She went in. It was warmer inside than she expected, and smelled of lumber.

Behind the counter, a man Dana assumed was Davey sat reading a magazine, an oxygen tank clicking beside him. His skin was pale, almost grey, and his hair clung damply to his forehead. He did not look well. He glanced up at her as she came in then looked back down.

She checked out the bandanas and sunglasses and fishing supplies, the leftover beach toys from the summer trade and the bin of old DVDs for sale. The store was deeper than she had thought it was, with rooms separated by arched doorways. She kept poking. In the back, past the bookshelves loaded with used paperbacks and the pegboard displays of toiletries and children's clothing was a door labeled "Private".

Dana looked toward the register, but shelves blocked her view. The only sound in the place came from a radio set on a shelf somewhere toward the front.

Curious, Dana turned the knob, and was surprised to find the door unlocked. She opened it to find a narrow hall and a staircase to an upper floor. Layers of footprints smeared the treads in dust. At the top of the stairs was another door, poorly fitted in its frame. Light slipped out in slices along its edges. She climbed toward it, drawn by the yellow light.

The door opened silently when she tried it. She stood for a long time on the threshold, taking in the contents of the room.

A pile of dry vines and flaking grey mud leaned in a tangle against the far wall, crowned with a small, unnervingly female figure. Dana stepped quietly across the room, plucked the figure from its nest, turned it in her hands.

It was carved of a greasy white stone, about ten inches tall, with rows of heavy breasts like animal teats, and a grossly swollen belly. The face was a swirl of scratches, and from the forehead two horns curved up in a semicircle. The figure's back and lower half were a mass of looping tendrils.

The stone was biting cold in her hand but she held it against the pain, studying the curves and lines that turned like a Möbius strip across the oval space where a face should have been. The pattern seemed to shift under her gaze. Uncomfortable, Dana put the figure back and tucked her hand underneath her arm to warm it again.

She turned away from the vines and the idol, and examined a shelf of books that stood below the room's single window. The languages of the titles eluded her. She pulled out a massive folio, examining the dark leather cover embossed with vines and beasts. It was spongy, and warm. She didn't want to open it.

She slid the heavy volume back and pulled out the one beside it. This one was beautiful, an octavo bound in stained, deep yellow silk with a winding silver pattern embroidered on the cover. She ran her fingers over the threads, and pulled them quickly away. Something in the design had slithered under her touch.

Wary now but drawn in, she opened the book and leafed through the heavy pages. Tucked between the leaves near the beginning was a sheet of lined notepaper covered in sharp blue lettering.

C.M. trans. Polyglot Lat. and Arab., some Grk.,

Germ.?.—Lord of the Wood, Black Goat of the Wood, Mother of the Wood and the Stars, Black Goat with a thousand young—incantation? Mother of Winter, End of the Sun, Ever Their praises, and abundance to the Black Goat of the Woods. Iä! Shub-Niggurath! Black Goat of the Woods with a Thousand Young!

Without thinking, she folded the sheet and put it in her pocket.

She flipped more pages. The words shimmered and turned, unreadable. She blinked, clapped the book shut and replaced it on the shelf. Still, her hand lingered on it. She wanted it. She pulled it out again and slid it into her purse.

She looked around, suddenly furtive. The sinking sun cut through the window above her in a wide pale beam, catching in her eyes, making her wince. The room seemed to close around her. Something could see her here. She knew it under her skin

She stepped to the door, and listened only a moment before pattering fast down the stairs. At the bottom the world filled with the thin radio music again, and Davey gave no sign of having seen her as she fled.

Days melted into days. Josh and Claire were often out. They did not ask her to come. Without them, Dana kept to the house. The days were too chilly and the town too empty for her to want to wander alone.

She spent her hours reading in the living room with the husk of Joe for company. He deteriorated slowly, like a great wet cake sinking in on itself. Sometimes he sighed, but otherwise he made no sound. As far as Dana could tell Joe never left the living room. She didn't want to be near him, but felt safer if she could watch him.

She finished the novel she had brought with her, and the magazines she found in the house. One dusky afternoon she pulled out the yellow silk book from where she had hidden it in her empty duffle bag under the bed.

She settled back in the living room and paged through it slowly, then got out the sheet of notebook paper. She tried to match it to a passage, but the language in the book was nothing she could grasp. She read the translation over, softly, aloud, her lips bending over the stranger syllables, her tongue halting at the sounds.

"*Lord of the Wood, Black Goat of the Wood, Mother of the Wood and the Stars, Black Goat with a thousand young—Mother of Winter, End of the Sun, Ever Their praises, and abundance to the Black Goat of the Woods. Iä! Shub-Niggurath! Iä! Shub-Niggurath!—*"

Joe moaned and leaned toward her, reaching. The hand he raised looked eaten away, the skin grey and peeling. Dana shrieked and leapt up, the book falling from her lap.

Claire stood in the doorway. She smiled, her lips wet.

"It's all right," Claire said. "Don't let him bother you."

"He doesn't," Dana said, gathering herself again.

"Josh, I mean" Claire said. She went to smooth the blanket over Joe's misshapen lap, pressing him back into the chair. "There now," she said to him.

She came over to stand beside Dana. She glanced down at the book on the floor, then up into Dana's eyes. "Josh knows what he has to do, and he doesn't want to do it. Family is hard, sometimes."

She lifted Dana's hand in her own, turned it over.

"Look," Claire said, pressing her finger against Dana's palm. "Do you see what's written there?"

"No," Dana said, pulling her hand back.

Joe snorted wetly in his chair, falling to one side. Claire moved to straighten him.

"I think you will," Claire said, bending to tend her father.

The evening was cold and still. Dana had talked Josh into leaving the house with her, to show her the quiet town. He had grown up here, after all. There were only six streets, and most of the small houses that lined them were dark. Some of the lighted ones were decorated with ghosts and plastic skulls.

"The way you talked, I always thought Newbrook was bigger," she said as they looped past the nursing home back to the main road. Her breath hung white in the air. "There can't be many trick or treaters. There's nobody here."

Josh smiled. "There are some," he said. "The town clears out after tourist season."

His voice dropped. "But twenty, thirty years ago, we lost a lot of people. They went...elsewhere."

"I guess that happens to a lot of small towns. The economy changes and it's hard to stay."

"Things do change, but our traditions...they make us," Josh said, and fell silent.

They strolled past Davey's, and Dana laughed with sudden bravado.

"You know there's some weird shrine in there?" she said, keeping her voice low.

Josh stared at her, no humor in his eyes. He stopped walking.

"What do you mean?" he asked.

Dana looked at him.

"Above the shop. Upstairs, there's a shrine set up. Fertility goddess, I think. And a collection of old occult books. I couldn't read them. Someone started to translate them and—"

"Why were you upstairs at all?" Josh hissed at her. "Did anyone see you?"

She stepped back.

"I was just goofing around."

"What is wrong with you?."

Dana blinked back sudden tears. She looked at her feet, then up over Josh's shoulder at the side of Davey's building. The narrow attic window was lit with a dim yellow glow. Shadows moved across the light. She wondered who was up there.

"I'm sorry," she said.

He pushed past her. "We have to go home now," he said.

He was trembling. She realized he was scared.

She followed him into the soft blue night, back up the road.

※

She heard him leave the house before dawn. She heard low voices from outside, then the crush of gravel under wheels. She rolled over and willed herself back to sleep.

Claire woke her before noon, standing over her, watching until Dana opened her eyes.

"I haven't been a good host," Claire said. "I've left you to your own devices all this time."

Dana blinked and sat up on the edge of the bed, pulling the blankets around her. She was groggy and pliant, beginning to feel unmoored in this empty town.

"It's all right," she said. "I've found stuff to do."

Claire sat beside her, her grey eyes huge. Dana could feel the heat from Claire's skin.

"Where's Josh?"

"Around," Claire said. "But I have something for you."

Dana opened the twist of paper Claire handed her. Inside lay a tangled clutch of roots, grey with dirt.

Claire grinned. Dana nodded, closing her fingers around it.

"This is the welcome you should have," Claire said. "You do belong here."

"I hope so," Dana said.

The afternoon was almost gone when Dana realized Josh had not returned. She had lounged away the time outside on the porch with the goat skull for company, bundled in her coat, too tired to read. Not a single car had passed. She felt as if she were waiting at the end of the world.

Claire walked out of the stand of leafless trees that edged the property, and waved.

"Dana," Claire called, "I have something else for you."

"Okay," Dana said, not moving from her seat.

"No, come with me," Claire said, coming closer.

"It's going to be dark. Josh has to be back soon."

"Maybe. We'll leave him a note" Claire said, pulling a crumpled ball of notebook paper from her front pocket. She smoothed it out on the hood of the car and tucked it under the wiper blade.

"He'll know what to do," she said.

Dana sighed and got up, following Claire across the yard. As she passed the car she glanced at the scrap of paper. The writing on was the same lettering as in the yellow silk book.

The sun slanted down behind the trees as the afternoon waned, the sky dissolving to a deeper blue. They walked into town, and then turned down Airport Road to follow its long loop. When they reached the nursing home Claire pulled Dana across the facility's parking lot toward the woods behind it.

As they passed the building Dana saw a line of slack figures propped in wheelchairs, drowsing in the deepening dusk. Their postures reminded her of how Joe sagged, boneless yet waiting. From where she stood it looked as if their skin was sloughing off like birch bark, peeling away and drifting across the concrete pad in shreds. Like masks, she thought. Like paper masks for Halloween. She wiped the back of her hand across her eyes.

"What's wrong with them?" she asked Claire.

Claire paid no attention to the nursing home patients. "Inbreeding. Cousins," she said, without glancing toward them.

Dana looked at the people in the chairs. Maybe Claire was right, and it was an ineffable weakness in the blood.

"Mason cousins?" she asked.

"Come on," Claire said. "It's not far."

Behind the home's parking lot a path snaked back through rough grass toward the trees. Claire tugged Dana along behind her, urging her to speed up, to reach the woods. Cedars and pines and bare maples grew over the path, blocking their line of sight, forcing them to push through the branches. Over their own noises Dana heard voices, and the sounds of other passage all around. Claire gave no sign she heard anything.

In less than a mile the trees thinned out, becoming sparse and unhealthy. The ground grew soggy underfoot as they walked into the swamp. Cold seeped through the soles of Dana's shoes. Claire stopped before they reached standing water.

"Here," she said, and pointed. "This."

The hulk of an ancient willow listed like a shipwreck a hundred feet from where they stood, rotten and broken but still alive. Where its roots had pulled free of the ground a great pit opened, greasy with mud. It gaped like a mortal wound to the earth.

Claire raised her arm and the sky suddenly dulled, the remaining light fading into ocher and purple and acid green. Night swarmed down.

Dana saw movement near the jagged pit. Long

branches whipped with no wind to drive them. Distorted figures moved through shadows. Across the shallow water voices rose and fell in ugly song.

"Iä! Iä! Shub-Niggurath! Lord and mother, hear us. Lord of the woods, hear us. Mother of Winter, hear us. Shub-Niggurath! Black Goat of the Woods with a Thousand Young!"

Dana recognized the words, and screamed. She turned to run but Claire grabbed a fistful of her hair and dragged her forward into the water. "No," she hissed, her grey eyes like lanterns, "You belong here."

Dana twisted, caught. Figures emerged from the cavern beneath the willow, moving to form a ring around them.

"Iä! Shub-Niggurath! Black Goat of the Woods with a Thousand Young," Claire chanted with them, and yanked Dana's head in time to the incantation.

Dana could see the approaching figures had heads and arms and swollen bellies, but a swarm of churning limbs where legs should grow. They had faces, with the skin grey and loose and slipping. As they drew closer, she thought one was Joe. Then the face she recognized fell off the misshapen head.

She screamed again, helpless, wild. Claire called out again, laughing.

The dimmed sky erupted in roiling black clouds, and withering cold washed over them. Water crackled and froze around them, crunching beneath the moving forms. Dana fell forward into the swamp, leaving a clutch of her hair in Claire's grasp. She struggled to rise, but the ground seemed to shift under her. She looked up.

Something had heard the chanting.

Shadows in the sky coalesced into a column of black mist, shot with lightning and scored with flickering tendrils of smoke and muscle. It descended, wet with a slime like an afterbirth. It pooled in the hole beneath the shivering tree. Smoke and ichor dripped over the figures as they called out to it. Where the dripping touched them they burned.

The chants howled into a frenzy. Claire had forgotten her, staring up at the blackness with joy and terror in her face. Dana gazed at the thing descending. She did not want to run, now.

"*Iä!*" she whispered. "*Shub-Niggurath!*"

She belonged.

A human figure emerged from the woods, dressed in a horned goat's skull and a still-wet skin, dancing and lurching and raising its bare arms to the thing in the sky.

Dana recognized Josh beneath the costume. He chanted, too, raising his voice to be heard above the roar of the tentacled cloud squatting over them, above the relentless chanting of the circling crowd. But his words were different than theirs. She stood unsteadily and reached for him, trying to answer.

Lightning cracked across the sky. Dana's senses wobbled as if she tumbled under waves.

She could see through Josh's eyes, under the edge of the skull. She watched his bare feet cross the rutted swamp to the fallen willow. She felt the weight of the dead skin hanging from his shoulders. She felt the fear that weighed in his lungs, and the need. He knew what to do.

Then she stuttered back, fell, and was in herself again as Claire lifted her and led her into the pit. There she pushed Dana to her knees in the icy mud, muttered an unintelligible string of sounds, and retreated.

Something squirmed in the slime Dana knelt in. She arched away, startled. Long flexing limbs slipped out and wrapped her body, binding her to a cold mass that moved over her skin, languid, lithe, slippery as water. There was foulness in its touch, a stirring of desires that should not be sated. The mass seeped into her flesh, displacing her. She cried out in mortal fear and delight. She wanted this.

Josh stumbled forward under his heavy wrappings, tangling with all her new limbs. She felt the crack of his head striking rock, felt flailing strands stretch from her and sink into him. He pressed against the slick resistance of her swarming muscle, blooming as the undertow of her swelling body bore him deeper into her. He dissolved like sugar in water. Like warmth in winter. He had to end, that she could begin.

She opened her mouth to sing out but another flowed in. Great ropy strands within her swelled, filling her, bursting her apart. Her flesh stretched and shredded, her mind scattered like dust. A million icy stars spilled out of her, a million cilia thrashed from her skin into blackest space. She rose in the column of her own wet flesh and smoke, seeing across the voids through a million lenses.

The chanting voices were so far away, the creatures that made their pleas so very small. She could not understand what they said with their small voices. What they wanted. But it didn't matter.

As she opened into the cloud and chaos, she saw the vast sweep of the sky above her, as deep as time, as empty. And the million scattered stars she birthed were still too few to dispel the dark.